CITY OF BEASTS

CITY OF BEASTS

CORRIE WANG

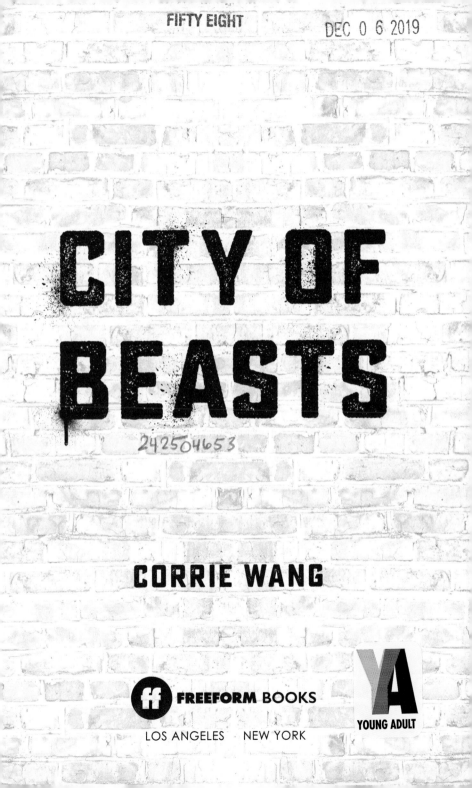

FREEFORM BOOKS

LOS ANGELES · NEW YORK

YA
YOUNG ADULT

for Shuai,
really, they're all for you

First Edition, September 2019
10 9 8 7 6 5 4 3 2 1
FAC-020093-19214

Printed in the United States of America

This book is set in 11.5-pt Adobe Devanagari, Veneer Two/
Fontspring; Century Gothic/Monotype
Designed by Phil Buchanan

Library of Congress Cataloging-in-Publication Data
Names: Wang, Corrie, author.
Title: City of beasts / by Corrie Wang.
Description: First edition. • Los Angeles ; New York : Freeform, 2019. • Summary: "Glori
has to question everything she's been taught when a desperate rescue mission brings her
to a strange city where she encounters men for the first time"—Provided by publisher.
Identifiers: LCCN 2018059645 • ISBN 9781368026628 (hardcover)
Subjects: • CYAC: Fantasy.
Classification: LCC PZ7.1.W3647 Cit 2019 • DDC [Fic]—dc23
LC record available at https://lccn.loc.gov/2018059645

Reinforced binding

Visit www.freeform.com/books

I'd go hungry, I'd go black and blue,
I'd go crawling down the avenue.
There's nothing that I wouldn't do
To make you feel my love.

—a male named Bob Dylan

Author's Note

All the science in this novel is fact-based.
Everything else is entirely made-up.

THEN

"**H**ey, Twofer, who loves you even more than she loves corn bread with berries?"

It was the deepest of the dark hours, and Two Five was hiding in the space next to my bed, scraping at a chip of paint that was flaking off the baseboard. I wedged myself in alongside it.

"Glori does," I answered myself.

The day had started fine. We'd gone to Costco, and I pulled Twofer around the empty aisles on the patched river float I'd scavenged a few years back. After, we'd played hide-and-seek for the thousandth time, then raced back to the house. Niraasha was on duty, and we had our lessons. Then everyone came home from career and school. All fine-ness crumbled at dinner. Su snapped at Twofer for eating too loudly. I scolded it for not saying *please* when asking for dessert. And Liyan shooed it from the kitchen when it offered to help with dishes. And Grand? She was avoiding it like usual and still hadn't come home yet.

"Hey, Two Five, who loves you more than she loves putting rocks in Liyan's shoes?"

I bumped its tiny shoulder. This time a muttered reply. "Glori does."

"That's right. Who loves you more than she loves drawing Su while she's sleeping?" I tilted my head back, mouth wide open.

A giggle. It was instantly happy again. "Glori does."

"And who loves *me* more than catching crickets for dinner?"

Standing up, Twofer pointed at itself and whispered, "Glori does!" then squealed with delight at its smarty-pants flub and flung itself into my embrace. And right then, I knew I loved that little beast more than the bright green of new growing things. More than temperate evenings or a full belly. Really, more than anything else in the world. So I suggested the one thing I knew it needed. Which also happened to be the one thing we weren't allowed to do.

"Want to go see the neighborhood?" I whispered.

Two Five gave a little gasp and nodded seriously with big, round eyes. So we did.

A few hours later, the beasts came and stole Two Five away.

NOW

"If you see a beast and you have the shot, don't hesitate. Kill it."

Su and I are sitting on our cracked driveway as her mom, Liyan, checks her bicycle tires. Forgoing her solar flashlight, she moves quickly and works mainly by feel. We're all used to the dark, but on this freezing, moon-hidden night this new cul-de-sac feels even more desolate than our last one, considering the nonworking streetlights and deserted houses are essentially the same.

Across the street, a section of broken vinyl siding flaps in the wind. We all jump.

"But if there's more beasts than you can handle," Liyan continues, glaring out into the darkness, "what do you do? Su?"

With a smirk, Su pretends to slo-mo swing a hatchet. "I chop them all into tiny bits."

I'm only half listening. We've been through this beast protocol what feels like every day of our last seventeen years. Prior to this morning, the lessons had begun to seem like superstitious safety precautions. Like not stepping on sidewalk cracks. Now the beasts had actually attacked. And they didn't only snatch Two Five. They raided the neighborhood, too. Killing seven of our most senior fees in the process.

Liyan smacks Su on the back of her freshly shaved head.

"Ow, Ma." Su winces. "Okay, okay. If there's more beasts than we can handle and we haven't been spotted, we stay hidden. If we have been spotted, we run."

"And how many is 'more beasts than you can handle'?" Liyan asks.

Su rolls her eyes. "More than one absurd, measly beast per fee."

Liyan nods curtly as my Grand Mati hurries from the house carrying her pack and both of their weapons. We call her Grand because with her signature messy braid and DNA-strand finger tattoos, she barely looks older than my mom, so grand*ma* has always seemed ill-fitting. Grand because with her sun-warm laughter and biting wit, she quite simply is.

Every single thing about her.

"Absurd," my grand snaps, "is getting killed because you put yourself in jeopardy when you just as easily could have kept yourself safe. Fees don't take uncalculated risks."

This is meant for me, but as my grand tosses Liyan the katana that usually hangs above the fireplace, I feign deafness. We spent the entire day moving from our old house to this one a few 'sacs over. We'd considered this house when we first moved out here years ago. Grand had liked the three-story roof's vantage point, but there had still been two corpses sitting at the kitchen table.

"Pass," I remember Su and me saying simultaneously.

Now the bodies are gone. And if my grand and Liyan would leave already, Su and I would be, too.

"We'll message as soon as we get to the labs," Grand says, affixing her arm-length electric cattle prod to her bike. "Keep your portables charged. Lock the doors. Stay in the same rooms but don't sleep at the same time.

No lights of any kind after dark. Obviously don't go near the shore, and if you hear screams coming from the neighborhood, stay put, you hear me?"

"Yes," Su and I say, both shocked by her tone. But because I am angry and scared, I also mumble, "It's not like we are inexperienced with the effects of a beast attack."

As one, we all look in through the living room window. Even in the pitch-blackness, Majesty's skeletal outline is visible on the sofa.

Majesty. That was what my grand named my mother. This was around the time when natural disasters were wiping out island nations and coastal shorelines. When fees were choosing names for their daughters that were wistfully optimistic. Prosperity. Peace. Hope. In every language under the sun.

Majesty.

It's been almost six years since she escaped from the beasts. More and more her name feels like a cruel joke. It's been months since I've even heard her speak. Until this morning.

"What about Two Five?" I ask, my voice breaking ever so slightly as they rush to leave.

Eight hours, Twofer's been gone. In that time, our EMS killed the two beasts that murdered our fees. My Grand Mati has made three trips into the neighborhood to console the victims' families. Twice she's gone to the labs to do "damage and retaliation control." She has exchanged countless heated PTT messages with various fees. Yet not once has she mentioned a plan for getting Two Five back.

Now she comes to me and puts her forehead against mine.

"Glori, I lost Two Five *and* seven of my closest friends today. I can't risk any more lives sending fees across the river to look for Twofer and . . ." She presses on as I try to protest. "I need all the EMS here protecting us. But I promise you—*I promise*—the beasts will not get away with this."

The wind picks up and blows in an unmistakable scent. Snow's coming. Soon and a lot. Of course she wouldn't attempt a rescue. Twofer being gone solves so many problems.

"Mati," Liyan says, releasing Su from a swift hug. "We have to go."

"I love you, Spark Plug," my grand says, a hand pressed to my cheek.

She waits a beat for me to reply, but I don't, and a moment later Su and I are watching their breath trail them in frosty clouds as they pedal away.

No sooner are they out of sight than Su asks, "You ready, Roach?"

It sounds more like *You sure?*

I get the hesitation. Not only does Su not love Twofer as much as I do, but our wing chung and cross-training and survival skills all assume beasts coming to attack us. Now we're going there. And truth?

We don't have any inkling what to expect.

Yet I nod confidently as I pull a knit cap on to cover my coiled braids. Running back inside for our packs, I kiss a nonresponsive Majesty on her dry cheek, then hurriedly write a note with our last working pen. My letters rough and unpracticed.

We leave it on the kitchen table.

Don't be mad.
Know you're busy.
Went to save Two Five.
Back soon.

Me, hoping most of that would be true.

3

tami is supposed to be on watch at the guard post that's closest to where Su and I are crossing the river. But when we arrive there, it's empty.

"Either it's our lucky day or we're all doomed," Su says, gazing up at the ruined bridge.

It's not like an EMS to leave her post.

Wasting no time worrying about it, Su picks her way down the rocky riverbank, then hauls branches off our family's hidden "emergency only" kayak. I'm halfway down to help when I catch a gleam in the grasses that have grown up around the old 190 highway. I almost ignore it but instead hurry back. It's a car. One that wasn't here before. One that I saw this very morning driving Two Five away.

"Holy crow," I say under my breath.

Both front doors and the back right one are thrown wide open, and the tiniest part of me expects to see Twofer inside. Alive. Sleeping, maybe.

But of course, it's empty.

"Glori, this is no time to scavenge," Su calls out urgently.

"This is the car that Two Five was taken in."

Incredibly, it's an old gas model. The tank on E. The ignition broken apart and hot-wired. I vaguely remember seeing it parked in a driveway a few streets over from the 'sac. And there's something pink on the floor, wedged beneath the driver's seat. I yank it out. It's a realistic animal mask. A pig. Up front, I find two others. A bear and . . . my brain reaches for the word . . . a gorilla. There were three of them, then.

I hold up the bear mask. "This is what Twofer saw when they grabbed it."

Su looks, then quickly busies herself with the kayak.

"That can't be helped now. Come on. Itami's pee break won't last forever."

Shoving the masks in my pack, we quickly change out of our fee tunics and leggings. Liyan said beasts still scavenged clothing instead of making their own, so we dress in pre-Night sweaters, sweatshirts, jeans, and trench coats I found crumpled in a closet of our new house.

"Su, I have something to tell you," I say once we're in the kayak, paddling against the river's frigid current. "Last night after everyone went to sleep, I took Two Five for a bike ride through the neighborhood. I think it's my fault the beasts attacked and stole Twofer."

"Glori, what were you thinking?" Su scolds, grunting as the current tries to veer us downstream, toward the Falls. But then she relents. "I doubt it's your fault, though. How could the beasts know you did that? And why would they wait a whole six hours to attack? Why not take Two Five right then?"

"Maybe they went back for reinforcements," I say, breathless.

"Then how did they know where *we* live? We're two miles outside the neighborhood. Other fees barely know where we live. The beasts didn't come because of that bike ride. It was just stupid dumb luck that they found us. Now stop amplifying your importance and please put your back into this."

Maybe she's right. Su liked to tease me that I could see a mosquito coming a mile away. And last night as we rode through town, not a single shadow shifted. Not one curtain in an abandoned house so much as shivered. I'm positive.

Perhaps we too vigorously followed Su's directive, because our kayak rams the far shore. We stumble out and drag it up the bank.

"Holy waste," Su says, giving each word extra syllables.

Our whole lives we've gazed across the river to this side, never imagining it was crossable and never caring to try. Yet now we're here on this cracked and rutted street. Derelict high-rise apartments loom above us. And as if it's meant specifically for us, a pre-Night highway sign reads:

WELCOME TO

BUFFALO

A SAFE HARBOR CITY

The City of Beasts.

"Tell me the plan again?" Su asks.

There is no plan. But as my grand said, fees do not take uncalculated risks. Nor do we function well under ill-preparedness. As Su's eyes flick upward to all the abandoned-yet-new-looking apartments, I reply with more confidence than I feel.

"We capture a beast and make it tell us where Two Five is."

"But what if it doesn't know?" Su asks.

"How could it not?" On Grand Island, every fee knows every other. "We have roughly the same population size. Can you imagine not knowing about something big like this in the neighborhood?"

"Yeah, Roach." Su snorts. "I can exactly imagine that, since that is exactly our lives."

"That's different."

We were a special case. Almost six years ago now, my mother went for a nighttime run along the river and never came home. Majesty was our fiercest fighter, and yet she became the first fee snatched by a beast in over a decade.

Months passed.

Then one dusky morning, as life was starting to feel normal again, one of our safety officers spotted her standing at the entrance to the remaining Grand Island Bridge. Battered. Bleeding. The SO ran out to retrieve her and even now, years later, I'm still not sure who they returned with. It's as if the brilliant, furious light inside of her has been entirely snuffed out.

We didn't find out until a month later that she was pregnant. That same day, my grand moved us out of the neighborhood to our cul-de-sac. Almost like she knew that when Majesty had the baby, it would be a beast.

We've been keeping Twofer a secret ever since.

"Mom calls these Die Rises, you know." Su stops and eyes all the apartment buildings. "She says the beasts didn't clear any of the bodies."

Realistically, how could they? On Nuclear Night, mass death was only instantaneous in some cities. Foul winds caught and orphaned the rest of us with their radiation poisoning. Since hospital staffs were as hard hit as everyone else, most people died at home. That means we are surrounded by hundreds, if not thousands, of corpses right now.

The wind picks up. I shiver.

"Let's keep moving."

A snowflake falls. Then another. Now that the snow's begun, it'll come fast. Accordingly, when we come to a wide-open intersection a few minutes later, fat snowflakes are already snagging on our eyelashes. We take cover behind a pre-Night garbage can. A Burger King *Green* is ahead on the left and another structure with faded yellow arches and the word *organic* cutting through them is on our right. An old newspaper box is next to the garbage can, the sun-faded headline barely legible: "WWIII: RUSSIA FIRES BACK."

"I'm all for caution," Su says when I put a hand on her arm and continue to observe our environment. "But we can't stop at every intersection we come to. This is obviously a dead zone. Not even a beast would choose to live here. Besides, this place is mammoth compared to Grand Island. It'll probably take us days to hunt one down."

"Gimme a minute."

I peer up at the buildings. Every window is dark, yet I can feel eyes nipping at us. Like gnats in the hot months. Across the street, a metal sign furiously swings in the biting wind. KINSEY'S FRESH CUT FLOWERS. Something's not right.

Su sighs. "Glor, we don't have time for this. The beasts could attack at any moment."

"Yeah. That's what I'm checking for."

"I didn't mean us. I meant home."

Before I can grab her, Su is sprinting through the intersection. Just as fast, I see what I missed before. There are tire tracks in the snow. Fresh ones.

"Su, wait!"

Halfway across the intersection, Su is suddenly bathed in light.

She drops to a crouch. Freezes.

The light comes from the Burger King *Green* parking lot. It's the headlights from one of the same driverless trucks that litter our roadsides. Which must mean the beasts figured out how to bypass the dead GPS and override the computer error screen. Oh good. Smart ones, then.

There's a plow on the front and a solar panel attached to the hood and bones painted on the tires.

Both doors open.

Enough smoke pours out to warrant a bucket of water. And with it?

Actual living *beasts*.

4

There are five of them. Three more than Liyan's stay-and-fight protocol allows. They all walk upright. Which I guess I knew but still didn't expect. One is noticeably larger than the others, and it takes point. And maybe it's a trick of the backlighting or the snow flurries, but from where I'm crouched, its skin looks blue. Like, old calendar photos of the ocean *blue*.

"Oye," the blue beast shouts. "You mayor's, little norm?"

English. I think. I recognize the words, but the meaning makes no sense.

Snubbing a lifetime of training, Su is still frozen in the middle of the street.

Music blares from the truck's speakers. If you can call it music. A flat high tone that has a drumbeat pounding into it, but no fee rapping or singing over it.

EEEEEE-DUNDUNDUNDUN-EEEEEE-DUNDUNDUNDUN-
EEEEEE...

"Glori?" Su whispers, petrified.

The beasts move toward her, like a swarm of hornets. There are smiley-face decals on the truck's headlights. They cast wicked grins on the building behind us.

"Coming to meet a mate?" the blue beast calls. "Get a bump, maybe?"

EEEEEE-DUNDUNDUNDUN-EEEEEE-DUNDUNDUNDUN-EEEEEE...

Su is more frozen than the icicles hanging from the street signs. The beasts are only ten feet from her. Then five. Goodness gracious. They're not even that big.

I stand up and shout, "Do Bye-Bye, Night-Night."

The beasts all spin on me. My command kicks Su's reflexes into gear. As the snow flurries lull, she fumbles a slim metal tube from her breast pocket. I take a similar one from mine.

"Oy! Hands where I can see them!" the blue beast shouts.

"Don't dart the leader!" I yell as Su brings the tube to her lips.

EEEEEE-DUNDUNDUNDUN-EEEEEE-DUNDUNDUNDUN-EEEEEE...

But it's too late.

Next second, the blue beast raises a paw to its face and fingers the tiny tranquilizer dart that's planted in its cheek. Around it the others crumple, each of them with one of my darts sticking out of their faces. Su darted the leader, and I got everyone else. The blue beast goes down a second later.

EEEEEE-DUNDUNDUNDUN-EEEEEE-DUNDUNDUNDUN-EEEEEE...

"Bye-bye," I say breathlessly as I run up to Su.

"Night-night," she finishes.

We grip each other in a tight hug.

"Sorry," she says as soon as I release her. "I got scared, then excited.

Thanks be that I preloaded. I didn't know I could blow that fast. And in this wind. I'd like to see Cocoa do that."

I can see the divots in the snow where most of her darts landed, but I won't ruin her triumph by telling her she *didn't* blow that fast. I did.

Instead I roll my eyes. "Yes. You are very impressive."

Just as I stoop to bind the beasts' hands and feet, a flash of color dashes from the shadows to the beasts' truck. So much for this area being deserted. There's another one out there. As I yank out Mama Bear the door of the building behind us slams open. A beast wearing an old bathrobe and hiking boots gestures at us frantically.

"In here. Quick. More will come."

The beast is shorter than me and less muscular than Su, with thin lips and a weak chin. Radiation-burn-induced keloid scars ravage the right side of its face, but the left is bumpy, like dozens of cherry-pit-size balls have been implanted underneath its skin. Radiation poisoning gave you mouth ulcers, peeling skin, fever, and lifelong lethargy. It took away your white blood corpuscles. It made you sterile. And if you were 95 percent of the global population, it killed you.

Radiation didn't do this *or* turn your skin blue.

"You're looking for the little one, yes? Them too. But Cutter knows where he is." It pats its own chest. "Cutter can help. Come. Come."

"*You* know where Two Five is?" I ask, not bothering to hide my disbelief.

At the sound of my voice, the beast shivers.

"Cutter saw him. At the river. Please. Come, come. Cutter means you no harm."

Still talking, it is absorbed back into the pitch-blackness behind it.

"Nice knowing you," Su says, and slaps a hand into my belly.

But then one of the tranquilized beasts lets out a groan. Another twitches and tries to roll over on his stomach. The darts are supposed to last ten times as long as this. Or, at least, they would have two decades ago when they were first manufactured.

"One third-person-narrative beast or five angry ones?" I ask.

"Let the record show, I do not have a good feeling about this," Su grunts as she unsheathes her hatchet.

"Don't worry. We won't be here long."

"Yeah. That's kind of what I'm afraid of."

The moment we step into the gloom and shut the door, Cutter is beside me.

"Miraculous. Cutter knows what you are. Cutter knew the minute he saw you." It leans in and breathes rank air on my face through rotten teeth. "You're women."

Women.

How long has it been since I've heard or read that word? It came from a different time. A time before the ice caps released their carbon. And the oceans rose. And the planet became a place of mainly insufferably hot and unsustainably cold regions. Before Buffalo's population exploded thanks to its facsimile of a spring and autumn. This was back before a hacker accessed our countries' nuclear codes and blew everything up. Before the ensuing retaliations. Before the majority of the world's population died or was orphaned practically overnight.

Women.

Back from a time when beasts and fees still lived together. When both weren't rendered (mostly) sterile by radiation. Before a beast named Fortitude Packer rose from the ashes that were Buffalo and campaigned for a lifestyle of scavenging and riches, drawing hordes of other beasts into his fold. Before a fee named Matricula Rhodes stepped forward and championed fairness and order. Back before things got nasty and

Fortitude introduced his ridiculous Breeder Bill. Before everything got violent and someone shot Fortitude in the head and fees fled to Grand Island for safety. To live separately.

It was only supposed to be temporary.

Women.

Back from when beasts were called something different as well.

Men.

5

The fifth-floor apartment the beast leads us to is a mess of clothes, empty aluminum cans, and antique posters of barely clothed fees. It smells like sweat and dust and something else that's dry and scratchy and gets stuck in my throat. Despair maybe.

As soon as we're inside, the beast locks the door behind us.

"For safety. I mean you no harm."

"You said you know where Two Five is," I say.

Its eyebrows furrow.

"The little one," I clarify.

"Oh yes." It smooths back its greasy hair, then wipes its paws on its pants. "He is here."

Su grunts with barely suppressed fight-or-flight.

Other than mold, there is no sign of anything living in this apartment. Post-Night has clearly made this beast mad. Luckily, fees have a saying—we have a lot, actually—*"Excellent preparation assures excellent results."* Which is why I didn't only bring Su with me, but three other fierce fees as well.

Hidden inside my boot, Baby Bear is strapped to my right calf. An exquisitely sharpened paring knife—drop a piece of hair on Baby's blade and she'll halve it as effortlessly as my grand shares advice. Slim, my boning knife, hangs out in a scabbard at my hip. Her blade is as thin and lethal as Su's patience during the heat months. And sewn into a special pocket on my backpack is my most valuable possession. My cleaver, Mama Bear. Her handle juts out enough to grab in a flash but not enough to be seen with a casual glance.

Liyan said since my girls were made from Japanese steel, they probably belonged to someone called a chef. I thank her daily but tonight a little extra as I slide out Slim.

"Right." Su nods. "Don't hesitate. Kill it."

The beast holds its hands out to me. "No, no, no. It's truth. Cutter was at the shore. Finding lunch. Cutter saw three bring him across. In a boat. Cutter hid. The little one fought, escaped. Cutter led him here. Same as you. He is here."

There *were* three masks. That didn't change the fact of the empty room.

"Not here," Cutter says. "Look."

It waves us over to a bedroom and gestures to a far wall where a door-size hole has been cut through the dry wall.

"This whole building is Cutter's. The little one is safe upstairs. Cutter gave him meat. Squirrel. He sleeps. Cutter will bring him to you. Wait. Wait."

Nodding and gesturing for us to stay, it hurries away.

"I do *not* like this," Su says. "Glor, please let's get out of here. There's no way that thing is coming back with Two Five. And I can practically feel all the dead bodies up in here."

My ears perk up. A few floors below, I hear doors opening and slamming shut. Someone calling, "Yoo-hoo." The other beasts must be fully awake and searching for us.

"It said there were three beasts. That can't be a lucky guess. Suze, if there's even a one percent chance it does have Twofer, we have to see this through. If not, we'll knock it out and get the hill out of here. Promise."

Su glances around the dingy living room and crosses her arms. She'll stay, but she's not deigning to take one more step. There are two candles lit in the apartment. I take one and run my fingers along a bureau. Su shakes her head no. On Grand Island, I never passed up an opportunity to scavenge. And this is a *beast's* stuff. I quietly slide open the top drawer.

I glance inside, then at Su, horrified.

"Su, get out. Now!"

It's filled with dozens of magazines that all have naked fees on the covers.

As Su spins toward the apartment's front door, it swings violently open. She screams in surprise, and right as the door bounces off the wall, I glimpse an equally surprised figure on the other side. A yellow bandanna is pulled up around its mouth and nose. Just as the door slams shut, Cutter runs out of the bedroom, cutting me off from Su and the exit.

At least, I think it's Cutter.

Now it's shirtless. Its pale belly flops over tight black leather pants and its head is covered by a see-through stocking. It's also carrying a whip.

As if nothing is out of the ordinary, it asks, "Did Cutter hear something?"

Its answer comes as the apartment door is kicked open again. This time Yellow Bandanna runs in toting a long tube with some kind of compression machine on the end. Faster than I can throw Slim, it fires two white missiles right into Cutter's stomach. The force flings the beast backward like congee whipped off a spoon.

"WHOO!" it shouts. "That was intense. Thank bumping heavens I found you when I did. Cutter was about to Temple of Doom your asses."

Everything about Yellow Bandanna is fast and loud. From its movements, to its speech, to its bright blue hat, puffy orange coat with all its buckles and straps, and shiny yellow sneakers that match the bandanna. As it walks over to Cutter and tosses the whip across the room, the only reason I'm positive it's a beast is that no fee would ever make such poorly camouflaged clothing choices. This must be the flash of color I saw outside.

It kicks Cutter in the ribs.

"That's for whatever it was you were about to do to these nags."

Cutter lets out a little poof of air. It kicks it again.

"That's for always stealing from my squirrel traps."

It kicks it again.

"And that's just karma, you dumb goit."

Cutter groans. The white things it was hit with lie next to it and have come unraveled.

"Are those . . . T-shirts?" I ask Su.

Yellow Bandanna swings its cannon-like gun at me. I twirl Slim so I'm pinching her blade.

"If you throw that knife at me," it says, "I'll shoot you, so help me Rhonda. And maybe they're poly-cotton blend, but the T-shirts leave a Lake Erie–size welt at this range and hurt like a father bumper. Let's all stay calm."

Slowly now, it lowers its bandanna. A beast no doubt, yet entirely different from all the other ones we've seen so far. Tall and lanky, it's about our age, with smooth unmutilated skin. Unlike Su, myself, and the rest of the Heinz 57 über-mixed multi-ethnic fees our age, this beast seems bred of a single race. Fully Chinese like Liyan, I'm guessing. I've never seen someone so young be so sole-racial. As if further letting us acclimate to its appearance, it takes off its baseball cap. Its haircut is short and neat. Except for the star that's shaved into the fade, it looks almost exactly like Su's hair.

Eyes flicking from me to Su, it studies us with as much interest as I study it. Or maybe it's simply making sure we don't attack. Regardless, it has absolutely paused Su. Mouth ajar, she hasn't moved since it kicked in the door. I lower my knife.

"There we go. You two all right?" When neither of us answers, it rolls its eyes and says louder and slower, "Are. You. Okay? I saw you cross the river. Let me guess, you're chasing after that little boy, right? Everyone's been buzzing about him all day. Comma said he thought it was bunk, but I told him if there *was* a little boy, someone would come after him. But *nooo*, he said. If there's a kid, Dictator Matricula and Mayor Chia will handle it diplomatically. My ass."

As it talks, it moves around the gloomy apartment, shoving things into its pack—duct tape, a small gold picture frame, a refrigerator magnet with a buffalo on it. When it finds the collection of magazines, it takes a thermos from its bag and pours hot water into the drawer. Naked fees must not be to its liking.

"Man, you two nags have bad luck. First, Mystique and his crew. What goits. Just because you tattoo yourself blue doesn't mean you have crime-fighting superpowers. It means you have poor judgment. The mayor's been telling Mystique to mind his own business for years. Now this scavenger rat? You are literally attracting the worst. Speaking of the worst, my name's . . . Wait. That didn't come out right. I meant, speaking of the worst, I'm the best. My name's Sway."

Su looks to me. I look to her.

It whispers, "This is where you introduce yourselves."

"What do you think?" I ask Su.

"I think it talks too much and will turn us in first chance it gets." Su brings up her hatchet. "Do you want to kill it or should I?"

6

"Okay, then!" Sway slowly moves to the door. "Not to ruin this uncomfortable and physically threatening gender bonding we're all engaging in, but since I have a paused *KillCrush C* game to get home to, I'll be leaving now. Alive. Please and thank you."

"Wait," I say. "Don't go. We need your help. We *are* looking for the little, um, boy."

"Yeah. You and everyone else," Sway says.

"But it's different for us. Two Five is my brother."

The word sounds so foreign on my tongue. I'm not sure I've ever heard it spoken before.

"Glori," Su groans.

"No use keeping it a secret anymore, Su. And this beast did kind of save our lives."

"Beast?" Sway's eyebrows dance upward. "That's a rapid and harsh character assessment."

"Maybe this beast is less creepy than that one." Su nods at Cutter.

"But it's no more trustworthy and no less unappealing. The only thing it saved is that Cutter beast from dying."

"Did we not establish that we all speak English here? And back up that verbiage. Did you say *brother*?" Sway pronounces it carefully so I can hear my mistake. Bruh-ther. Not BRO-ther. "So, A, the kid actually does exist? And, B, you're related to him?"

"C. Yes." I nod. "Now will you please tell us where Two Five is?"

"Ha!" Sway laughs. Just once. Then looks between us, confused. "Wait. You're not joking? How should I know where he is?"

"Ask someone," I say impatiently. "I mean, aren't there only four thousand beasts?"

"You're telling me you know every single fee?" he says.

"Of course we do," Su sniffs.

"At least by sight," I clarify, though I also know everyone's name, age, and address. But that's how my brain works. "Plus, they wore animal masks. I'm assuming they had to check those out of a library or borrow them from Supplies...."

Sway gives that lone laugh again—*ha!*—then shakes his head. "Y'all are delusional."

Su steps forward, and he quickly holds his hands out in surrender.

"Also, seriously, nags?" he adds. "Two Five? You've been hiding possibly the only child on the entire eastern seaboard and you don't even give him a proper name outside his citizen number?"

I'm too stunned to register his criticism. Our entire plan was based on the assumption that all beasts knew each other. I hadn't even considered otherwise. Seeing as I quite literally can't imagine what else I don't know, how can we expect to last another two minutes here, let alone find Twofer?

"Look," Sway says with what seems like sympathy. "If I had to suggest a starting point, you could go see the mob. Rage has his hand in pretty much everything in Buffalo."

Far below, we hear the sound of glass breaking. Su and I rush to look outside. Three massive, well-maintained black E-SUVs are all parked at varying angles on the street. Doors open, engines idling. Meanwhile, the beasts from the smiley-face truck are getting to their feet and seem to be debating whether to follow the new beasts inside or leave.

"How did these ones find us?" Su asks.

"See those little black boxes on the traffic lights *and* on the corner of the building across the street?" When I nod, Sway cups a hand to its mouth and shouts, "They're called cameras."

"You mean yours work?"

Sway snorts. "Yep, and that means the mayor's patrol saw your conspicuous, trench coat-wearing selves the second you rolled up. Anyway, nice meeting you. Thank you for not killing me. Good luck with dying."

Just as its hand touches the doorknob, I call out, "Five thousand dollars."

I know instantly from the way its head rocks back that this is a huge sum of money. But how was I supposed to know? Unlike the beasts, fees use a point system for commerce. It only goes up to a hundred. Sway spins back toward us in one fluid movement.

"What now?" it asks.

"All you have to do is show us where Rage is, and I'll give you five thousand dollars."

"I'm not sure what Matricula Rhodes teaches you in history class, but over here, we all learned that while everyone else was hoarding food immediately after the Night, Fortitude Packer and his boys spent an entire month emptying banks in case the government ever came back. No one except the mayor has that kind of cash anymore."

A few floors below I faintly hear someone shout, "Clear!"

I lift my pant leg. Tied to my ankle are fifty of the hundred-dollar bills that I skimmed from Liyan's hidden mattress hoard. I have another fifty secured to my other leg right above Baby Bear. Sway's nostrils flare like the money is fresh-baked bread and it can smell it.

Suddenly, it comes at me. One hand extended.

I quickly swipe its leg. Next second, it's on the floor with Su's hatchet leveled at its neck.

"Okay." It winces and laughs. "Let's *not* shake on it. I must be bumping crazy, but you nags got yourself a deal."

7

"**C**lear."

As Sway pulls a crowbar from its pack and pries off the lock on a supply closet that's down the hall from Cutter's apartment, Su and I run ahead in the dark toward the next stairwell, then double back on our tracks in the dust. It doesn't take my exceptional hearing to know that the beasts from the E-SUVs are now on the fourth-floor landing. It's like no one ever taught them the word *stealth*. No sooner are we all inside the closet with the door shut than we hear footsteps and the sounds of heavy boots kicking in doors.

"Got something here, Risk," a beast shouts.

"Risk?" Sway whispers. "He's not mayor's patrol. He's mob. That was fast."

"If Risk is mob, shouldn't we go talk to it?" I ask.

Sway shakes its head. "There's different kinds of mobsters. Some are more socialized than others. Risk is the kind that doesn't 'do' talking. He more does murdering."

"Oh, I really do not like this," Su groans, pacing.

Sway shushes us as a cacophony of voices and radios crackle right outside our door. Then a beast hollers, "Downstairs! Downstairs!"

Footsteps pound past the closet. Then it gets quiet again. After a few minutes, Su turns on a crank flashlight, and we all warily eye one another. In this tiny space, filled with more upcycling-worthy items than all the closets on Grand Island, the air crackles with Sway's presence. I can practically see Su's brain working. She was expecting carnivorous mutants that solely wanted to jump our bones, and instead we're met with this fast-talking mess of right angles that, thanks to the haircut, kind of looks like her. For the past five years, I'd been trying to convince her that maybe beasts weren't so different from us. Now, given everything we've seen, I'm not entirely sure which of us is right.

"So, are y'all sisters?" it asks.

My left foot is only an inch away from its right; they're *almost* touching. It clears its throat. I jerk my foot away. Su continues to stare straight ahead. But I can't bear the awkward lingering silence. I mean, it asked a question. It's rude not to answer.

"No. We're cohabitators. Her mother and my grandmother were friends and chose to live together after the divide. My mother lives with us, too."

Su elbows me. "It doesn't need to know all that."

Sway snorts. "Yeah. Stop telling me such valuable information. Hey, everybody. These nags live with her grandma."

Su's grip tightens on her hatchet handle. "Mouthy, scrawny beast."

"Aggressive, thick-skulled nag," Sway replies.

"What's a nag?" I ask.

"It's what the older norms call you." Sway licks its thumb and wipes a minuscule speck of dirt off its sneaker. "*Nag* means to annoy or irritate with persistent faultfinding. And apparently it also used to mean an old, useless horse. By the way, men don't wear what you're wearing."

Men. The way it—he—speaks is so fascinating. *Him. His. He.* Not *it.* Su had advocated for calling Twofer *they*. Majesty had insisted on *it*. But I'd always simply thought of Twofer as a *she*, same as everybody else on Grand Island.

"We only had dated information to work with," I reply.

In all actuality, we had no information to work with. Fees cleared and burned any evidence of beasts in our first few years on the island while they were consolidating all the remaining goods. Massive bonfire marks still charred almost every street. Sure, some of our mothers kept things back, hidden away in attics and storage totes—contraband magazines, fiction books, and photos of passed loved ones—but otherwise fees had completely bleached beasts from the fabric of our lives.

"It's not the information's age. Norms never wore what you're wearing. You look like an old Dress Me app set to Joke Mode. Or like you stepped out of an old *Dick for Hire* episode. No, no, I've got it. It's like you scavenged bodies that had been trying not to freeze to death."

Su's head whips toward me. "Don't even tell me..."

"Ew," I say.

Maybe the two bodies were no longer in the house we moved into, but Liyan must have stripped them before she burned them. These were their clothes I found in the hall closet. Su pounds me one in the shoulder and it hurts. A lot. No delicate breeze will ever blow me or anyone in our year over, but I am a dainty (albeit lethal) seedpod compared to Su. Plus, she's wearing her gardening gloves with the license plate strips sewn into the knuckles.

"Here." Sway digs around in his bag and pulls out jackets and shirts that are a hundred times less warm than the ones we're wearing. "This will help a little. At least for any cameras you walk past, because no norm your age would be caught dead in those."

"You just so happen to have two full sets of clothes on you?" Su says.

"You don't?" Sway replies, then slaps a hand over his eyes when I start to lift my shirt.

"Glori!" Su yanks the closet door open and tosses Sway out. She slams it shut behind him. "You can't be fee-like around them. Stop acting so . . ."

"Like myself?" I fill in.

"Exactly." She nods.

"You think a beast that normal might have Twofer?" I whisper hopefully as we change.

A pitying look is my only reply.

To avoid the cameras, we exit out the back of the building.

Ducking down, we follow Sway and race across the street.

"The subway line used to end at University Station, but ten thousand people came here after Hurricane Maria hit Puerto Rico. Then a few years later, those twin tsunamis hit Japan. By the time the arctic shelf fell off, Buffalo was awash—Ha! get it?—with coastal and island refugees. All those apartments over there went up and the city decided to extend the subway tunnel out to the river. This was right when Buffalo was picked to be the next smart city and all that grant money poured in, which means something actually got built here in a timely fashion." He laughs, like he made a joke. "Or, you know, at least half built. Since the tunnel doesn't need any power to stay merely coolish in the freezing months and only warmish in the heat months, it's pretty prime real estate."

We've stopped in front of a brick building with glass entrance doors that are needlessly chained considering all the glass is missing. Neat white lettering next to the shattered doors reads: NIAGARA RIVER STATION. Bloodred kanji cuts through the words.

怒り

Ikari.

Rage.

How very not subtle.

"Voilà," Sway says. "I present to you the mob. Just follow the tunnel. Once you get to the red lights, you're there. You can't miss Rage. He's the size of a two-car garage." He holds out his palm. "That will be five thousand dollars."

Su smacks his hand away.

"Don't give him a nickel. You could have pointed us here."

Sway shrugs. "You said all I had to do was show you where Rage was. And now I did."

Suddenly, I can see individual snowflakes and how dirty my hands are and that the very outside of Sway's irises are indigo rather than black or brown. We are bathed in light. For a moment, I only think how marvelous it is to see perfectly clearly at night. Then I notice that a happy face is illuminating Su's chest.

Then I hear the music.

EEEEEE-DUNDUNDUNDUN-EEEEEE-DUNDUNDUNDUN-EEEEEE...

"Oh waste," Su says.

The truck is parked a half block back. The engine revs. That music cannot be helping their headaches any. The driver floors the accelerator, and the truck's tires spin on the fresh snow. A moment later, it's careening toward us. Sway dives in through the glassless door, Su a half beat behind. I duck in, barely with my feet pulled through, when a mound of snow is pushed in after me. Sway jogs three paces down the stairs as Su and I fall into defensive stances. But outside, the beasts continue to plow more snow against the door. They're barricading us in.

"Cowards," Su spits.

"No." Sway groans. "Smart."

For the first time, his chatty, easy facade falls away. He looks genuinely upset.

"They're forcing us into the tunnels?" I ask, and he nods. "Why?"

"They're betting what's up ahead will kill you for them."

"There are no other ways out of here?" Su asks.

"Nowhere viable before you get to Rage."

Su slaps Sway in the chest as she passes him and heads down the subway stairs.

"Welcome back aboard," she says.

"I'll lead you there. But as soon as we get to the mob, I'm out. Y'all are tourists, but I have to live here. Generally, I make a habit of not putting my neck on the line. I happen to dislike when it's horizontally spraying blood."

8

Chipped orange-and-red tiles decorate the walls around us, along with framed pre-Night advertisements that are faded but otherwise intact. In one, a beast stands in front of a high-rise with the words: COME HOME TO THE PLEASANT TOWERS. SECURE. SUSTAINABLE. FUN! Another shows a mixed family—fees and beasts—sitting down to eat a meal of Farm Safe Goods, both "delicious and or-genic."

I can't help but stop and stare. Nowhere back home can I think of a single place that depicts beasts and fees together. I'd always thought this was because cohabitating had been awful and thus fees scrubbed out all reminders of it. But . . .

"These fees look happy," I say to Su.

"They must be drugged."

"Everything all right back there?" Sway calls over his shoulder.

"Hardly," I say.

"Ha!"

We follow Sway out onto the subway platform. Since it's the start of the line, there's only one direction to choose. We need to go right. Right into a gaping maw of darkness. The smell, even from here, is atrocious. Waste mixed with unwashed feet mixed with festering decay. This is what beasts consider an optimal place to live?

Vaulting off the platform, Su executes a somersault midair and lands on the tracks. I can't help myself. When I jump down, I do two somersaults.

She rolls her eyes but then grins. "Touché."

When we glance back at Sway à la *Top that*, he just stands there with his jaw dropped open, as if running leaps wasn't first-grade material. I wonder if he's joking, but then instead of following our leads, he *walks* the entire length of the subway platform to a set of stairs.

"Tell me I haven't been doing two hundred squat thrusts a day for nothing all these years," Su says. "They can't all be this weak, right?"

"You want them to be stronger?" I ask, then call out to Sway, "Take your time!"

"That's a twelve-foot jump. Some of us value our knees."

At the mouth of the tunnel, Sway takes a solar-charged headlamp from his pack. If it's anything like the ones Su and I pull from ours, the light will stay strong for about five minutes before fading to a glow barely more illuminating than a freshly lit match. With these as our only sight aids, we enter pitch-blackness.

"I'll take first scout," Su says. "Best to stay quiet back here."

She gives me a meaningful look, then silently runs up ahead.

When we can no longer see her headlamp, Sway says, "She, like, your bodyguard?"

I'm surprised he's picked up on it, but I shake my head. "Older cohabitator syndrome, I guess. She's always been that way. I'm also a little smaller than most fees my age, so . . ."

"Why?" Sway asks. "How old are you?"

This time I flat-out lie, "Nineteen."

We're told never to reveal that we're part of the Miracles, aka the last group of fees born after Nuclear Night. Sway snorts with disbelief, but then must realize I'm serious and drops it.

"Now that Lumber Jane's gone," Sway says, "you know I have to ask about him."

"Twofer?"

Sway nods. "Are there more like him?"

"No. He's the only one."

I was in Majesty's bedroom when Two Five was born, so I witnessed it firsthand. My mother *didn't* give birth to a beast. She gave birth to a regular old baby. Only its vagina was pushed out instead of pushed in.

Liyan laughed when I pointed this out. *"Beasts have penises. You know this."*

"Well, we didn't know they looked like that," Su said for me.

When I questioned Grand Mati, she was more serious. "It's not that they look like beasts, Spark Plug. It's that throughout the entire history of the world, they have acted like them. Not all of them. And not all the time. But enough. Especially after the Night. And since the world has reset itself and we can now choose how to make our lives, we have chosen to be done with them."

Sway waits for me to continue. I dutifully tell him the lie Su and I prepared, about the fee from Canada, coming in a boat with a baby. How we thought that was why she was still fertile. Canada was farther away from any direct detonations. How she died shortly after. Late into the dark hours on the day Twofer was born, my grand told me all the survivors of the Night knew sterility was an effect of radiation. The last few broadcasting news sources had said as much before they went off the air. Grand said in Buffalo, once Fortitude's shaky government was up and running, he elected her to run fertility tests on the remaining fees. Although she never told him, she cut the study short after more and more of the results came back negative.

"Imagine," she said, "the life a fertile fee was destined for in that environment."

Which meant Majesty probably wasn't the only fertile fee.

It was the only time we spoke of it.

"And Matricula Rhodes knew about this?" Sway continues. "I mean, of course she did. She knows about everything over there, right? And she let him stay? And no one thought to tell the mayor?"

Grand always teased me that I lied like I sewed: sloppily and unjoyfully. It was partly why I never returned to school with Su after Twofer was born. It was hard enough seeing fees at the gym or at my grand's labs. Two Five was a secret I'd never be able to keep.

Well, that and I didn't want to leave him home alone with Majesty.

My headlamp goes out. A moment later Sway's does, too. I must not have lied convincingly. Why does he still have so many questions?

"Why tell anyone?" I say into the darkness as I wait for my eyes to adjust. "We weren't even sure if he would survive."

That part was true. Still, we gave the baby a citizen number—2584-0612—but no name. And when it became clear Majesty wouldn't be taking care of her baby, *I* tentatively washed, clothed, and fed it. I was there for its first smile, first laugh, and first steps. It was me who answered its first proper question: *"Why's a bird called* bird *and not* cat?*"* I taught it the names of the stars we could see and the planets we couldn't. I cuddled it at night when it had nightmares and made it take naps when it balled its hands into fists and got cranky.

Out of the murk, another subway stop appears up on our right. Fine living room furniture is neatly arranged on the platform. A couch, end tables, ottomans. A nonworking chandelier even hangs from the ceiling.

Strange. Even stranger, barbed wire blocks off the exit. Yet in the very faint ambient platform light, I'm more interested in who's next to me. Sway has small ears and a freckle right below his left eye, and his teeth still seem to be in good shape.

"Staring," Sway says.

"Excuse me?"

"You're staring. At me." My cheeks get warm and tingly with embarrassment, but he just barrels on about Twofer. "But he did survive. What if more nags are fertile? We could have been making babies this whole time. I mean, with your consent. Naturally. Okay, yeah. I guess I can see why you wouldn't tell us. But how come *your* family kept him?"

"We were the ones who found the fee," I stammer.

How could we not keep him? Even if my Canada story were true. Even if he hadn't been Majesty's. As much as Su and Liyan, hill, as much as my Grand Mati, I wholeheartedly, fiercely loved that little beast. Even as I waited for the day he began exhibiting some kind of violent tendencies. Instead, to my surprise, he simply loved me back equally as much.

First thing when we get home, I'm taking Two Five before the common council, telling them everything, and petitioning that he be granted immunity from the ban on beasts. Once everyone sees how sweet he is. How kind. How *not* beastly. They'll fall in love with him, too. They'll let him stay. I hope.

Beside me, Sway unzips his coat. It's about thirty degrees warmer down in the tunnel. Underneath, he's wearing fitted pants, a black hoodie, and an orange T-shirt all in pristine condition. A thin yellow tie completes the look. Yet for all his finery, Sway is slim, on the border of underfed. One of his collarbones becomes visible as he adjusts his ensemble and for some reason I can't stop looking at it.

"Still staring."

I finally avert my eyes, flustered.

He continues, "I mean, you have a *child* on the island. I'm surprised fees aren't coming over here in droves. Doesn't, like, everyone want one?"

"Oh, most fees don't even know he exists."

The words are out before I can stop them. Sway is so surprised, he slips off the track he's standing on. Thanks be that Su is not here. The bruise she'd inflict would be monstrous. Sway shakes his head like there are keloid scars in his ears. From the subway platform a sluglike sleeping-bag shape suddenly sits up on the couch.

"Some of us are trying to sleep," it shouts.

"How is that possible?" Sway whispers as we hurry on.

"No more questions."

I walk faster. He jogs to keep pace. Up ahead the tunnel glows.

"No more questions." He is lightly out of breath. "Heard."

He trips on an aluminum can, then immediately gets tangled up in a plastic bag.

"Are your eyes even open?" I ask.

"Hey, question: When you said you know all fees, did you actually mean that?"

Once more we stop walking. I'm not only imagining the tentative hopefulness on Sway's sweaty features, now I can actually see it. Hanging from the ceiling is a thin string of twinkling red lights. Even from our cul-de-sac, I'd seen the faint nighttime glow that meant beasts used more electricity than we did, but I'd never imagined they were using it continuously.

I click off my headlamp.

"Pretty, aren't they?" Sway asks softly.

Back home, power is our most precious commodity. Grand said that even pre-Night Buffalo was infamous for its cloud cover, but now the near-constant gray skies make our solar grid unreliable at best. We have a few windmills on Grand Island, but that energy is routed straight to the labs. As a result, we wash all our clothes manually and have strict dusk curfews, which, in the freezing months, means being inside by the late afternoon.

I've always thought it was weird we hadn't figured out an alternative source of energy, especially considering all the classes we took in water, wind, and solar power, but when I asked Liyan about it, she said it wasn't that we didn't know *how* to produce energy. It's that we didn't have the *supplies* to produce energy. The beasts did. And over the years, regardless of who the mayor was, they made it abundantly clear that if we wanted to share in any of their power, we had to give up ours and move back across the river to do so. A choice that hardly made individual refrigerators worth it.

"Wasteful is more like it," Su's gruff voice says from the left side of the tunnel. "Illuminating an empty tunnel like this."

I jump. Sway squawks. Normally, I would have heard Su waiting for us a full minute out. I quickly realign my expression to match my friend's. Because for a moment there, I'd agreed with Sway. Despite the color, the twinkling lights remind me of fireflies. Twofer would love them.

"First of all," Sway says, "it's not an empty tunnel. Second, you have to think of them more like a trail of bread crumbs."

"Who would leave bread crumbs lying around?" I ask. "You'll get roaches."

"Ha! Not actual bread crumbs. It's an expression. The lights are like a signpost."

"Yes, but what does the signpost say?" I ask.

"Right this way to the mob."

Only then? The mob comes to us.

9

One second there is *not* a giant, decapitated head floating in front of us and the next second there is. Rationally I know the blinking, breathing face in front of me can't be real, because it's nearly the size of me. Yet it looks as lifelike as Sway. It's so huge, I can see every weird half-grown face hair running along its jaw. Each tiny bead of sweat near its temple. A level of detail I do not appreciate, considering its left eye socket is empty and looks like it was hacked out by Mama Bear.

Su, however, does not rationalize the head.

Hatchet out, she immediately slashes it in sixteen different places, then ends with a perfect roundhouse that sails her through the beast's cheek.

Sway points at the head. "Um, that's a hologram."

And then he starts to giggle. Soon he's laughing and then coughing harder than a generator on its first start of the year. This does not prevent him from talking.

"They used to be for subway ads, but the mob repurposed them when they moved down here. What did you think it was going to do? Burp on us?"

"It could have head butted us," Su says seriously. "Or, like, bit us."

A tiny whiff of laughter escapes me as Sway begins to outright cackle. Really, it's rude. I have to stop looking at him. I run a hand through the beast. The image doesn't even flicker. Liyan once mentioned that beasts still used pre-Night technologies, but she never got specific.

"You'd think they'd find a less damaged spokesperson," I say.

"And completely defeat the purpose of being an antiestablishment, terror-spreading gang that strikes fear in the hearts of every norm?" Sway hiccups. "Nah. All the mobsters self-mutilate. We think it's an initiation thing. I mean, what says you're more committed to a cause than carving out your own eye?"

"When you ignore the minority," the head rumbles in a low voice, "you get mob rule."

"Yeah, yeah, yeah," Sway mumbles, then says louder, "Mob rules. Quick, you have to say, 'Mob rules,' too, or it'll go into alarm mode and scream in angry Japanese."

"Mob rules," Su and I say together.

The head nods. Up ahead, I can make out market-style stalls. Sway zips back into his orange parka and flips his hood up. Su pulls her face mask on. I pull my own homemade mouth mask from my bag and loop it over my ears. Then I bend down and untape a wad of bills from my calf. I put another in my pocket for Rage and also slip Baby Bear out of my boot and tuck her up my sleeve.

"Oh right, thanks," Sway says when I hand him his cash. "Yes. This is where I'll be leaving you, then. Once y'all get your info, you can leave out the mob's subway platform. I think I'm gonna head back to that floor display platform and negotiate my way . . ."

Su doesn't wait for him to finish. She simply keeps walking ahead.

"Hey, a bit of advice," Sway quickly says. "The way you walk, all tense like that, you two practically scream Jump Me and Take All My Money. So try to be chill. Keep your heads down—they don't like when you stare—let your money do your talking for you, and don't suplex anyone without good reason. Oh! And for bumps' sake. If you're gonna pass here at all, you can't be calling males *beasts* all the time. It's derogatory."

"And *nag* is any better?" I ask.

Sway's eyebrows lift in surprise. His head jostles back, the way it seems to when he's had a realization.

"Oh snap," he says. "Heard. Okay then. I guess this is goodbye."

I knew he wasn't coming with us. Still I feel weirdly disappointed that we're leaving this quirky, fidgety anomaly behind. I envision bringing Twofer *and* Sway home. Stunned awe shining out from every fee's expression. Except fees tried that once before at the divide. Matricula Rhodes brought a group of young males with them to Grand Island. Those beasts ended up being loyal to Fortitude and horrifically maimed a number of teenage fees. No one much talks about it, and yet, it hangs over every beast-related decision that fees make.

"Good riddance is more like it," Su says.

Then, without further ado, she spins on her heel and continues down the tracks. I hold up a hand in goodbye. Sway slaps it with his own, realizes that's not what I meant, and laughs. He laughs almost as easily as Twofer. I'd always thought my brother learned that from me. Then Sway pulls his bandanna up over his nose and, with one last over-the-shoulder glance, disappears into the dark.

"Officially on our own again," I say, catching up to Su.

"You sound worried. We don't need Sway, Glor. Based on what we've seen so far, how bad can this mob really be?"

10

Rows of stalls line either side of the tunnel. Dozens of strings of lights, all red, crisscross back and forth along the ceiling. Fire spits out of metal drums behind every merchant, half of whom are still asleep under their tables of wares. It is hot and smoky, like a cast-iron skillet left too long in the flames.

Back home, fees would normally be waking up, sharing breakfast, walking in to their careers at the labs, hydroponic farms, libraries, schools, co-ops. (That is, if we weren't on lockdown because of a beast attack.) Right about now, the fees of my household might be finding a brief note left on the kitchen table. Or maybe we still have a few hours before that happens. Regardless, here it looks like everyone just went to bed.

Another old subway platform is a few yards past the stalls. Faint dawn gloom creeps down from the outside entrance into the tunnel as a beast—*male*, I guess—blows into his hands and stomps down the stairs trying to dislodge snow from his boots. While all the vendors are either heavily tattooed or mutilated in some way, this male's face and body seem completely unmarred.

Mob versus norms.

Got it.

The norm male hurries directly to a stall where a giant stock pot is on a grate over the metal drum. The mobster who runs it is missing both eyelids and ears. Carcasses hang along the wall behind him. What species, I can't deduce. Cat, maybe. When the male orders, the mobster turns and carves off a hunk of meat, tosses it into a metal bowl, then spoons hot soup over it. The norm crouches next to the stall to eat.

I glance at Su. "You have to admit, that smells delicious."

"You mean the dead endangered animal flesh that would give us mild radiation poisoning? Yum." But her stomach gurgles. Loudly. Her eyes cut to me. "Shut it."

Sway was right. It isn't hard to spot Rage. His stall is in the middle of all the others, right across from the subway platform. Only there is no "not staring" at this beast. I've seen smaller houses, shorter trees. And every inch of him is inked. On his neck, chest, and arms, males are being hung, tortured, and burned. On his right cheek is a graphic and bloody torso. On his left is an equally gory lower half, as if Rage's mouth ripped it in two. He seems about Majesty's age, and I briefly wonder what he was doing when the Night hit. If he was something innocuous like a bus driver. I wonder which lifestyle he prefers.

For all his bulk, he sits on a tiny stool, hands crossed over his king-size-bed chest, sleeping.

"What's the play?" Su asks.

"Ask if he knows where Twofer is, then keep adding money until he tells us. All we need is a name or a location. Oh, and you should do the talking."

Above her face mask, Su's eyes grow large with concern. "Why me?"

"Your voice is beastier."

I palm her a wad of cash. She discreetly peels off a one-hundred-dollar bill, then puts the rest in her pocket. What was it Sway said?

"Be chill," I murmur.

Su cracks her neck side to side. Taking deep breaths, we step up to Rage. I clear my throat.

It all rests on this.

Just as Su is about to speak, Rage, eyes still shut, points to a sign above his right shoulder that has two kittens on it waving. CLOSED. We pivot. Our backs to him.

"What now?" Su hisses.

"I guess we browse until he's open," I whisper back.

I expected a mob leader to sell weapons or drugs, but Rage's wares more resemble a makeshift pharmacy. His tables are filled with everything from socks to homemade bars of soap to only lightly used-looking razors. At the very end, even more unbelievable than the still-packaged toothbrush, is a stack of pre-Night children's books. I play with the paperclip necklace that Two Five made me as I sift through them and stifle a happy murmur when I see one titled *Plucky and Lucky Go to the Park*.

I read to Two Five from the same children's books I grew up on. They were all non-gender-specific about vegetables or colors or animals. His favorite was also mine. It was a story that my grand must have overlooked, about two ducks that went out to play in the rain. Their names were Plucky and Lucky. They were brother and sister.

"How come Plucky and Lucky get to live together?"

"Well, because they're animals."

"And I'm a beast? That's why I'm kept separate from everybody else?" He sighed, world-weary. *"I wish I was a duck."*

"No you don't, Twofer. All the ducks are dead."

Grand was always adamant about the truth. Half truths did no one any good, she said. We kept Two Five because Grand thought raising him might help Majesty heal. (It didn't.) And we kept him hidden because we couldn't have the males knowing fees were fertile and we couldn't have fees falling in love with one of the very creatures they'd been raised to fear and despise.

"And what do we do when Twofer isn't a baby and starts asking questions?" I asked.

"Hopefully, I'll have figured out a solution before we get to that point," Grand replied.

But she hadn't. Or if she did, she never told me.

"Kore wa toshokande wa arimasen."

Jarring as a hail storm, Rage's voice shakes me from my reverie. Yet I secretly feel a little thrill. Japanese is my favorite of the surviving tongues. Thanks to Itami, I'm fluent.

This isn't a library.

Funny. I thought libraries were a fee-only creation. And that's when I look at the book in my hands and realize the tattooed hulk is speaking to me. Rage still appears to be sleeping, yet now the kitten sign behind him reads: OPEN.

"Suze?" I murmur, taking money from my sock. "I think I'm buying this book."

I can't imagine the look on Two Five's face when he sees it. A grimy sticker on the cover reads $120. Instead of putting two hundred-dollar bills on it, I lay down five of them. I also let Baby Bear drop into my hand, then nod encouragingly at Su.

"We'll take the book and some information about that boy," Su says gruffly.

"Anata to hokanohito." *You and everyone else.*

Itami always said Japanese was the perfect post-nuclear language. It used the fewest words possible to get a point across. Yet now there was so little left, we barely needed any words. Except Su slacked off in her language classes. Her eyes flick to me in panic.

"I said, it will cost you more than five hundred dollars for that information," Rage says, then adds, "Sono naifu o oku ka, watashi wa sore o tsukatte anata no kanzō o kirudeshou."

His eyes open, then close. He told me if I didn't put away my knife, he'd carve out my liver with it. I tuck Baby Bear back up my sleeve.

"Will this do?" Su asks, and lays down her entire big stack of cash.

Her fingers have barely left it before Rage swipes the money from the table and puts it in a fanny pack that's clipped to his stool. Just like that. A quarter of our cash is gone.

He refolds his hands over his chest and closes his eyes.

"Hai. Thank you very much."

"You were supposed to pay him in increments," I say under my breath.

"It wasn't impressed by increments."

I take another wad from beneath my pant leg. "Otokonoko," I say, dangling the stack.

"Speak English. Your Japanese is offensive to my ears."

"The boy. All we want to know is who has him."

Rage cracks his knuckles. It sounds like a car backfiring. Sighing, he readjusts in his seat and opens one eye.

"A male, I'm guessing."

"Which one?" I ask. "And what are they going to do with him?"

A shrug. I hand him the money. When he reaches for it, I jerk it away. Now he is fully awake. His midnight eyes gleam in the red lights.

"I imagine," he says, "they'll do whatever they please."

With a swiftness a beast his size shouldn't be capable of, Rage grabs my wrist. As fast, I jab him in the throat. For a second, we simply stare at each other. If I did that to a fee, she'd be gasping for air right now. Rage smiles and takes the cash from my hand. I desperately try to jerk out of his grasp, but he holds on tight. I can bench 225 pounds, but there's no getting away from this beast. His bicep weighs 225 pounds. He yanks down my mask and tilts my head back.

"Suppressed your apple, did you, little swan?" he asks, inspecting my throat.

"A little help," I call to Su.

"Yes, thank you," Su replies urgently.

Her back is to me, hatchet out. From tables and stalls, mob beasts have formed a loose half circle around us. Rage stands up and dangles me in the air, turning me this way and that, like I'm a sweater he's considering trying on. I desperately reach for my leg.

"Īe," Rage muses. "Soredewa nai." *No, that's not it.*

Rage's eyebrows go up with mild surprise as he considers the better reason my throat wouldn't look like a beast's. My fingers touch duct tape. Ripping it from my calf, I fling our last stack of money into the air. The paper bills waft down like dandelion fuzz caught in a thick, hot breeze. The tunnel is stunned into silence.

Then?

It's mayhem.

"Clever swan," Rage calmly says as behind us a mobster stabs a norm in the eye with a spoon and yanks cash from his hand. "Only you aren't a swan, are you?"

"No, you dirty subpar species. I'm a fee."

11

The words have the desired effect. Rage drops me like I'm scalding hot and backs away. I grab Su's wrist and yank her into the writhing crowd. Rage is on his portable just as quick.

"Watashi no mise ni wa josei ga imasu. Koko ni kite kudasai."

"He's calling backup."

My eyes roam the tunnel as we hurry farther into it. There are three clear options.

Go back. Go forward. Or take the subway platform outside.

"It's like trying to decide how we'll not die the longest," I say.

"Outside will have more escape routes," Su says, then adds, "I can't believe you told that beast you're a fee."

"I think he already knew. And I didn't see you chopping off limbs to help me."

As we hurry toward the subway platform, a wiry mobster ducks out from a stall and cuts us off. He whistles at Rage, who whistles back, then the wiry one strolls toward us, an anticipatory hitch in his step. A jagged scar slashes across his face and mouth, so when he smiles, his lips pull apart vertically to reveal crooked, rotting teeth.

"Gross," I say, because I can't help it and it's true.

"Hellos to you, too, little flower," he lisps. "My name's Jackal. What's yours?"

"Glori," I say as Su simultaneously says, "It's Kiss My Ass."

She glances at me. "Geez, Glor."

"Why, you're both even sweeter than Rage said," Jackal lisps, then announces loudly, "Mob calls these two."

Just like that, the tunnel thoroughfare clears. Where males had stood, there are now dropped soup bowls, still-burning cigarettes, and empty spaces. Some of the norms make a beeline for the outside, clutching our cash to their chest. The rest hover against the walls to watch. Like this is sport.

Ahead of us, two mobsters slide out from behind a set of tables loaded with bags of cigarettes. They're only a little older than us, but their eyes are as lifeless as a dead body. One has a sharp-toothed fish tattooed over his entire face. The other a skull. Both are hoisting heavy chains. They block the south end of the tunnel. Jackal, the subway exit. Rage blocks the north, simply standing in the middle of the tracks, arms crossed, waiting for the others to get us. There is no escape. Jackal watches me realize this and laughs. It is exactly the laugh that Liyan gave the beasts of her campfire stories, high-pitched and malevolent.

Su and I go back-to-back, dropping into our defensive stances, knees bent, hands loosely up. Jackal does a sidestep dance over toward us, shimmying his shoulders.

"Don't come any closer," I say.

"Or what, sweetheart?" He grins.

"Or we'll hurt you." I twirl Baby Bear.

"Is that so? With your widdle knife?"

"Yes. My grandma says honesty is the only acceptable form of communication."

"Like it couldn't tell," Su mumbles.

Jackal throws his head back and belts out more laughter. Seconds later, he hits the ground hard when I drop into a roll and knock him off his feet. Before he can get up, I have a foot on his throat. I press down with all my weight. Su holds her hatchet out to the two males with chains.

"I warned you," I say.

But then Su drops her hatchet and holds her hands up in the air.

"What are you doing?" I hiss.

She nods at Jackal in horror. When I look at him, I see why.

Jackal's holding a gun. And it's aimed at my head. If I wasn't cutting off his air, I know he'd be spewing that awful laugh again. Instead his split lips part, and I get his widest of teeth-exposing smiles. *Click* goes some kind of mechanism on his gun.

Shocked, I say, "Those are banned."

"Oui, but only on Grand Island, sweetheart."

"Oh, waste."

I fling Baby Bear.

But not before Jackal pulls the trigger.

12

The sound of the gunshot inside the tunnel is like a solitary car alarm honking on an uninhabited street. Wrong and eerie and creepy as waste. The force of the bullet striking my arm knocks me off Jackal and onto my butt. My ears pulse from the noise. My left bicep feels like someone dragged a blisteringly hot iron from my elbow up to my shoulder. Blood runs down my arm, drips out my jacket cuff. Gritting my teeth, I grip the wound, then force myself to my feet. Jackal is rolling on the ground shrieking, Baby Bear run through his wrist.

Rage shouts, "Take them alive!"

But Jackal isn't listening. Still screaming, he aims his gun at my chest. Suddenly, a moped flies down the subway stairs, vaults off the platform, and lands right next to us. The back tire spins the bike around, kicking up debris and soot.

It's Sway.

He smashes Jackal in the face with a helmet. Teeth spray into the air like that time Two Five tripped and every last kernel of popped corn flew from his bowl.

No more screaming. Jackal's out cold.

"What are you doing?" Su shouts. "I thought you left."

"What are *you* doing?" he shouts back. "I told you to be chill."

I point at Jackal. "I *stabbed* him," I say, still utterly shocked by the fact.

"He probably deserved it seeing as he *shot* you. Did you see that jump I took?"

"Maybe let's get out of here," Su shouts, then screams and swings her hatchet as the cook mobster comes at her with two cleavers.

"Glori, look out!" Sway yells.

The mobsters with chains are sprinting at me, their eyes still dead.

They must sense this won't end well for them.

Forgetting my wound, I run at them, Mama Bear and Slim drawn. Seconds later, their chains are on the ground, and they both have deep slashes across their brachial arteries at the crooks of their arms. The tunnel floor is splashed with their blood. It's thick and viscous, and the smell fills my nostrils like hot garbage. My stomach somersaults.

"Glori, hop on the bike," Sway says.

Rage is coming toward me. Two normal fee strides for his one.

But I can't move.

"I don't know what to do with my knives."

They are coated in blood. I don't want to wear them or put them in my pack. I barely want to hold them. Whenever I practiced beast counterattack moves with our EMS, they always wore padding and I fought with sticks or wooden spoons. This isn't like practice at all. Across the way, Su has no such qualms. I'm the better fighter, yet her conscience isn't hobbling her. She's already taken down three more beasts.

"Wipe them on Jackal and go," she shouts.

I do as I'm told, only pausing to yank Baby Bear free from Jackal's wrist. It makes a wet slurping sound that is identical to Liyan eating noodles. I'm officially ruined on ramen for life.

"Beast, take Glori. I'm right behind you," Su adds.

"Boto wa wasurenai," Rage's voice booms after us.

"I don't even want to know what he's saying," Sway shouts as I straddle the seat behind him.

"He's roughly saying the mob doesn't forget."

"Fantastic. Of course you speak Japanese."

"It's an eighth of our population's first language. You don't?"

"Are you seriously lecturing me right now?"

Driving over the railroad ties makes pain flash through my arm like heat lightning searing the summer skies. I must black out for a second, because when I open my eyes, the glow from the red lights is gone and we're swerving around a cluster of white stones that are arranged across the tracks. I'm nearly thrown from the moped and let out a surprised cry.

"It's safer if you hold around my waist," Sway shouts.

"You'd like that, wouldn't you?" I shout.

"You not falling off? I'm kinda fifty-fifty on the idea."

I look back over my shoulder. Su is sprinting after us, about sixty yards back. We swerve around another pile of white-and-gray stones. Maybe it's a pain-induced hallucination, but I could swear one of the stones had teeth.

"Was that a pile of skulls?" I ask as my eyelids flutter.

"Uh-huh. It means the Charleston refugees are up ahead. They decamp down here every winter. They're total babies about the cold."

Tiny white dots cloud my vision. They're almost as pretty as the mob's lights, though a lot more hallucinatory. Suddenly, smooth wood planks are set out over the subway tracks, making an actual road. As soon as Sway drives up a homemade on-ramp, and the moped goes silent, then glides to a stop.

"No, no, no. This is a very bad time to be breaking down."

He taps the bike's electric gauge, then hops off and fiddles with the engine wires. I slide off and do a little two-step on wobbly feet. Ten paces ahead of us is another subway platform. In the faint gloom from the upstairs windows, I can make out another pile of skulls in the road.

"I don't hear any pursuit."

Sway shakes his head. "It's not the mob I'm worried about anymore. They'd never risk coming this far in. The Charlestonians require a toll to pass through here."

"So why don't we pay it?"

"Do you have an extra hand lying around?"

"The toll is a *hand*?" I ask, my vision blurring.

"Well, it prevents you from coming this way, doesn't it? Bumping electric mopeds. Easy to steal, useless to drive. I thought this one had more charge. I had a backup plan, but . . . No, no, no," Sway says as the tunnel flips, and I'm forced to sit down. "No local stops."

But then Su is there. Immediately, she rips off her jacket sleeve and ties up my arm.

"Are you crazy?" Sway cries. "That's Gucci!"

Suddenly, a birdcall echoes through the tunnel. It's coming from about thirty feet up and on the left. A second later, another bird replies even farther down. *Birds!* Since birds were as badly affected by the Night as humans—cataracts, small brains, sterility—I've only ever seen photos of most species. Not including all the crows that somehow managed to survive.

"How wonderful," I murmur.

But then shadowy figures slink out from the dark tunnel.

At first there are three.

Then five.

Then ten.

And then there are too many to count.

"Glor," Su says in awe. "I don't think they're all beasts."

She's right. While most of them have immense face hair that reaches down their chest, a few are entirely face-hair-free. But more telling is the shape of their bodies in the old pre-Night fitted coats they wear. The Charlestonians' brutality now makes sense—why hide in subway tunnels and exact gruesome tolls unless you had something invaluable to protect?

Su laughs and waves her hands over her head, walking forward. "Hello!"

"What are you doing?" Sway calls, panicked.

"Some of them are fee," Su says. "They'll help us."

Suddenly, a brick strikes her in the shoulder. Another smashes into the moped. Just as a Charlestonian roars, "Attack!" a bright floodlight illuminates the tunnel. We and they cringe and shrink in the blinding light.

"Hey, Holy City goits," a voice calls from up on the subway platform. "Sorry. I'm a little late. I was deep in a Snuggie-and-Denzel marathon when the call came, but those are my friends, and this box of fresh veggies plus this automatic weapon say it's in your best interest to let them leave here fully intact. I'd fire a warning shot for effect, but I don't want to waste the bullets. So trust me, okay?"

Behind the floodlight, a lean male holds a gun that's half the size of his body. He kicks a box over to the edge of the platform. Two Charlestonian males come forward to take the produce, but I can't take my eyes from the three fees behind them. Though filthy, they seem healthy enough.

Grand said not every fee crossed with them at the divide. Some had sons or husbands. Some simply favored their survival chances with the beasts. Determined, Su again runs forward. To save them or be embraced by them, I can't tell. But a beast steps out and blocks her, hefting a two-by-four with nails driven into it.

"Back the hell off," he growls.

"Maverick," I hear a fee behind him say. "I think that's a girl."

"No. That's a ghost, Charity. We don't mourn or help ghosts."

Without a single backward glance, they leave us. Matricula Rhodes has a saying, all fees for one or no fees at all. These fees have chosen a side and it isn't ours. Su lets out an anguished cry and looks at me with brimming eyes. She thought all our problems were solved. Now not only are we still mired in them, we're not even a little better off.

I go to pull her into a hug, but before I can, the new beast levels his gun on us.

I put my hands up in the air, my vision cutting out as I raise the wounded one.

"Comma." Sway sighs. "Don't you dare."

"You SOS'd me—in a snowstorm. That gives me every right to dare."

Swinging the gun around to Sway, the male pulls the trigger.

A steady stream of water squirts Sway in the chest.

"Great." Sway throws his hands up. "Now I'm gonna catch a cold."

And maybe it's relief or maybe it's the blood loss or maybe it's that we almost died three times in about as many hours, but that's when I vomit on Sway's feet, then pass out cold.

13

"What's the difference between a beast and a fee?" I ask my grand.

She is sitting outside on the back porch, surrounded by her usual assortment of portables, all with varying degrees of charge. I'm dreaming. I know that immediately. Not only because it's suddenly the hot months, but because there are cows in the yard behind our house and I've only ever seen those in Twofer's picture books. Never mind these cows are purple.

But my relief at seeing my Grand Mati feels very real.

Her face lights up when she looks at me, and she immediately puts her work aside. "That sounds like the setup for a joke."

"I'm serious. Because it's not so obvious to me that there is a difference."

This conversation happened. In waking life. Many times, in many different ways. But this one specifically so that I know in another moment, Grand will get up, stretch, and motion toward the pitcher of sun tea that lives on the back porch in the hot months.

She does.

"Glori," Grand warns as she sets my tea beside me. In my dream it is the exact shade of blood that coated my clothes after I slashed the two mobsters. "We've been over this."

Yes. Fine. We couldn't send him over because the beasts might guess some of us were fertile. Yet keeping him was a double standard that *might* jeopardize everything we'd been striving to build. Still I didn't see why, a year later, we couldn't figure out how to integrate him.

"Matricula Rhodes always talks about how we're creating a new world. Why can't fees accept Twofer like they accept Lovie or Harmony? A fee with different sex parts?"

Suddenly, as it did that night, the screen door whines open and slaps shut. Only now all the ambient light gets sucked out of the air. In the pitch-blackness, I suddenly have the weight of Twofer in my arms. I hold him tighter, as I did that night, when Majesty sidled out onto the porch.

"Save yourself the resentment and tell her the truth, Mother," my own mother says.

When I was growing up, Majesty's voice went up and down the scales with a vivacious musicality. After she was snatched, it always played the same flat note. In my mind, my mother existed as a pair of opposites. There was the Majesty from before she was taken. And the one from after.

Her skin, like crepe paper dusted with ash, suddenly glows luminescent.

"What truth is that, Maj?" Grand Mati asks.

"The truth," Majesty says, so quietly that Grand and I both lean forward, "is that even when there were appropriate amounts of food and water and beautiful things in the world, like the color green, beasts were power-obsessed, narcissistic, philandering monsters. The truth is that Nuclear Night did not change them as much as it *freed* them and all their most primal urges."

"But maybe Two Five is different," I say, cradling and shushing him so his little toddler ears won't hear her hateful words.

"And maybe tomorrow I will wake up a cat."

Majesty steps into the backyard grass, and suddenly a swing is beside her. The same type as at the island's old amusement park. The ones she likes to sit on, twisting the chains around and around until it seems they might snap. This is how she's spent a large portion of every day for the last six months. Just silently twisting.

"Glori," she continues, "do you know why we do not talk about the beasts or our history with them? Because they are not worth the breath. We do not live with the beasts because we are finally free. And we do not tell you about the beasts because you can never fully know how evil they were and we hope you never have to. This is much bigger than *that*." By *that* she means Two Five. "This is about power. With no males, for the first time in history, our power is finally our own."

Suddenly, we're standing in the kitchen. Majesty is in the doorway wearing a cat mask, as realistic as the ones Two Five's snatchers had on.

"I saw you," she says.

It's the morning after I rode Twofer into the neighborhood. This is what she said. It's the first words, never mind complete sentence, she's spoken in months. Twofer's no longer in my arms but out in the yard catching crickets for dinner just as he was that morning.

"Hi!" I hear him say as I fill our water glasses from a jug by the sink.

I try to peer out the window, but Majesty steps in my way.

"I saw you. On your bike. You took it into town."

"Please don't tell Grand." I try to get around her. "No one else saw. I'm positive. It's just that Twofer had a bad day yesterday and . . . I think it's going a little crazy out here."

"Aren't we all?" my mother asks, the cat lips lifting up ever so slightly.

Outside, car doors slam.

Next comes Twofer's panicked call. "Glori?"

I drop our water glasses and scream, "Twofer, run!"

Only by the time I get there, the car is gone. In real life I ran after it. In my dream I simply stand there until Majesty comes to the door.

"Don't forget," she calls. "They always see."

I wake drenched in sweat, my left arm throbbing. I am in an enormous room in an enormous bed that is covered by an absurd number of pink-and-green comforters. I pull my knees to my chest and rock myself the way I rocked Two Five every time he had a nightmare. But the only thing that makes me feel better is repeating my pledge again and again.

"I'll find you. I promise. I'll find you. I promise. I promise. I promise. I'll find you."

14

"**S**uze?" I quietly call out as if she might be hiding somewhere among this menagerie.

Around me, floor-to-ceiling windows line an entire wall and are covered by sheer pink, blue, and yellow pastel drapes that remind me of a sunrise. The fabric hangs from metal pipes that encircle all four walls of the room, clearly hiding shelves. Colorful carpets haphazardly coat the floors, and everywhere there are life-size fake animals. Wood-carved giraffes. An entire herd of stone sheep. An enormous stuffed lion. And in a throne-like chair in a corner sits a bizarre sculpture of a fee in a dress with a shark head. I must be high up. From where I lie, hazy late afternoon sky is my only view.

It's then I hear the whispering.

"Do loafers go with cutoffs?" a voice hisses. "Of course I'm mad, Sway. The only reason we get by is because no one knows we're here. And now…"

"You're the one that said we should bring them back, Comma."

I quickly check myself. Though I do not see my girls or my pack, my clothes are in place and my body feels undisturbed, with the exception that the left sleeve of my shirt has been cut away and my arm has been wrapped in clean cloth. Wincing, I peel back the bandage. Where the bullet grazed my bicep, it scooped out a pecan-size divot of flesh, which is now tidily dressed with four neat stitches. It looks well cleaned. Good. I highly doubt males make their own antibiotics like fees do.

"Well, you're the one who helped them to begin with. Hanging around the river like some scavenger creep. And I get it, I do. You're hoping to get information about *her*, but that big one looks like he wants to eat me, Sway. And not in a good way."

Sway laughs. "I wouldn't worry, you're too bony to eat."

"Joke all you like. But if this goes bad or you get hurt, so help me, I'll give you a choppy fade."

"No, you won't, Com. You love my hair more than you love me."

"Well, today I hate both you and your marvelously straight, ethnically unambiguous locks." The male lets out a puff of exasperated breath. "No, I don't. I can't even pretend. Do you think he's awake?"

"You mean, do I think you screaming about loafers woke her? Yes, yes I do."

Footsteps. Sharp. Light. I jump out of bed and position myself behind the door. When it's thrown open a second later, the curtains along the walls billow, and before I can properly grasp the wonders beyond, a beast charges into the room.

"Rise and whine, little nag! Wait. Where'd he go?"

No sooner does he turn to look for me than I have his arm pinned behind his back and his face pressed to the wall. It's the same male who rescued us from the subway platform. He doesn't look much older than Sway, but he couldn't be more different. Whereas Sway is tall and thin and lithe, this one is more compact, leanly muscular, and much darker. His curls are shaved close to the side of his head, but on top they're picked out and messy. Half are an orangey yellow; the other half look more naturally black. He's wearing tight, shiny pants and a loud, bright blue shirt that hangs off a toned shoulder. Rings decorate every single finger, and he's wearing what looks like a wand in a holster across his chest.

"You're right," he says with his face smooshed to the brick wall. "This one is much less frightening than the other."

Sway leans against the doorjamb. Savory cooking smells waft in after him.

"Glori, Commander. Commander, Glori."

"Don't say it," Commander says. "I couldn't command my way out of a dark room. But I am excellent at making my way *into* dark rooms, if you know what I mean."

I look to Sway.

He laughs. "Clearly, she doesn't."

Commander shushes Sway, then says, "You can call me Comma. Everyone does."

"Is that a wand on your chest?"

"Sacrilege. It's a Majesterial horn replica from the Unicorn Warrior films, which were based on the acclaimed and beloved television series *Unicorn Warrior*. This horn is the only good thing those films produced." He puts a hand to his mouth and fake whispers, "*Unicorn Warrior* is my life. And if that statement doesn't assure you I'm not the threatening one in this situation, nothing will. Can you maybe release me now?"

I hesitate, but then Su is there.

"You can let it go. As far as I can tell, it's safe."

"Did he just call me an it?" Comma quickly steps away from me, rubbing his wrist. "You're right, Sway, this *is* worth risking our lives over."

Su pulls at the bandages on my arm.

"You probably shouldn't remove that yet..." Sway says.

"That is going to be one wicked scar," Su says enviously.

"I'm sure we can get you your own gunshot wound soon enough," I reply.

"Promises, promises." She puts her forehead to mine. "Thanks be you're okay."

"This is not how they described y'all in nag class," Comma says.

We both turn our heads so our cheeks are pressed together.

"Nag class?" I ask.

I feel my forehead crinkle into what Su calls my get-out-the-way face, but I can't help it. The beasts are taking classes on fees?

"It's a program Mayor Chia started for all us younger norms," Comma says, and then ticks off on his fingers. "So far we've learned that you're sensitive. That you love talking about how things make you *feel*. And how to be a good listener—smile and nod—also, that you're weaker than we are..."

"Huh!" Su laughs.

"Terrible drivers..." Comma continues.

"Who drives anymore?" I ask.

"And bad at fixing things," Comma says.

"Okay, now I'm getting annoyed," Su grunts.

"Oh! And that you're very emotional and cry at the drop of a hat."

"Who would cry at a hat dropping?" I ask innocently. "Did the hat get hurt? Was it the last hat to survive and now there are no more hats?"

"Sway." Comma grabs at him. "I can't tell if she's joking or not. Interpret."

"I couldn't be joking," I say. "Didn't you know? Fees aren't as funny as beasts, either."

But that last one gets me. Twofer teared up a lot. When he skinned his knee. If he stepped on an ant. If Su jumped out and scared him. Was that not normal? Thinking of Twofer crying over the small nothings of day-to-day life, I can't imagine how terrified he must be right now. As if reading the shift in my expression, Sway gestures out of the room.

"Should we eat? There's a lot to talk about."

I nod gratefully. As I follow him out, I ask under my breath, "How often do you cry?"

He shrugs. "I don't know. Whenever it's appropriate, I guess."

Behind us, Comma sidles up to Su like a fly to half-eaten fruit.

"Now *you* tell *me*," he says. "What do you learn in your classes on males?"

Su considers, then replies, "Primarily how to kill you."

15

Some minutes later, we wary four sit around an island in an open kitchen that is bigger than the entire Costco bakery section, in a loft that is at *least* the size of a soccer field. More floor-to-ceiling windows line the wall facing the river. Which is strange, because the males—boys, as they keep calling themselves—seem so much smarter than enormous windows that let out the warmth in the freezing months and let in the scorching sun in the heat months.

As in Comma's bedroom, the loft is filled to excess. There are at least twenty different guitars, a deflated jump house, too many half-built Gundam models to count, and an enormous framed canvas covered in paint splatter that is longer than Su and me standing an arm's length apart.

"Matricula Rhodes says ownership breeds discontent," Su says, surveying the loft.

"Then she's clearly never sat in a massage chair," Comma replies.

Sway clears his throat. "Everyone, dig in."

Laid out on the counter before us in red glazed ceramic bowls is a veritable feast. A spicy Japanese curry with eggs and kale, various pickled root vegetables, a clay pot of porridge, a stack of homemade scallion pancakes, and a bowl of little circle pastas in a bright red sauce. With the exception of the pasta, it smells similar to the food Liyan cooks and looks one hundred times more delicious than the cabbage soup that is my Grand Mati's specialty.

Su leans back, arms crossed. "Sorry. I'm allergic to poison."

Sway shakes his head and scoops porridge into his bowl. "Let me guess, Matricula Rhodes says that's how we kill you. Fine. More for us. But please tell Madame Rhodes that if we were gonna poison you, we wouldn't waste SpaghettiOs doing it."

It's just an offhand comment—still, Su and I exchange a look. It goes unnoticed as the males fill their bowls. After clinking their spoons together, they begin inhaling their food with their mouths practically right to the edge of their dishes.

It is, quite frankly, gross.

"Learn some table manners," Su grunts.

"What for?" Sway asks.

Su's eyes track back to me as I put a little curry on a scallion pancake. "Don't even..."

"I'm no help to Twofer if I starve, Suze."

Before she can stop me, I take a bite.

I press my eyes shut.

"Are you okay?" She leans across and shakes my arm. Luckily not the wounded one. "Roach? Roach!"

I look at Su and smile. It's not like Liyan's cooking. It's better. I quickly spoon curry into my bowl. After a few more bites, Su grabs my wrist and takes my pulse. When it's clear my heart is not seizing up, she slips a pancake onto her plate. Sway meets my eyes and grins. I quickly look away, the rich food suddenly flipping in my belly.

"So, what have you learned about where Two Five is?" I ask.

"Not much yet." Sway slurps porridge. "Through the pipeline, we've heard lots of theories, but none worth men—"

"Aristotle bets he's going to be the prize at this week's Road Races," Comma interrupts, spraying scallion pancake crumbs across the table. "Flux Capacitator bets he was traded to the Charlestonians for one of their women. Which makes sense why those Holy City goits came at you so hard. And Fuego insists your bruth was taken to the Fortress. That he's being cloned."

"Cloned?" Su repeats. "Beasts have that capability?"

"No one has that capability," Sway says, and I try very hard not to look at Su again. "Don't listen to Comma. The Charlestonians would never trade a fee. Period. A human child is too big a prize for a Road Race. And the stuff that goes on at the Fortress is all urban legend."

"What's that mean?" I ask.

"The Fortress is this giant end-of-times bunker that's past the farms, down the road from where we grew up," Sway explains. "It's the place everyone's dad threatened to send them if they misbehaved. What happens inside changes on a family-by-family basis. A mad scientist runs it. A mad scientist runs it as a torture palace. A mad scientist runs it as a torture palace that churns out AI. Take your pick." Sway rolls his eyes at our blank expressions. "*AI* means artificial intelligence."

"Robots," Comma says loudly, as if volume and not vocabulary are the hindrance to our understanding. "Maybe they're not making robots, but, Sway, you know the Fortress is up to some kind of no good." To us he adds, "My dad, Rugged, thinks it's where our first mayor, Mayor Grim, sent all his dissenters after he took office. Fortitude's leftovers, if you will. Rugged used to let us set bear traps in the woods, Sway. He wouldn't make us stay away from the Fortress if the stuff that went on inside it was just urban legend."

As Sway helps himself to more curry, Comma takes his bowl to a gunmetal-gray garbage can and drops it in. Not the unfinished food. The *entire* bowl. Su wails in protest. Unperturbed, Comma returns and plucks my knit hat off my head. I'm so shocked by his flagrant wastefulness I don't even flinch. And then panic flutters in my chest like moths at our solar porch light. I'm no closer to finding Twofer now than I was on the other side of the river.

Comma stops picking at my hair and leans a heavy hand on my shoulder.

"Oh my Gray Grantham Hallow. That's it, Sway. Dissenters. Take them to the Influencer."

Sway snorts. "No way."

"Why not? The Influencer ticks every box. Close to the mayor. Ear to the ground. He's probably the one who saw the little boy. . . . What's your brother's non-name again?"

"Two Five."

"Right. The Influencer probably spotted Little Digit coming over in the first place."

Sway taps his spoon against his lips. "Huh. Except the Influencer hates fees."

"Who's the Influencer?" Su asks.

Sway stands up, stretches, then retrieves Comma's bowl from the garbage.

"This goit that broke into one of the old television stations a few years back and rerouted things. . . . Honestly, I don't know what he did. Anyway, now he's one of the most powerful people in the city, in charge of the programming on every screen. You want to binge *Chef Down* on the ad board in Ellicott Square? You talk to the Influencer. The only problem is, Euphoria, the place he holes up in, is impenetrable. Even if we got in, you two wouldn't last five seconds."

"Great." I stand up. "Let's go."

"Didn't you hear the 'only problem' part of what I just said?" Sway laughs.

"Sure, but impenetrable? I doubt that."

"You also forgot," Comma says, "the Influencer hates nags."

I sigh, frustrated. Then I have an idea.

"Then make us less fee." Su starts to protest, but I hurry on. "In the tunnel, for a second, Rage thought I was something called a swan. Why can't I pretend to be that?"

"That's actually not a terrible idea," Comma says.

One second Sway's wiping out Comma's bowl, the next he's right beside me. As fast, I have his upper body pinned to the table, the pointy end of a chopstick pressed against his throat. Just as quick, Su has one pressed to Comma's heart. A bowl of pickled root vegetables spins off the table and breaks on the floor. Despite the threat of being impaled by a chopstick, Comma squeals and applauds. My arm is thrown across Sway's shoulders and neck. The lengths of our bodies are pressed together. Our faces inches apart.

"I admire your confidence, slick, but if you want to get your brother, you can't do *that* every time some norm approaches you. *I'll* go talk to the Influencer. You two would need way too much desensitization to ever make it work."

"Desensitization to what?" Su asks.

"Males," Sway says.

Absurdly slowly, he raises a finger up to my face. It takes every ounce of self-control I have not to break it. Finally, he presses it to the tip of my nose.

"Boop."

I can't take it. I spring off him. He pushes himself off the table and whips his torso around, cracking his back. Su slowly lowers her chopstick.

"I might need a little desensitization," I say. "But if anyone is going for Twofer, it's me."

Before Sway can respond, his portable chirps with an incoming PTT. Although what Grand called cellular service went out with the Night, as long as the correct app had been previously downloaded, the walkie-talkie-style push-to-talk voice messaging feature still worked on most portable devices.

Now Sway's portable says, "Nice coat, you goit. Turn on your TV."

Cursing, Sway hurries to the far end of the loft, where four giant leather recliners are set in front of a tennis court–size screen. Comma grabs a remote and clicks play. A windowsill-mounted wind-powered generator whirls, and the screen flickers to life.

I gasp. "What the . . . ?"

"Chill, sweetie, it's only the news," Comma says.

Now Su gasps. "You mean this is a *live* feed?"

"Oh my Hallowed Horned Halls," Comma murmurs as he watches the screen. "You two are famous."

"I don't know what any of that means," I say.

Sway clarifies, "They're onto you."

"Who?" Su asks as I hold my breath.

"By now?" Sway says. "Everyone."

16

"We're back with continuing coverage of this morning's female sighting and an update from the mayor. . . ."

This comes from an elderly male who is sitting in his living room in his underwear and a ratty T-shirt. You'd think maybe he'd dress for the occasion. But then the screen flashes and suddenly is filled with a burly male with slicked-back salt-and-pepper hair. He wears a clean, pressed, pre-Night suit that he makes look rumpled. *Mayor Chia*, the caption beneath him reads. This is the males' equivalent of our Matricula Rhodes. Only he's been in office for a third of the time. I expected him to look evil or corrupt, yet he just looks tired.

"Fellow citizens, we are considering these females armed and dangerous. If you see them, you are instructed to call the patrol immediately. Do not engage them. They appear to be assassins sent here to retrieve the child who was erroneously reported to have crossed the river."

"Erroneously?" Su echoes, her eyes flicking to me with worry.

"That means wrongly reported," Comma says. "Goodness gracious, read a book."

"I repeat, there is no child in Buffalo. Granted, this is a condition we are working to change. Raiding Grand Island or attacking females will not help these pursuits."

"Why does he keep calling us fee-*males*?" I ask.

"Like he thinks he owns us," Su adds.

Sway mumbles, "Bump me."

Comma shushes us all, squints at the screen.

"I cannot be clearer," Chia says in a steady yet slightly impatient voice. "If you see these females, you must call or hand them over to your local patrol immediately. Any males found abetting them, holding them hostage, auctioning them or their body parts off for profit, or using them for sex will immediately be subject to death. Hand them in, though, and as a show of my office's appreciation, you will receive a fifty-thousand-dollar reward."

"Whoa," Comma huffs. "Not to say you aren't worth every penny, but that is . . ."

"Astronomical," Sway finishes for him.

Su is glaring at me. Lest her hot gaze sear off my face, I finally look at her.

She mouths, *What if they figured out who you are?*

I tug my ear. *I can't hear you.*

If Comma and Sway think we're priceless solely for being fees, how fast would they turn us over if they knew which fees we actually were? This is not good.

"As you know, our talks with Matricula Rhodes have stalled these last few years. I hopefully do not have to explain how important a little bartering leverage is. So let me repeat—again—there is no reward if we have to take them from you. Or if you turn them in dead or in pieces or harmed or damaged in any way. This includes bruised, cut, violated . . ."

As the mayor continues validating everything we've ever been taught about beasts, the screen cuts back to the newscaster. He blows his nose on a not-clean-looking sock.

"You'd think maybe he'd try to look a little more presentable," I say.

"Why bother?" the males say together.

"We do have a photo of one of the females," the newscaster says.

"Holy waste," Su curses.

Because suddenly, she is looking at her hatchet-wielding self.

It was snapped in the tunnel. I'm next to her but as barely more than a vertical blur. Sway, meanwhile, is a fuzzy bright orange cloud on a moped.

"You look fierce, boy," Comma says to Su, nodding approvingly at the photo.

"Thank you." Su blushes, pleased.

"Eyewitnesses describe the other female as five feet nine inches tall, one hundred and sixty-five pounds, with medium brown skin and dark brown eyes...."

I scoff, "That describes more than half of the fee population."

"We do not have a description of the male that is aiding them other than that he is wearing a loud orange jacket and a bright yellow bandanna."

"Loud?" Sway echoes.

"Told you," Comma says.

"Do you think Matricula can see this?" I ask Su.

She shakes her head. "I don't think so. Stuff would have exploded by now if she had."

Su's right. At this point, someone should have found our note. Which meant, one way or another, Matricula had to know we were gone. And while I'm sure she was highly displeased, she wouldn't risk fees' lives trying to bring us back. But if she found out the *beasts* knew we were here?

And were offering that big a reward? Well, that would certainly change the game.

"And this just in." The newscaster holds a finger to his ear. "The mayor is issuing a reward for the male as well. Thirty dollars. Alive or dead. Now back to our rebroadcast of the 1989 AFC Divisional Playoff Game between the Buffalo Bills and the Cleveland Browns."

Sway clicks off the television, stunned.

"Thirty dollars?" he says. "I own toothbrushes that cost more than that."

His portable immediately chirps, but he silences it before we can hear the PTT message. Comma glances at the front door. Which is when I realize that not only do I have no idea where my girls are, but that we are locked in a monstrous warehouse with two well-connected males who have recently learned that we're worth enough money to sustain them for at least a decade. Never mind that if I were in their position? With my own life at stake? I'd turn them in faster than water evaporates off the sidewalk in the heat months.

Clearly having identical thoughts, Su slowly takes a flashlight off a side table and goes back-to-back with me. As if beasts might suddenly rappel in through the windows or spring up out of the aboveground pool the males filled with plastic balls. Sway holds his hands out the way I do when I approach skittish feral cats.

"Everyone, calm down," he says.

"If you get me to my brother," I say, "I can get you double that amount of money. Not the thirty dollars. The really big number. Our number."

"Rub it in, thanks," Sway says. "No one's turning you in. Comma, you're up."

"I'm what now?" Comma asks, eyeing Su and her flashlight.

"Swanify Glori. Full treatment with as much desensitization as you can squeeze in." Comma starts to protest, but Sway stops him. "It'll only get worse if we wait. They'll be expecting us to go to ground. They won't be expecting us on the street. Su, you'll stay here."

"My left breast, I will." Both males look. She rolls her eyes. "It's an expression."

Sway reddens and continues, "That's the only way I'll do it. They have your picture, and you're too protective of Glori to pass. You'd need a year of desensitization around norms, and I'm not sure that'd even be enough. You'll put everyone at risk."

Su spins on me. "We don't need them. Let's go back to the Charlestonians. I remember the route. They're fees, Glor. If we explain who we are and what we're doing here, they have to help us. Plus, you heard that one." She nods at Comma. "They might already have Twofer."

The choice is between my best friend and a scrawny, fast-talking beast. No doubt Sway knows his way around the city. But even if he can get me in to speak with the influencing beast who hates fees, he might also backstab me at any moment. Or decide something is too dangerous and leave. Even as my brain murmurs that he rescued us from the mob, it more loudly reminds me that he left us to defend ourselves against them in the first place.

Only coincidence has aligned me with this male. Yet I have spent my entire lifetime with Su. There's no one else I trust more implicitly. Maybe we don't have Sway's connections, but we shouldn't split up. There is no choice here.

But then Su quietly says, "Think about what Matricula Rhodes would do."

What would Matricula Rhodes do if Twofer were in danger and she had to choose between sticking with fees or rescuing an innocent child?

She'd stick with the fees. At all costs. Without veering off course for love or family. She'd stick with the fees.

I should know.

After all, Two Five and I aren't some random children to Matricula Rhodes.

We're her grandchildren.

17

"**S**orry, Suze. I'm going with Sway."

Su flinches as big as if I'd swung a surprise right hook at her.

"And what am I supposed to do?" she asks.

"Maybe you can go back home and try to run interference with Grand."

Although this is what would be most helpful, going by the I-will-murder-you expression that settles over Su's face, it's not the answer she was looking for.

"Or you can stay here with Comma," Sway quickly says. "And be an integral part of the next portion of the rescue plan."

"Right." Comma snaps his fingers. "And in the meantime, you have lots of vital catching up to do. We won't have long enough for all twenty seasons of *Unicorn Warrior*, but we can start the HP reboot, *Harriet Potter*. And she's *Black*. They only made three films before the world ended, but Snape alone will turn these lemons into lemonade. Hu-buh."

"Sure, why not." Su wipes at her eyes. "Better than going anywhere with this traitor."

She doesn't say it lightly. And she isn't kidding. But I don't blame her.

Su risked the ire of our entire community, never mind her own life, to come here. Yet she came without question, because I asked. Now I have chosen a beast over her. And not for the first time. Kind of ever since Twofer came into our lives. No wonder she never liked him.

"I'll be on the roof if you need me," Sway quietly says. "We'll leave at dusk."

Hoisting up the window next to the generator, Sway wiggles out onto the fire escape. As the burned smell of fresh air fills my nostrils, his foot catches on the windowsill and he stumbles to one knee. Only after manually unsnagging his leg does he spring to his feet and give a thumbs-up, his face flushed bright red.

"Solid choice, Glori," Su says.

She bangs into my shoulder as she heads to a tire swing the males installed over the aboveground pool ball pit. Hand over hand she climbs the swing's rope to the ceiling.

"Don't worry about her," Comma says. "Of all the bumps and scratches, bruised egos hurt the worst. She just needs to climb out her anger, apparently. In the meantime, lesson number one. The three things you will need to pass as a male, swan or any other variant, are confidence, ownership of place, and balls."

"But I'm a fee. I'll never have testicles."

Comma's eyes go wide. "You murder me! It's like you speak in T-shirt slogans."

He goes to take my wrist, but I smack his hand away.

"Sorry." I take a deep breath. Let it out. "I know I have to stop doing that."

"Let's try again, shall we?"

This time I hold still as his fingers lightly encircle my wrist. His touch is soft. Gentle. No different from Twofer's or Grand's.

"Very good," he says as he guides me across the loft back to his quarters. "And no, dolly. By balls, I do not mean the actual physical accoutrements. How do I je ne sais quoi this? What I mean is the gravitas they deliver. The brashness. Oomph, essentially. Like this..."

Comma stomps his foot, throws out his hands, then shimmies his shoulders. When I do not seem impressed, he sighs.

"Anyway, little fee, luckily the balls part you already have covered. You walk like a mobster, fight like the patrol, and scowl better than Sway. If it weren't for those tiny little boobies and the fact that you practically rip males to shreds every time they so much as breathe near you, I'd say you fit right in."

At the door to a white-tiled bathroom that's spacious enough to house a co-family of ten, Comma stops and calls out to Su, "Are you coming, Spidey? You'll definitely want to see this. I'm about to give Glori the one thing that remains sacred, honored, and adored across all genders, rivers, and weather-ravaged countries."

Having climbed to the ceiling, Su is now doing pull-ups on the metal rafters.

She calls out, "A seven-inch axle-to-axle slingshot tech crossbow?"

"A giant piece of corn bread?" I guess.

Comma pinches the bridge of his nose. "Remind me never to bring either of you to a party. No. Even better than a crossbow or food, I'm giving Glori... drumroll, please... a makeover."

Su and I immediately look at each other. Normally, we'd laugh. A makeover? *What is that?* But then she remembers she's mad at me.

"I'd prefer the crossbow," she grunts.

"You're going to make me look ridiculous, aren't you?"

Comma tsks and says, "I do believe the *o-u-s* word you're looking for is *fabulous*. It's how you carry it off that determines the prefix."

18

"Oh dear," Comma says.

"Please stop saying that."

Two hours later, we're all staring at my reflection in the mirror of Comma's bathroom wondering if it's too late to go back in time and reverse this entire thing. I have been shaved, plucked, deodorized, and perfumed in regions that have never before said hello to the sun and if you ask me, were better left that way.

For the hundredth time, I hold my arms above my head. My underarms look so underdressed, like being naked at the dinner table; my legs the same. But when I tried to resist shaving them and insisted that hair insulated us, Comma shot back that so did another neat invention called clothing. And that no swan would ever be caught dead with my Chewbacca level of body hair. So now I stare mournfully at my goose-pimpled arm divots. Because I can't quite manage to look at my face.

After hacking off my butt-length braids with three heavy scissor cuts, Comma powered up a pair of solar clippers. Now my head looks almost like his, nearly bare along the sides, with what can only be described as a mane on top. It starts at my widow's peak and goes to the nape of my neck. Mounds of shaved curly brown hair lie scattered at our feet. After the haircut, I actually thought I resembled Two Five a bit. But then Comma went and put bleach on my hair—apparently an all-the-rage trend for males my age—and now it's so yellow it's almost white, gelled upward so that it swoops into a peak.

"Glori, bruth," Comma says, gently directing my chin until I meet my eyes in the mirror. "No one knows better than me what it's like to be attached to something disastrous. In my case, his name is Fuego. Don't play with fire, lesson learned *many* times over. But, dolly, you look so pretty without all that extra-ness."

"Except I don't want to be pretty, Comma."

"Who doesn't want to be pretty?" He squints at me as he sweeps up the floor.

I thought I'd made that clear.

Me. I don't want to be pretty or anything it entails. Back home, anytime Liyan let slip a compliment about how lovely my hair was, Grand would go off on a rant about how beauty standards were the first thing that should have died with the Night.

Beauty was a yoke, she would say, that's harnessed us since the dawn of time. Then she'd list a bunch of procedures I didn't know the definitions of and didn't care to. Hair dye. Hair straightening. High heels. Liposuction. Tummy tucks. Botox. Teeth whitening. Electrolysis.

Back then, Grand told me *pretty* meant every fee always thought she had to lose five to ten pounds. *Pretty* meant we took hot wax and applied it to our vaginas. As far as I was concerned, Beauty could toss her high-maintenance ass over the Falls.

Now *pretty* was a fiery sunset after a day of hard rain.

A clean leg sweep.

The golden crust on a loaf of fresh-baked bread.

Thanks be, *pretty* no longer had anything to do with us.

Jostling me aside, Su inspects her teeth in the mirror.

"I, for one, think Glori looks absurd."

"Let's agree on absurdly beautiful," Comma says. As my inner voice rebuts, *Beautiful is watching a cell divide through a microscope,* he adds, "I know thirty different boys who would kill for your eyelashes."

Su stops picking at her teeth.

"Not, like, literally, though, right?" I ask, as much to reassure Su as myself.

I mean, the mayor *did* warn his citizens against breaking us down for parts.

Comma laughs. "Glori, dear, you have to release this go-to assumption that all boys want to slaughter anything that moves. So, no, not literally. In fact, lesson number two is: Males love them some innuendo. Especially when it references their privates."

"By privates, you mean penis, testicles, and anus?"

"Oh my Gilded Gruff," Comma squeals. "You're murdering me! To wardrobe! To wardrobe!"

Tugging us along like we're maces to his chain, Comma yanks Su and me into his bedroom, where he immediately gathers sections of the pastel curtains and slides them back along the pipes with a flourish. Comma and I smile at each other. Even Su grunts with admiration. Because hidden behind the fabric are racks and racks *and racks* of clothes. They are all sorted by color. Apple-red jackets, garnet shirts, and flaming fire-hydrant-colored skirts flow into an array of orange items all in the same vibrant jeweled order until at the very end of the rainbow is a section—double the size of the rest—of black garments.

Beyond the clothes, on their own individual shelves, is an entire boutique of hats. Shell hats with ruffles. Top hats with thick patterned bands. Plus, more than a few hats that look like they could take flight for all the feathers.

And the shoes.

Boxes and boxes stacked at least ten feet high with the front flap cut away so you can see inside. Brightly colored sneakers, fringed boots, and so many glittery, colorful pairs with tiny heels that have to be solely decorative, because what male in his right mind would choose to walk around in tight shoes balancing on the equivalent of chopsticks?

"It's okay to happy cry." Squinting at me, Comma plucks a tiny white-veiled hat off its shelf and sits it on the very tip-top of my hair at a jaunty angle. "Please tell me you're a size-eleven shoe."

"Eight."

"Close enough. Now listen, little nag. Sway won't tell you this because it's not his style, but it's very important. Lesson number three: If things ever get out of hand, don't be afraid to fall back on your feminine wiles."

"Her what?" Su asks.

"You know"—Comma pulls out a gold, sparkly shift and holds it against my chest, then crinkles his nose and lovingly hangs it back on the rack—"play up your sexuality. Be alluring."

He bounces his shoulders, drops his chin, and winks.

"She needs to pretend her head is heavier than usual and there's something in her eye?" Su asks. "Are you trying to tell her to flirt? Because no fee flirts like that. Glori, sexy isn't this waste. Sexy is a look. Or a touch. It's chemistry. Passion. Racing pulses. Secret kisses."

Comma has literally dropped what he's doing to listen. "Go big or go home, I guess."

"I mean"—Su blushes—"at least that's what it's like in my experience."

"She's right, though, Comma," I say. "No fee acts like that. Ever."

"Perfect, because you aren't trying to be a fee, are you? At least not today's model."

He presses a black sweater and a pair of sparkly leggings into my arms along with a pair of shiny white thigh-high boots that have only moderately absurd heels on them. He also tosses me a warm-looking melon-green puffy coat with an enormous ostrich-feather hood.

"All I'm saying is with your face, boys were going to look at you no matter what I did. But if you get into trouble and any of them seem to recognize the king beneath the queen, then you can't go acting all awkward, freezing up the way you do around Sway."

"I don't freeze up around Sway."

"Trust me," Comma says. "You do."

I look to Su.

"Like a tongue to a light post in winter," she confirms.

Comma snorts as he pulls back another section of curtains to reveal a screen that's only minutely smaller than the one in the living room. It's surrounded by shelves filled with hundreds and hundreds of DVDs and VHS tapes. Even though he must have seen these countless times, he sighs lovingly.

"And if you freeze up around other males, they'll be onto you in a minute because—and I'm speaking from experience—hot swans are never afraid of the glittering God-light that the heavens cast on us. Ah, here it is. I leave this one queued up."

"What is all this?" I ask.

I run my fingers across the covers as he takes a VHS tape from the shelf and puts it into a player. One of his well-plucked eyebrows lifts when he looks at me again.

"My job. I have the largest collection of porn in the whole city. I rent titles out for twenty bucks a pop. Though half of that is a deposit."

"We are not watching porn," Su says, not quite shouting, but not quite not shouting.

Comma taps play. There's a soft electronic purr. I shield my eyes and peer through my fingers. On-screen, a substantial blond fee is sashaying across a stage in a bright pink dress singing about diamonds.

"This isn't porn," Su says, confused. "This is a regular movie."

"Does it have nags in it?" Comma asks. "Yes? Then it's porn. *Gentlemen Prefer Blondes*. 1953. That, Glori love, is the patron saint of swans everywhere. Mr. Marilyn Monroe. *That* is femininity."

Only it isn't. As Comma scans all his other DVD cases, pulling out movies I *must* watch while there's still daylight hours, I can't help wondering if we are now totally divorced from what we used to be as fees, or if back then we were subjugated to be fees that we weren't.

Outside, the sun is setting, and along with it, any momentary comfort I felt while wrapped up in Comma's preening. I'm not simply playing dress-up. Lives are at stake. Two Five's. Mine. Sway's. And to succeed I have to pretend to be something that I couldn't be less similar to. With all this powder and gloss, I have never felt so unconfident or more exposed. It is neither a feeling I am used to nor one that I enjoy.

Just then, Comma's portable blips, and Sway says, "Mayor raised the reward to sixty-K."

"Comma, I'm never going to pull this off, am I?" I ask.

He pauses as he thumbs through DVD cases and gives me a weak smile. "Well, little nag, it would seem you're certainly going to have to try."

19

I slip away and leave Su with Comma. Over the last number of minutes, we watched an array of the best clips from some of Comma's favorite pre-Night films as a last-ditch effort at desensitization. Only, unlike Su, I haven't enjoyed any of the best parts. Or any of the films, period. Weirder than seeing the old-world fees with their painted faces, skeletal wrist bones, and unserviceable, weaponless attire was seeing them interact with the males.

"Boy, stop hiding your eyes. This isn't *Eighty-Nine Killings*, it's a rom-com."

But I couldn't help it. All those started-then-stopped sentences, held breaths, long looks. The tension between the genders made my insides feel squishy, and I kept asking, "Are they going to fight *now*?" only to watch the two actors kiss instead.

Outside on the fire escape, I can finally breathe again. I also instantly know where we are. The boys have taken up residence in the massive redbrick factory with the smokestacks that's right across the river from the oldest house on Grand Island. The place where Two Five and I used to play hotel. My brother and I have stood directly across from this exact spot trying to guess what this factory used to produce. I told Twofer it was where clouds were made.

"Is that why there are so many?" he replied, eyes wide.

Tonight, those clouds are burning red with sunset. And when I climb up to the roof, I see that what is actually being produced here is something I'd never have come up with in my wildest fabrications. Stunned laughter burbles up from my chest. It's like stepping back in time, but like, *way* back. Back to when Comma's movies were new. Back to a world when people "holiday shopped" and went to something called buffets that were "all you can eat." (Thank you, Liyan, for the nostalgic bedtime stories about the old world.)

A row of greenhouses runs to my left, each lit with solar-powered pink lights that illuminate rows of crops in their warm party glow. I can see peas, beans, beets, and kale. Behind the greenhouses are stately rows of wheat sheltered from the snow by giant tarps and warmed by solar heaters. Beyond that is a grove of fruit trees, now barren, along with a lone scrappy pecan tree like the ones we have on the island. Our farms are impressive as well, but they are entirely indoors, maintained by lab techs. Here, they have a massive chicken coop and an enclosure with goats milling around. The animals cry plaintively when they spot me.

How amazing would it be if Two Five could grow up in a place like this?

Thunder booms not far off. Yet there isn't a single rain cloud in the sky. Only the normal haze. Strange. And that's when I hear something even stranger.

Barking.

It's resonating from a woodshed that would make a great fort for Two

Five. I peek inside. Sway is on the ground being knocked over by a swarm of bread loaf-size, wiggling, yapping, fawn-colored animals.

Liyan said there were rumors that post-Night, an "activist" liberated the surviving non-predator animals from the zoo. That now buffalo actually roamed around Buffalo. (Though, as everyone knows, the animals are actually called bison.) And for a moment I think, *Wolves.* But no. I'm looking at dogs. Actual, tame dogs. From the library books that Twofer had me check out on a weekly basis, I know dogs were plenty common before the planet crash. But after the Night, most domesticated animals died either from radiation sickness or because their food supply couldn't be sustained.

A grown dog growls at me from inside a wooden pen. Sway pushes the puppies off and reaches for a pair of nunchakus, which do not seem like the most effective weapon for him, seeing as he can barely coordinate his blinks.

"Yo," he says when he sees me. "You know you're not allowed up here. Comma's downstairs, novio."

He thinks I'm a male! The puppies bombard him again as he tries to get to his feet.

"You need me to draw you a map, slick?"

"Sway, it's me."

Calling it flamboyant camouflage, Comma painted a cream streak across one of my eyelids. From another tin, he dusted some pink high up on my cheekbones. My nails are a delicate blue. Grand would be horrified, but the colors are the one thing I love. Twofer would as well. Telling from Sway's expression, he is not a fan.

"Staring," I say as I wobble in my ridiculous high white boots.

"Sorry," he says. "But you look so ..."

My fingers find the paperclip necklace Two Five made me. "*It's like us*," he said when he gave it to me. "*Hard to part.*" Comma said it looked like I found it on something called "the dressing room floor of an H&M" and ruined my look. I told him it was nonnegotiable. As Sway searches for the right words, I realize I'm holding my breath.

Oh my mother. Held breaths, awkward silences? I'm rom-com-ing! With a beast.

"I look so *what*?" I ask Sway, my own voice sounding strangely choked.

"Weird," he finishes.

Not good or bad. Weird.

Which is true.

I could take weird. And I could definitely take him not analyzing my looks anymore.

"You know," I say, "Twofer and I used to play right across the river. We've always wondered what this place was."

"It used to be a coal-fueled power plant. It was called a steam station. Do you ever get angry at our ancestors? Comma's dad said even before the Night, people knew the planet was dying. Knew it. But they didn't do anything until it was too late. I kinda never believed him."

Before I can respond, a puppy scampers over to me. Unlike its fawn-colored siblings, this one is black except for its speckled white paws. It jumps on my leg. I back away. The sudden lack of support makes it topple to the ground. It rolls over once. Yaps. Comes at me again.

"He won't hurt you." Sway watches me in that way that tells me, fee *or* male, I'm doing something distinctly strange. "You can pet him."

I lean down hesitantly. The puppy nibbles my finger. Something taps at my memory, like drops of water from a broken faucet.

"I think we raised dogs, too."

But it was at the labs and I don't remember them being very nice.

Sway goes still. I'm telling him something new. I force a laugh, sit down. The puppy immediately climbs into my lap and chews on my sweater.

"Sway, before we leave, I need to ask you something."

He nods; his eyes are expectant. "Why am I helping you?" he asks.

"Well . . . yes."

When it would be so much easier to turn us in. When the boys had built such an incredible situation for themselves here and were risking it all by hiding us. When Comma disagreed with the decision. *Why?* Why in the world help us?

"Did Comma tell you how we came to live together?" he asks.

I shake my head.

"A man sold me to Comma's dad shortly after the divide. Just knocked on their door and asked Rugged what he'd trade for me."

"Was he your father?"

"I don't think so. He said he found me in a camp outside of Batavia. A mix of men and nags. That my mom was dead, that everyone in the camp was dead. He said he couldn't raise a toddler. But couldn't leave me there. Who knows? Maybe he *was* my father. Anyway, he saw the lights on in Rugged's house, and did Rugged want me?"

I rub the puppy's tummy as I wait for Sway to continue. This isn't surprising. No one had good stories right after the Night. But it doesn't make it any less sad. At least the beast saved Sway's life.

"Rugged could have been anyone," he says. "Living that far out from the city. I mean, if I saw lights on in a house now? I wouldn't go to that house. I'd skirt a mile around it. But, luckily, Rugged wasn't anyone. And he had another child in the house—he had baby Comma. So he gave the guy some cans of food and a few hundred dollars, then told him if he ever saw him again, he'd shoot him in the face."

Sway rubs his nose with his fist. Then plays with a necklace at his throat. Unsurprisingly, his is fancier than mine. A pale green rock attached to a bright red knotted cord.

"I don't know what my heritage is. Or when my birthday is. Or really how old I even am. Rugged guesses about nineteen. But that man said my mom was dead. Which means I had a mom. She raised me for at least a year or two of my life. And maybe she *is* dead. Or maybe that goit lied, and she made it across the bridge to a place where all nags... where all *fees*, lived in peace. Except I can't exactly walk over and ask."

And then I understand. I *could* walk over and ask.

"Is that why you were waiting at the river?" I ask. "Why you wore that coat and a tie?"

He nods. "I wanted to make a good impression. I guess Cutter wasn't totally lying. He said he saw a little boy cross the river and blew up all our portables about it. I knew if he was telling the truth, someone would come to get him back. I mean, he's the first child anyone's seen in over a decade, since Comma's age group came of age. Someone, maybe a lot of someones, would think he was precious." If only that were true. "And then you showed up."

From under his hat, his eyes dart to mine. He smiles, almost sheepishly.

Part of me wonders if this isn't some kind of sympathy ploy. What better way to relate to me than to also be searching for a lost loved one? Except, as we sit together rubbing puppy bellies, I realize I trust this boy. What's more, I also think I kind of like him.

"Seems like you're risking your life for a giant maybe," I say.

"Are you telling me not to help you?" He laughs. "Because don't get me wrong, Glori. I was kinda hoping you'd choose to go with Su and I could go back to playing video games."

My name on his lips is like sweet maple sugar butter. My words drop off. I suddenly feel like I'm wearing my winter coat on a day that's turned fireball hot and I'm sweating under too many layers. Except now the layers are my skin. As if he's experiencing this strange heat as well, Sway's cheeks turn pink. He takes off his hat. While I was passed out, Comma must have shaved his hair. The star is gone, the sides almost bare.

Unlike me, he does not look weird. He looks nice.

The black puppy snuggles even deeper into my lap. Trying to dispel the awkward, Sway reaches out to rub the puppy's rump. He has lovely hands with long, elegant fingers meant for playing piano or making complicated braids or giving fees pleasure. Oh my mother, where did *that* thought come from? As if he had it, too, we both suddenly realize how close his hand now is to my crotch.

"Sorry," he says, withdrawing his hand.

In our flushed awkwardness, without thinking, I press a finger to his nose. "Boop."

Only it doesn't have the same comic effect that it did downstairs. Instead it increases the tension. I let my finger drop. My hand rests on the floor between us. I am ever so slightly tilted forward. His eyes meet mine. I feel like I'm made of two selves, and one wants to jump out of the other.

"Glori?" My name catches in his throat.

"Yes, Sway?" It takes everything I have to force these words out.

Only he never finishes the thought, because that's when the building explodes.

20

The entire steam station shudders. I grip the puppy tight to my chest. Sway grabs his backpack. We run outside. With the river at our backs, we look toward the sprawling mass of warehouses that stretch out around us. A plume of smoke rises from an abandoned factory about a quarter mile away. More from another a half mile past that. A little—and then a lot—of smoke billows up from the side of our building a few dozen feet from where we stand.

Again, thunder. Yet I haven't felt a drop of rain and there is no humidity in the air.

The roof falls silent as all the animals listen with us.

"Apocalyptic lightning storm?" Sway ventures.

"Final world-ending earthquake?" I guess back.

Sway cuts the generators that operate the greenhouses. The roof goes dark as the rumbling gets louder. It's not coming from above us. It's coming from the ground. Crouching low, we run to the side of the building and look over.

"Oh bump," he says. "Worse."

It's not thunder. Or an earthquake. It's motorcycles. At least fifty, each mounted by a pair of heavily armored males, all of their faces and chests painted red. Half of them are carrying torches. The other half guns. Even from ten stories up I recognize the lead male. His motorcycle looks like a personal tank, fitted with metal plates that protect his arms and legs. He is shirtless and, unlike the rest, he is painted white, only his features are red.

It's the tattooed beast from the market. Rage. And it looks like he's brought the entire rest of his mob with him.

"Why doesn't the mayor get rid of the mob already?"

"Because all the other mayors tried, and they're all dead. Mayor Chia's take is that we spent the last ten thousand years killing people over different ideologies. If the mob wants to keep Fortitude's ideals alive and scavenge for existence, so long as they stay in their zones and scavenge only outside the city boundaries, that's their choice. Besides, even though no one really knows where they come from, their numbers keep growing."

Sway curses as a lone motorcycle breaks from the rest and drives up to our building. The passenger heaves something flaming that shatters a window. The pair quickly drives back to the pack. The building quakes when their bomb explodes a few floors beneath us.

"Remember that thing you said about leaving at dusk?" I ask.

"Right. This is dusky enough for me."

Another bomb explodes while we race through a miniature vineyard and head straight for the wheat field. As we enter the tall grasses, the goats bleat with terror.

"What about the animals?" I ask.

"They'll be fine. The roof's fortified and the mob doesn't know this is up here."

"It sure seems like they do."

"Nah, all those goits know is that Comma and I squat in a warehouse

somewhere along the river. No sane male would ever choose this building. I mean, all those windows are a nightmare. They're only trying to
flush us out."

Wheat lashes at my face and hands. Sway parts a particularly thick
clump to reveal a perfect, narrow, snow-dusted path. It would be nearly
impossible to find this standing at the edge of the field. They're not only
growing this wheat for sustenance. It's camouflage. Smart males. Another
bomb goes off. Sway is now wheezing, which is weird. We've barely run
a quarter mile. I'm about to comment on it, when something suddenly
launches itself out of the wheat and attacks me.

"Horns tougher than thorns," it shouts.

We crash to the ground. I quickly have an arm wrapped around its
neck. Sway skids to a stop, slips on ice, and goes down, too.

"Comma, are you trying to get yourself killed?" he yells as another
bomb explodes. "She could have broken your neck. Would you please
wear your glasses already?"

"Not so long as you think they make my eyes look 'balloon-like,'"
Comma says as I pull him to his feet.

Sway tsks. "I make one comment and you hold it against me forever."

That's why Comma squints? I've seen older fees with glasses but didn't
even know poor vision was still a thing. Not a single Miracle has sight
issues. And then, as if by magic, the wheat parts and we're all standing
in front of a prefabricated metal shed. Su is already there digging out the
shed from the mound of snow piled against it. Sway types in a key code,
then strains to open the door against the remaining snowdrift. Once we're
all inside, even in the dark, I can see the boys beaming.

I let out a low whistle. "Well done, nags."

"That is a fee-only word," Comma says.

"Yes. And I'm a fee. So I can use it however I like."

All the walls are lined with gas canisters. Hanging from the ceiling is a rowboat, a canoe, and a fast-looking motorboat similar to the ones the EMS use when they go scavenging. Beneath and to the left are two sleek motorcycles and two solar glider riders. And next to them, unbelievably, is a brand-new, glossy black SUV. I can't even imagine how they got it up here. All I know is *that* is a thing of beauty.

"Let's take that one." I point at the SUV.

"Good choice," Comma says. "It can drive underwater."

"The Rinspeed?" Sway laughs. "Not on your life. Why are you still holding a puppy?"

I look down. It licks my chin. "I panic clutched it."

"You'll need one for the Influencer anyway," Comma says, then hands me my pack. "He'll be safe in here. Also, I included a few wardrobe changes that should cover just about any social situation this boy lands you in. And the nail-polish colors that you thought Twofer would like. Can we all please agree? That is such a heat hairstyle."

Su leans against the shed door. Normally, she would be all about this room. Now she crosses her arms, looking bored. Which is a feat, considering there are literal bombs exploding outside. I unzip my bag. Inside, along with everything previously mentioned, is the book I bought Twofer as well as all three of my girls. Freshly washed.

With a squeal of delight, I slide them into place, saying their names as I do.

"Mama Bear. Baby Bear. Slim."

"Slim?" Comma asks.

"Well, I couldn't have two Mama Bears, could I? And Goldilocks was such a drip."

"Ha!" Sway says.

As Comma puts the puppy in my backpack, Sway weaves through the bikes and pulls a dust cloth off a third very fast-looking motorcycle. It is entirely pre-Night except its tires are covered in snow chains.

"The Indian?" Comma asks. "But that's your baby."

"And it's the only bike that can outpace Rage's pack."

This time I don't hesitate. I climb on behind Sway just as the bike rumbles to life. The males clutch hands. Comma brushes at imaginary dust on Sway's shoulder. Sway blinks back tears. This has all the awkwardness of rom-com-ing, but it isn't. It's genuine affection. I didn't know beasts felt that. I look to Su, but apparently now she's highly interested in the battery on the solar gliders.

"Have I mentioned this is insane?" Comma sniffs.

"Com, if you don't hear from me in a few days . . ."

"You shush your mouth."

With a swipe at his eyes, Sway takes a small remote from his pocket. It looks like the same temperamental garage door opener we have at the cul-de-sac.

Comma waves it off. "You know I don't like to. Let him do it."

Sway tells me to push the red button. I do as I'm told and off in the distance there's an earth-quaking series of booms followed by the sound of glass shattering. All those times we heard "heat thunder" out on the cul de sac, it was probably the males blowing things up. Grand would be repulsed at the waste of it.

"Congrats, sweetie," Comma says. "You just torched a few city blocks."

"Don't spoil the puppies," Sway says, giving the bike gas. "It makes them impossible to train."

Su is suddenly beside me. She clutches my arm, panicked now that we're leaving.

"Don't let your arm fall on your parries," I say.

"And don't forget to floss," Sway adds as Comma pushes open a back door.

"And remember, you stab up and through."

"Good Galena, we know." Comma flaps his hands at us to leave, then tucks an arm through Su's. "Don't stay up too late watching porn. Always go for the groin. For bumps' sake, we're not the ones to be worried about. Remember what I told *you*, little fee. Embrace your femininity. It's the only thing that will make you seem like a male."

21

Getting down from the roof of a seven-story power plant on a motorcycle involves a series of not very sturdy, homemade ramps and bridges.

"This is like Chutes and Ladders but instead of sliding back ten squares there's death," I say as we coast through a rickety coal chute on an even more rickety conveyor belt.

"I'm surprised you're allowed to play that game. Aren't there pictures of boys on it?"

"You mean the ones wearing dresses?"

"Ha!"

Angry shouts come from the street below. Suddenly, a deep amplified voice rises above them and booms into the frigid dark air.

"Sway, we know you have the fees. Tank recognized your orange coat. This is too big a task for a small-time dog breeder. Give them to me and in exchange, I'll trade you two new dogs to grow your pack and you will live to see many more days. Keep them, you will die."

"Small-time?" Sway curses. "Bumping Rage."

"Boring clothing choices must look pretty good right about now."

"Must you always state the obvious?"

Before I can reply, another amplified voice lisps, "If you hand them over now, *I* promise to only hurt you in ways you'll enjoy."

Jackal.

"Yeah, yeah, yeah," Sway says. "It's all talk. You're too valuable to damage."

"Right. Good."

"They'll sell you to someone else and *they'll* damage you."

When we come to the edge of the power plant, Sway cuts the engine. We're still two floors up and apparently all out of bridges and chutes. We dismount and he pushes the motorcycle out onto a four-by-six plank of wood that has a pulley system attached to it. The whole contraption swings wildly when Sway steps on.

"How much weight does this hold?"

"So far? Comma's massive bed frame plus me. I think we're under that."

There's no way that's true. But I don't debate him on his math. Two trips isn't an option. Sway grunts and, hand over hand, begins to lower us down the side of the building. It takes all of his body weight hanging from the chains to get us to drop an inch. Though we're at the back of the building, we're not well hidden. If anyone drives beneath us and looks up, we're made.

"Can you hurry this up, please?"

"You think you can do this faster?"

"My grand could do this faster." He glares at me. "What? I'm only being honest."

"Bruth, sometimes you make it really difficult to be pleasant."

But I've already taken the chains. Soon we're dropping at triple the speed, the pallet cracking beneath our weight. Motorcycles rumble, too close for my liking. A bomb goes off only a block away. From my pack comes a pathetic puppy whimper.

"They're only frustrated by all the smoke," Sway says, then, "Hold your breath."

We've reached the first-floor windows. Thick black smoke pours out of them. Sway said the roof was reinforced, and I hope his math is better concerning those physics, because once all the fires go out, there's not going to be much steam station left to his steam station. Sway starts the bike. I give a few more tugs on the pulley. We both put helmets on. Just as the wood we're standing on gives, we launch off the platform.

I barely have time to flip my visor closed.

Leaving the headlight off, we race along a back road in the growing darkness. Every second I expect Jackal to turn a corner and be there with his split smile. Yet we're still all clear a half mile away when we cut down a path that leads to a hole in a chain-link fence.

"Glori?" a mini Sway voice in my ear says.

My hands go to my ears as if I can trap his voice.

What magic is this? Our helmets can communicate?

"You okay back there? It sounds like you're trying to blow up an air mattress."

"Scared" is all I can manage.

"Me too."

Behind us, the warehouses are lit up like the pyres fees built to burn all the bodies. I search the upper windows, hoping to see a light or flicker that somehow indicates Su and Comma are okay, but something else catches my eye. About a thousand yards behind us, coming along the same path we took, is a lone headlight.

"Oh waste. Sway, I think we have company."

Sway checks his mirror, speeds up, and swerves onto an on-ramp to the highway.

They'd begun to build a proper highway on Grand Island when Nuclear Night hit. It had one exit, and I never went on it. Partly—no, entirely, because the side streets were faster to bike on, plus weren't littered with abandoned, rusted cars that used to be filled with dead bodies.

This highway is different.

All the old vehicles have been cleared or pushed to the side of the road and it's *lit*. Roughly a third of the streetlights work. That feels like thousands compared to the dimness we traveled in back home at this hour. Scooters and mopeds race along with us. A giant E-SUV speeds past. There are too many cars on the road to count and almost all of them have *single drivers* inside. Never mind that the highway is actually *plowed*.

"Have you males learned nothing about pollution?" I ask.

"Oh sure, we've learned that at this point, a little more's not gonna matter. Just because Matricula made y'all go cavemen doesn't mean all of the pre-Night tech is bad. Half of these vehicles are electric and we have a working power plant, so why not use them? We're a dying species, we might as well go out in style."

"Fees have very different views on this."

"And that surprises no one."

As if to be further wasteful, Sway revs the bike and drives faster than everyone else. Every now and then he checks his rearview mirror. I look back, too. There are so many headlights, it's hard to tell if the one tailing us is still back there. A four-wheeler flies past us, then drops back. Two norms are on it. Unwisely, neither wears a helmet. Even worse, the passenger is aiming a gun at me.

"Sway!"

"Stay calm. It's fine."

Sway flicks up his visor. "Problem, mate?" he shouts.

"No problem," the male with the gun yells back. "Spot-checking for that boy or those sweet nags. Your little passenger mind giving a visual hello?"

"Not at all," Sway calls. To me he quietly says, "Glori, you're up."

"You want me to stab him?" I ask.

"No! I want you to flirt with him."

I hear the worry in his voice. He doesn't think I can do it. I remember the blond fee in the film. Maybe I'm as different from her as the planet was pre- and post-Night, but she's still my ancestor. If she could do it way back then, and Comma can do it now, why can't I?

Whipping my helmet off, I shake my hair into the wind and blow the bikers a kiss just like I'd seen her do. The four-wheeler swerves into oncoming traffic and misses colliding with a Prius Solar by an inch. Its horn toots plaintively. When the ATV pulls up next to us again, rider and passenger are both laughing, gun lowered.

"Bump me," the passenger calls. "He's dynamite."

"Actually, my name's Commander," I shout back. "Because I know how to command my way in and out of the dark."

"Nope," Sway mumbles. "That's not what that means."

"Huh?" the passenger shouts, confused.

"I mean," I quickly add, "now you know who to call if you do find that little one."

He laughs. "Sorry. We're turning him in for a reward."

"Oh, well." I falter, trying to imagine what Comma would say. "What reward is bigger than me?"

The driver whistles loudly. "You got a point there, bruth."

The passenger salutes us. I flit my fingers in goodbye and put my helmet back on. The bikers speed away. Up ahead they level their gun on another motorcycle.

"Glori, that was terrible *and* excellent. Points for having them hit up Comma."

My breath is coming fast and shallow. I try to muffle it so Sway can't hear it through his microphone. Meanwhile, he is totally unflustered, like it's a daily occurrence to have a gun pointed in his face. Thank goodness Su isn't here. The beasts' population would have shrunk by two if she were.

"I'd like to never see another male again, please."

"This might not be your favorite, then," Sway says.

Taking the next exit, he drives us right into the heart of a habitation zone.

22

They're everywhere.

Bundled-up older males sit in front of a café clutching chipped mugs of steaming tea. Despite the snow, right in the middle of the street, males are engaging in a game of throw-the-ball sport that I don't recognize. Other males gather on the sidewalks tossing down coins at every play. This isn't mob territory. Not one of these males looks mutilated. These are regular males, going about their regular evening activities. On Grand Island, we'd almost be at curfew. Everyone would have to be inside. But I guess unlike us, the males' night isn't consumed by darkness. Nor do they have anything to hide inside *from*.

I try to picture my Grand Mati here. She lived in Buffalo for ten years before the Night. Telling from the magnificent dead trees that line the streets, it must have been beautiful at some point. Quaint three-story brick buildings butt up against the buckling sidewalks, while newer steel and solar high-rises reach into the sky like fingers behind them. (Do not calculate the dead, I tell myself.) Across the street, a handwritten sign is tacked to the porch of a Victorian home. Warmly dressed males line up, waiting to get in.

"What's Hope's Home?" I ask.

"It's this new experience that this norm, Exemplar, came up with. For an hour, you sit in this completely pre-Night room while a house-cleaning AI vacuums and asks you about your day. Near the end, Exemplar sends in a meal. Ratloaf, or, like, tamales. And you get to watch twenty minutes of uninterrupted television. It costs the equivalent of two days' work. I've never done it, but older norms are way into it. Exemplar will be set for life with that idea. The goit."

I have no words.

But I don't need them. There is plenty of other sound here. Everywhere, on almost every building no matter the age, screens play pre-Night advertisements. They all must run off solar batteries, because they function about as well as our solar tech does, blipping on and off every few seconds. But regardless of the reception, almost every screen that isn't showing the blurred photograph of the three of us in the tunnel is playing a video of a pre-Night fee.

There is a hum in the air. The kind fees get when the clouds build up, meaning a big storm is rolling in. Anticipation. Worry. Excitement. Sway lets the bike idle in the middle of the street as a group of males crosses right behind us. I hear the words *nags* and *children* and *sixty thousand dollars*. And then I hear, quite clearly, "Kid's probably dead already."

"Maybe we should keep moving," I say.

"You want me to draw more attention? The light's red."

"That's what those things are for?"

"Ha!"

Graffiti on the building next to us reads: CHIA SAYS ABSOLUTION, BUT

WE WANT RESTITUTION. Apparently, not everyone looks so kindly on the mayor's mob leniency.

A screen underneath the graffiti flickers and shows fees walking along a narrow stage. Two midthirties males, both smoking, stop to watch. Although they're all varied in skin tone, the fees are almost identical in size, shape, and hairstyles. They're also all wearing similar skimpy undergarments and—oddly—enormous wings on their backs. They are completely unlike any fee I have ever met.

"You said the Influencer is in charge of these screens?"

"Yeah."

"For someone that hates fees, he sure shows a lot of them."

"He never used to. He must be following the mayor's orders. This is probably part of Chia's last-minute effort at reverse desensitization. Naturally, because he's against the whole thing, the Influencer's picked exactly the kind of footage the mayor wouldn't want shown."

"Last minute until what?"

But then the light turns green. As we drive away, one of the smoking males begins pressing his genitals against the screen. They both laugh. So much for desensitization.

"I think I hate it here," I say.

"Join the club," Sway replies.

Moments after the surrounding buildings turn from brick commercial to stately colonial, we drive around a traffic circle. Sway nods at a massive white marble building on our right.

"Chia's official headquarters."

Ten patrol soldiers dressed all in dark blue with BPD on their chests stand out on the steps holding machine guns. Sway slows the bike.

"I will break your neck if you turn me in."

"Good to know," Sway says, and keeps driving.

Shortly thereafter, we stop in front of a building that used to be solar-panel-coated but is now all rusted bolts and facing.

MAIN PLACE LUXURY APARTMENTS.

"What's *luxury*?" I ask.

"It means fancy."

"Then I'd hate to see plain. This is Euphoria?"

Sway laughs. "This is a building. Euphoria is what happens *inside*."

I stare at him blankly. His nonsensical words don't matter. This building is the best thing I've seen since I arrived. Maybe Two Five isn't in here, but someone who knows how to find him is. I'm getting closer.

23

The front doors are plastered with more anti-mob posters that read I'LL TAKE MY CITY THE WAY I TAKE MY PEAS AND CARROTS—PERFECTLY SEPARATED so that it's impossible to see inside. Sway knocks five times rapidly, then makes a series of loud sounds that can best be described as yawps. After a brief pause, a male the size of a tree trunk answers, a cigarette dangling from between his lips. He has thick, ropy locs and is wearing Band-Aids horizontally—frivolously—under each of his eyes. Back home, only a major health emergency would necessitate use of such precious medical supplies. He's also sheathed in an enormous blue tarp. When I step inside, I see why.

The average (generous) life-span of a roof is twenty years. Strange are the times a house on Grand Island *doesn't* have weather damage. But this building doesn't solely suffer a few leaks. The three-story foyer has twisting stalactites of ice stretching from the ceilings almost to the floor. Drips of water, like a perpetual frigid spring rain, have turned the lobby floor into a skating rink. Which might explain why the male picked to guard this place is in such a glacial mood. He stubs out his cigarette on the handlebar of Sway's motorcycle.

"Uncalled for, Wreckage," Sway protests.

"File a complaint." Wreckage sticks the butt behind his ear. "Pat-down time, mates."

Sway's eyes immediately flick to my groin. I purse my lips. He blushes. But he's right. This can't happen.

Sway laughs. "Not necessary, Wreckage. We're not here to party. We're just dropping off payment for the Influencer."

"That's nice," Wreckage grunts. "But since Matricula Rhodes is losing kids no one knew existed and sending assassins to retrieve them? Everyone gets a pat-down. Don't tell me you're suddenly shy."

Spinning Sway around like he weighs no more than his good intentions, Wreckage runs his hands up and down his legs, like, right into his penis parts, then roughly along his rib cage, chest, arms. As discreetly as possible, my fingers slide over Slim. If this male is the "impenetrable" that stands between me and finding my brother? There's no way I'm not getting past him.

Stab? I mouth to Sway.

He frantically shakes his head.

"Geez, Wreckage, if you wanted to go to third base, you coulda at least got me flowers."

Wreckage grunts. "It takes more than a Tater Tot to get me hungry, Sway."

Sway's eyes flick to me.

"Harsh," he mutters.

This is that "innuendo" that Comma said males like so much.

"Next," Wreckage says.

Remembering Comma's advice about embracing my glittering God-light, I take off my helmet and smile.

"Helloooo, handsome," Wreckage says.

"Hello to you. If it's big potatoes you're looking for, I have two of them and, um, a very large carrot you might like."

"Good to know." Wreckage laughs but reaches for me all the same. "I'll call you next time I want to make a stew. Arms out."

"By potatoes," I quickly say as he spins me around, trying not to cry out as he unintentionally grabs my bullet wound, "I meant testicles, and by carrot I meant penis."

Sway begins furiously coughing, but Wreckage laughs again. Considers me anew. He crosses his arms. Which means, his hands are *not* patting me down right now.

"Is that so?" he asks, his eyes alight with play.

I nod, pretend seriously. "It is."

"You know now that you mention it, I might have some meat to put in that stew."

"Oh, but I'm vegetarian," I say before remembering what we're actually talking about.

Sway coughs again and pulls me away.

"Wait," Wreckage calls after us. "What's your name? You're hysterical."

"It's Busy," Sway shouts back. "His name is Incredibly Busy. Valet my bike, would you?"

As Sway leads me to a nonworking escalator that is entirely covered in ice, I wave goodbye to Wreckage. His face lights up. He waves back. Then Sway and I start to climb, both hands clutching the slippery handrail. My white boots have zero traction. Apparently, neither do Sway's bright blue sneakers. One second, he is standing on the step above me. Next, he is kneeling on the step below me. From the foyer, Wreckage laughs.

"Bump me," Sway says, righting himself, then angrily whispers, "What was all the vegetable nonsense about?"

"Oh! I was fitting in. Comma said males are extremely fond of penis innuendo."

"Yes. Innuendo. Not straight-up anatomy class. That was ridiculous. *And* gross."

"It got us past Wreckage, didn't it?" I ask as my feet do a quick criss-cross on the ice beneath me. "You know, I don't agree with the way you criticize. Criticism is supposed to be helpful and constructive. You're supposed to say something nice, followed by something to correct. Followed by one last nice thing. And for the record? It's all gross. Do you realize how absurd it is? The need to constantly reference your genitalia? Look! I have a vagina. Still have a vagina over here." Sway hums loudly to drown out my words. "Maybe if your penis is so gross, stop drawing attention to it."

When we finally get to the top of the escalator, a male is waiting for us in a pre-Night suit that is impossibly clean and pressed. His thick black hair is short, neatly combed back from his face, and held in place with some kind of gloss. He smiles with perfect gleaming white teeth.

I'm so surprised, I gasp and then brandish Mama Bear.

Sway pivots on his heels, clears his throat, and says, "Glori, you smell nice today. Please stop gasping every time you see something new. It's like you were raised in a barn. Oh, wait! You probably were. Also, you have nice wrists. There. How's that for criticism?"

"You think I have nice wrists?"

Sway's face turns bright red. "It was a theoretical example."

Before I can further reply, the male says, "Hi, my name is Eugene. Welcome to the Main Place Mall. May I assist you in your shopping needs today?"

"Bump off, Eugene," Sway shouts, then walks right through him.

Downstairs, Wreckage hollers, "Bump off, Eugene, you bumping mother bumper."

"All right," the hologram says cheerfully. "Thank you for your input. Have a great day."

Sways eyes flick to me. I let out a "Huh" of laughter. One corner of Sway's mouth lifts up higher than the other in a grin. Just like that, our argument about penises and vaginas and constructive criticism is forgotten. Su and I would have been wrapped up in that sucker *for days*, and I don't know if this is a difference between Sway and Su or between male and fee.

From the level above us, a thumping emanates through the floor like a heart beating in an otherwise dead body. We ascend another escalator. Darkness replacing the ice. At the top, young males stand in front of a store called Applebee's. The only letter that's lit up on the sign is the first *E*. All the windows are intact but painted black so it's impossible to see inside, yet music pours out as thick as a hot breeze.

"Maybe I should wait out here."

Putting a hand on the back of my neck, Sway presses his forehead to mine. It's exactly how Su does, only much harder so that it makes a clonking sound. It's also different because Su is fee and Sway very much isn't. And while I can't help noticing how warm Sway's breath is and how tingly his fingertip skin makes my neck skin feel, what I'm mainly thinking is . . .

"I can't tell if you're being nice or aggressive right now."

"Sorry." Sway lets go. "I saw you and Su do it. I thought that's how you conveyed a meaningful message. Listen, forget what Comma told you. Being male doesn't mean using gross innuendos or being a super flirt. It means being yourself. It's not like it was before. Not here, at least. Nowadays, *everything* is considered male. Besides, you're not *that* fly, little swan. I know at least a dozen boys that give off more heat than you. Nobody'll even notice you're here."

Then to let me know he's teasing, he presses a finger to my nose. "Boop."

A water droplet splashes on my shoulder, and I half expect it to sizzle. Then we're through the door and Sway is knocking fists with a gigantic male standing right inside who's wearing a headdress made entirely out of tiny silver spoons and hardly anything else on his body below that.

"I think this is a huge mistake," I shout at Sway.

He nods his head along with the music as he takes in the room.

"'Course it is. This is Euphoria. *Everything* that happens here is a huge mistake."

24

Liyan told me that after Nuclear Night, even with everyone sick, they heard news that some places in the world nonstop partied. Cities in countries I'll never see. Mexico. Greece. South Africa. Brazil. This is what *that* must have been like. Everywhere there are males. Dancing, drinking, and singing along to music that is loud, fast, and a lot more enjoyable than I expected.

"K-pop," Sway shouts as my shoulders twitch to the beat.

"No thanks. We poured all our pop out years ago. Grand says it rots your teeth, causes cancer."

"Ha!"

An oval bar sits in the center of the dark club. It's strung with colorful blinking lights that illuminate canning jars filled with murky liquids the males are lined up two rows deep to get at. High-backed booths ring the outside and teem with males playing with cards and dice and—in the black corners, where the bar lights don't reach—kissing.

"Staring," Sway calls out.

A norm in a pink frilly bralette and skimpy bathing suit bottoms presses up against me.

"That's a heat hairstyle," he shouts, then pats my rear end and moves on.

As we squeeze through the crowded dance floor, Sway slaps hands and bumps chests with half the males we encounter. A male in a plain gray T-shirt and jeans puts a cup in my hand. Before I can so much as sniff it, Sway says, "Nope," and hands it off to someone else.

On Grand Island, when I lived in the neighborhood, I went to talent shows, concerts, and crafting classes. Boot camp, yoga, and sparring tournaments. We had a few bands and bonfires and dancing at sleepovers and lots of hours of productive relaxation, but there was nothing as chaotic and vibrant, careless and carefree, as this.

A petite male, plainly dressed but with yellow color over his eyes, loops his arm through mine.

"Well, Sway Me Off My Feet," he purrs to Sway. "When did your preference switch to swans and how come I wasn't notified?"

"Brontë, you're always my preference."

After doing a fancy hand slap, the males talk about a team sport they're both on—something called Frisbee golf—and that's when I notice two figures dancing on either end of the bar. Males are gathered around, looking up appreciatively.

"Holy crow," I murmur.

I wedge my way through the crowd to get closer. Although they're wearing elaborate eye masks with pale blue feathers and silvery sequins, they aren't wearing much else. Which means those dancers? Undoubtedly fees.

They can't be here of their own free will. The one nearer to me has silky straight black hair and a placid smile that no sensible fee could maintain in this environment. It's only as I push aside a male twice my size and stand right in front of her that I realize my mistake. One moment she's dancing with her arms above her head, then she shimmers and restarts her dance with her hands on her hips.

Yet another hologram.

In the few hours I've been here, I've seen more undressed fees than I had in my entire childhood on Grand Island. I mean, no. That is a gross overstatement. We are not shy, especially in the hot months, *and* I spend a lot of time in gym locker rooms. Yet the amount of bare fee flesh here is astonishing. I can practically hear Comma telling me it is purely out of aesthetic appreciation, but then where are all the naked males? Are their bodies not equally beautiful?

This isn't desensitization. It is one-sided hyper-sexualization. I know Grand will never allow it, but if ever fees and males did reacquaint, how could the males ever see us without seeing *that* scantily clad, breasts-out fee at the same time?

Suddenly, my hips are grabbed from behind. A male with slicked-back hair and a dozen safety pins through his ears dances me side to side with his groin pressed right up against my rear end. This isn't acceptable fee behavior. But I don't know if it's normal here or not. My eyes scan the crowd for Sway.

"I'm here with someone," I shout as the entire club belts out the chorus of a song.

Only males would create a social environment where it's impossible to hear one another. And then Safety Pins pulls down my ostrich-feathered hood and runs his tongue from my collarbone up my neck. I can feel the slimy trail his spit leaves even when he's done. I don't know what a swan would do right now. But I know perfectly well what a Glori has been trained do. I turn and shove him off.

"Feisty!" He grabs my wrists. "I like that."

"As much as you like broken noses?"

"Huh?" He leans his ear toward me.

"If you don't leave me alone, I'm going to break your nose with my forehead," I shout.

In response, he throws his head back and howls. Then he darts at me again. I keep my promise and next second, he's slumped in my arms with blood pouring out of his face. And then Sway is there.

"It wasn't my fault," I shout exactly as Sway shouts, "What did Brando do now?"

"He licked me."

Turning his snapback cap around, Sway takes Brando from me and hands him off to a big male in a bright red sweat suit.

"Here. Happy Hanukkah, Mozart. I always said you'd get what you deserve, Brando."

"You'll pay for this," Brando mumbles, coming to.

"You know where to find me," Sway says.

Gone is any trace of the overactive, slightly clumsy male I'm used to. Standing there with his fists and muscles tensed, Sway actually looks kind of dangerous. As dangerous as a one-hundred-and-forty-five-pound anything *can* look. I get that squishy belly feeling again, and suddenly, I don't want to be here anymore. I desperately wish Su had come. I miss her, and Liyan, and my grand, and just *home*. I miss being told what to do and when to eat and the absolute certainty both instructions would be safe. I miss fees and our form of affection, which does not involve rubbing your genitals on someone unasked. I miss our sagacity. Our simplicity of dressing and our complexity of speaking. I miss how we respect one another's me space.

I miss all those things desperately. Like I'd miss water on a long run in the heat months.

Except I miss Two Five more.

The crowd now moves in some kind of synchronized dance, yet magically opens before us as Sway pulls me to the back of the club. He pounds on the door of an antique phone booth. Two males exit, giggling. Sway holds the door for me, and when I hesitate, he barks, "Geez, it's safe. When will you stop suspecting I'm trying to kill you?"

The booth is lit with a single red lightbulb. The walls are covered in crushed black velvet.

The beasts' city is everything our teachers warned us it was. The violence, the sex. And yet the chorus of that song spins in my head with a male *and* a fee singing. *No eres tú, no eres tú, no eres tú, soy yo. No te quiero hacer sufrir.* And I wonder if Comma knows how to do that synchronized hip-swaying dance that went with it. I feel frightened and disgusted, but also for the first time in a long time, I feel noticeably *alive.*

As soon as Sway closes the door behind us, another red light blinks on: OCCUPIED.

"You okay?" he asks tightly.

"Nothing a good scrub with a pumice stone won't fix. Are you mad at me?"

"Bump no. I've wanted to do that to Brando since we took shop class together in the sixth grade. But I turned around and didn't see you and ... you can't go wandering off like that. Okay?"

"Okay," I say, and he takes a deep breath. "Won't people get suspicious if we're in here too long?"

"Nah, that's kinda the whole point."

Sway feels along the bottom of the phone-booth panel until his fingers find a latch. He lifts up and the back wall of the booth springs open. It leads into a narrow hallway that ends with a silver door. Furious barking greets our approach. It's as if every remaining dog in the world is beyond that door and none of them slept well.

"So, hey," Sway says. "Remember when I said the mayor's official headquarters were in that big building in Niagara Square? Well, these are kind of like his unofficial headquarters."

"You mean the mayor who is offering the sixty-thousand-dollar reward for me and the thirty-dollar reward for you?"

"Technically, your reward is only thirty thousand dollars. Sixty is for both of you."

"And you thought it was a good idea to bring me here?"

The barking has now reached a fever pitch.

From the inside of my pack comes a pathetic puppy whine.

"Don't worry." Sway's talking even faster now. "Chia has offices all over town. With everything going on, there's no way he's here. But the Influencer *is*. He barely ever leaves, which is part of the problem. Narrow worldview. But that's why you're here. To convince him of one very crucial point."

"What's that?"

"That he should stop hating fees." Sway gives me a once-over, and telling from the crinkle of his nose, he doesn't have high hopes. "Now remember what I told you in the tunnel before you went and took on the mob?"

"Be quiet. Keep my head down."

Sway nods. "This is exactly the opposite. The more you talk, the less they'll see you."

"What kind of strange beasts ignore you the more you speak?"

With a grimness that I've only seen equaled by Su at exams, Sway utters one little word. "Adults."

And then the door swings open.

25

Adults.

Adult *males.* Who have seen fees before. Who have lived with us. Adult males who won't be fooled by a haircut and some fake bravado. Adult males who work for the mayor and are tasked with actively searching for me.

"My babies!" Sway throws his arms wide as a pack of whining mutts immediately swarms us, each vying to be the first to lick his face.

As I try to keep them from planting their noses in my crotch, I quickly survey the room. This isn't a *few* adults. It's a minor battalion.

"Gang's all here," Sway says through bared teeth.

I count thirteen males right off the bat, and I'm sure I'm missing a few that are sitting down. These are the beasts I've been expecting. All brawny and in good health. Roughly Liyan and Majesty's age. With guns harnessed across their backs or at their waistbands. It's a room of beards and radiation-burn-induced keloid scars and musky sweat. And every single male looks at us when we enter.

"S'up, y'all?" Sway says loudly, forcing his grimace into a grin. "Chilly weather we're having, huh? I haven't seen my balls in weeks."

As one, the males all turn back to what they were doing.

Applebee's must have been a restaurant and this space its kitchen. Stools and chairs are pulled up to all the counters and pass-throughs as if they were desk space, which only slightly lessens the fact this room looks better suited to hosting a coming-of-age party than running an all-male regime. The walls are crammed with old fluorescent beer signs and pre-Night band posters. A wooden plaque that says WELCOME TO THE MAN CAVE hangs crooked above a bathroom doorway, while holoscreens, each at least three solar panels wide, play non-work-appropriate sports on the back wall.

Or at least three of them do.

The fourth holoscreen is paused on the photo of us in the tunnel.

"Staring at it doesn't help," Sway murmurs.

Having said their hellos, the dogs disperse. Broadening his smile, Sway shoulder-punches a grizzled male with a bushy red beard who's doing bicep curls with a fifty-pound barbell. It's all I can do to suppress an eye roll. What a septic tank.

"Hey, Quarry."

Sway bobs and weaves at the bearded male like a boxer until Quarry puts a heavy hand on Sway's face, stopping him. It knocks Sway's hat to the floor. He makes a distressed grunt and eyes me gratefully when I pick it up. On Quarry's veiny forearm is a blistered keloid scar that looks like a pair of lips. A tattoo of a mustache sits right above it.

Through Quarry's meaty palm, Sway says, "Crowded today."

"Yeah, well, it's not every day we have fees to hunt," Quarry grunts, continuing his reps.

Fees to hunt? From the rapid number of blinks that Sway's eyes perform, I can tell he is trying very, very hard not to look at me.

"You recognize the little blurry turd that's helping them? He look familiar to you?"

"Nah," Sway says. "His coat is pretty heat, though."

Quarry snorts. "You're as blind as Comma."

Behind me, covering an entire wall, are dozens of grainy head shots of young males. They're all taken from a distance. Some only catch a profile. Yet each one has a note card next to it listing what looks like the male's height, weight, and address. In the upper-right-hand corner of each is a number. Next to the photos is a pre-Night map of downtown Buffalo. Two blocks along Delaware Avenue are heavily circled. Each number from the note card is matched with a corresponding downtown house.

I have no idea what I'm looking at. A most-wanted list? A neighborhood crime spree with profiles of the victims? Or the perps? Blurry as the photos are, I do see one similarity. All the males are about the same age.

About my age, in fact.

Quarry drops his hand from Sway's face so that he can do reps on the other arm. When I hand Sway his hat, he carefully dusts it off before putting it back on his head exactly so. Quarry watches this process, lips curled with derision.

"You know..." He nods at the wall. "I almost feel sorry for them little nags. Imagine their surprise when they come back and realize they're stuck with the likes of you."

My gaze quickly travels to the wall of photos. This time, it lands on a grainy picture of a familiar wide nose, sturdy chin, and furrowed brow.

"Oh my mother." I cough into my hand.

It's Su.

"Nothing says they can't trade up," says a male whose upper-lip hair hangs past his mouth in two braids. "Get themselves a real man."

"Don't be a pedophile, Berserker," Quarry snaps. "Mayor says they can't trade up."

Sway tries to lead me away, but I shake him off. Now all the other faces make sense, too. I just haven't seen them much these last five years. But that's Chardonnay with the button nose. Cinnamon Toast with the 'fro. Cocoa with the freckles. All of them named after luxuries their mothers missed. That's our Miracle class. The last group of fees born after the Night.

Radio. Chenin Blanc. AC. They're all there. How did the beasts have all this reconnaissance? These aren't old photos. Su told me about Olive's new buzzed haircut only a week ago. Were the males hiding in the woods snapping photos? Using drones? Suddenly, Grand's insistence on abolishing old-world tech seems so . . . stupid. Didn't she realize the advantage it gave our enemy?

"Me?" Quarry grunts as he works his triceps. "I'm praying that brunette is still alive."

"Which brunette?" a bald, paunchy male asks.

"The one with the phoenix tattoo," Quarry says.

The bald male looks to the board. But the fee Quarry's talking about won't be up there. He isn't talking about a Miracle. He's talking about my mom, Majesty.

"Nah, you don't want her," Braided Lip-Hair says. "She's damaged goods, remember? She was in that pack of nags those boys messed up right after the divide."

Sway tugs on my coat. Nods toward a door in back covered by emerald-green beads.

"Hold on," I say, waiting for Quarry's reply. "I want to hear this."

"No." Sway sighs. "I promise, you don't."

"You're talking about that one with the gargantuan tits, right?" asks a beast wearing a fur coat that I can smell from here.

"Quarry, you don't need to cross no river for big titties," calls out an enormous beast with four chins as he bobbles his breasts. "I've got some right here for you."

"If I wanted fat, Everest..." Quarry grabs his genitals.

This time I don't protest as Sway steadily guides me away from the males.

"Just keep swimming, just keep swimming," he sings under his breath.

I have never in my life felt this way. It's like being dirty, but on my insides. I need to go home and warn everyone. No, correction. I need to get Two Five and then go home and warn everyone. No, correction to the correction: I need to kill everyone in this room, grab Two Five, and then go home and warn everyone.

"You know what I miss more than a nice pair of breasts?" the bald male muses. "Watching Neo Simone make three-pointers. What do you think happened to Neo Simone?"

"He's dead," multiple voices say simultaneously.

"You miss the news eighteen years ago?" Quarry asks. "Everyone's dead."

And then it all falls into place. All those posters out front. The reverse desensitization that all those fee videos were meant for. Nag classes. Forget the mob. There's only one group the males are truly separated from.

Fees.

Next to all the ordered head shots, I spot one last photo tacked up off-kilter, as if in a rush. It's snapped in the darkest of the dark hours but still clearly shows a fee riding a bike with a tiny tot clinging to the handlebars.

Twofer's smile glows brighter than a dozen solar lanterns on a pitch-black night. We're both circled in red marker. Our note card has a giant red question mark on it.

As Sway finally corrals me through the doorway hidden by the emerald-green beads, I don't know which realization is worse. That the beasts are planning a reunification with fees that we know nothing about.

Or that I was right.

Twofer's kidnapping *was* all my fault.

26

"**Y**ou didn't tell me the males had an entire reunification campaign going on," I hiss to Sway as soon as we step through the beads.

It takes my eyes a second to adjust to the darkness. Previously either a storage closet or a walk-in freezer, the room is now entirely taken over by pre-Night tech. Loose DVDs. Film reels. Countless pieces of equipment I don't have names for. They're all piled on top of filing cabinets and dressers that are filled with even more of the stuff. And yet there's not one working lamp. The space is solely lit by screens that are stacked like blocks on an incredibly messy desk at the far end of the room. A high-backed swivel chair is rolled up tight to it, and a cot piled up with coats sits to the left. If his lair is any indication, I imagine the Influencer looks like one of those ancient albino crustaceans that Twofer and I read about in that book on caves.

Also? Apparently, the Influencer does leave. Because he's clearly not here.

"I didn't think I *needed* to tell you about reuni," Sway says, doing his surprised head jostle. "How can you possibly not know? That's like not knowing what the Breeder Bill is."

"I know what the Breeder Bill is."

It's why we had the divide to begin with. It was legislation Fortitude Packer tried to enact that called for all fees between the ages of seventeen and forty-five to solely focus on making babies. No role in the government. No outside jobs. Just baby making and child care. When Matricula and the other fees balked, Fortitude threatened to burn down their labs unless they complied. At which point, Matricula pulled a semitruck up to the labs, cleared out the fees, then fled Buffalo in the middle of the night. Fortitude was so angry, he burned the labs regardless. The following day, someone shot him in the head.

Karma, Su always says at this point in history class.

"But what does the Breeder Bill have to do with males wanting to reunify now?"

"Um, because of the Seventeen-Year Truce." Sway doesn't bother commenting on my blank expression. Instead he simply—graciously— continues. "After Matricula left and Fortitude was murdered, Mayor Grim came to power and begged fees to return. His mantra was 'Whatever keeps them happy.'"

"Except then Grim was murdered," I say. "Like a half minute later. Naturally."

"Right. Chaos ensued. And when Mayor Bull replaced him, he left the divide alone. Because what did it matter? By then everyone had figured out the Night had made fees and males sterile and the babies Matricula took were too young to think about in reproductive terms. But to prevent human extinction, everyone agreed reunification would be revisited when the babies came of age. And a few months back..."

"Chardonnay turned seventeen," I finish for him, stunned.

The Seventeen-Year Truce. Why hadn't anyone told us about this? Where was this history lesson? Yet even as my brain forms these questions, it responds with this answer: Who'd want to grow up with a deadline like that hanging over their head?

"Does Matricula know about this?"

Sway nods. "I mean, she was there, so I'm assuming..."

"No, not about the truce, I mean does she know about your reunification plan?"

"I think Chia has brought it up? I'm just not sure Matricula has, um, agreed to it."

My ears burn. "And that map of downtown Buffalo out in the office, with the dark circle and the numbers that correspond to each of my classmates. What's that for?"

Sway takes off his hat and uncomfortably scratches the back of his head. High above the messy desk, three holoscreens run with code. On the desk, two screens show traffic footage while a third plays a film of a male in a bat suit flinging tiny bat-shaped objects at a male in an equally strange penguin costume.

"Well." Sway clears his throat. "I think that's the fenced-in community where they're planning to relocate y'all once you've moved across."

"Sway!"

Never mind hearing those beasts objectify my mother over her breasts. Over. Her. Breasts. They had note cards that read like an ingredient list. Like we were cans of beans that could simply be plucked off one shelf and thrown onto another.

"Maybe it's not as bad as it sounds, Glor," Sway says.

"Or it's worse than it sounds," a quiet voice says. "Unless you appreciate your life as you know it being entirely blown to bits."

I spin. Mama Bear out. "Who said that?"

The desk chair pivots ever so slightly.

"Oh good," Sway says. "You are here. Glori, this is Reason, aka the Influencer. Reason, this is—"

"Yes, Sway," Reason calmly interrupts. "I heard the first part of your introduction. Unfortunately, *Glori*, as I mentioned in earlier PTTs to your friend there, I've already helped more than I wanted. *No, Chia, I swear, the tunnel photo came to me blurred.* You'd better have burned that coat, bruth. Nag, Sway wasted your time. You both need to leave."

"No," I say.

"No?" Reason repeats with a soft laugh.

"If you have access to information about my brother, then the fastest way to get me to leave is to help me."

Reason yawns. "Actually, the fastest way to get you to leave is to call Quarry."

And then Reason leans forward to tap at one of his screens. Dark cowlicks stick up every which way beneath bright yellow noise-canceling headphones. I'd been expecting an adult. On Grand Island, only mid-aged fees were adept at pre-Night tech. Plus, I figured anyone who hated fees so passionately had to remember us. Yet Reason can't be much—if any—older than me. His curiosity getting the better of him, he turns to give me a quick glance. Heavily lidded, soulful dark eyes begrudgingly take me in, then lock on mine with surprise.

"Oh my," I breathe out, my tongue suddenly thick in my mouth.

With his cut cheeks, smoky complexion, and tousled hair, Reason looks caught beneath the wheels, as Grand likes to say. While his tight, ratty T-shirt only too finely accentuates that his upper body is as thickly muscled as a fee's, his baggy sweatpants do little to hide the fact that his right leg is withered and frail. Without question, Reason is the most attractive human being I have ever seen. In my entire life. Ever.

Just as I step forward—to do what, I have no idea, congratulate him perhaps—one of the coats on the cot growls. It's the dogs. All curled into one another so it's impossible to tell where heads start and tails end. The biggest of the group—a mountainous brown mutt with jowls larger than Grand's flapjacks—hops off the cot and plants its head in Reason's lap. It breaks the spell. As does the fact that as striking as Reason is, he looks back at me with an equally arresting amount of dislike.

Reason absently rubs the dog's ears and says, "Sway, have you at all considered how coincidental it is that as the truce is up, two fees cross who are stronger than any norm? Speak the mob leader's first language? And also happen to need info that can only be accessed in the war room of Euphoria? I cannot believe you brought him here. I mean, Chia might be clueless, but there are limits."

Sensing my annoyance, Sway holds a hand out to calm me.

"Maybe she speaks Japanese, Rea, but it's not because she's some assassin or in cahoots with the mob. . . ."

"I also speak Spanish, Hindi, French, Chinese, and a little Burmese."

"See?" Sway points at me. "It's because she's insufferable. No one knows better than you how ill prepared the fees are. And Chia *might* be clueless? He still hasn't figured out that you're the one printing anti-reunification posters. And you two live under the same roof. The peas-and-carrots one is hysterical, B. T. Dubs."

Reason's head twitches with begrudging acknowledgment. "Thank you. It's my favorite."

The enormous dog has now joined me to sniff my crotch.

"I told you, bruth," Sway says with forced patience, crouching next to Reason's chair. "The steam station has been temporarily compromised. I know how you feel about fees, but I didn't know what else to do. Be *reason*able."

"You know that's not helping your case," Reason grunts.

Suddenly, Reason's massive dog lurches up and puts his baseball-mitt-size paws on both of my shoulders and starts sniffing my pack, whining loudly.

"Mastodon, off," Reason commands.

When the dog doesn't listen, Reason grabs a crutch from the side of his desk and gets to his feet. The other dogs are immediately beside him. He steps forward so we are eye to eye. Exactly the same height. And I know in that moment that however nicely he intends to word it—which, given previous evidence, won't be nice at all—Reason is about to tell me no. He won't help us.

And then it occurs to me what Mastodon was after.

"Wait. I also brought you a gift."

Gently, swinging my bag to the front, I unzip it and take out the puppy. He's delighted to be back out in the world, his tiny paws and pink tongue all aflutter. I hold the puppy up so it and Reason are nose to nose. Reason's chin drops to his chest.

"Oh my Great Gatsby. Look at his little white paws. Come here, lover." Gently taking him from me, Reason inhales the puppy's warm popcorn smell and sighs. "My only regret in life is that I'll never pet the little heads of every animal before I die."

Reason snuggles the puppy to his cheek, then meets my eyes again. Su used to anoint her crushes with various hues of green. The darker the green—*Mochi is so moss*—the more she liked them. Reason is all the shades of green. Every single one. He is *that* fine. How could someone so stunning, someone who loves dogs so much, so thoroughly hate fees?

As the puppy chews on his thumb, I notice a tattoo of a lightbulb on Reason's palm.

"What's that mean?" I ask.

He holds his hand above his head, lightbulb facing out.

"So I'll never run out of ideas."

Clever. But when I smile, Reason's eyes cut away from mine. He sinks back into his chair and resumes staring at his screens.

"What will you do if you find your brother?" he asks.

"Take him home."

"And tell all the nags about what we're doing here? About reunification?"

I glance at Sway. He nods, encouragingly. *Tell him.*

"Yes," I say reluctantly.

"Fine, I'll help. If telling nags about reuni doesn't stop it from happening, I don't know what will."

What did we ever do to you? I want to ask, but settle instead for a flat "Great. Thank you. So do you really think you can find my brother?"

"Do I *think* I can?" With a glance over his shoulder at the main office, Reason grins and turns the volume all the way up on the man-bat movie. "I know I can. 'Cause I already did."

27

"**Y**ou found Twofer?" I ask with disbelief.

"What do I look like, some tech-inept nag?" Reason laughs. "Of course I found him."

Ignoring both his gibe and my impulse to flip his chair over, Sway and I gather in tighter around Reason as he clears the rest of his screens.

"I don't have footage of him coming ashore. When nags blew up the first of the two south Grand Island Bridges, we lost all those toll cameras. I mean, obviously. But if Cutter saw him, that must be where they crossed, so I scanned other footage in the area. And I found this."

On two of the holoscreens a dozen different traffic intersections pop up. Suddenly, the same Prius E drives through each video. This car is a lot nicer than the gas-powered clunker the beasts used to take Twofer on the island. Reason lets the footage run through once, then replays all the screens and pauses each one when the car is perfectly centered. He pulls one of the shots to a holoscreen and zooms in.

This can't be right. There's only one beast in the car. Yet three took

Twofer from home. But then I clutch Reason's shoulder. He yelps with pain. A little head of curls just popped up in the backseat of the Prius, and I'd recognize those chubby cheeks anywhere. I squint and lean even closer to the screen.

"What's that on Two Five's window?"

Reason increases the size by 50 percent and slows it down. The image isn't sharp enough to see if Twofer's crying or tied up or even if his mouth is gagged, but on the breath-frosted glass next to him, it's clear that my brother drew a series of shapes. Two boxes. One on top of the other. With a triangle at the very top tilted sidewise.

"Looks like a house," Reason says. "Maybe he's drawing home."

"Our house looks nothing like that," I say.

"Harsh much?" Sway asks. "He's five."

"It's probably just a doodle," Reason says. "I always doodle dogs."

"And that surprises no one," Sway says.

Two Five does love to draw, but then the whole window should have been covered. This means something. I'm sure of it. It's supposed to mean something to me.

"I lose him here at this New York State tollbooth."

We watch as the Prius flies through the abandoned toll stop. Its tires crush the hand of a disintegrating corpse that lies half out of the booth. Reason pauses the screen. This camera angle is from the front and better shows the driver. He's wearing a knit ski mask. A thick braid of long black hair hangs down his shoulder.

I peer at the still. "Where is this?"

A street map of Buffalo is instantly on-screen.

"We're here"—Sway jabs at the map—"and that's right . . . here."

There is a cucumber-size amount of space between Sway's two fingers.

And not a gherkin. A proper English cucumber. As a shaggy, copper-hued dog only slightly smaller than Mastodon hops into Reason's lap and licks his cheek, my stomach gets tight and panicky. Twofer is even farther away than that?

"Okay, so where are they headed? What's out in"—I squint at the map—"Orchard Park?"

"Not a lot." Hugging his dog, Reason moves his cursor and circles something that's called New Era Field. "The farms, primarily, and then a whole lot of nothing."

"I heard a rumor Chia was letting the mob work at the farms now," Sway says.

Reason shrugs. "Yeah, but I already checked the stadium cameras. Nothing. No one but the normal workers in or out all day."

"Sway, back at your loft, Comma said there was a place out past the farms. Where bad things happen."

Sway points at what looks like an empty patch of land. "Got any cameras here?"

Reason nods. "Rugged's security systems..."

Reason swipes and clicks, and then we have a ten-camera view of a house and the outlying surrounding streets. Reason rewinds the footage, until suddenly, in the very corner of one of the screens, a Prius E careens into view and then back out of sight.

"That street only leads to one place," Reason says, pushing back from his desk.

I tap the screen that still shows Twofer's window drawing.

"I don't think that's a house or a random doodle."

"The Fortress." Sway whistles. "Which means, this is a worst-case scenario come true."

Reason nods. "Last I heard, the mob was using it as their butcher shop. And I'm not talking steaks. I'm talking you cross them, you get sent to the Fortress and get cut, then nobody sees or hears from you again."

"Excellent," I say. "How do I get there?"

"Well, first you'd book a transport—that will at least take you to the farms. . . ." Reason's words fall off, and he spins to face me. "Nag, you can't go to the Fortress. If the mob does run it, you'll need firepower, money to barter with, and at the very least a guide to get out there."

"I have Sway," I say.

"Sway?" Reason rolls his eyes. "Bruth can't even find his way out of his own clothes."

"Insult noted," Sway replies, then looks at me. "Glori, I think you should talk to Chia."

I snort. "You mean Mayor Chia, who might have killed seven of our smartest fees yesterday and stolen my brother? Chia, who's offering a sixty-thousand-dollar reward for me and Su? Who's planning an entire reunification that fees haven't agreed to?"

"Chia didn't kill any fees," Reason interrupts. "The *mob* killed your fees. And the mayor only offered that huge reward to guarantee you'd be brought in safe. Chia's one of the good guys."

"Right," Sway says. "If we tell him where your brother is, we wouldn't even need to leave this building. Everybody would win. You'd get your brother back. Chia would get in the good graces of the fees. Neither of us would be murdered by the mob."

Reason is devouring his thumb cuticle. "Unfortunately, he kind of has a point."

Before I can answer, a door slams open in the outer office.

"Boys?" a voice booms. "Today is a good day."

Reason's pack of dogs tumbles off the cot. Nails scraping, they run into the other room.

"Not today, you damn mutts," the same voice bellows.

Moments later, they're all back with their tails between their legs. I peek through the beaded doorway. Even if I hadn't seen him on Sway's television, I'd still know this was the mayor. Never mind the frizzy salt-and-pepper hair that crackles off his head like he's been electrocuted. Only someone with a world of responsibility on their shoulders can look that weary. Grand wears a similar countenance all the time.

Chia stretches, then sits at the sole proper desk in the room and kicks his feet up.

And then? He starts whistling.

"You're in a good mood." Quarry sits on the corner of Chia's desk as the mayor pulls two crystal rocks glasses from his bottom drawer along with a decanter of brown liquid.

"Why shouldn't I be? All these years, I've been trying to figure out the one thing that would make Matricula come back to us without resorting to force. And then this morning we find out she's been hiding a kid. The terrible and vicious mob reacts." He says this with mock horror. "And now self-righteousness is our ally. Terror our common adversary. Safety and enforcement our bargaining chips. And guess who PTTs me this afternoon? Apparently, Matricula Rhodes is ready to talk. Fees will be swarming over here in no time."

"And all it took were some murdered nags and a kidnapped child," Quarry says, eyeing the mayor as he accepts a glass of liquor from him.

"Exactly." Chia laughs, throwing back his drink. "I should have good-cop-bad-copped her years ago."

Sway holds me back. I shrug off his grip and glare at him, then at Reason. This was who they thought I should ask for help? But the Influencer is so focused on his screens, I might as well not be in the room.

"Reason, you awake back there?" the mayor shouts.

"Oh, he's awake," the male with lip braids says. "Your boy has company."

"He does, does he? Well, stop twiddling your diddles . . ."

"That is not what we're doing," Reason mutters, and sighs.

". . . and get me eyes on the herd."

With a glance at me that would be guilty if it wasn't so self-righteous, Reason swipes at the top right holoscreen. It zooms in on fixed grainy footage of a familiar-looking neighborhood. One house, with its long front porch, stands out in particular. Grand told me she and Liyan broke down the shutters and garden shed for firewood our first few years there, but they left the porch alone because we deserved one nice thing in our lives. I've missed that porch every day since we moved. I grew up in that house. That's *the* neighborhood. Where all the fees live.

Those aren't grainy photos hanging on the wall in the office. Drones didn't snap them. They're video stills. Telling from the footage, there are six cameras total. Three on traffic lights. The rest on businesses along Whitehaven Road. Having watched Reason navigate his way around Buffalo via traffic cams, I can't say I'm surprised. Maybe *appalled* is the better word.

"All these years, the beasts have been watching us?"

"Whoa," Sway says. "That is messed up."

"No," Reason replies. "Apparently, that is survival of the fittest."

The herd.

Chia means us. Like we're sheep.

"It looks normal," Reason calls out. "Except they have four—no, five nags up on rooftops. Light weaponry. Bows and arrows. Two homemade spears."

This is our protocol during a beast-attack drill. Some fees guard the riverbanks. Some hide along the roads and some go up on roofs with long-range weapons. It always seemed efficient to me, but I can tell from the males' snorts that five is a ridiculous number of sentries. Considering all the males' guns, our bows and arrows are a ridiculous type of weaponry.

I peer at the screen. "Reason, zoom in."

Is that . . . Grandma Lucy? She does most of the baking for the neighborhood. On another rooftop, I'm certain I see Grandma Aruun. She likes to DJ at our block parties. Why would Grand put such elderly fees on guard duty? What would they do if beasts attacked? Overload them with carbs and killer beats?

"Reason." I jostle his chair. "How are you so certain it was the mob that killed our fees? Do you have footage of the invasion?"

"Yeah," he says hesitantly. "But I don't think you want to see it."

"Didn't I just specifically ask to see it?" I snap. Still smarting from his survival-of-the-fittest comment, I add, "I'm not some weak thing."

"Fine," he says shortly. "It's your emotional funeral."

With one swipe, it's suddenly early morning on-screen in Grand Island. The footage is from far away, yet it's easy to see the two beasts that run down the center of Whitehaven Road. The scarring on their faces is apparent even from this distance. Reason was right. Mob. One kicks in the door at Ruth's house. The other runs farther up the block and shatters a window at LaVaughn's. Both beasts come back out moments later. Calm. Collected. But hurried. One goes into a house a few doors down. The other cuts down a side street.

When Liyan told us beasts raided the neighborhood, I'd imagined chaos. Randomness. I imagined doors being smashed down. Wild gunfire.

This looks planned.

"I'm so sorry," Sway says.

Ruth's family now races out of the house, weapons drawn. Down the block, a beast pushes Josie Baker out into the street, a gun to her back. Her cohabitators follow, all armed with knives and crowbars. Sway lets out a cry of distress. Reason quickly presses the fast-forward button. Growing up, I went to Josie Baker's house whenever Grand worked late. I still dream about her zucchini bread. She said it was seasoned with a little love and a lot of elbow grease. My eyes fill with tears. Reaching over Reason, I press play.

On-screen, Josie Baker's body hits the ground. A moment later, the mobster falls next to her. An arrow impaling his head. A short, thick fee comes on-screen. She is dressed in a formfitting uniform. It looks dark gray in the footage, but I know it's still a vibrant scarlet. Never mind that it's patched in more places than it isn't. She wears a balaclava, a face mask that I have never seen her without. A skull is drawn on the front. A long bow and satchel of arrows is slung across her back.

As Josie Baker's family cries over her body, the fee in red places a foot on the beast's head and yanks the arrow out.

"Who is that?" Reason asks.

"Muerte," I murmur. "She's one of our EMSs."

"That's ironic." Sway coughs a little. "A paramedic named Muerte."

Except EMS doesn't stand for Emergency Medical Services. It stands for Elite Murder Squad. In Spanish, *muerte* means death. I think that's a perfectly appropriate name considering Muerte is a mercenary, one of our most elite soldiers.

Grand Mati formed the squad after the first time beasts attacked us on our island, leaving violence and heartache in their wake. And yet it has returned to our door regardless. And Mayor Chia's in a good mood.

"Stetson," Chia barks out in the office. "What the hell did you get into?"

With Slim in my hand, I go back to the doorway. A male in a cowboy hat is now present. He has a rifle slung across his back and a red blistered rash on his arms.

"Don't know," Stetson says, studying his forearms. "I went drinking in the tunnels last night and today I woke up with this. I'm itchier than a wool sweater. Probably contagious, too."

Grinning, he scratches the sores right over Quarry, who swears and pushes him away.

"Well, I kind of need my security chief not to infect the entire team right before we bring the fees over. Get to the medic and see if he's got anything that helps...that. Everyone else," Chia shouts to the room at large, "it's time for the finishing blow. Quarry, cut their power and any feeds you think they might still use. Put double security along the bridge and waterfront. Give them food and water to hand out. Get DMX on the bullhorn telling the nags we offer peace and protection. I want them to feel the mistake they're making, keeping their daughters there."

I look at Reason. "Chia's one of the good guys, huh?"

"Yeah, well." The shock in his eyes is so palpable, I look away. "Color me disappointed."

"And if one of you doesn't find me those runaway fees in the next hour," Chia shouts, "I'll string you all up by your johnsons and feed you to the dogs. I want no loose ends on this. Check the transports. The clubs. The sex dens. They are here somewhere. Probably right under our got-damn noses. Find them!"

28

"**M**aybe we should go," Sway says.

"I couldn't agree more," Reason replies. "And that says a lot. We'll go out the back."

"No," I say. "*We'll* go out the back. I'm not going anywhere with you."

"Don't worry, I'm not sabotaging you. Only trying to get you to the station in one piece. If anyone spots us, being with the Influencer will buy you a few minutes of protection. It's the least I can do."

"Great, thank you," Sway says before I can protest further.

From a metal lockbox in the top drawer of his desk, Reason takes out two blue raffle tickets from a pile of various colored ones. Grabbing his crutch, he then hops to his feet and takes a leash off a hook on the wall. The dogs immediately swarm him. Ignoring them, he uses his crutch to pull a hover board out from under his desk, then slings a backpack over one shoulder.

"Carrot, Mastodon, Eggnog, to me."

The three biggest dogs gather around Reason. He clicks the leash attachments to each of their collars while I scoop up the puppy. As soon as Reason steps on his hover board, his dogs lurch forward. When we emerge back into the common room it's cleared out by half. Chia is spinning one of the empty crystal glasses on his desk.

We move to a back door. As Reason's hand touches the doorknob, Chia lifts his head.

"Didn't you think I'd notice?" he says.

I freeze.

"What's that?" Reason asks.

"You don't say goodbye anymore when you go out?"

"Like *anything* I say matters," Reason says over his shoulder.

Chia lets out a hollow belt of laughter. "You think I don't listen, huh? 'Bump the matriarchy. Bump future generations. We're happy with the way things are. Nags would cramp our style.' I hear you loud and clear, Reason. I just don't agree with you. Life looks a lot different when there's less of it in front of you. And when we save the human race, I don't think future generations will be too picky about what methods we used to do it or who our allies were."

"What's that supposed to mean?" Reason asks as Sway pales.

Chia spins his glass. It skids perilously close to the edge of the desk. He catches it a moment before it plummets to the floor.

"It means you might not like me right now, but one day you'll thank me."

Reason shakes his head. "Keep telling yourself that."

The moment we're out the door Reason's dogs pull him forward on his hover board at such a fast clip that Sway and I have to jog to keep up. It's like they can sense his fury.

"You know what I always wonder?" Sway asks, puffing as we trot down a service corridor. "How come no one ever says: 'Let the fees have what they want'? Like the supplies and power and stuff. I mean, y'all have spent the last seventeen years on an island. Why doesn't anyone ever say, 'Maybe we should leave them alone to have their cake and eat it, too'? Oh my bump nuggets. What's *he* doing here?"

At first, I don't understand the transition. But that's because I'm looking at the ground. When I look up (and up and up) it's to find that we've popped out from our little service hall into the main promenade. To our left, Rage is about to enter Euphoria.

"Here for Chia," he tells the bouncer.

Seeing as we've just dashed out into the open with three dogs not ten feet away from him, there is no *not* seeing us. But then Rage does a double take and *sees* us.

"Ahh," he says quietly.

Just that. "Ahhh."

And then he is on his portable.

"Influencer," I say. "I think we could use a diversion."

"On it," Reason says. "Eugene. I need immediate assistance."

"Hello." The hologram is instantly next to Reason in his clean suit and gleaming teeth. "How may I help? Do you need directions? Fashion advice? Please say: Eugene, I need blank."

"Eugene, I need the entire building to evacuate." Panic makes waves in the calm river of Reason's voice. "Full emergency protocol. Safety procedure override code six-nine-two-four-N—bump, I can't remember it."

Rage doesn't bother pursuing us. Clearly he's either not used to moving quickly or simply never has to. But I can perfectly hear the PTT he sends.

"I have her. White hair. She looks like a swan. Coming to you."

"Reason, now's not a good time to stop being a know-it-all," Sway says as he looks over the third-floor banister to the lobby below.

I join Sway and look as well. Three floors below us, Wreckage has his hands up in the air and is backing away from the entrance as Jackal and two other tattooed mobsters walk in.

Reason closes his eyes, "Safety procedure override code six-nine-two-four-N-five-six-one."

Eugene blinks. Smiles. "Safety procedure overridden. Emergency protocol in effect."

Red emergency lights begin flashing. Over a loudspeaker, a voice not unlike Eugene's loudly directs everyone to calmly and quickly head to their nearest exit. The club music screeches to a halt. A moment later, drunk, loud norms pour out into the third-floor hall and swarm around Rage. Moments later, like a burst pipe, they pour down the escalator around us. Reason sends his dogs ahead. I zip the puppy into my coat. Then we three join hands and let the masses consume us. Seconds later, we're all tumbling down the escalators.

At the entrance, Jackal slips on the icy floor as he grabs a norm with white hair.

"Hello, little precious," I hear him say as we slide past him out into the freezing night.

29

"Can we safely assume Rage is in Chia's pocket?" Sway grunts.

"Or the other way around," I reply.

"Seems like a leap," Reason says, then adds begrudgingly, "but maybe not a far one."

We lost the cover of the revelers from Euphoria a few blocks back. Now Reason leads us down deserted streets, his hover board skimming the top of the knee-high snow. I'm following close behind in the trenches left by his dogs' bounding bodies. Sway is even farther back, his breath coming in harsh rasps. When I ask what's wrong with him, Reason simply says, "Asthma," as if that strange word explains anything.

A few blocks over, I hear the whine of snowmobiles and someone calling out, "Here, kitty, kitty." More worrisome are the footsteps I hear crunching snow about half a block back. Someone is following us. But every time I look behind us, expecting Jackal or Rage, all I see is Sway's pained face and an empty street past it.

Honestly, I don't care whether Chia and the mob are covertly aligned or not. *"Beasts are beasts are beasts,"* I remember Majesty saying before she was snatched. What difference does it make *how* they're teaming up? What shocks me is how completely unprepared my grand is. Matricula Rhodes has backup plans upon backup plans if the wheat fails. She couldn't be caught this unawares. Except I've never heard her mention any of this.

"All I know," I say, "is that Chia is crazy if he thinks our mothers would ever voluntarily sign us up to live in fenced-in neighborhoods."

"Don't you already, though?" Reason asks. "Seriously. I don't see the difference."

"Glori," Sway kindly interrupts, puffing, "you haven't lived in the neighborhood for five years, right? I think maybe things have changed while you were gone. From everything I hear, fees are starving. You're out of food. You have no power."

"Thanks to you males."

"Actually, can we stop?" Sway wheezes, his face violet. "I have to stop."

Reason and I exchange an anxious glance. The street is wide and eerily desolate. Dark light boxes run along the buildings with posters for things called *Miss Saigon* and *Hamilton*. An enormous vertical sign that spells BUFFALO in half-smashed lightbulbs hangs above our heads. A half block up is a forest-green street sign with white lettering that reads BUFFALO NIAGARA MEDICAL CAMPUS, along with an arrow pointing north. I never thought I'd get this close to them. My Grand Mati's old labs.

"All right," I say. "But we can't stay here."

The snowmobilers are one block closer now. "Here, kitty, kitty, kitty."

"The late transports don't leave until midnight," Reason says, looking around.

Sway glances at his portable and rasps, "Two hours to kill trying not to be killed."

"Fuego's place is close," Reason suggests.

He meets my eyes. Sway won't make it far.

"Can't," Sway pants. "Comma would kill me. Though that might be preferable to this."

"How much farther to there?" I point at the medical campus sign.

Reason shakes his head. "The labs? No thanks."

Gauging from the sound of their engines, the snowmobilers are now only one block over. The dogs whine. Waving the males to the building with the Buffalo sign, I kick out a pane of glass from the front door. Reason sends his dogs in first. The puppy whimpers to run after them. When I put him down, he scampers off into the darkness. As both males crawl inside, I try to clear our tracks from the snow. I've barely snuck through the glass when four snowmobiles turn the corner.

"Where are the dogs?" I whisper, sinking back against a wall.

"Dinnertime," Reason quietly replies as he crouches behind a dusty couch. Seeing my questioning look, he adds, "Rats."

The building must have plenty to spare. It's enormous and anciently decadent with marble floors and walls, chandeliers with hanging baubles, and intricate carved molding that fees would have burned ages ago. All of it is coated in a half inch of dust. Covering his mouth with his sleeve to muffle his ragged breathing, Sway stumbles up the steps and hides next to a bathroom.

One moment the males are shouting, "Here, kitty, kitties." The next it's silent.

Putting a finger to my lips, I use a mirror from my pack and carefully peer outside. Four snowmobiles sit empty at the corner. Otherwise, it's wind, snow, and nothingness.

"They must have gone another way." I hunker down to keep watch, Mama Bear at the ready. "Reason, what do you have against the labs?"

He considers not answering but then taps his leg with the crutch.

"I was one of the ones your elder fees left behind. I was in the day care when Fortitude started his fire. Chia rescued me, but not before my leg was crushed by a fallen beam."

Reason says *fee* like someone else might say *spontaneous diarrhea*. I guess I don't blame him. When I heard it growing up, this part of the story made perfect sense to me. Why save beasts when you could save fees? But now, looking at these males, knowing Grand knew this is what they grew up into, I suddenly get why she spent so many sleepless nights on the back porch staring off in the direction of the river. No wonder Reason resented us. Except for one problem.

"What day-care center?" I snort. "When fees fled, they took the fee *fetuses* from the labs."

"No," Reason says. "Chia's told me this history a thousand times. It's why I live with him. He saved me from the fire that Fortitude set at the *day-care center*. I'd bet my puppy on it."

"Great. You're on."

"Technically, I didn't give the puppy to either one of you." Sway rubs his chest. The violet deoxygenated flush in his cheeks is being edged out by his normal creaminess. "So can we please agree that you both have different names for the same thing?"

"Why would I agree with a fee about anything?" Reason snorts. "You have no idea how weird they are, Sway. Every other day they do this bizarre dance ritual in the intersection of Grand Island Boulevard and Baseline Road. They're always hugging. You've heard Quarry talk about how hard they are to please. How critical. There's a reason they call you nags, you know. I mean, what did we ever do to you anyway? I say, if males are so terrible that you couldn't even handle the baby version of us, then we have absolutely no need for any of you now."

He is breathless with this rant, and I have to suppress the urge to shush him. The Here-Kitty-Kitty beasts *are* still out there. But all I can hear is Reason's subtext. When I reflected on our history with the beasts, I thought about how badly fees were affected by the divide. Our lack of electricity. Our diminishing goods. But I never felt unloved. I never felt abandoned.

As calmly as possible, I say, "First of all, day-care centers don't have babies that are all born in exactly the same year. Second of all, it's called Intersectional Zumba. Third of all, yesterday wasn't the first time beasts attacked the island, and fourth, Matricula Rhodes *didn't* only take fee babies with her at the divide."

Simultaneously both males say, "Come again?"

"Jinx," Sway says. "Also, that's what he said."

"When Matricula Rhodes fled to Grand Island," I continue, "she took a handful of teenage males with her. One was the son of a fee. The others were his friends. And they were loyal to Fortitude. Their first night on the island, they killed two of our teenage fees and so badly beat up a handful of others that we still don't talk about it."

"I've never heard about this," Reason says, shocked.

"What a surprise," I say.

Though in all actuality, I never heard much about it, either. Majesty was there that night. She was one of the girls who was hurt. Grand created the mercenaries the very next day.

Suddenly, a shuffling sound comes from the back of the theater. I bound up the steps with Mama Bear ready, but it's only the puppy. Dragging something long and white with him.

"Whatcha got there, little pup?" I pick it up and immediately fling it away.

It's a decaying human arm bone. Flesh dried to it like jerky.

Scooping up the puppy—wiping my hand on my pants—I follow his tracks behind a mahogany bar where a corpse is zipped into a sleeping bag, its mouth yawning open in agony or sleep. Empty liquor bottles and candy wrappers are littered around it. Reason scavenges. Finds an unopened box of something called black licorice.

"How did that survive?" I ask.

Reason eats one and spits it out. "Because I don't think it's food."

I dig into my bag looking for the snacks Comma packed. Instead I find the animal masks from the car.

"Do these mean anything to you?"

I offer the bear mask to Reason, but he won't take it.

"I know what that is," Sway says. "Those are why y'all call us beasts to begin with. Rugged told Com and me that Fortitude's followers traded them around and wore them when they attacked fees. Stole things. Scavenged. The masks made it so you could never be sure who was a safe male and who was a beast. Until eventually, it was safer for fees to assume all males were beasts. Where'd you get those?"

"They were in the car that took Twofer from our house." Quietly, I add, "And you think males don't hurt fees?"

"I had no idea," Reason says, his dark eyes liquid with apology.

Nodding, I shoulder my pack and zip the puppy back into my coat. It immediately attempts to disassemble my hood.

"Where are we going?" Sway asks.

"To the labs. I want to see where my grand worked and settle this daycare-versus-labs debate once and for all. Twofer will love his new puppy."

"You can't take back a gift," Reason says, whistling for his dogs.

"I'm not. I'm winning him. You'll be embarrassed when you realize how wrong you are."

As his dogs return, licking their chops and wagging their tails, Reason laughs, and the unexpected playfulness that illuminates his expression does so many miraculous things to his features, I look away.

Sway rolls his eyes, mutters, "It's *my* puppy."

Outside the door, there's a flash of movement. I slide out Baby Bear.

"There's just one thing I have to do first."

"What's that?" Reason asks, eyeing my knife.

"Catch whatever septic's been following us."

30

Back outside, the moon makes a rare appearance and casts an otherworldly light on the deserted street. I squint down the block. The snowmobiles remain, but now there's also a shadow crouching behind the garbage can across the way.

"I need to pee," I say loudly. "Here, Sway. Hold *my* puppy."

As Reason laughs and hooks up his dogs, I meander my way to the garbage cans. I'm only two steps away when whoever is behind them springs out. I launch myself at his core. He's wearing a black knit balaclava and has me by at least three inches and forty pounds, but I'm faster. As we tumble backward, I'm able to flip around and put him in a headlock.

"What is happening right now?" Reason shouts.

"He's been tailing us since we left the club," I shout.

"No, I meant, it's like someone pressed a Berserker button."

"Told you," Sway says as they both come running to help.

"I've been following you longer than that," my abductee grunts. "You got sloppy, Roach. Now who's this new beast? And how friendly are its dogs? I want to mush that big one's face."

I yank off the mask, never feeling so relieved in all my life. It makes me think about my grand. How she must be feeling the exact opposite right now. For all the talk of what she knows or doesn't, one thing is certain. Twofer and I are gone. And she has no idea if we're safe or not.

But then my head is being roughly noogied. And I'm being hugged so hard I kind of wish I were still wearing those smelly dead-body layers of clothes to cut me a little extra breathing space. Because here—fierce and angry, relieved yet hurt, and don't let Comma hear me, but beautiful in her lipstick war paint—here is my best friend.

Su.

31

squeal like Twofer seeing his first butterfly. Then we are both talking at once.

"I'm sorry I chose Sway over you..." I say.

"No, it was the right choice..." Su says.

"I know you get mad that I always favor Twofer, but that doesn't mean—"

And then Su slaps me. Reason and Sway both take a few steps back.

"Maybe let's give them a minute," Sway says.

"Just stop it already. You want to know what I get mad about? That right there. That you think there's only one kind of love to show Two Five and it's yours. That I'm such a monster"—her voice breaks—"that I feel nothing toward someone who laughs so hard it gets the hiccups when I tell a joke. Someone who told me it *liked* my log-like qualities when Cheerio broke up with me. That logs built happy homes."

I can't help it, I laugh. "Cheerio called you log-like?"

Su nods. "Wooden, thick-skinned, and prone to ignite. You think I am only here to support you? I am here because Twofer is and that is the only true thing we know. I love it—" She rolls her eyes. "*Him*—I love him, too. Okay? You aren't the only one."

Most of what I want to say is a rebuttal of blame that ends in more dot, dot, dots. *Then why didn't you...? How was I supposed to know...? Why haven't you ever...?* But if this is Su's truth, I have to respect it. And while I could have done without the slap, her words are also insanely wonderful to hear.

"His hiccup thing is really adorable," I say. "Especially considering your jokes are terrible."

She pulls our foreheads together. I lightly bite her nose.

"Fees are *so* weird," Reason says.

"Now," Su barks. "What are you doing standing out here in the open? Did Liyan not teach you how to cover your tracks? Did Itami not teach you the art and value of doubling back?"

"The snowmobilers?" I ask.

"Not dead. Knocked out in an alley up the street. They'll probably want to find some pants and shoes when they wake up, though."

"What about Comma?" Sway asks. "Is he okay? Why aren't you at the steam station?"

"It's totally fine. It tried to convince me to stay and watch more movies, but I figured you could use the backup."

That was the headlight I saw. She's been following us this whole time.

"Su, you shouldn't have come."

"No. I shouldn't have let you go by yourself to begin with. You're out here risking everything, and I'm supposed to stay back there eating popcorn, watching television? Though if we make it out of this alive, from what I've seen, we've got to watch that *Unicorn Warrior* show. The fees are so diesel. Swoon."

Suddenly, Su punches me in the shoulder.

"Ow, what now?"

"Don't *what now* me." She points at Reason. "Now there's two beasts we have to worry about turning us in. You can't keep collecting beasts because you're attracted to them. Influencer, my ass. I see why you brought this one and it's obviously not for his fighting skills." She knocks his crutch with her hatchet. "Why are we all still standing around in the open?"

"I've changed my mind," Reason says as Su tromps off in the snow, heading in the opposite direction from the labs. "I'd like to not help anymore."

"You get used to her," Sway says. "Kind of."

32

At one time, the medical campus must have been a beautiful sprawl of brick and glass and curved steel and oil-slick-shimmering solar roof tiles. Potential for scientific advancement still radiates from the structures like fumes off the river in the heat months, and this is despite the fact that most of the buildings looked like they took direct hits on Nuclear Night. I can't even imagine what a mind like Grand's could have done if she'd been able to access this space for the last seventeen years. The diseases she could have cured. The crops she could have brought back into existence. I wouldn't put it past her to make a molecule that cleaned air.

All my life I've been told of Fortitude's viciousness, but it is something else entirely to see it firsthand. It looks like he stood in the street and haphazardly launched Molotov cocktails in every direction, only the flaming bottles were the size of cars. Enormous chunks of the buildings are missing. No wonder we fled.

"Sorry," Sway mutters.

"You don't have to keep apologizing," I say.

"I know, but I feel like it keeps needing to be said."

On the jog over here, I filled Su in on everything that happened in the last few hours. Now we spin, taking in all the labs, trying to figure out which one Grand used to call home.

"That one," we say together.

"Excellent," Sway says. "The one with the protective twenty-foot-tall iron fence capped by the triple row of razor wire."

"No," Reason says, "the one with the lights on in the top-floor windows."

As we watch, the light goes off, then another goes on a few feet away from the original. Then that goes off and another light switches on a few windows down. Reason's dogs whine.

"Maybe it's a faulty circuit," Sway says.

"Only one way to know for sure," I say. "Apologize to Comma for me."

Taking off my coat—fly away, little hood—I throw it on top of the razor wire. Then, gripping a single iron post, I plant my feet on the bars and walk up the fence. When I reach the top, I push off the bars, use the momentum to flip over the barbed wire, and fling myself to the other side, landing neatly, gymnast-style.

Applause meets my landing.

Sway and Su are standing next to me, grinning with almost identical smiles.

"Loose spoke in the fence," Sway says. "Like, a foot that way."

Switching off his hover board, Reason also slips through the fence, telling his dogs to wait. Reluctantly, I leave the puppy with them. Then we all hurry to the entrance doors. Unlike the other lab buildings, this one is missing any noticeable holes. Only a few second-floor windows are shattered. NEUYUE is etched in white on the black-tinted glass.

"How do we get in?" Reason asks.

Intending to see how thick the glass is, I walk up to the doors. When I reach my hand out, they soundlessly slide open.

"The building has power," Reason says, halfway between a question and a statement.

I pull Slim from her sheath. Reason twirls his crutch upside down and pops off the rubber tread to reveal a sharp spike.

"Nice," I say.

"I do okay." He shrugs. His eyes cut to Su. "Despite first impressions."

"I'll be sure to call you when I need a hole punch," Su grunts, hatchet out.

We all look to Sway. He pats his pockets.

"I think I left my wine key at home. Don't y'all look at me like that. A corkscrew's a great weapon."

"Actually, Glor," Su says, "if I were you, I'd go for Crutches."

With both males' complexions traffic-signal red, we step inside. Since the outside windows are tinted against the sun, the lobby is pitch-black. Yet a soft yellow glow emanates from a bank of elevators. Sway presses one of the glowing buttons. It turns green.

"How did you know to do that?" I ask.

"Ha!"

As sharp red numbers above the elevator count down, the males cluster behind me as if any distance greater than one inch between us isn't safe. They're probably right. The elevator dings and we all crouch defensively.

The doors glide open.

Gentle music drifts out.

The elevator is empty.

"It could be a trap," I say.

"Oh, it's most definitely a trap," Su says.

"Maybe we should go straight to the train station," Reason says. "There have to be better places to kill an hour and a half."

"You goits." Sway laughs. "It's an *elevator*. A working one. Any of you ridden in one of these before?"

He steps inside, bounces.

"See? Perfectly safe."

With no time for subterfuge or sneak attacks, once inside, I press fifteen. The button for the top floor. As Su attempts to identify our blind spots in a simple square box, the mirrored doors glide shut. Suddenly, we're all staring at ourselves.

In the ambient lighting, Reason takes off his hat and sheepishly uses it to rub a smudge of dirt off his cheek. Realizing his hair is even more of a disaster, he quickly puts his hat back on. Thanks to Comma, I'm remarkably cleaner than usual, but my hair has flopped over and I can't help noticing that the used clothes I'm wearing are starting to smell. Su fixes the lines of lipstick she drew under her eyes, then frowns intimidatingly . . . at herself.

"This is why I stopped working out with you," I tell her.

Sway, meanwhile, is spotless. With his blue shoes, camo parka, neat haircut, and bright red snapback cap, he looks like he stepped out of one of Comma's magazine ads. He quietly whistles along with the elevator music but stops when we all turn to stare at him.

"What? Backstreet Boys. Classic."

The elevator dings. We collide into one another in our effort to be the first out, only to be bathed in immediate bright light. Reason wields his spike. Su swings her hatchet. I tug Mama Bear out to fight alongside Slim. Sway grabs hold of my sweater. But nothing happens. The hallway lights above us have simply turned on. As one, we shuffle forward. When we've gone three feet, the lights behind us go off and the ones directly above us flash on.

Su lets out a muffled scream. "They're following us."

"Energy-saving lights, bruth." Reason grins.

Nothing on Grand Island was outfitted with this level of green technology. Yet a quick look around tells me the motion sensor lights are the least remarkable fixture of the space. No wonder all the fees spoke so highly of these labs. In the very first room we pass, on gleaming stainless-steel tables, there is an ultracentrifuge *and* a tabletop one *and* a microfuge. Sterile tubes and cryovials sit on neat shelves on the back walls behind a swinging bucket rotor for gradient purification. In the second lab, there are ultra-cold freezers and refrigerators. Biosafety cabinets and autoclaves. And actual proper nitrogen tanks. Eight at a glance, so unlike the ones Grand and her staff rigged back home.

"Someone's keeping this place up," Sway says.

"No, it's more than that," I whisper. "Listen."

But telling from everyone's blank expressions, they don't hear all the purrs, beeps, and hums that I do. To me, they sound as loud as doorbells.

"The machines are on. Someone is actually using them."

I follow a cord that runs from one of the ultra-cold freezers. It ends in a room filled with fans and generators. If the power went down, the backup generators would instantly kick on and no cells would be lost. Reason moves to the next room and peers in through the glass door.

"Yeah, but using them for what?"

We all crowd around to look. Inside, plastic tubs with metal grated tops are stacked on shelves running five wide and six high. Each tub houses a rat. And each rat is covered in angry red sores. A few are dead. This was either very sloppy lab work or these animals died so recently the techs hadn't had a chance to remove them yet.

"I don't want to go in there," Sway says.

"Probably a good idea," Su grunts.

"That looks important, though," Reason says.

He points to a cord that's as thick as ten ropes braided together. It runs through a hole in the wall to a room next door. As Sway and Reason push through the next set of double swing doors, Su remains staring at the rats.

"Suze?"

"Gimme a minute."

Inside the next room is a desk with a holodisplay. It sits in front of a plate-glass window that looks into darkness. Reason immediately goes to the computer. One by one, I turn the lights on. Except I stop as soon as I see what's on the other side of the glass.

"Holy crow," I say.

"Holy bump," Sway adds.

Reason looks up from the computer. "Holy bumping bump."

Not only was someone still using the labs, they were still using them for their originally designed purpose. In the room on the other side of the glass, heavy clear plastic bags hang from the ceiling. And inside each one . . . is a fat perfect fetus.

33

"**H**oly waste," Su says, rejoining us.

"This finally proves," Sway says, "that there is no end to the uses of Ziploc bags."

Su rolls her eyes. "Those aren't Ziploc bags, numbtits. They're SymSacs."

Maybe Symbiotic Sacs don't physically resemble wombs, but they do incorporate all the same key components. The clear plastic bag holds and protects the fetus while tubes pump in an electrolyte solution that doubles as amniotic fluid and helps it exchange carbon dioxide for oxygen.

"Suze, the males are making babies."

"Yes. I see that."

"Those *are* babies, right?" Reason asks. "Actual babies? Growing in a bag."

"The word is *gestating*," Su says. "I mean, where did you think babies came from?"

"Fees!" Reason cries.

"They do," Su says. "Fifty percent of all those fetus's genetics come from a fee."

"No, I mean . . ." Looking sheepish, he gestures to his groin.

"Oh, you mean from our vaginas?" Su snorts. "That's so old-school."

Originally, Symbiotic Sacs were solely used for premature babies as a way to incubate them longer in the "womb." Then fees began using them out of medical necessity—if they were too old to carry children in vitro or if their womb was inhospitable. When their babies came out fat and strong and healthy, the entire world took note. Grand told me eventually a few "movie stars" used them for very public births. After that the practice took off.

Looking at them, I think, No wonder they called us the Miracles. They are exactly that. Miraculous.

"Suze, why are males making babies?" I ask.

"I really don't—"

"*How* are males making babies?"

"Glor, I don't know."

"I know for a fact," Reason says, "that Chia knows nothing about this technology."

"Just like you knew he was one of the good guys?" I ask, then immediately regret it when Reason's peevish expression falls off. "Sorry. That came out meaner than I meant."

Yet Reason was probably right. NeuYue was an entirely fee-run company. Of course, there were males in the world who had this technology, but they didn't work out of Buffalo. Only fees did. That was NeuYue's whole mission statement. NeuYue made procreation a right for everyone. No matter their age, relationship status, sexual preference, or gender. The power of conception was entirely in fee hands.

The only question was *how* and *why* and *when* did males acquire that power, too?

Despite everyone telling me not to, I pop open the door to the gestation room. There are fifteen fetuses all together. They look to be about six months old.

"Chia called us the herd," I say. "You think he was referencing the fact that initial ex-utero birth trials were all with fetal sheep?"

Three sets of eyeballs simultaneously roll upward.

"Right," I say. "Probably not."

"How come you two know so much about this?" Sway asks.

I try very hard not to look at Su. Playing it equally cool, Su walks to the farthest end of the gestation room as if she hasn't heard the question. The answer is simple.

It was my Grand Mati's life's work.

"Every fee does," I say. "It's conception. Plus, since the buildings were hermetically sealed, everyone working here during the Night survived. We've been learning the science behind ex-utero births for as long as I can remember."

"Man, this whole thing creeps me out." Reason shudders.

But Twofer was born the old way, and all I remember is blood and more blood and the sound of Majesty screaming. Compared to the Symbiotic Sacs, the natural process is so barbaric. Then it occurs to me. I nudge Reason's arm.

"I told you Chia didn't rescue you from some day care. He rescued you from these *labs*. You're a Miracle baby."

I almost say, *Just like me*, but stop myself. Reason is not impressed.

"I came from a sac?" he asks flatly.

Sway ever so lightly touches one of the bags. The little fee inside has the hiccups.

"You guys notice anything particularly striking about these babies?"

He wiggles a pinkie finger in the air, then lowers it like it died. I walk around to the next-closest bag. She already has wisps of dark hair on her head. The next one is sucking her thumb. They're all so beautiful. But as I look into the next bag, then the next, my heart sinks.

"They're all fee," I say.

34

Out in the observation room, a timer goes off on an autoclave.

"Hey, fees," Su says. "Remember why we came up here in the first place?"

"The lights were on," Sway says.

"The motion sensor lights," Reason corrects. "We're not alone."

"Don't we *want* to see who's working here?" I hiss as we hurry to the outer room.

"Sure, we do," Sway says, switching off the lights. "And I'm sure they will gladly let us leave with this obviously public knowledge that they're breeding baby girls."

"Shh," I whisper. "Someone's coming."

"Don't tell me you can hear them," Su says, always a little jealous of my better-tweaked senses. "This room is sealed."

"No." I point. "I can see them."

Out in the hall, the motion sensor lights outline two figures against the frosted glass. Inside the room there is nowhere to hide, only one storage cabinet and the desk. I motion toward the gestation room. Once everyone's in, I lock the door behind us. There's a camera in the corner; thankfully, the lens is shattered. We press ourselves against the wall beneath the observation window, our knees tight to our chests. Each sac gives off a blue ethereal glow until the lights go back on around us and in the outer office as well. A shadow slides across the floor. It's a big shadow.

"Progress report?" a familiar male voice intones.

"The fetuses are two months out."

"That's a fee voice," Su says, surprised and loudly.

Shut it, Sway mouths, then, *something...something...crazy?*

I'll shut you...something...something...numbtits, Su angrily mouths back.

"How is the environment?" the fee asks.

"Not ready yet. But the mayor is pleased with how things are progressing. It won't be long now before they submit or are all dead."

"Good. This is cutting it close."

The doorknob shakes. Then shakes again.

"Do you usually lock this door?" the male asks.

"No." The fee sighs. "But none of us are operating on much sleep. My keys are downstairs in my room."

I take the mirror out of my bag again and angle it so I can see through the observation window into the outer room.

"Glori!" Su hisses. "They'll see."

But I have to know who the traitor is. When I get the reflection to work, Reason's and Sway's heads are pressed right alongside mine.

First, we see a giant male, tattoos.

"Rage," Reason murmurs.

"And?" Su whispers.

Curly hair pulled back into a quick knot. Midfifties. A weary expression and a too-tight lab coat buttoned over pajamas. I shake my head. Her face is familiar, but I can't place it. Like I've only seen it in a dream.

Moments after they leave we are on their heels, popping open the outer office door. As soon as we hear the elevator ding shut behind them, Su points at a stairwell across the hall.

"Go," she says quietly.

Needing no second invitation, Reason is down the hall and through the door, nimbler on his crutch than Sway is on his own two feet, as is evident when Sway skids and trips on the polished floor. Su and I go together. Every lab we run past, I expect someone to jump out and snatch us.

Just like that, I know who the fee is.

Her name is Esperanza. She was one of Matricula's most brilliant protégées. A self-described loner, she never cohabitated with anyone. Instead she preferred the solitude of the labs. The companionship and stimulation of progressive science. Which is why no one immediately knew she was missing when the beasts raided her home and snatched her shortly after Majesty was taken almost six years ago. Espe was discovered missing a full day after the other five fees who were also kidnapped.

Thanks to all the blood, our EMS declared her dead.

I guess they were wrong.

35

We steal Rage's car to get to the transport station. Yes, it's stupid. And dangerous. But we're late and Sway insisted that by the time Rage found his car we'd already be on a transport a few hours away. Plus, Rage's ride is a Hummer, which impressed Su and the males. Unfortunately, it is much smaller on the inside than it looks. Which meant the dogs didn't fit, and after lengthy hugs, Reason commanded them to "Go home." Next second, they were loping off through the snow. All but the puppy, who I hid inside my coat.

Now the Hummer is parked in a driveway a block behind us, and we're running through snowy woods across from a street lined with dead trees and enormous brick houses the likes of which I've never seen on Grand Island. I'm sure they're what used to pass for "luxury" housing, but I can't imagine keeping their massive rooms warm right now. Accordingly, they are all dark. Reason says the transport hub is through this park. Whatever transports are, they must be at least ten times bigger than cars. I've heard them rumbling for a mile now.

As we race through the woods, Sway as ever a few feet behind, I tell the males about the fees who were snatched right around when Twofer was born. I don't include the fact that my mother was also snatched months before that. Alone.

"Esperanza was supposed to be dead," I say.

"Does that mean the other five snatched fees aren't dead, either?" Reason asks.

"Well, Espe couldn't grow and monitor all those fetuses herself."

"So they've all been stuck there? All these years?"

"Stuck?" I ask. "You mean imprisoned. Still think your mayor and the mob aren't teammates, Reason?"

"I'm highly considering the possibility. But I don't get why Chia would go through all the trouble of reunifying, if he's able to make babies?"

Maybe because it killed two birds with one stone. It rejuvenated the population, and it took away our bargaining chip. Previously, we were the only ones who could make babies. Both the regular lab way and the old-school physical way. That meant the males had to respect it when we said, *Leave us be on Grand Island.* But now that males had that power? We were a lot less relevant, which meant we were far less safe. I can still hear the glee with which those males in Chia's offices discussed Majesty's breasts.

"Glori," Su starts to say.

"Don't worry, I know." I grip her hand. "Those labs change everything, and we need to tell our community about it immediately. But we don't need two people to warn Grand, Suze. I'll go for Twofer. Reason, you make sure Su gets home safe."

"*I'll* make sure Su gets home safe," Su snaps. "Though I will let you point me in the right direction."

Reason mumbles something about he'll point her in the right direction all right, but then more loudly says, "We're in luck. Bertha hasn't left yet."

When we step from the woods, we're met with rolling snowbanks. Tops of green SAVE THE PLANET signs poking out here and there. We had those, too. Until fees used them all to patch roofs. Beyond the snowbanks is an imposing building of stately marble columns and grand steps. A partially snow-covered sign reads: BUFFALO ALBRIGHT-KNOX-GUNDLACH ART MUSEUM. On the side of the museum, a huge screen shows an old broadcast of the throw-the-ball sport that plays on every station. Despite the cold, males stand scattered in front of the screen, occasionally yelling advice. There's at least a dozen patrol soldiers between us and the transports. All with guns. All on alert.

"Beasts turned an art museum into a bus station?" Su asks.

Reason blows into his hands. "The common thought was if the air wasn't breathable, animals were nearly extinct, and nags amputated themselves from us, what's the use of art?"

"A lot of it's been looted anyway," Sway adds with a grin as he and Reason slap hands.

Su sighs with disapproval, but I'm too transfixed by the transports to care. There are four altogether, and each one is a massive, armored, prehistoric-looking creature cobbled together from pre-Night vehicles, farm equipment, and building parts.

"How long did it take you to make these?" I ask.

Sway laughs. "*We* didn't. A fee did. A sculptor. They're pre-Night. Having to do with our monstrous need for transportation destroying the planet like the asteroid that took out the dinosaurs. Or something. They all run off furnaces that burn garbage. We use them to reach the farthest parts of the livable zones, since most vehicles' charges don't last that long."

The giant screen on the museum has switched from sports to the tunnel footage. BREAKING NEWS, the feed on the bottom of the screen reads.

UPDATE: THE REWAURD FOR THE FEMAILS IS NOW $75,000. THE REWAURD FOR THE
MAIL A BETTING THEM IS RAISED TO $35.

"Come on," Sway says. "Now they're just being mean."

"I hate when Chia puts Regulator at my terminal," Reason moans.
"Dumb goit. I'll never live this down."

The males who had been watching the sport now turn and survey the
lawns. Each of them is holding some kind of very professional-looking
weapon. Hunting knives, a crossbow, semiautomatics. They aren't ran-
domly standing out in the cold at all. Exactly like the patrol soldiers,
they're here waiting for us.

Having recently burst from the woods, we've attracted attention. A
few eyes narrow as they take us in. A cinder block of a male with a cord-
less nail gun ambles our way. Reason is instantly on his portable. The big
screen cuts out. Males groan. When it resumes playing, it's a scene of a
group of males on a stage doing a coin toss. One of them says, "Man, I'll
go first against this choke artist." The norm headed our way looks back
over his shoulder, then says, "Oh nice!" and stops to watch.

"The *Eight Mile* rap battle." Reason grins. "Works every time."

"You have an easy fix for all the patrol soldiers?" Su asks.

"In fact," Sway says, "we do. Bon Jovi?"

"Geez, Sway." Reason rolls his eyes. "Of course."

After looping an arm through his crutch, Reason throws both arms
around my and Su's shoulders, then belts out: *"Tommy used to work on
the docks."*

Weaving side to side, we stumble away from the woods, the boys
singing at the top of their lungs. And I realize that these males aren't
male. At least not like any we learned about. That's why one sequestered
himself in the outskirts along the river and the other kept himself hidden

in the back room of a club buried in his screens. As Sway yells directly into my ear—"*Whoa, we're halfway there. Whoa, livin' on a prayer*"—I can't help thinking they don't belong in this world of Rage, Chia, and Charlestonians any more than Twofer or I do.

When we reach Bertha moments later, we are wounded by nothing more than annoyed or longing glances, and I am getting increasingly excited to ride this transport. Bertha's engine room is the cab of a semi-truck. Giant steer horns are affixed to her roof. A patrol soldier is checking tickets. Disentangling himself from us, Reason lurches forward.

"Hey, Escalade, look," Reason says, slurring those three words in seven different places. "I found them. Here's the fees. You can go home now."

Su shoots me an alarmed look.

I shake my head slightly and murmur, "Trust."

"Is that right, Reason?" Escalade asks as he writes down the name and citizen number of the male behind us, then hands him a worn blue ticket.

"Yup. I'm a hero."

Nodding like his head's come loose, Reason suppresses a burp and not so subtly takes a hundred-dollar bill from his pocket, wraps it around the two blue tickets he brought from Euphoria, then presses the whole packet into the guard's hand.

"Now that you're in my debt, my friend Benjamin asks that you let *me* put my friends on *this* transport without telling Chia about it." Leaning into Escalade, he wetly whispers, "Chia hates Sway and Caliente here. Hates them. Come on. What do you say?"

"I say you need to learn to hold your liquor, Influencer."

Yet he hands back the tickets minus the hundred-dollar bill.

"You are a true diamond in the rough, Escalade. Always one step ahead of the breadline. One swing ahead of the sword. Hey, can I get a moment here? To say goodbye?"

Pivoting toward me like a wobbly spun nickel, Reason pulls me to him. His eyes alight with mischief, he lightly presses his nose to mine. Our lips are only a finger's width apart.

"Hey now," Sway barks.

"It's the alcohol." Reason hiccups.

Su shockingly makes no protest. The guard, however, holds his hands up and resolutely turns his back to us. Reason immediately drops the dopey drunkenness.

"Su," Reason says. "Watch our perimeter for a sec, would you?"

Su considers him suspiciously, but the request so aligns with her natural instinct—always watch your perimeter—she does as she's told.

No sooner is Su's back turned than Reason urgently says, "Glori, there's something I haven't told you. I know Chia didn't send the mob across to steal Two Five or kill those fees, because I didn't tell anyone that I saw you and your brother on that footage until the next day. We've all watched the film a hundred times since then, but the night it was recorded? The night you took Two Five out for that bike ride? I was sleeping."

This is not what I was expecting. "I don't understand."

"Everything that records overnight, I watch in one lump over breakfast. Which would have been about five or six hours later, around the time the neighborhood was getting raided."

"So someone else was watching your screens?" Sway says, then squats to clean a smudge off his shoes.

Reason hesitates. "Maybe? Though not likely."

"I keep thinking," I say. "About how precise the mob's attack was, like they weren't looking for more children, but for specific fees. It almost seems like the mob was planning to attack anyway, and Two Five was a last-minute bonus. Is that what you mean?"

Su sighs loudly and glares at us over her shoulder. *Wrap it up.*

Quickly, Reason says, "I guess what I'm saying is maybe you're right. Maybe Chia and Rage are working together, but I'm not sure it was a *male* who put the word out that you have Two Five." He glances at Su. "I'm not sure you should be trusting anyone right now."

Next to us, Bertha roars to life. I cover my ears. I've never heard an airplane engine, but I imagine this sound can't be too far off. Su comes back over.

"Your video ended." She nods at the museum screen and the males who are all coming out of a freestyle daze.

I clear my throat. "Take good care of *our* puppy."

Taking the puppy out of my coat, I kiss his head and hand him to Reason. Holding the puppy to his heart, Reason takes off his hat and dips toward me in a mini bow. A lock of hair falls over his eye, and before I can think better of it, I pull him in for a hug. He is muscles and tension and heat, and he embraces me back without hesitation.

"I'm sorry they left you behind all those years ago."

"It's okay," he murmurs. "I'm sorry I held it against you. Please take care."

"Time to go," Sway says loudly.

And then Reason lets me go and Su is filling his void, hugging me even tighter. There are no last-minute instructions this time. When she lets go, we simply stare at each other.

"When you see Grand, tell her I'm okay."

"So long as you promise me you'll do everything in your power to stay okay."

"I promise."

I've known Su my entire life. She loves Two Five, she said so herself. Granted, on good days, she treated him like he was a time bomb, keeping him at arm's length as if he might explode and turn into one of *them* at any second. Could I see her venting to one of her crushes? And could one of those crushes have ties to a fee that worked on this side?

The question is so easily answerable, it doesn't need to be asked.

"Word of advice?" She casts a glance at the males. "I know this is your intro to having working hormones, but don't get your hopes up, okay, my little straight-arrow cohabby?"

"Suze, I'm hardly here to rom-com."

"No, I know. I'm only saying, as much as you might like these males? Reunification is never going to happen."

36

"This is by all counts the weirdest day of my entire life," Sway says as we board Bertha. "And that includes the time those goits wandered in from Chicago and tried to sell me and Comma lakefront apartments."

Bertha's interior looks like a child's drawing. Aisles abruptly end. Flights of stairs take us up, only to lead us immediately back down. Sliding open a door, we exit the first car and step into what looks like a pre-Night school bus that's been sliced down the middle. Seats and windows line the left-hand side, while a metal wall with two doors for restrooms is on the right.

"This can't be right," I say. "Every seat is taken."

"We wouldn't have tickets if there weren't seats."

It's so different here. Back home, there would have been handshakes and "Hello!"s among all the passengers. Fees would have been splitting sandwiches and sharing dried fruit. Here everyone averts their eyes as we pass. But then I catch the gaze of a male in a kelly-green cap. Fifty or so, and a norm, he seems to recognize me but then quickly looks away. I glance at him over my shoulder as we cross into the next car. Likewise, he furtively looks back after me.

"Sway," I murmur. "I think I've been spotted."

"Let's just get to our seats."

Except when we make our way to the end of the next car, it turns out I was right. There are no more seats. Sway checks the tickets again. Thirty-two and thirty-three. I point to a solid metal wall with the same numbers on it and a tiny eye-level knob. Sway gives it a tug and the wall slides open.

"You have to admit," I say, "Reason is very everything."

He booked us our own private, hidden compartment.

"I guess on paper," Sway says. "Comma's had a crush on him for years. I never got the attraction. I mean, did you notice how Reason tries never to say his name in a sentence? He'll be like, 'The purpose of my being here . . .' What a goit."

I yank down one of the bars from the luggage racks above our seats and wedge it under the door handle. Once the door's secure, I press my ear to it. But I hear nothing outside.

"I don't think he followed us," I say. "False alarm?"

"Or he was into you. People watch you when they like you. I mean, you're no *Reason*, of course. . . ."

I bat my eyelashes à la Marilyn. "But who is?"

Sway pretends to vomit. After he puts our packs up on the remaining luggage bars, he offers me the window seat. Meant for school-age children, the bench is so small that when I sit on it, my knees are almost at my chin. I can't help laughing. Sway joins me and his grin breaks even wider than mine. We shouldn't be in such good spirits. Males are making babies and planning to force fees into a reunification they don't want. Still, we're on our way to get Twofer and also? It's nice being back to only the two of us.

Out in the hall, a male announces the various travel times to every stop on our route, then shouts, "Last call."

Scrunching farther down in his seat, Sway pulls the brim of his hat lower over his forehead. There's that freckle again under his right eye. It is perfectly round, and I have the insatiable urge to press it.

"Staring," he says, but softer than before, sleepy. His eyes hold mine. He breaks the stare first. "We should get some sleep. We've got at least a two-hour ride until we get to the farms. Maybe longer if the snow's piled up."

"Sway?" I ask.

"Sleeping."

"If Reason's right and the mayor didn't know about Two Five, then why hasn't he put up a reward for him? He knows he crossed. Why is he claiming he isn't here?"

"Good question. Let's ask him."

I breathe on the window, then draw Twofer's fortress on it. "Sway?"

"Mhh?"

"I'm not nineteen. I'm one of them. A Miracle baby."

Yawning, Sway takes off his jacket and tries to snuggle under it like a blanket. "Yeah. I figured." He closes his eyes again.

"What? How?"

"Aside from the fact that you barely look thirteen? Reason and Comma are both attractive, but I mean, Comma needs glasses and Reason's kinda short and he has those big ears. You're like the Maybach of designer babies. You've obviously been CRISPRed."

If ex-utero births were old science, CRISPR was ancient science at this point. It was first detected around the early aughts. The acronym stood for Clustered Regularly Interspaced Short Palindromic Repeats. Essentially, it was molecular scissors. It let you recognize and select a virus, disease, or character trait in a line of DNA and effectually snip it out. Muscular dystrophy. Alzheimer's. Sickle cell anemia. All cured by CRISPR in the midtwenties.

"If this is about that fighting stuff, I've trained every day for almost my whole life."

"Yeah, but no offense, it's not that you're not normal for a fee. You're not normal for a human being. Your eyesight. Your sense of smell. Bruth, you speak, like, four languages."

"Seven," I softly correct.

"Not to mention how strong you are. I mean, that crazy flip over the barbed wire fence? Do you know how long it'd take me to get down one of these luggage bars? Try infinity. It would take me an infinity of life to work one of those suckers off."

"How did you not know about SymSacs, but you know about CRISPR?"

"I knew about SymSacs. Comma's dad told us all about them. Comma's a sac baby. He was a six-month-old fetus when the Night hit. I don't know why Chia lied to Reason. It never occurred to me other goits didn't know."

Sway yawns, smacks his lips together, then says, "Fortitude and Matricula weren't so different, you know. They both saw the collapse and planetary reboot as an incredible opportunity to make something great. Fortitude was just more old-school. Or at least that's what Rugged always told us.

"Rugged said the Breeder Bill didn't require a fee's primary focus to be on making babies; it emphasized that the primary focus had to be on the 'natural' way of making babies. I think Fortitude was trying to outlaw CRISPR."

"But who would want to do away with CRISPR when it makes the best humans?"

That was the thing. CRISPR didn't only cut. It let you add. In 2017, the Chinese were the first to use the science on embryos. Shortly after, in 2018, they were also the first to CRISPR an actual fetus, making the DNA of a baby girl impervious to the HIV virus. Initially, people the world over feared the implications. They worried about the exact super race of "designer babies" that Sway pegged me as. Yet when babies (and adults) began dying—actually baking—in the insufferably, unsustainably hot regions of the world, or developing subpar immune systems in the most polluted, people minded a little less that scientists could adjust their baby's DNA to cope with it.

"Maybe," Sway says as delicately as if he's knitting lace, "Fortitude wanted to do away with the idea of 'best.' I've talked to old males about pre-Night times. How competitive it was. How there was this pervasive feeling that someone always had more than you, was doing 'better' than you. How no one was satisfied with their share, no matter what portion they received. If that's what always striving for the best of everything got us, I can kind of see Fortitude's thinking and why he and Matricula clashed so hard."

Seeing the blood drain from my face, he quickly says, "I'm not saying I agree with Fortitude. But I mean, maybe there's not a right or wrong way to do things anymore."

I bristle. "Of course there is. Habitation zones, for instance, shorten commute times, build community, keep everyone safe. They are the *right* way to live. And obviously there are efficient and more sustainable ways to eat, drink your water, wash your clothes."

"I guess. *Or* maybe we're only making up these rules to feel less scared about the fact that we survived. Maybe the only rule is 'wake up.' After that, everything else could be based on what makes that waking-up experience a happy one."

Now Sway bats his eyelashes at me.

I snort. "Sounds great, until the day everyone in your society wakes up and decides food production no longer brings them joy. And as lovely as the singular goal of existing to be happy sounds, you've never had to live on an island because you feared for your safety. Hey, Sway?"

"Yes, Glori?"

I suppress a smile. My name on his lips. Welcome back, sparkle up my spine.

"I think Matricula knew about the cameras you had on us."

Sway shakes his head at my abrupt swing in conversation. But I can't stop thinking about it. When Majesty discovered she was pregnant, Grand moved us to our abandoned cul-de-sac less than a day later. After Twofer was born, she was always adamant that I never take him into the neighborhood yet lax about letting us go to Costco or Fantasy Island. Despite the fact that a fee could have happened upon us at any moment. I don't think it was fees she was truly hiding us from. I think it was beasts.

But I can't exactly tell Sway any of that, so I take a different route instead.

"Matricula used to come to my school on her lunch breaks," I continue. "She'd stand in the back of my math class, with this little smile. Once, when I asked her about it, she said she still got a kick seeing young fees learning complex science and math. That in the past we'd been told we weren't inherently smart enough or genetically suited to it. She said some days she needed a reminder of what this was all for. I'm positive she would never let us be as unprepared as Chia seems to think we are."

Same went for putting Grandma Lucy and Grandma Aruun up on the roofs for guard duty. It was a poor defensive strategy and Grand didn't make those. Sway listens while trying to peel a sticker off the wall above him.

"I hear things like that and it makes me think we're better off now," he says.

I sit up a little straighter. "I think that, too. I know it isn't right or charitable, but sometimes I don't mind that there's so few of us left. Listening to what Grand said it was like before the Night—the stress, the inequality, the conflict, all those screens—I've always felt kind of lucky. Not just to be alive, but to be alive *now*. But I wouldn't have minded living in a world where there weren't quite so many dead bodies."

I've never told anyone that before.

"What would you have more of?" Sway asks.

"Swimming pools. I would definitely have more working swimming pools."

He laughs. "Nay to dead bodies. Yea to swimming pools. Heard."

He rips off the sticker, gives a little cheer, then wads it up and throws it on the floor.

"Hey," he says. "For the record: You know I'm not like that, right? Those pre-Night beasts who thought y'all couldn't science? Neither is anyone else I know. I mean, we all grew up fee-less. Reason aside, we have no expectations of you. I just want to be me."

He gives me a sleepy smile, and there's nothing stomach churn-y or sparkly about it. It's solely sweet and comfortable. And it makes me realize that's exactly what I want, too. For me to be me. And him to be him. And for Twofer to be Twofer. And what I really want—what would make me wake up happy every day—is for us all to do that together. Because how can I possibly go back to living my solitary life, my fee-only life, now that I know he's over here? How can I possibly dream of robbing Two Five of the exquisiteness that is being friends with Sway?

"We should get some sleep." I scrunch down and shut my eyes.

"Boop," he murmurs, and then ever so quietly says, "Honestly, Glori, if Matricula is prepared? Good for her. She'll need to be."

Next second, he's snoring.

37

"Can of peaches for your thoughts," Grand offered, setting aside her portable.

I flopped down on the couch across from where she was tucked into her "reading" chair. I didn't want to tell her this, but there was no one else *to* tell. Liyan would have said to ignore it. *"Who cares?"* And Su had already told me that instead of being sensitive, maybe I should try a little harder to fit in. Only, I *had* been trying.

I pressed my face into the couch's seat cushions, vaguely wondering at the pre-Night butts that had sat there before us. This was before Majesty was snatched by the beasts. Before we moved to the cul-de-sac. When for as long as I could remember, there was something that made me different from everyone else.

"The Miracles started this thing," I said into the cushions of the couch. "All the friend groups are making names for themselves. The Tricky Switch Stance Nine. The Sensational Sevens. The Gaudy Arties."

"What's your group called?" Grand Mati asked. I could hear the smile in her voice.

I pulled my face from the crack in the cushions to look at her.

"The Optimal One."

Her bemused expression sank.

"Oh, honey, no. Want me to talk to everyone?"

"No." I inhaled, mortified. "Don't you dare."

Clicking an empty pen that she kept specifically for this purpose, she was quietly thoughtful, then leaned toward me in her chair. "Glori, did I ever tell you why I went into genetic biology?"

I shook my head, riveted. On Grand Island, new stories were as rare as bright colors.

"My mom, your great-grandma, was something of a celebrity. The creator of this thing called a fashion blog. She began it in high school as a side project, and it skyrocketed her to something called celebrity. Which meant lots of people who didn't know her envied her. But she was not a happy person. She had a horrible relationship with her parents and I grew up believing she had me if not entirely by accident, then at least partially to infuriate them.

"Anyway, even though it was still controversial, my mom signed unborn me up to be CRISPRed. I was one of the first in the US.

"Looking back, I'm sure it was mostly a publicity stunt, which means a thing you do for attention. And yet, it gave us our height, eye color, and good metabolism. Plus, it eradicated our Rhodes family's susceptibility to breast cancer and depression. There were about twenty-five other adjustments they made as well. I honestly can't remember all of them. I still have the documentation in a drawer somewhere around here."

Grand quietly played with her braid. We called that style the Matricula Rhodes. I'd been wearing mine the same way since I could remember.

"When I started school, it was at something called a private school in a place called Brooklyn. Since my mother made no secret of my enhancements—there were entire magazine articles written about it—my competitive classmates knew me long before I knew them. You'd think with time, you would become inured to certain words like *freak* and *monster*, but you don't. Honestly, I think I envisioned our life here on Grand Island decades before the Night. A place where no fee ever had to temper her intelligence or athleticism or interests ever again."

She clicked her pen for a few beats.

"How come you've never told me any of this?" I finally asked.

"For starters, the world ended. All those people are dead. It seems silly to hold a grudge against them now." She laughed at herself, at how serious this conversation had become. But then her eyes narrowed. "No, that's not entirely the truth. I've never told you because it felt like letting their memory endure was an honor they didn't deserve.

"Anyhow, when it was time for me to decide my career, I went whole hog into genetics. My goal was to make CRISPRing so common that the freaks became the people without it. You are all called Miracles for the fact that you survived. But *you* are *my* miracle, Glori. My special girl. Optimal One sounds like the perfect name to me."

In the transport, a voice comes over the loudspeaker and shakes me from my reverie.

"Our next and last stop will be the farms. This transport will go express until then. I repeat, our next and last stop will be the farms."

As we pass old snow-covered highways, and as Sway snores beside me, I can still hear them arguing.

"What is wrong with you?" Grand Mati quietly seethed on more than one occasion when Teacher Paz brought me home from school—again—because Majesty had neglected to pick me up. "At least try to engage her."

"Like you 'engaged' me as a child?" Majesty did not keep her voice down. "You never had any use for me until she came along and now I'm supposed to pretend to—"

"Glori is your daughter, Maj. You shouldn't have to pretend anything."

"Oh really, Mother? In what sense is she mine?"

Which was weird, because of all the Miracles, I was the only one who wasn't adopted.

38

As if it's keeping rhythm with my heart, Bertha shudders to a stop. The effort of the brakes unexpectedly being called into action sounds like a building collapsing. We must have been on this transport for at least a few hours, yet the sun is still some time away from rising. Sway jolts awake.

"Please don't kill me. I'll pay you whatever you want."

"Bad dream?" I ask as he wipes drool from his mouth.

Sway shrugs. "Nah, that's how I usually wake up. The nightmare varies, but the paying my way out of it stays the same. Are we there?"

He leans over me to peer out the window. His breath smells like socks and not the clean kind. It is now the darkest of the dark hours. From what we can see, both sides of the transport are surrounded by old, dead cornfields.

"It doesn't look like we're anywhere," I say.

Suddenly, a patrol soldier walks past our window. Sway and I both fall out of our seats and drop to the floor, but the windows must be mirrored because even though the soldier looks in—right at me—he simply uses the glass to smooth down his lip hair (which is prodigious).

"They're probably checking for stowaways under the transport. Sometimes goits try to get out of paying the fare. Happens all the time."

"I don't think so."

I clutch the neck of Sway's shirt and tug it until he's looking where I am. The color leaches from his face when he spots the gloriously long-limbed figure clad entirely in red. Her balaclava is stitched together rag-doll-style. Heavy chains crisscross her chest, covering the fact that she's a fee. Though her baseball bat embedded with nails and her razor-studded brass knuckles make her gender the least interesting thing about her.

"Isn't that one of your paramedics?" Sway asks.

"No," I say quietly. "That is one of our mercenaries. Sway, EMS stands for Elite Murder Squad. There are five altogether. Misère. Niraasha. Itami. Muerte. Ann. Which translates into English as Misery. Despair. Pain. Death. And Ann."

When I still lived in the neighborhood, every young fee had a favorite mercenary. We might not know what their faces look like beneath their balaclavas, but we knew all their weapons, stances, and battle card kill ratings by heart. Yet it was impossible for me to choose a favorite. Tasked with watching us while Liyan and Grand were at work, the mercenaries became my teachers, my sparring partners, my bodyguards. Later, seeing as they were the only other people outside my family who knew Two Five existed, they were also my confidantes and friends.

"That's Misère. She's a refugee from New Orleans and was something called an ROTC cadet in her past life. After my lessons we'd sit on the steps and weave tiny animals out of dead blades of grass and talk about pre-Night food like pizza and something called suicide wings."

"That doesn't sound so scary," Sway says.

"She also taught me how to kill someone with one punch."

And she's not alone. Another mercenary is with her. Shorter than

Misère, she has a longbow and arrows across her back and a skull on her balaclava. Muerte. Considering the note I left Grand on the kitchen table, I've kind of been waiting for them this whole time.

In the hall, males are shouting as the soldiers clear them out of the transport. Our door rattles but stays shut. Outside, the patrol soldiers arrange the passengers into a line.

"Why is an elite murdering fee here? Working *with* the patrol?"

"Maybe Su made it home," I say. "Told them we were on this transport?"

"And they made it here already? No way."

"When I left Grand Island, I wrote my Grand Mati a note. Chia said he spoke with Matricula Rhodes. Maybe she was requesting that the mercenaries be granted permission to come and look for me. My grand would do anything to get me back."

"And what, the mayor gave his permission for extra good-guy cred?" I nod. "Well, your grandma must be pretty important if she can deter a couple of elite fighting machines from protecting the shore right now."

"Every fee is important. Regardless, we should get out of here."

Now that all the males on the transport have been herded outside, the mercenaries walk up and down the line, knocking off hats and holding their portables up to faces, which doesn't make sense since they both know what I look like. They stop in front of the male with the kelly-green cap. The one who made eye contact with me when we boarded the transport.

Muerte gently takes off his hat. The male's hair is black and choppy. Misère uses the razor blades on her brass knuckles to slice open the front of the male's coat, then shirt, then flicks aside the fabric. I put a hand over my mouth in horror. His chest is wrapped with cloth. It's not a male at all. It's a fee.

"Things just got interesting," Sway says.

"Holy crow," I curse. "Of course. That's Rauha. She used to live a block over from us in the neighborhood. She's another of the fees who went missing years ago."

And it looks like she isn't happy to have been found.

Rauha says something to Misère, sharp and harsh. As Misère takes off one of the chains that cross her chest, Rauha kicks her in the wrist and follows that with a swift punch to Misère's face. It's a classic defensive move that every young fee knows. Only problem is, Misère is one of the mercenaries who taught it to us, and Rauha is not a young fee. As Rauha bolts into the tall cornfields behind her, Misère tentatively feels her nose, then says something to Muerte.

"Glori, don't watch," Sway says.

Languidly, like honey dripping off a spoon, Muerte unsheathes her bow. Before I can shut my eyes, three arrows stick out of Rauha's back.

"Sway, we have to get off this transport. Now!"

"Or we could keep hiding."

Except we were always taught it was easier to fight in the open. Never to get trapped. I don't think the mercenaries are here because of my note. I'm not sure they know I'm here at all. Or whether they'd take me home or kill me if they did. But I know I can't stay in this tiny space where we wouldn't have a chance against Muerte's arrows or Misère's bat.

Yanking the bar from under the door handle, I slide the door open an inch and look out. The car is empty. Telling from the windows on the other side of the transport, more dead cornfields flank us, the stalks over ten feet high. If we can reach it, it's a good place to disappear.

"The field," I say.

The exit is right down the aisle at the end of this transport car. Twenty feet, tops. There isn't a patrol soldier in sight. I pull Sway after me. We've just run past the restroom when suddenly, he makes a choking sound. I look back and cry out. A patrol soldier with a clown face tattooed over his own stands behind Sway with an arm around his neck, a knife pointed at Sway's head.

"He came out of the bathroom," Sway says. "Don't kill him."

The soldier laughs. "He'll be lucky if that's all we do to him."

I roll my eyes. "He wasn't talking to you. He was talking to me."

Next second, the butt handle of Mama Bear hits the soldier smack in the forehead with such force it knocks him out cold. Only he wasn't alone. The other bathroom door opens.

"What the . . ."

The soldier sees us, then his fallen friend, then goes for his gun. Sway sinks to his knees in a bomb-shelter crouch, arms over his head. I dive over him and tackle the soldier. We fall into the bathroom stall. It reeks so strongly of urine, it's like no one's aimed for the pee hole at all in the last ten years. Next second, I have the soldier in a headlock. He elbows my ribs, but it only takes twenty-five pounds of pressure to the carotid arteries to cause instant unconsciousness, and I have a very strong grip.

When his body sags, I lay him on the floor, then drag the other soldier in and hoist him on top of the first. The second soldier has a lightning bolt scar zagging over his features.

"Sway, both soldiers have mob marks on their faces. You think Chia's let them infiltrate his patrol?"

"Not our biggest concern right now, Glori."

That's when I hear the growl.

Back out in the hall, Sway is facing off against a creature unlike any my worst nightmares could have conjured up. This is truly a beast. Neither wolf nor bear nor tiger, but some mix of all three. With a bear's claws and teeth. A wolf's muscular body and tail. And a tiger's size and coloring. It makes Reason's Mastodon look like a flea. It growls once, then charges straight at Sway, slashing out with its giant claws. Sway cries out and falls backward, the beast on top of him. Just as it lunges for Sway's throat, I manage to grab its massive head. Its jaws snap at my face. As it springs off Sway onto me, I violently twist its head, breaking its neck.

With a whimper, Sway scrambles to his feet. Our eyes meet. Sway almost died. His chest and arm bleed profusely. Clutching him against me, I run to the door. This side of the transport is still empty. We hop off and are about to run for the cornfield, when Muerte steps between the transport cars.

There is no hiding.

There is no her not seeing us.

And even though her face is always, always covered, she recognizes mine immediately.

"Glori?" she asks, and steps forward.

I almost run to her. Pre-Night, Muerte wanted to be a history teacher. Which meant once a week, when it was her day to watch me and Twofer, she taught us all about the wars fees used to fight in the battlefields *and* in the courtrooms. But also how to expand the kelp beds in the river to help decontaminate it and all the bad Spanish phrases that weren't in my language learning books. Hearing the surprise in her voice, I know she didn't come here for me. Which meant that she was sent solely to kill Rauha.

Now, as she unsheathes her bow, pulls an arrow, and aims it at Sway, all I can think to say is one little word.

"Please."

I'm not sure if I'm begging for my life, or Sway's, or Twofer's, or simply one more chance. Because now that Death literally stands in front of me, I don't care so much what rules I live by or if I wake up happy or not, so long as I get to wake up even one more time.

"He's helping me find Twofer."

Her breath catches. "Glori, Two Five is dead."

The pain is the same as if she shot an arrow straight through my heart. "No."

"Yes." She nods curtly. "Itami found his body on the beasts' shore."

"When?" Sway asks. "When did she find his body?"

Even under the balaclava I can see Muerte's snarl. She doesn't owe a beast any answers.

Yet she growls, "Right after he was snatched."

Quietly Sway says, "Can't be. Reason's footage was from after that. You hear me?"

He grips my arm, shakes me. No wonder Grand made no move to save him. No wonder Chia offered no reward. Everyone thought Two Five was dead. But why would Itami lie?

"Please," I say again. "I at least have to know for sure."

Muerte looks back between the transport cars as sounds of a struggle come from the other side.

"Go!" she whispers, lowering her bow. "But take my advice, little fee. *If* your brother is alive and *if* you manage to find him, keep running and do not stop. Whatever else you encounter out there will be better than what is waiting for you back here."

39

"Just a little moment...just a little moment...just a little moment."

Instead of going straight to look for Twofer, we decide to stop at Comma's father's house to stitch up Sway and find either weapons or bribes to use at the Fortress. We run. Then jog. Then walk, and I would have looped Grand Island twice by now, but we still haven't gotten to Rugged's house. Yet the whole time Sway follows behind me, panting and murmuring, "Just a little moment."

Finally, weary of dead cornstalks hitting us in the face, with the transport long behind us, I suggest we move out onto the road only to discover an exodus of snow-covered, stranded cars. Telling by the silhouettes in the ones closest to us, none of them have been cleared of bodies. I can make out skeletal heads in every car for the next half mile. On and on until the foggy darkness takes them.

"Back home, we used to call this a grave road," I say.

"Here we say corpse road."

Sway looks near dead himself. His eyes are hollow and ringed with gray. His lips colorless. And his fingers keep trailing up to his claw wounds. They're not life-threatening, but they're bleeding nonetheless, and the extra shirt Comma gave me that he's pressing against them might be helping to contain the blood loss, but it's doing nothing for the pain. He's on the constant brink of tears. So am I, for that matter. Sway says he is 100,095 percent certain that Two Five is still alive. That we have videographic proof.

I wish I had even 1 percent of his confidence.

Yet he laughs as I walk cozied up to the guardrail. "If you get any farther away from these cars, you'll be in another state. You can take out two soldiers and a demon dog, but you'll let some dead bodies get you down? Nah. You know what I do in scary situations?"

"You repeat, 'Just a little moment,' over and over and over again?"

He nods seriously, ignoring my gibe. "I say it to remind myself that no matter how awful my life or a certain situation is? It doesn't last forever. I read that pre-Night, suicides were higher than in the entire history of the world. Everyone's always had things they were stressed about or lost sleep over or that made them hate their life. Now they're all dead anyway. None of it lasts forever. Not the fear or pain or anger. Definitely not the life."

Maybe it's the painful chest wound, but it's the grimmest I've ever heard Sway be.

"Well, you know what Su says," I say, trying to lighten the mood. "She says if you do ridiculous things in terrifying situations, it makes the terrifying ridiculous."

"All right, let's name them," Sway says as we pass a car that has a family of four in it. "Then you can't call them scary anymore. Look. That one's name is Clyde, because he's as big as a horse and laughs like one, too. Now you do one. Who's that next to him in the passenger's seat? What's she like?"

She. Right, because old families had fees and males.

"That's Sky. She's in health care, and she likes to eat people, and she's a dead body."

Sway laughs. "Maybe it takes a little practice."

I hold out my hand. "Do you mind?"

"Never."

We link hands, our fingers entwining as tightly as our fates, then walk in silence as farmland switches to tree-covered streets and suburbs around us.

Finally, Sway asks, "Did you know that fee who died?"

"You mean the one Muerte murdered?" I nod. I know every fee. "That was Rauha. She was one of our original founders and very close with Matricula. Their families spent Chriskwannukah with each other every year."

"Chriskw ... never mind. Now's not the time. You said the fees who were murdered on the island were also founders. Seems like Matricula's losing her inner circle pretty fast."

In my head, I replay the scene right before they murdered Rauha. She said something to Misère, almost like a command or like she was goading her. We're missing something.

"Unless Rauha wasn't part of Matricula's inner circle anymore. Mercenaries would never kill an innocent fee. But maybe she wasn't innocent. Maybe they found out that she was helping the males make babies."

"But then why would the patrol be helping the mercenaries hunt her down?"

"But they weren't patrol, were they? You saw their faces. They were mob. But the mob killed our island fees and our mercenaries killed those mobsters."

Sway considers this. "Think about when you first came here. You didn't know the mob mutilated themselves. Maybe the mercenaries thought they *were* working with the patrol. It seems like the mob is working lots of sides all at the same time."

I stop walking. Next to us is a car with two adult bodies in the front and two little bodies in the back. Another family. Males and fees. Suitcases are piled on the roof. There shouldn't be traffic like this in such a faraway suburb. Yet the street is clogged worse than a shower drain in a ten-fee household.

"Where were all these people going?" I ask.

"To the very place built to survive mass extinction."

"The Fortress," I say with awe. "We're actually almost there?"

I wonder what Twofer is doing right at this moment. I close my eyes and send out a little wish that he is sleeping. That his bed is comfortable and he's warm. I wish that his dreams are sweet and his belly is full. When I open my eyes, I catch the tail end of Sway's gaze as he studies me. It looks fevered and sad.

"Yes, Glori. Almost there."

40

The clapboard house is a few hundred years old and has managed to maintain every ounce of its rustic charm. When no one answers our progressively louder knocks, Sway kicks around in the leaf and plastic-bag debris on the porch until he finds a Coke can. The idea that I might actually have a pop, as he'd earlier suggested, is squashed when he twists off the lid and shakes out a key that's hidden inside.

"That's the most amazing invention I've ever seen," I say.

"Says the fee who knows how Symbiotic Sacs work," Sway replies, opening the door.

I cover my nose as a funk comes out of the house, like an anti-scented candle.

"Hello?" Sway shouts. "Anybody home? Rugged?"

Silence.

Contrary to the moldering smell, the inside is well maintained, with woodsy, dark paneling, braided rugs, and printed ducks everywhere. Curtains. Blankets. Upholstered dining room chairs. Grand would love it here. Kitschy, she'd call it.

"Maybe he's out hunting," Sway suggests.

"At dawn?"

"Yeah. That's kinda when you go."

"I wouldn't know. Fees don't make a habit of killing endangered species."

"You are the literal worst."

Our bickering is halfhearted. I don't care why Rugged's not here. Though I'd love a peek at the man responsible for Comma, the sooner we stitch up Sway, the sooner we get to my brother. I only wish Rugged had composted his garbage before he left.

We drop our packs by the door. After turning on Rugged's flashlights and electric lanterns, I grab my mending kit. Sway roots around in a dining room cabinet and cheers when he pulls out a fresh, completely unopened bottle of clear alcohol. He joins me at the dining room table.

"Rugged's been saving this for a momentous occasion." Using his teeth, Sway twists open the top, spits the cap away, then holds the bottle aloft. "To Two Five and chest wounds."

"Off with that shirt," I say, threading my needle.

He takes a healthy drink, but his shirt stays on.

"What?" I ask. "Don't tell me you're shy. Would it make you feel better if I took my shirt off?"

"Yes, but not for the reasons you're imagining."

Still looking like he'd rather not, he lifts his shirt over his head. I can't help but stare. His chest and stomach are flat but concave. His nipples are small and pink. He smells lightly like pickles and some kind of pre-Night manufactured scent. The small opaque green necklace on the red thread practically glows against his pale chest.

"You look like one of Two Five's stick drawings."

"Ha!" Sway takes another drink and crosses his arms so his chest is covered. "Never mind. I don't want the stitches. May I have my shirt back, please?"

"Stop being a baby and hold still."

I flatten the skin of his chest to inspect the claw marks. He sucks air through his teeth.

"I didn't even start yet."

"It's not that. It's the touching."

Turning bright pink, he drinks from the bottle. Suddenly, I get that sparkly feeling again, but now it's *more* than sparkly. Hovering over Sway's scrawny chest, with my face inches from his bare skin, and his breath on my neck, it's like the entire precious canister of gold glitter that Twofer and I hoarded was poured into my bloodstream and is coursing about, running through each and every one of my internal organs.

"Oh." I squirm a little in my chair. "I see what you mean."

We stare at each other. Breathing. Swallowing hard, I pour a little of the vodka on a scrap of my shirt, dab it on his skin. He tries, and fails, to stifle another gasp. It comes out sounding more like a groan.

"Bottle," he rasps.

Before I hand it to him, I drink from it, too.

"This is ridiculous," I say. "You're only a little naked. I'm around naked fees all the time."

"Not helping."

To change the subject, I finger his necklace. "What's this?"

"It's jade. I looked it up with Rugged a bunch of years back. Jade's a protective stone. It's supposed to bring peace, harmony, and luck. This one's meant to look like a money bag. It's big in Chinese culture. Or was, I guess. I think my mom gave it to me."

"Su's mom is Chinese," I say, brightening. "She was a flight attendant on one of the last flights out of Beijing when the Night happened. It was on this private jet. She insists the Night was a global conspiracy, because this billionaire had her and the entire crew on retainer under something called a doomsday clause. Everyone was allowed to bring their families, because they knew they would never get back home. But since there wouldn't be a home to go back to, Liyan said she was okay with it. Plus, she got paid a million dollars. Apparently, my Grand said lots of billionaires had contingency plans like that.

"Anyway, they were in the air when the Night hit. They were destined for a compound in Canada but made an emergency landing in Buffalo. We don't talk about it, but Su's not actually a Miracle. Liyan was pregnant with her when the divide happened. The birth almost killed her."

"She was pregnant at the divide? And she left Su's father for Grand Island?"

"I don't think *father* is exactly the right word. No one hates males more than Liyan."

"Oh. I'm sorry."

After she moved to Grand Island, Liyan learned wing chung from old videos she found while scavenging. She proudly said (every chance she got) that it was a perfect fighting style for fees since it relied on dexterity, speed, and quick thinking. That it was, in fact, based on techniques created by fees for self-defense. She made sure we all excelled.

Maybe it was Reason telling me not to trust anyone, but I can't help wondering if Liyan hated males enough to turn in Twofer. Enough to send the mercenaries to kill fees that helped the males make babies. If I could slap myself, I would. Liyan is like a surrogate mother to me. She isn't capable of either of those things.

Guiltily, I clear my throat. "If I ever get home, I'll ask Liyan and my Grand if they know of a fee who has a story like your mom's. Who knows, stranger things have happened."

We finish in silence after that. There's not a whole lot else to say.

41

After I finish stitching up Sway, I go in search of food while he hobbles to the study to look for bribable goods that might help us at the Fortress. Like the rest of the house, the kitchen is neat and well maintained, yet the decaying stench is so much worse in here. The sink holds a dirty cup and plate that, telling from the crusted sauce, looks at least a week old. It's out of line, given how spotless the rest of the house is. My arm hairs prickle. The garbage is empty. The cupboards bare. Something must have died in the walls.

I hurry back into the study. It's a cozy space with a worn plaid sofa and four full walls of books. Sway has a small fire going in the fireplace and is taking books off the shelves, then putting them back, displeased. He looks like he was dragged by a bus.

"Hope you like air," I say. "The kitchen's empty."

"Oh, the pantry's in the basement. I'll check it before we leave."

He drops another book on the floor, titled *Doom*. Like we don't have enough of that.

"You really think a few books will be worth the price of a boy?" I ask.

This is Sway's plan. To walk into the Fortress and try to bribe the first male we meet.

He shrugs. "It's a lot easier and less dangerous to sell multiple books than it is to sell one boy. Besides, whoever is guarding the entrance is most likely a lackey that gets no cut for whatever Two Five brings in. Maybe he'll have always wanted a box set of the *Game of Thrones* books."

Though I won't be much help knowing what's valuable, I inspect the books with him. They're crammed onto the shelves. Some are leather bound, others flimsy paperback. It all looks like fiction and it might be dumb to say, but I'd never realized there was so much of it. My hand rests on a beautiful copy of something called *Dorothy and the Wizard in Oz*. I only understand what three of those words mean and they're the short boring ones.

"Staring," I say over my shoulder but smile. "What?"

"It's fun to watch you see things for the first time. It's like it wipes a film off my own lenses. Makes the world new again for me, too."

Clearing his throat, he eyes the half-empty vodka bottle, veers toward it, but then thumbs through a shelf of records instead.

"Let's have a little music. Have you ever heard Prince? He will blow your mind."

"Prince is a he?" I ask.

"Ha!"

"Sway, how many bodies do you think it takes to keep a medium-size pyre burning for a week straight?"

As if this is a normal question that normal people discuss all the normal time, he says, "I dunno. Maybe a few hundred? When they're dried out they burn fast, like kindling. Why?"

"When we first moved out to the cul-de-sac, my grand and Su's mom said they went around removing all the bodies from the surrounding houses. They said we couldn't help because a virus related to the bodies had been going around. Mochi almost died.

"But I don't think they were only burning bodies. The bonfire they built was massive and fees already went through those houses right after the divide. I think they were burning anything that had to do with males. I knew they did this when fees first fled to the island. But I was eleven when we moved to the cul-de-sac. . . . I mean, I know they couldn't risk anything disproving that you were all beasts, but seeing evidence of how we used to interact wouldn't erase all the newer history we had. It seems like such a waste."

Surrounded by all these books, I felt shortchanged.

And lied to.

"Or maybe it wasn't about that at all," Sway says. "Maybe they thought it was a waste to always be living in the past. Look at us. Males are all addicted to things that won't ever be manufactured again. We could be creating, pioneering, instead we're . . . clinging. Yes!" He suddenly exclaims. "He still has it."

Ever so gently, Sway blows off a record, then delicately puts it on the turntable. I've never seen another being have so much respect or awareness that we're in a world of finite antiques. After turning on a desk-size solar generator, he plugs in the phonograph. When the needle touches the record, there is a slight thrum, and then a piano plays, rich and melancholy. And then a fee starts singing about rain blowing in her face and the whole world being on her case.

"Adele," I whisper.

He nods. "Originally Bob Dylan sang this song. But I like this version better." He wipes dust off the record player lid. Swipes the dust on his pants. "Glori? I know this probably isn't the time or place, but will you maybe dance with me?"

He holds out a hand. I bite my lip, then take it. After a confusing second of figuring out where our hands go, we settle for each other's back, like a hug.

When the evening shadows and the stars appear,
And there is no one there to dry your tears.
I could hold you for a million years,
To make you feel my love.

Fees slow-dance all the time. Since Su is taller, I usually rest my head on her chest. But Sway stays back, looking into my eyes. We rock back and forth. Finally, I rest my head on his shoulder. And then in this deserted house, in the middle of nowhere, we stop dancing and instead simply hold on to each other. It is loose at first. But my grip gets tighter as I think of how starved Comma was for affection. How Reason told his jokes with a glare, guarding against no one laughing at them. I think about Twofer and how he would cuddle into my side every night, play with my fingers and give them all names. But mainly, as I feel my eyes fill with tears, I cling to Sway because I cannot imagine a life without this clumsy yet gentle, sweet yet loud, silly yet amazing male in it.

Ever so quietly, under his breath, Sway sings parts of the last verse. *"I could make you happy, make your dreams come true … go to the ends of this Earth with you."*

"To make you feel my love," I murmur.

He does not have a good singing voice, yet it is the most beautiful sound I've ever heard. When the song ends, I pull away only to find that Sway's eyes are wet, too. He wipes at them with the hem of his sleeve, then takes a wad of cash from his back pocket.

"I'd like to make a donation to the Rescue Two Five Fund." Its rubber-banded with the same blue band I had bound it with. He puts the money in my hand, then taps my nose. "Boop."

"Boop," I repeat, staring at the cash. "Sway?"

He laughs. "Yes, Glori?"

"Matricula Rhodes is my grandmother."

42

"I knew you had to be someone," Sway says. "But I didn't know you were *someone*. Oh man. I don't feel so good."

Dropping to his knees, he grabs a wastepaper basket and vomits into it, waving me off. The study is filling with early dawn light and precariously tilts when I drop the money in his pack. My urge to vomit is so strong, it could beat Su in an arm-wrestling competition. I will never, ever, *ever* drink alcohol again.

"Now we're even," I say. "We've both seen each other throw up."

"For us to be even"—Sway retches—"I need to dump this on your best pair of shoes."

"Do you want to talk about what I just told you?"

"Honestly, Glor?" He spits into the garbage can. "What's there to say?"

"How about I go get us some water."

"Perfect." Then he calls after me, "Basement."

When I open the basement door, I take an immediate step backward. It's like opening a bag of vegetables that decomposed in the hot sun. I look back into the living room and consider calling Sway. But there's no need for us both to experience the shock of whatever's down there. And to be honest, he wouldn't be much help anyway. I find a tiny pen flashlight on the top step and click it on.

The stairs creak beneath me. I pull my sweater up over my nose.

Regardless of the early morning light upstairs, the basement is still almost pitch-black. Yet I see the male as soon as I'm off the last step. He's sitting in a chair in the corner, as if he's waiting for me. The air is filled with a persistent buzzing. My flashlight catches him in the face. I aim it away.

"Whoops, sorry. Hello, Rugged?"

The male in the chair moves.

Slowly.

Sickly.

"Are you okay? Rugged? Ma'am?"

I inch closer, shuffling forward one foot at a time, the flashlight illuminating my feet. Rugged must have sat down to fold laundry and couldn't get back up. He must be so very sick. When I'm only a half step away, I reach out to shake his shoulder. His flesh moves beneath my hand. But not in a natural way. It's writhing.

I jump back.

"Name your scary, Glori," I whisper. "This is Rugged. He's like Comma's mama."

I lean closer and nudge him in the chest. Rugged's head drops forward. The buzzing reaches a fever pitch as a swarm of insects fly into my face. Something white and wet falls from his mouth and lands squirming on his lap. I slap a shaking hand over my mouth. It barely kills the scream on my lips. A curtained window is above the washing machine. I yank down the cloth to be sure.

Yes, Rugged is definitely dead.

I fling open the lid to the washing machine and vomit into it.

When I've completely emptied my stomach, I glance back at Rugged. It's the first fresh dead body I've ever seen, and it's so much worse than the skeletal ones. It's almost like he could open his eyes and talk to me. There is a box of plastic bags on the shelves next to the stairs. Taking two, I cover my hands, hold my breath, and gently inspect his body, trying to decipher if his death was natural. He's handsome, like Comma. Rugged must have elected to have Comma. He looks like his actual birth parent.

I don't see any wounds, but this is no natural death.

Rugged's body is covered in red sores.

Like those rats in the lab. Like Chia's security chief, Stetson. And maybe it's because Sway and I were just talking about the pyre Su and I built, but the sores remind me of the itchy red splotches that fees broke out in so long ago. How our lab techs thought it originated from Twinkie and Radio finding that skeleton in the house by the river. How it came from the house's contaminated pent-up air.

"Glori? You down there? What is that smell?"

I jump back. My foot kicks an empty paint can, and it clatters around the basement. The flies covering Rugged swarm again in agitation. Sway is at the top of the stairs.

"Don't come down here." Biting my knuckle, I manage to say, "Um, jars of fruit fell off the shelves and are rotting. It'll make you sick again."

Blindly, I put cans of food in my pack and grab a few bottles of water. Taking a blanket from a stack on top of the dryer, I cover Rugged with it, then I hurry up the stairs and guide Sway to the door.

"What did you say Rugged did again? He has such good supplies."

"Promise you won't get judge-y? He's Chia's security designer. He blows things up."

"Only beasts would keep destroying things at the end of the world."

"Ha! Told you. Judge-y. Bump. My mouth tastes like I drank the run-off at the bottom of a garbage can. But, like, hot."

Sway scribbles a note on a pad next to the front door, then locks up behind us. Neither gesture is really necessary anymore. Maybe it wasn't only Matricula who was losing her inner circle. Somebody was covering all their bases.

No wonder Muerte told us to run.

43

In the creamy pink-and-gray dawn, we can see the Fortress from Rugged's front porch. Sheathed in gunmetal-gray solar tiles, its oil slick exterior rises above the dead tree branches, at least ten stories tall and equally wide. It looks like a massive firebox. But one of the good ones. The kind you can't crack open with an old safety pin.

"The grounds of the Fortress used to be a country club," Sway says. "That's a place where wealthy people went to play golf. But when all the environmental refugees started pouring in, a Taiwanese billionaire bought up the land and all these surrounding houses and began building one of those luxury end-of-the-world compounds. Unfortunately, it was only half-ready when the actual end of the world struck."

"I hate when that happens."

Sway snorts a laugh. "Rugged never let us go near it. Sometimes Comma and I would sneak out in the middle of the night, see trucks pulling up and leaving again. But we never got close enough to see what they were unloading."

The temperature is at least twenty degrees warmer than yesterday and hot steam evaporates off the road. The sun is coming up steadily now. But it gets caught behind the towering Fortress and casts a dark shadow over us. Without discussing it, we hold hands. Three streets later, the houses fall away and we are met by rolling fields. The grass is so tall it's above our heads.

"This was the old golf course," Sway says.

No wonder Sway was so sure where the corpse-road vehicles were headed. Cars are stalled bumper to bumper, some driven off the road, others badly smashed. Luckily, these have no bodies inside. In fact, all the cars are empty for as far as I can see. Which, you know, is far.

"Were they always empty like this?"

"I dunno." He hitches up his pack. "Com and I were never brave enough to come this far in."

Feeling too exposed on the road, we cut through the grass. The thin blades wick our hands and faces, leaving little tracks of blood. We emerge only ten feet from the front entrance.

"Gasp," Sway says.

"I couldn't have said it better myself."

All the cars crash right into the front of the Fortress in a massive fifty-car pileup. A monster truck with enormous tractor tires crushes the first two cars in line and still manages to be the worse for wear. A spiked security gate skewers its hood while bullet holes pepper the windshield. I look up at the Fortress's windows. Any one of them would have offered a near-perfect straight shot onto the masses below.

"This place was supposed to protect people."

"These cars go back for miles, Glor," Sway says. "If they let all of them in, they would have been out of supplies in weeks, not years. You can't always protect everyone."

Sway's words ring so close to my grand's rationale for leaving the

SymSac male fetuses back at the labs all those years ago that it feels like déjà vu. And I can't help thinking, Shouldn't you at least try? But then I see it. Parked on a dirt utility road that intersects with the main one is a Prius E that looks exactly like the one from Reason's traffic footage. I open the back door, breathe on the window. In the condensation from my breath, the faint outline of a child's drawing appears.

"He's here," Sway says.

It's obvious from the awe in his voice how little he thought he would be.

Yet he came anyway.

"Sway, Rugged was the smell at the house. He was dead. In the basement."

Sway shuts his eyes. Sucks in his lips. After a few beats, he says, "Did it look accidental?"

"It looked like he caught some kind of disease. Like those rats back at the lab."

Sway's mouth works like he has many things he'd like to say but doesn't. Rugged raised him. He was the only parent Sway knew. He sniffs a few times. Wipes his eyes. Then nods, like, *Okay, ready*. That's the thing about the world we live in, nothing is shocking for long.

And everyone dies.

Behind the monster truck and security gate, the front entrance has been boarded up with plywood and metal siding. But there's a thick steel door next to it that's open a half inch. When I push on it, warm, dry air gusts out, like we're unlocking a long-buried tomb.

I glance at Sway. "I'm scared."

"Nah, almost done now," he says.

He squeezes my hand. I squeeze back. We go inside.

As if an end-of-the-world bunker couldn't be anything but dark and intimidating, every surface in the lobby of the Fortress—the floors, the walls, the ceiling—is shiny black marble shot through with fissure lines of gold. Or maybe they planned to have potted plants and fancy crystal chandeliers, but the world blew itself up before the decorator arrived.

At the far end of the room, up on a black marble dais behind a black marble reception desk, sits a male in a well-fitted entirely dove-gray suit. It is hard to tell if he is young or old as his hair is exactly the same shade of gray as everything else on his person. The only exception to his monochromatic color scheme is his bright red-framed glasses, which I can't help thinking Comma would love. His skin is a jaundiced yellow. Someone's been in this room way too long.

"Hi there," Sway calls.

The gray male looks up and smiles. Or, it's like he's heard what a smile is and this is his best imitation. He sets down a gold pen. From what I can see, there is no paper on his desk. He stifles a cough, then clears this throat.

"Ah yes, welcome. We've been waiting for you."

And then the door slams shut behind us.

44

As if we weren't thoroughly trapped enough, an impenetrable blast door slides down over the Fortress's impenetrable outer door. Yet Sway pounds on the steel like his slim fists might have an effect when a nuclear bomb wouldn't. Working a different kind of steel, I pull out Mama Bear. The gray male lets out a light cough of disappointment.

"We've come for Two Five," I say.

"Who?" he asks mildly.

"The little boy," Sway says. "We know he's here. The car that brought him is dumped out front. We're prepared to trade for him."

He tosses his pack toward the dais. Books, records, and cash tumble out. The gray male peers over his desk at it.

"My, my, that *is* tempting." Suppressing another cough, he picks up his gold pen and twirls it between his fingers. "Did you know that prior to the Night, the Fortress was slated to be the most technologically progressive building in the entire world? Our solar cells are so advanced they can run the entire building for two weeks of overcast days before systems start shutting down. We have more audio and digital files in our cloud than the Library of Congress had. Our heat-sensing technology picked you two up a mile away. So while your rucksack of secondhand items is surely impressive, forgive me if I do not find it appealing."

"What do you find appealing?" I ask.

Holding a handkerchief to his mouth, the gray male adjusts his red frames, points his gold pen at Sway, then swirls it like a wand and points it at me. He smiles.

"New walk-ins never hurt." Slightly louder than before, the gray male says, "Security."

Behind him, the black marbled wall instantly slides open. Two guards emerge. Both are dressed entirely in tan and look like they store rocks under their uniforms. One carries a Taser, the other a dart gun. As if doing nothing more urgent than crossing the street, they move on us.

"Come any closer and I'll hurt you," I say.

"I don't know why you bother warning people," Sway says as Taser comes at me.

"Because I keep hoping it might actually deter them."

As Taser reaches for me, I slice his thigh with Mama Bear. He goes down screaming. The other guard fires his dart gun. Sway throws his arms over his head and makes a thin warbling sound. I dodge the tiny missiles, trying to find an opening to attack. Before I can make my move, one of the darts strikes Sway in the forearm.

"Glori," he murmurs.

Next second, his body topples sideways. His cheek strikes the floor so hard I hear his teeth crack on the marble. Blood pools around his face.

The guard and I look at each other. Both surprised. Then I charge.

"Get him," the gray male coughs.

I tuck and roll as three rapid-fire darts sail past me. I grab one out of the air. Dodging behind him, I twist the guard's arm up behind his back.

Growling, he tries to stomp on my foot, then smash my face with the back of his head, but he's so big and predictable, I see each move coming as if in slow motion. A moment later, he is facedown on the marble tile with a dart sticking out of his neck.

Two more guards come out.

"Get him," the gray male repeats, then adds, *"Now."*

I am only five feet away from him. If I can grab him and create some kind of hostage situation, maybe we can get Two Five *and* get out of here alive. I dodge another dart, then launch myself over the desk. My hands are on the lapels of the gray male's suit when something clips on to my shoulder. There's a clicking sound. Suddenly, it feels like every nerve in my body is being rubbed with coarse flaming sandpaper.

"That's enough." The gray male stands. "We don't need him swallowing his tongue."

Through blurry vision, I watch a guard carry Sway out, slung over his shoulder like he's nothing but a wet blanket to be hung out to dry. Blood runs out his mouth and ear. With drool spilling uncontrollably from my own mouth, I reach for my calf. For Baby Bear.

"This one will need a lot of work." The gray male sighs.

Then he takes the Taser from the guard and presses the button until I no longer see or feel, or *care* to see or feel, anything at all.

45

I wake on my stomach and peer out one eye. I'm in a bedroom that is barely longer than it is wide. Next to my bed is a compact metal nightstand. Past that, there's a plain metal desk and chair. There are no windows. Not that the room needs to be brighter. Every detail in here is shockingly well illuminated. The walls are literally glowing with blinding white light. I have no idea how long I've been out.

Considering the gray male's speech about the state-of-the-art nature of the Fortress, I'd expected the rooms to be enormous, plush like Comma and Sway's loft. But this is a narrow, claustrophobia-inducing room. It is also a mirror image of itself. Which means that on the other side of the room is another desk and nightstand and a flimsy metal-framed bed with a bare mattress, its footboard almost touching mine. And on that bed, staring at me through thick, round tortoiseshell glasses, is either the youngest-looking seventeen-year-old male I've ever met, or it's a twelve-ish-year-old boy.

Nearly a foot shorter than me, he has wiry, close-cropped black curly hair, round cheeks, and a sour expression. Shielding my eyes against the light, I look above me for a hologram projector, because this boy should not—*cannot*—exist. Twofer is the last child.

Although I guess that's also what I thought before I saw all those fetuses in the lab.

"Are . . . ?"

His plum-size eyes widen beneath his heavy frames. He puts a finger to his lips. *Shhh.*

"Are you real?" I whisper.

Comma and Sway said one of the rumors about the Fortress was it churned out robots. At this point in my journey, nothing would shock me.

In a raspy whisper, he replies, "No, I'm a wooden boy who wishes he was real."

I stare at him blankly. "Is that a movie reference?"

He pushes up his enormous glasses using his whole hand. "Duh."

"Motor," a calm voice says. "What do we say about sarcasm?"

I jump. The voice sounds like it's next to me, yet the boy and I remain alone in the tiny room. The boy's bitter expression immediately changes and becomes beatifically blank.

"Sarcasm," he parrots, "is aggression with a bow on top."

"Yes," the room says. "Very good. Very good indeed."

Suddenly, a male in a pale blue suit materializes against the wall to my right. As with the gray male at the front desk, it isn't only his suit that is powder blue but also his shirt, tie, shoes, hair, and eyes. I bolt up in surprise and immediately regret it. The liquor. The electricity. I feel like the twisted sheets of paper we use to start a fire. Which must be why I don't quite understand what I'm seeing.

The blue-suited male didn't appear *against* the wall. He *is* the wall. The entire room is one big screen.

"What's going on?" I ask. "Where's Two Five? And my friend Sway?"

But it's like the blue-suited male is on some kind of prerecorded track, because instead of answering my questions, he cheerfully says, "Welcome to the Fortress. You may call me Doctor. While you are here, I ask that you follow a few simple rules. Motor?"

Motor sits up straighter, like a tame cat bringing its owner a mouse, then studiously says, "No roughhousing. No back talking. Always drink your milk."

Always drink my milk? Why does every male environment have to be *so* strange? Rubbing at the ache in my forehead, my hand quickly moves across the rest of my skull. My hair is gone. Shaved off entirely.

"Lice preventative," Motor murmurs, and rubs his own shaved head.

I look down. I'm now wearing a baggy gray sweat suit. No shoes or socks. Same as Motor. And then it hits me. Someone has *changed me into* a baggy gray sweat suit. I look back up at the doctor. His gaze is directionless, yet the corners of his lips rise ever so faintly.

And right then, knowing this or some other equally strange male saw my bare body. Knowing they have Sway and Twofer, yet prefer to keep us frightened and separate. Suddenly, my fear, sickness, and confusion burn off, and all that's left is seething rage.

"Look, Doctor Blue Male," I say. "I don't know who you are or what it is you do here or why you can't mix and match your colors. I honestly don't care. Sell me or turn me into a robot or force me to drink all the dairy you want. I. Don't. Care. I want my brother and my friend Sway, and until they're with me, I don't plan on following any of your garbage rules."

Motor lets out a gruff squeak of distress and curls into a ball with his hands over his ears. His reaction is so severe, I spring from my bed and ready myself for more guards or electric volts. Instead quiet chimes sound throughout the room.

"Recess time," Doctor says pleasantly.

As Motor stays curled up, I walk to the screen and peer at Doctor.

"Can this dumb goit even hear me?" I ask.

The doctor blinks once, then shifts his gaze to stare straight at me.

"Yes, Glori," he says quietly. "I can *always* hear you."

I freeze. "How do you know my name?"

"As it turns out, we have a mutual friend. We've agreed to keep you here for them until they arrive. In the meantime, break whatever rules you feel you must. But be warned, as you witnessed earlier today, we do not tolerate dissent at the Fortress. Instead I think you'll find that you get along easily if you go along easily. I'd hate for a tragedy to befall you—or anyone else you cared about—simply because you could not do what you were told."

I can still hear the smack of Sway's face hitting the floor.

"Although I would love to give you a personal tour, I regrettably have much to do. Motor, however, shall accompany you during your stay. Given the right motivation, Motor is my most helpful ward. He will keep me apprised of your every concern. Won't you, Motor?"

"Oh, yes, Doctor," Motor says fervently.

"You mean he'll tell on me if I step out of line?"

The doctor's laugh sounds like an un-oiled door screaming open. "I can see the back-talk rule will be a hard one to follow."

"Wait." I ask, "How long do I have? Before my 'friend' gets here?"

Doctor smiles. "Six hours, perhaps. Depending on traffic. But please don't waste your time trying to escape. The first-floor doors are all impenetrable steel. The windows are constructed from the same glass that aquariums used for their ocean tanks. Aquariums, if you don't know, were places fish were kept for people to stare at and study."

"Let me guess," I say. "Fish never escaped their aquariums."

Again, that laugh. "You *are* a quick one. I think you will enjoy this."

Once more, the chimes sound through the room. Doctor softly clasps his hands. "Time to play."

Then he blinks out.

46

Six hours. Six hours to find and free both my brother and Sway and then escape from a place that is inescapable. SIX HOURS. Part of me wants to curl up on this mattress and sleep the minutes away. Six hours is only a little longer than a good rainy-day nap. It isn't nearly enough time to figure out, let alone complete, this impossible task.

As fast as the doctor disappears from our wall screen, the obedient fervor drops from Motor's expression. We warily eye each other as he resumes a seated position. I have a thousand different questions for this male. How old is he? What is this place? Are there more males like him? Who is the doctor?

But honestly, there's only one thing I care about in this second.

"How the hill am I supposed to get out of here in six hours?" I say aloud.

"Weren't you listening? You aren't. Duh. Want me to set a timer?" Before I can answer, he says, "Set timer for six hours."

Softly glowing blue numbers now count down on the wall above him. They're the same blue as the doctor's suit. The chimes ring again.

"Third chime," Motor says. "We gotta get to the yard. Lateness is not tolerated."

Grabbing a keycard from his nightstand, he hops out of bed and waves it at the door. It pops open with a soft hiss. The outside hall is pitch-black. When we step into it, a warm ambient light glows from the baseboards.

"Terrific," I say. "More environmentally friendly lighting."

"Being friendly is always good. But being environmentally friendly is the best."

This must be what I sounded like to Sway when we first met. Motor gives me a flat, satisfied smile, then hurries off down the hall. I follow after, glaring at the back of his head, trying very hard to suppress the urge to squash it. As we trot along, the baseboards light up in front of us like they know our route. Considering Motor's timer is now floating along beside us on the wall—5:58:02. 5:58:01—maybe they do.

Now, *this* looks like a luxury compound. Charcoal walls meld into plush charcoal carpeting that is swirled with deep cranberry-and-black flowers. Wide doorways are spaced evenly along the hall, all with copper keycard sensors to the right. After every fourth door, an identical hallway branches off and seems to go on for miles. I try running a blue fingernail along the wall, but Comma's nail paint doesn't even chip. Likewise, there are no other distinguishing markers to give me my bearings. No decorations, no room numbers. Nothing.

I'll never find Two Five.

"This tour doesn't come with a map, does it?"

Behind his thick glasses Motor's eyes grow even bigger as he waves his hands in front of him. But it's too late. The doctor is suddenly on the wall next to us. Motor smacks his forehead.

"Is there a problem?" Doctor asks.

"Walk-In asked for a map."

Doctor considers and nods. "All right, understood. Continue to monitor. Proceed."

Interesting. So Doctor can't hear what you've said. Only that you've spoken. Motor shoots me a dirty look and hurries on again.

"Motor," I whisper. "What *is* this place?"

"Geez," he quietly rasps. "Pay attention. It's the Fortress, the most technologically progressive building in the world. It was gonna have a VR climbing wall, a skydiving room, and an Olympic-size swimming pool on the top floor—"

"There's a pool?" I can't help but interrupt.

"Nah, none of that stuff got built. But the Butler did. It's a Household Smart Assistant. It can go anywhere. Except the bathrooms, obviously. Can you imagine? Oh, hey, Doctor." He makes a fart sound with his mouth and lets out a soft guffaw of laughter. "Back when all the Littles started showing up, Doc reprogrammed the Butler with his image. Now we self-police."

"Who are the Littles?" I ask.

"You'll see." He glances at me over his shoulder. "You walk funny, you know that? And too close."

I hold up my hands in surrender and drop back a pace. In the lobby, the gray-suited male raised his voice to call security. Given Motor's whispering and propensity for shushing me, it was safe to guess the Butler only activated at certain volumes. And thank you, Motor, I now knew there was one place he couldn't go.

"So how do I know a bathroom from a regular room?" I ask.

"A bathroom has a toilet." He snorts. "Duh."

I roll my eyes. "I mean from out here."

"The keycard light next to a bathroom is yellow"—Motor snickers—"like pee."

He waves his keycard, and we take a stairwell three flights down, then walk along more gray corridors until we turn a corner and are stopped by impressive white-ash doors. EXERCISE YARD is written on them in gold script. Motor waves his card. As the panel next to the doors beeps green, I realize just how stuck I am. Not only will Motor tell on me if I step out of line, but I also can't go anywhere without him. He sees me eyeing his keycard and smugly tucks it in the elastic band of his underwear. *Waste.*

5:53:26. 5:53:25.

We push through the doors.

"Whoa," I whisper as every thought of escaping escapes me.

Behind his enormous glasses, Motor's eyes cut to me and he flashes a trace of a smile. His first genuine one.

"Welcome to the Yard. Nice, right?"

Considering we're in a nuclear fallout building, I'm not surprised the yard is inside. But I certainly wasn't expecting it to perfectly re-create the outdoors. The space is roughly the size of the athletic field we have at school, but this one is wrapped, floor to domed ceiling, with wall screens that play a lifelike video of a pre-Night park. Vibrant green trees sit in lush emerald grass as orange-chested birds fly past. At the very top of the dome, the sky is construction-paper blue with puffy white clouds. I have never seen such color.

But that's not what's left me speechless.

It's that the cavernous room is *filled* with children.

47

Dozens of young males crowd the yard as more trickle out from a doorway on the opposite side of the room. I do a quick count. Despite the silence, there are almost seventy males in this space. All of them look younger than me. A couple dozen seem younger than Motor. It is a miraculous sight that brings tears to my eyes. Except I don't understand how it is possible. It can't be, unless fees never stopped making babies. Except we'd never purposely make more males. Grand had guessed that Majesty wasn't the only fertile fee. (Liyan was proof of that.) But telling from these numbers, there were a lot more out there. But how and why did their children—all sons—end up here? And where were *they*?

"Motor, where did all these males come from?" I ask.

"Admissions, duh."

"But from where before that? Like, who are their parents?"

"I literally have no idea what you're talking about." He starts pointing around the room. "The Sixteens are over there on the exercise court watching the MMA practice wall. Fifteens are the ones doing kickboxing where that park couple is sharing dinner meal. If you watch the couple long enough, they kiss. It's disgusting."

As we move into the space and Motor continues to break down the yard by age group, my eyes frantically scan the room for *my* males. With all the shaved heads and gray sweat suits, they—we—all look identical. Yet since everyone is as Heinz 57 as a Miracle, Sway should be easy to spot. Only, no matter how many times my eyes sweep the room, I don't see him.

"And," Motor finishes, "last but not least, the Nines are the ones over there lying on their backs staring at the sky. They're more useless than an empty candy wrapper."

Trying to steady my breathing, I say, "Empty wrappers make pretty good origami."

I didn't see Sway. And there was no one here younger than nine, so that meant no Twofer either. Panic fills my chest as swiftly as floodwaters took the world's shorelines. A sensation that isn't lessened when, one by one, every single male in the yard stops what he's doing to turn and stare at us.

Despite the Fortress's perfectly regulated temperature, I shiver. For as little as I know about the gender, these males are not behaving like males. Males shout and laugh and bicker. At Euphoria, they sang and danced and provoked. On the streets, they played sports and talked trash. Yet here, during *playtime*, never mind the silence, there is no joy or amusement, let alone fierceness. Instead every gaze turned on me—which is all of them—is sleepily blank.

"Motor, what's wrong with everyone?" I ask.

Before he can answer, a ripple subtler than a leaf falling into a puddle goes through the yard. A boy holding a ball a few feet away leans forward and whispers, "Breaker calls dibs."

"Excuse me?" I ask.

"Who are you talking to?" Motor looks around. "Did they start a murmur? What did it say?"

With a quick glance, I realize there are no guards in the room. Motor said they self-police. The males must be purposely quiet to keep it that way. So quiet that even though we're standing side by side, Motor can't hear them.

But I can.

Another murmur goes through the room.

"Breaker is coming."

Like a hand squeezing into a fist, all the males in the yard move in tighter around us.

"Motor, how do we get out of here?" I ask as my flight instincts dial up to high.

"Can't. They remotely lock the doors once we're all inside."

The timer he set unobtrusively hovers in the park air above where we came in.

5:49:58. 5:49:57.

Why is there so much time left?

The crowd parts and makes room for a tall, muscular male who must be a Sixteen. Breaker, apparently. Unbidden, I think of Liyan cracking walnuts, unsure if this male is the nut or the nutcracker in the analogy. Because while Breaker is obviously fit—his sweatshirt sleeves might burst at the seams for his muscles—he isn't healthy. His shaved hair is badly thinning, and his cheeks are so sunken they could hold a quarter cup of water. His emotionless dark brown eyes are equally cavernous and rows of black spots crisscross half his face, like someone wanted to play connect the dots but had no paper.

"Oh no," Motor breathes. "Not Breaker."

Other similarly worn-down-looking Sixteens bunch behind him. All with sickly little potbellies despite their toned physiques. All with varying patterns of black marks on their skin. It's like I'm being approached by a bunch of underfed sewing patterns. Just as Breaker steps into the empty circle of space that's around me, the doors at the far end of the room swing open.

Two guards enter. Both were in the foyer when Sway and I arrived. Only now they aren't toting Tasers or dart guns. Instead two neat lines of males, all about Twofer's age, trail behind them. I do a quick count. There are sixteen altogether, ranging in age from three to five. These must be the Littles.

Just like that, the flood of panic that drowns my chest rushes out in one swift breath. Because there, bringing up the rear, chatting happily as he swings the hand of a little boy with a very large head, is a slight figure I thought I might never see again. His long curls have been shaved off, but his chubby baby cheeks remain. I laugh out loud with relief. It makes Breaker take a step back. Finding Two Five was the goal of this entire journey, but only now do I realize how thoroughly I'd never expected to achieve it.

As if he can feel my eyes on him, Two Five looks over. His little mouth drops open. Then, like seeing me here is no more extraordinary than if we'd casually met in our kitchen back home, he brightly waves and gives me a thumbs-up. I laugh again. It's him all right.

My silly lovely sweet *alive* baby brother.

48

"**W**here are you going?" Motor whispers.

Two Five is right there. Only forty feet away. You can sure as waste bet I'm going to him.

The only problem is, a mob ten males deep separates us. And they have other plans for me. I motion for Two Five to stay put.

"Breaker's got dibs," they all murmur. "Breaker's got dibs."

As the guards who brought the Littles in leave—Negligent, I think. Who leaves something so precious alone?—I try to push my way past Breaker, but his mixed martial arts training is obvious. It's like pushing against a solid wood door only to have it push back.

"Seems to me, we kinda, like, have not yet begun, Walk-In," he says.

It's now so quiet in the yard, you could hear dust settle. Across the way, Two Five is acting out something that looks a lot like hopscotch for the enrapt Littles.

"Fine." I roll up my sleeves. "You called dibs? Hurry up and get yours."

Breaker tilts his head to the side and considers me. "All right, then."

With no caution in his advance or anticipation in his eyes, he comes straight at me almost like some kind of horrible reanimated dead body. I've seen something like this before, but there's no time to remember when. Instead I grab the ball from the boy that murmured at me and bounce it once. It comes back true. Then I chuck it into Breaker's face.

Even his yelp of pain is nearly silent. The ball returns straight into my waiting palms. Breaker holds a hand to his nose. Blood seeps through his fingers.

"Don't do it," I murmur to the second biggest of the group.

This male has an amoeba-like pattern of black marks on his face. He doesn't listen any better than Breaker. Fists raised to protect his face, he charges. The ball nails him in the groin. He instantly keels over. It works as beautifully as Liyan and the mercenaries always told me it would. Why have I been wasting my time doing anything else?

Scooping the ball up, I hold it out in front of me as I back my way through the crowd. If you could hear dust settling before, now you can hear dust being *made*.

"Stop him," Breaker whispers.

More Sixteens move in, but I easily dodge them. Then I am through and running to Twofer. He throws his arms wide, bouncing, waiting for me. The Little with the big head mimics him. I'm a dozen feet away.

"Fight!" Motor shouts. "Fight!"

No sooner does the room register his words than everything changes. The park view flicks off, and the wall screen becomes a brilliant white. All the males drop into a crouch. I skid to a stop as the two guards hurry back in. One has a mug of what smells like tea. The other has a Taser out in front of him.

"Everybody, out!" he barks at the Littles.

Two Five flings a small hand out to me. "Glori!"

"No," I cry.

Muerte said if I found Twofer, I should take him and run. But where? When Grand and Liyan mused about what other cities might have survived the Night, the scenarios they dreamed up were always horrific. Look what happened to us, after all. But we didn't have to live in a city. Considering all those empty houses we passed on the way to the Fortress, what did it matter where we went?

Yet if I grab Twofer now, then what? Steel blast doors and concrete-block-thick windows and no way out. And worse, no Sway. He'd be trapped here. Maybe always. I am only here because of him, and as much as I love Two Five, this isn't an either-or scenario.

Holding hands with both a guard and the male with the large head, Two Five looks back at me over his shoulder. Helplessly, I do nothing but watch him leave.

When the doors close behind the Littles, I turn on Motor.

"Why did you do that?" I fume.

He shrugs and adjusts his glasses. "Doc said to keep him updated. Duh."

As I move toward him, intending to squeeze every last drop of sour smugness from his face, a booming voice fills the room.

"STAND DOWN. STAND DOWN. STAND DOWN."

The words grow louder with every repetition. Around me the males crouch tighter to the floor, covering their ears with their hands. Compared with all the previous silence . . . I drop to my knees. Curl over. I'm certain my ears are bleeding. It's so loud, yet it's never-ending.

Minutes and then more minutes pass. There is only the voice.

"STAND DOWN. STAND DOWN. STAND DOWN. STAND DOWN. STAND DOWN. STAND DOWN. STAND DOWN. STAND DOWN. STAND DOWN. STAND DOWN. STAND DOWN. STAND DOWN. STAND DOWN. STAND DOWN. STAND DOWN. STAND DOWN. STAND DOWN. STAND DOWN. STAND DOWN."

Finally, it stops.

Doctor's calm voice fills the room. "What do we do at the Fortress?"

"We listen," all the males chant together.

"And?"

"Do as we're told. Always. Without question."

The doors open. Two different tan-uniformed guards enter. Except they're not different. I recognize them as well. The one shot me with a dart gun. The other's thigh felt the bite of Mama Bear. He has a knife wound. That doesn't allow him an afternoon off?

If anyone knows where Sway is, they do. But I don't know what to do with that knowledge.

Motor points both at Breaker and at the male with the swirls. As one guard drags them away, the other takes a slim cocoa-colored bar from his pocket. Hershey's. After unwrapping the foil, he breaks off a single piece and hands it to Motor. It's been years, but I'll never forget the scent of chocolate. It must have been cryovacked, because it doesn't even smell. The doctor said with the right motivation, Motor was his most helpful ward.

"Chocolate?" I say to Motor. "*Chocolate* is your motivator?"

As the other males in the room slowly come back to a sitting position, Motor ignores me and crams the candy into his mouth. A few cast scornful looks at him. Everyone else is too shaken to bother. My ears ring. Yet I can't help but notice that as the guard leads Breaker out, he whispers something to the nearest male. Moments later, a boy roughly Motor's age turns to me, smiles blankly, and in a singsong voice murmurs, "As they say, Walk-In, to be continued."

It's then I know where I've seen males like these before. The weird lack of emotions. The tattoo marks on the Sixteens. They remind me of those two younger mobsters that tried to attack me in the tunnel. They had that exact same glazed look in their eyes. Everyone here speaks with the same disinterested calm that Rage uses. Sway said no one knew where the mob came from. But maybe that's not true anymore.

"Motor, is this where they make the mob?"

I expect a blank stare. Or a comment about how dumb I am. But as chimes sound and Motor's tongue probes his teeth for every last taste of chocolatey sweetness, he pushes up his glasses and whispers one little word.

"Duh."

49

4:59:00. 4:58:59.

The Fortress is where the mob comes from.

And they know who I am.

And they have my brother and Sway.

Realistically, that means the friend who is coming for me, in just under five hours, can only be one of a few people. Chia or Rage or Jackal.

Although I tell myself it's not important, that I need to focus on figuring a way out, instead my brain picks at how this is all possible. The more I think about it, the more I'm convinced all these males came from my grand's old labs. Except maybe fees *didn't* make these males. Maybe the males did.

Or tried to.

Judging by Breaker and the other Sixteens, whoever began the process clearly didn't get it right. But they must have kept trying. Why they stopped at the Nines, I don't know. But maybe it explained why our fees were snatched six years ago. The males needed help getting the baby-making process right.

Regardless, as the chimes sound again and recess in the yard leads to recess in an enormous screening room replete with lush red velvet curtains and reclining chairs, the only other thing I know for sure is that I should have taken Two Five when I had the chance. Because as the seats fill with males around us, the Littles are noticeably missing. Luckily, so is Breaker and the Sixteen with the swirl pattern on his face.

My timer now floats on Motor's armrest.

"Can we please get rid of that thing?" I whisper, interrupting him as he goes on about why our seats are exactly the best seats in the theater.

"How you gonna know when your friend gets here?" he huskily replies.

"How *will* I know," I automatically correct. "Trust me. I'm sure I'll know."

"Congratulations. So, anyway..."

As ordered, Motor hasn't left my side. But he is not a silent shadow. It's like his betrayal in the yard was so second nature he's not even aware he should have the courtesy to at least *act* guilty. Instead he cheerily goes on about how great life is at the Fortress. I've already learned that Sway and I arrived on something called weekend day. That the meal he likes best is yellow. And the classes he particularly excels in are all of them.

It's like he's waited his whole life for someone to talk to.

Actually, he probably has.

Yet as the overhead lights dim, no matter how I pry or interrupt, he refuses to say another word about the mob or where they might be keeping Sway or the Littles or precisely how many doors his keycard can open or how many guards the Fortress has on staff.

The movie screen lights up.

"What the hill...?" I whisper only to be shushed immediately by the row in front of us.

It's the same kind of cartoons that we watched back home. Either the Fortress didn't enforce single-sex viewing the way fees did, or else the males in charge thought the mouse in shorts was a male and therefore audience appropriate. How they explained the character's high-pitched voice, so clearly a fee's, I don't know.

When the mouse cartoon ends, a new title screen comes up. It's so pink, it hurts my eyes. An excited murmur goes through the theater.

"What are the *Powerpuff Girls*?" I whisper.

"Only the best thing ever." Motor sighs. Elbows on knees, face in hands, he smiles as three squeaky-voiced fees fly across the screen. "They're heroes. *Super*heroes. Buttercup is my favorite. I'm gonna be just like him someday."

"A tiny flying fee?" I ask.

He did have the bulbous eyes down. I'd give him that.

"What's a fee? And no, I'm not gonna fly. Duh. I'm gonna be a hero."

I snort. "Last I checked, heroes didn't rat on their friends for chocolate."

"And last I checked"—Motor frowns, even as he remains absorbed in the screen—"males who get sent downstairs don't come back up."

I freeze. Did Motor just tell me where Sway was? He shoves up his glasses, oblivious to the dirty fingerprints he leaves on the lenses.

As offhandedly as possible, I snort and say, "What's that supposed to mean?"

Half glancing at the timer, Motor whispers, "One hour and eleven minutes ago you told Doctor you weren't going anywhere without Twofer or your friend Sway. If that Little in the yard was one of those names and the other one isn't here, then he must be downstairs. Du-uh."

My entire body tenses, as if it might run to Sway without my permission.

"What happens downstairs?"

"They correct males with attitudes."

"Correct them how?"

Motor laughs at the screen and shrugs. "The angry kids wake up blank. The sarcastic kids wake up dull. Everybody wakes up . . . less *them*."

More than the fear of the doctor coming, this explained all the males' lack of emotions. The Fortress was "correcting" them. But if the eventual goal was to turn them into the mob, why make them less angry or violent? Jackal had plenty extra of both those qualities and he rose through the ranks perfectly fine. Although I can't imagine he's easy to control.

As if on cue, Breaker walks in. A bandage is neatly taped over his nose. Blood still flecks his sweatshirt. His expression is even more remote than before. I know, because he takes a seat at the end of our row and proceeds to stare at me. Unblinking.

"See?" Motor rasps. "Downstairs."

"How do I get there? And don't you dare say I take the stairs down."

Motor's eyebrows rise up above his large glasses. "You said it, not me. But you don't wanna go there. Last week, I told on Adventure for selling his dinner milk. When he found out it was me, he gave me two purple nurples and threatened to kill me." He snorts. "I told on him for that, too. That's why they moved me from the bunks to my new room."

"What happened to Adventure?"

"I dunno." He shoves up his glasses and looks back at the screen. "No one's seen him since."

Just like Sway.

50

4:05:00. 4:04:59.

Chimes. Cartoon recess goes straight to dinner meal. Motor pushes me so we're first out of the theater. Breaker is right at our heels.

"Hurry," Motor says, though I need no encouragement. "First cuts of meal are the biggest."

The cafeteria is an airy room of high ceilings, stainless steel, and warm blond wood. At the center of the steepled space is a "meal station." It's shaped like a cube with rails for trays running along the outside. Matching steel-and-wood tables and chairs ring the cube in concentric rows. Running along the outside of the room are honey-colored wood cabinets.

Again, I scan the room for Sway.

Again, there is no sight of him.

Inside the cube, dressed entirely in white, are the two oldest males—never mind people—I have ever seen. With shaking hands, one slices into a square block of red-colored substance that kind of resembles Liyan's homemade tofu. If it was made of blood. The other elderly male puts the slices on plates and hands them to us. At the end of the line are tall glasses of milk.

"What is this?" I ask, sniffing the red lump.

The substance wobbles unappetizingly.

"What do you think it is?" Motor snorts. "It's dinner meal."

"Yeah, but what *is* it? Like, what is the food that the meal is made out of?"

He shakes his head, exasperated. "It's red dinner meal. Duh. For breakfast there's flakes and milk. For dinner there's meal. Pink dinner meal. Green dinner meal. Don't even get me started on brown dinner meal. Eat fast. Flakes and milk are portioned out, and you can only get one. But dinner meal they let you get seconds."

"Yeah, but who would want to?" I ask.

Motor snorts laughter as he takes two dishes of meal and a glass of milk.

Always drink your milk.

I wonder where the males get theirs from. Grand told me all the cows died after the Night, but that they were harmful to the environment anyway, which was why she and her lab techs made our milk from a soy base. Just as I put a glass on my tray, I am jostled from behind by Breaker's friend. The Sixteen with the amoeba-like black marks on his face. Only now they're not black marks anymore. They're oozing, raw burns. It looks like someone took a hot iron poker and traced the previous pattern. The welts are raised and inflamed.

"Downstairs?" I murmur to Motor.

"You think?" he dryly replies.

Only after he's gone do I realize the male dropped four little pieces of paper on my tray. Single words that look like they're all cut from separate books.

milk

the

drink

don't

I mentally rearrange them as I follow Motor to a table. Each itera-tion tells me the same thing. I glance around the room. Every Sixteen is staring at me. Their glasses clearly pushed away. *Don't drink the milk.* Understood. Yet I'm so parched, I'd drink my own bathwater—and at home we used ours a half-dozen times—and I wish I knew if this was a beneficial message or a harmful one. Because I can't imagine after the yard that Breaker's crew wants to help me.

Still, when we sit, instead of drinking, I cut and taste a tiny piece of red meal. Its flavor is identical to how it looks—squishy, bland, and lukewarm. No wonder Motor would do anything for a bite of chocolate. Yet he hovers over his plate like the meal is as delicious as Liyan's kimchi stew with preserved greens. Watching him take a hearty drink of milk, I reach for my own glass. But then he looks around and spits the liquid onto his second plate of meal and mixes it in.

"You don't like the milk?" I ask.

"It makes me itchy."

I glance at the timer, which is floating above the cafeteria door we came through. It's been five minutes since we sat down. All the males from the theater are here. But no Littles.

"What's on the agenda after dinner meal?" I ask.

"What's an agenda?" Motor asks, bits of meal flying out of his mouth.

"It's like a schedule."

"Oh." He shoves up his glasses. "Why not say *schedule,* then? Bedtime's on the thing."

"*Agenda.* Isn't it too early for bed? It can't even be dusk yet."

Motor's brow furrows. "What's dusk?"

"You know, pre-dark."

Again, the blank look.

"Motor, how long have you been in here?" I ask, exasperated.

He rubs at his eye beneath his glasses, then pushes them up again. "My whole life."

"But, I mean, you've been outside. You've left this place, right?"

He pokes at his red meal. "Duh, where would I go?"

Before I can reply, milk and red dinner meal crash down onto Motor's head. The Sixteen with the facial burns is standing over him, an empty tray in his hands. His now empty glass of milk in Motor's lap. His plate of meal broken on the floor.

"Hey, watch it!" I push back in my chair as Motor's lip quivers.

"I work here," the male says calmly.

I try not to look at his oozing face. "Good for you. You okay, Motor?"

Motor stands up, his arms held out at his sides. He is covered in milk and meal. The Sixteen's expression is emotionless and vague. He looks back to the cafeteria workers.

"Motor spilled his meal," he calls. "Permission to take him to the restroom?"

"Permission granted, Maximum," one of the cafeteria workers croaks.

The other worker slowly gets a mop and bucket from a slim cabinet inside the cube. And yet, Doctor doesn't come. Motor looks back over his shoulder at me as Maximum leads him away. They stop near the cabinets that run along the room. Maximum opens a few until he finds a stack of neatly folded gray sweat suits. The rest are all empty.

You can't always protect everyone.

"I'll be right here," I say.

The moment Maximum and Motor are out the door all the males in the room silently point at the opposite exit door. A murmur goes through the room.

"Breaker has a gift."

I glance from the ancient cafeteria worker with the mop to the door. Another murmur goes around. This one whispered more urgently.

"Go now."

Since I really have no other options, I do.

51

Outside the cafeteria I find myself in the usual endless charcoal-gray hallway. Except this one leads in three different directions. As I debate where to go, a door opens on my right. A boy with blue eyes, somewhere around the Tens, steps out. With a finger to his lips, he points farther down the hall. Breaker has a gift. It can't be good. *Just a little moment*, I hear Sway sing.

Right. Whatever awfulness Breaker has in store, it won't last forever.

I jog ahead. Another boy around Motor's age is waiting at the next corner. He gestures for me to make a left. At the next corner is yet another boy. He holds out a hand to me. *Wait.* Together, we peer around the corner as a guard and a Little come out of a room. The Little is sobbing, his pants thoroughly soaked at the crotch.

"Hush, Crusher," the guard says in a much softer voice than I'd expect. "Megatron didn't mean to spill his drink, and we have more pairs of pants."

"But these are my favorites," the Little wails.

Doctor immediately appears on the wall next to them. The Little cries harder.

"Honor with a Little, Doc," the guard says. "Going to the restroom to clean up."

Maybe it's the name or the fluidity of his voice or that his ponytail looks identical to Liyan's, but for a split second, I can't help thinking, *That guard is a fee.*

"All right," Doctor replies. "Proceed."

When the guard and Little turn the far corner, the doctor's image disappears. I'm waved on. The door to the room the guard left is still cracked open. Inside, it's painted a sunshine yellow. Overflowing toy chests, books, and games are stacked against the walls. Farther in, two long tables are surrounded by the Littles eating dinner. A Sixteen I recognize from Breaker's crew walks around and helps them cut their food. On dirty plates in a tub by the door, I glimpse a few bites of broccoli and something that looks like a nut cake.

At least the Littles get to eat real food.

I'm about to push open the door when another male comes out of the room directly across the hall. Freckles pepper his nose. He waves me to him. After a brief hesitation he puts his lips to my ear.

"We gotta help them watch the Littles. It's too much for one guard." Then he gestures to the room he just left. "You got eight minutes. Doc can't go there. I'll knock."

The room I step into is steeped in darkness and isn't finished like the others. The walls are only beams. Plastic covers the windows. Yet it's the most fantastic room I have ever been in, because there, at the heart of it, working on a puzzle on the concrete floor, is Two Five.

"Hey, little cricket," I whisper.

He startles. "Glori, is that really you?"

Then he's standing up and I'm kneeling down, and a moment later he launches himself into my arms. I scoop him up and swing him around. I didn't know joy and love could ever feel painful, but I'm having a hard time breathing through them as Twofer and I simultaneously laugh and cry with relief. I'll never let Twofer out of my sight again.

"I can't breathe," he squeaks, but then hugs me tighter.

I kiss his head. Too many times to count. Finally, we sit. He stays in my lap the way he hasn't done since he was a toddler. There's so much we need to discuss, but for a minute I simply thrill in his voice and smell and warmth and chatter and *him*.

"You look like Su!" He pats my shaved head. "But why's it yellow? And how'd you get here? Do you want to know how I got here? First, masks came to get me and I was scared. I called for you. But they said you were coming. And I said, *'Oh, okay.'* Then they gave me something called candy. It hurt my teeth but made me really excited. Then we went in a boat. Well, first we went in a car. *Then* we went in a boat. And then they had an argument about who was going to kill me."

I put a hand to my mouth, but Twofer simply continues to tick off his memories as nonchalantly as he lists objects in that game I made up called Everything I Can See.

"Finally, Pig said it would do it. Then Pig and I ran and got in another car, and Pig said it was only joking about that killing stuff, it was actually taking me to a place called the Fortress that was like something called camp. But I already knew what one was, because remember? We used to build them in the living room? And did you see? I drew a picture of it on the window."

"I did. That was very smart, Twosie. It helped me find you." He smiles, happy I'm impressed. "Did you happen to see who Pig was under the mask he wore? Like did he have any tattoos or special markings?"

"No, Pig didn't like when I looked at it. But its voice was real deep. Did you know they have different books here than the ones we used to read? Everyone in them is a beast! Isn't that so weird? I can't wait for you to meet my roommate. Her name is Hercules."

"*His* name, Twofer."

The pronouns would take him a minute to learn, too.

"Oh, okay." But then he is suddenly serious and whispers, "Glori, I have to tell you something. Don't get mad. But they let me have a real name here. I'm Mouse Scooter! Isn't that great? I don't have to be a number anymore."

My eyes tear up. How could I have thought his name never bothered him? Like as much as I loved him, a little part of me still thought he was less human than me somehow. I feel sick.

"Mouse Scooter, huh? That's a great name. Did you pick it?"

He nods proudly. "Mouse just like Mickey. Scooter 'cause Bicycle was already taken. It's my name, but it's two names!"

"That is very green." There's a Band-Aid on the crook of his arm. "What happened here?"

"Oh, I got a shot this morning. Honor told me it was just for me and all the big boys. It's called a vaccine. Don't worry. It didn't hurt. And guess who went first?"

"Your roommate, Hercules?"

He cackles. "I said only the big boys got shots. No, it was me! But then Hercules cried 'cause she felt left out. And one of the Sixteens felt bad and he gave her—I mean, him—one, too. Isn't that great?"

This is not my favorite information, but before I can ask him if he knows what they were vaccinating against, there's a knock on the door. My time can't already be up. That was barely a couple of minutes. I hoist

Twofer—*Mouse*—into my arms. Yet when the door opens I immediately put him down and shove him behind me.

It's not the freckled boy.

"Seems like we meet again, Walk-In."

It's Breaker. With a flat smile, he locks the door behind him.

52

My personal wing chung fighting stance is not impressive—standing sideways, knees bent, arms at the ready in front of my chest. For this confrontation, I borrow Itami's stance instead. A low side lunge, my hands balled into fists, one over my head and the other out in front of me. Following my lead, Mouse raises two little fists in front of him.

"What game's this one?" my brother asks, laughing.

Breaker rubs his balding head. Dandruff flies everywhere. He looks behind him. "What are you doing?" he asks.

"Getting ready to fight," I say. "What are you doing?"

"My memory ain't great, Walk-In, but if it serves me right, in the yard I was merely approaching you the way I am now. *You* went violent. No hard feelings, though, or feelings of any kind. This *is* the Fortress."

His shoulders silently shake up and down. He opens his mouth. Except no sound comes out. Wait. Did Breaker just make a joke?

"That's how he laughs," Mouse whispers. "It's so Doc don't hear him."

"It's so Doc *doesn't* hear him. Breaker, why did you bring me here?"

"Little here's been telling us when you came for him, you'd escape."

"You knew I was coming for you?" I spin on Mouse and put a hand on his head.

"Of course," he says brightly, then nods encouragingly at me with big serious eyes. "Go ahead, tell him. Breaker watches us at breakfast. He's fun. Except for his weird laughing thing."

"Mouse, don't be rude," I scold. "Manners."

"Oh, that's okay, Glori. Beasts don't have any. Isn't it great?"

Ever so slightly, Breaker smiles at Mouse. With his hands held up in an I-won't-hurt-you style, he nods toward the window. Thick opaque plastic sheeting is stapled over it, yet a faint outside glow manages to permeate. When we get to the window, Breaker leans into the diffuse light.

"Yes," I whisper, though I don't need to in here. "We're leaving."

"How?" Breaker asks.

There's a knock on the door. Freckles pokes his head in.

"Five minutes."

"I'm not sure. I haven't got much further than stealing Motor's keycard. I also have to get my friend Sway. Motor thinks he's downstairs."

Breaker lightly touches the perimeter of his bandaged nose, then nods. Not like Sway does, as if in time to a beat that no one else can hear. Just once.

"Walk-In, your friend *is* downstairs. I ain't seen him, but I heard him plenty."

"You *didn't* see him," I automatically correct. "Oh my mother."

Mouse pats my leg consolingly.

"What I mean is," Breaker continues, "he was screaming—loudly—in pain."

"Yes, thank you, Breaker. That was clear the first time."

Doctor told me if I stepped out of line, he'd hurt someone I cared about. But I hadn't. I hadn't done one single thing wrong. Well, except for being here right now. And plotting to escape. And smashing Breaker's nose. But other than that, I'd followed his rules. But he'd hurt Sway anyway. My nails bite my palms until Mouse takes hold of my pointer finger and shakes my hand out, making me relax.

There's another knock on the door.

More urgently: "Three minutes, Break."

"It never used to be like this. Doctor's just doing what's necessary to manage everyone."

"By putting sedatives in your milk?"

It's a guess, but Breaker nods.

"It calms us, makes us feel . . . happy. But over the years, we kinda, like, found that cooperation is the only dependable thing. If you try to escape alone, you will get caught. If you trust us, we can help you get your friend *and* your brother, and you will leave here alive. But you gotta, like, do exactly what we say."

I look to Mouse. He nods at me. As if it's that simple, trusting this strange male.

"Why are you helping us?"

Breaker palms his head again.

"What else we got to do?"

I take a deep breath. "All right. What's the plan?"

53

Considering he's had years to formulate a getaway, Breaker's plan is much better than mine. In an hour, when everyone goes to sleep—guards included—I'm going to swipe Motor's card. Go down six flights of stairs, into something called the Room with the Pants, and free Sway. Meanwhile, Breaker will take Mouse to the cafeteria. Once I have Sway we'll meet up, then use Maximum's employee keycard to let ourselves out the loading dock.

That was it. Keep quiet. Rescue my friend. Then leave.

"Wait. Maximum has a keycard that lets him outside?"

"Yes. So the elders don't have to haul heavy trash bags. I'm unsure what to do, though, if a guard stops any of us."

"Breaker, you do know there's a lot more of you than there are them, right? And wait, if Maximum can leave, why are any of you still here?"

Breaker shrugs. "Most of us have never even seen the outside. We kinda, like, didn't know there was even anywhere else to go. Here. I drew you a map."

He hands me sheets of construction paper. Each one has a floor plan of the Fortress traced on it in crayon. One per level, marking all the hallways, bedrooms, and common spaces with tiny boxes and lines. I commit them to memory and hand them back. The plan's simple enough. Except it means leaving Mouse.

"Mouse, you think you can keep all this a secret until I see you again?"

Hearing me say his new name makes him smile. He gives a thumbs-up.

When we follow Breaker back out into the hall, Mouse happily skips ahead.

"Thirty seconds," Freckles murmurs, mild concern flashing across his features.

Breaker and I both look down the hall. He seems to hear it, too. The distant soft sound of shoes on carpet. The guard and the Little are coming back. The guard is quietly humming "John Jacob Jingleheimer Schmidt." Still, I give Mouse one last quick hug.

"Glori, can I bring something with me?" he wetly whispers against my ear.

"As long as it travels well, Mouse."

"Oh, it definitely does."

Rejoining the other Littles, he shouts, "I'm back, guys!" which helps make the fact I'm leaving him again only slightly less awful.

As the chimes sound indicating the end of dinner, Breaker tugs on my sleeve. Silently—reluctantly—I jog down the hall after him, away from the returning guard.

"Breaker," I whisper after we turn the corner. "Seriously. Why are you helping us?"

"Many moons ago, it was told that a walk-in would come and set us free."

"What?" I ask, shocked. "Really?"

"No," he says as his shoulders move up and down. For a male that's had his personality corrected, Breaker is actually pretty funny. "But I kinda hoped if you got out, you'd maybe send someone back to help the rest of us."

When we get back to the cafeteria he squints inside, then sets a timer of his own. It floats on the wall above him. It's a quarter of the size of Motor's and green, but it keeps the same time. He wants me to send help. *If* I get out of here, who exactly would I send back? No fee could come to their aid, even if they wanted to. (Which I'm sure most wouldn't.) Meanwhile, Chia and/or Rage run this place. They *want* these males locked up.

I can hear Sway sigh with exasperation. Breaker and I had a plan. It would work. I just needed to stick to it. *You can't save everyone.* But shouldn't you at least try?

"How you aiming to do it?" Breaker asks, interrupting my thoughts.

"Do what?"

"Dispose of Motor."

According to Breaker, the Butler system was only capable of recognizing the keycards the males held, not individual voices. Any words it picked up were transmitted back to the doctor as a text message along with the cardholder's ID. Which meant as long as I could passably fake the way Motor spoke, if Doctor appeared and asked me why I was going downstairs when I should be sleeping, I could say I needed a Band-Aid and be by Sway's side five minutes later.

"Think you can talk like Motor, Walk-In?" Breaker had asked.

To which I'd replied, *"Duh."*

We'd both had a good silent creepy non-laugh laugh over that one.

Now I say, "I figured I'd tie him up and leave him in the bathroom."

"Tie him up with what?" Breaker asks.

"I don't know. Bedsheets?"

My room didn't have any, but Motor and I were both recent additions to the space. Surely other rooms had bedsheets. But Breaker shakes his head.

"Ain't any. Not since Excelente hanged himself up with them."

"All right, then I'll knock Motor out."

"How long's that last?"

"Well, I can't be sure, Breaker. Last time I concussed someone I didn't exactly stick around to time it."

His eyebrows lightly furrow, yet somehow his expression manages to convey a disappointment far greater than one of Grand's ten-minute-long guilt trips about the importance of upcycling.

"What are you suggesting," I ask, "that I kill him?"

I laugh. Breaker merely blinks.

"Oh my mother," I say, incredulously. "That *is* what you're suggesting."

All too seriously he says, "You aim to leave here, right, Walk-In? And you aim to do that under Doctor's nose with your friend and brother? Doc always says it only takes one loose thread to unravel a sweater. And Motor is as loud and untrustworthy as a loose thread comes. Ask me? You gotta remember what's at stake."

We both stare into the cafeteria, where Motor sits with his back to us. From the hunch of his shoulders and his swift side-to-side glances, it's clear he's plotting how he'll take down the whole lot of them.

I sigh. "I'm sure I can think of something other than murder. Either way, wish me luck."

Breaker spits on the floor. "Don't believe in it. What'd luck ever do but land me here?"

A moment later, when I hurry back into the cafeteria, Motor is literally on the edge of his seat waiting for me. He's changed his clothes but clearly didn't bother to wash. His scalp looks tacky, and his face and arms glisten with dried milk and meal. He's also starting to smell. Like rotting fish. His mood is just as foul.

"Geez," he wheezes in his raspy voice. "Where'd you go? We're almost at third chime."

"I had to use the bathroom. Meal ran straight through me."

"Well, next time at least leave me a murmur."

When we get back to his bedroom, the wall is now a deep midnight blue and offers just enough illumination for us to get to our beds without bumping into anything. It also makes the timer more blinding than the sun on a rare cloudless day.

2:51:15. 2:51:14. 2:51:13.

Breaker said to wait until the even two-hour mark to make sure everyone's asleep. He said the milk helps with that. I'd rather go now. I wonder how close my "friend" actually is. Regardless, I tell myself two hours is plenty of time to execute our plan. I might even be able to shut my eyes for thirty minutes. Yet after I lie down I immediately feel a light depression on my mattress. Motor has crawled over his baseboard and is sitting at the foot of my bed. Doctor gave all the males sedatives to drink, but Motor dumped his. No wonder Motor is so . . . Motor. I sit up. He holds up a hand in a silent wave.

It unleashes a new flood of pickled funk into the room.

"Doesn't the Fortress have showers?" I whisper.

"Right across the hall." He nods as he pushes his glasses up. "But I hardly ever use them. It's not like I get dirty in here. They're too hot, anyway."

Biting his lip, he picks at my scratchy mattress.

"You okay?" I ask.

He doesn't ask what I'm talking about.

"Yeah. They do stuff like that to me all the time. It's not that big a deal."

Motor's been here his whole life. I wonder if in that time, he's ever had anyone who loved him. Tucked him in. Was happy to see him in the morning. I hope so. Even if he can't remember it, I hope Motor at least had that. From where I'm sitting, the clock is positioned right over his head. *No loose threads*, I hear Breaker say. *Remember what's at stake.*

"Motor, you know there are better motivators in life than chocolate, right?"

"Oh yeah," he says, pushing up his glasses. "Honor told me. Egg tarts, right?"

A surprised laugh escapes me. "No. I was thinking more like friendship."

Motor lets out a begrudging laugh. "Oh, duh."

Then he snorts, and for brief second, we're grinning at each other and I realize I kind of actually like this odd, surly little gruff-voiced tattle-tale male. Too bad I still haven't thought of a way to humanely "dispose" of him. *Remember what's at stake.* Mouse. Sway. I let out a wide yawn, stretch.

"Bedtime, Motorhead."

As I lie back on my bare mattress, Motor looks reluctantly over at his.

"You want to sleep here tonight?" I ask. "You know, as a favor. So I feel less homesick?"

Rolling his eyes, Motor sighs heavily but then quickly crawls to grab his pillow and hurries back to the foot of my bed.

"Just for tonight."

"Thanks," I say. "I really appreciate it."

As Motor hunkers in, he lets out a fart and laughs. "Doc almost showed up for that one."

"And here I thought it couldn't smell any worse," I murmur.

2:46:15. 2:46:14. 2:46:13.

My eyes blink, heavy with sleep. It's been over two days since I've gotten any decent rest. But if everything goes well, this will all be over soon. Just as I'm about to make my move, I feel two little feet press up against mine. Somewhere in the building, Breaker is getting ready to take Mouse to the cafeteria. And that decides it for me.

I know exactly what's at stake.

"Hey, Motor." I sit up. "Can I borrow your keycard? I need to use the bathroom again."

54

Leaving our bedroom door open a crack, I walk across the hall to the bathroom. My hands shake as I leave that door popped open as well. As I wait, I stare at the showers. Motor said they were too hot. I can't even imagine what that feels like. Never mind the last time I bathed was at Comma and Sway's. Or that it was more of a hand bath than anything else. Or that the water was frigid. On Grand Island, *hot* and *shower* were words that didn't ever go together. It'd be like running a quick marathon.

Before I can think twice about it, I turn on the faucet in the last shower stall. Within seconds the whole bathroom is steamy. Quickly disrobing, I hop in. I should have a solid five minutes before Motor comes to investigate what's taking me so long. That's four minutes longer than I need.

I step into the scalding water and let out a quiet groan. Maybe the food comes in bricks of color and they use sedatives and sensory overstimulation to keep the wards in check, but the water at the Fortress is piping hot. And the feel of it is . . . delicious.

Which is maybe why as I soap up under the scorching spray—with actual soap—I find myself thinking about milk. When I was younger and Grand was testing out her recipes for the milk substitute, she'd call me into her lab to be her official taste-tester.

"If you like it," she'd say, *"then the pickiest drinker in the world will like it."*

And I did like the milk. Except it always tasted the same.

Of course, I never told my grand this. Not after all the time she spent perfecting the recipe. So I'd make things up. *That one was creamier than last time.* Or *This one was sweeter.* They were happy memories for me, because the milk tasting meant I was allowed into her lab. The time went by so quick in there, I'd leave without realizing that half a day had passed.

My knees give a little, and the soap slips from my hands. Even given the almost unbearably hot water, a shiver runs down my back as an awful thought occurs to me. Maybe the reason nothing is adding up is because I've been calculating all the wrong sums. Because now, as I quickly think everything out, point by point, it all clicks into place.

The bathroom door creaks open.

Waste. I turn off the tap.

Grabbing my towel from the curtain bar, I wrap it around myself, then step out into the locker room, where I come face-to-face with Motor.

"I know what you're doing," he says.

"Bathing? You should try it. Truly."

"No. You're escaping, aren't you? You're gonna steal my keycard and escape."

I try to get past him to my clothes. Half-naked was not how I envisioned participating in this conversation.

"Motor, listen . . ."

He blocks my way, wiping at his steam-fogged glasses in annoyance. "No, you listen," he says in a voice that's more raspy than usual. "I'm not some dumb septic tank. I'm right. Aren't I?"

As I dart around him and reach for my clothes, he grabs my arm to stop me. Right on my stitches. I cry out. I feel my towel loosen, and next second it lies in a lump on the floor.

I'm naked.

"What are those?" Motor shrieks, pointing at my chest. "And what happened to your ding-dong? Mutant! Mutant!"

I lift him into the air by his shirt, my hand covering his mouth. *Remember what's at stake.* It would be so easy to break his neck right now. I could hide his body in an empty wing of the Fortress. It would be weeks before anyone found him. Sway, Mouse, and I would be a lifetime away by then. Maybe he can see all these thoughts rush through my head, because he stops struggling.

"I won't tell," he quietly whimpers.

"I doubt that," I say.

Putting him down, I quickly grab my towel, then turn my back to him and slip into my clothes. He cranes his neck, trying to get another look at my body.

"And I'm not a mutant. I'm a fee. Same as your Powerpuff Girls. And you're right, I am going to steal your keycard and escape. So now what?"

His nose is running and his forehead is dotted with sweat. "Take me with you?"

This is not what I was expecting. "Why would I do that? You've spent the entire day solely telling me how great the Fortress is. You're the doctor's most helpful ward. You love it here."

"No. I'm done with being helpful. I want to be a Buttercup—a real hero. And if you won't take me with you, you're gonna have to break my neck. Because otherwise, I'll go out into the hall and scream for Doc, and you'll never see your brother or friend again."

Minus the request to tag along, this is exactly what Breaker predicted Motor would do.

"Motor, I think you're confused on the definition of a hero. Heroes don't blackmail their friends."

"I don't want to mail black at you, but I have another six years until I'm of age. That means another six years staring at gray walls. Six years of everyone thinking I'm a septic tank. And waiting for yellow dinner-meal days. You know, I don't even like yellow dinner meal? I think I actually hate it. I just like pretending I have something on my *agenda* to look forward to."

His voice is high and wobbly, as if the very idea of staying here one more minute, never mind six more years, is enough to make him cry. I laugh with relief. His eyebrows go above his glasses frames as a small snot bubble forms in his right nostril.

"Geez, rude," he sniffs. "What's so funny?"

"You're in. You passed."

"Of course I passed. I'm super smart."

"Though I need you to promise that you'll help me with my brother, Mouse. If he doesn't make it out, we're not making it out. Understood?"

"Geez, yeah. I get it. Only Mouse matters. Not me. Understood." He wipes his nose on his arm. It leaves a trail of wet. "So wait. What am I 'in'?"

"My escape plan. I needed your help, but I didn't know if I could trust you or if you'd even be willing to lend a hand. But now I do and you will and we really have to get moving."

Motor pushes up his glasses with shaky hands. His little sour mouth is a mess of smiling and trying to look tough and suppressing stress tears.

Luckily, the process of telling him Breaker's plan and having him comment on how dumb it is and how it'll never work snaps him right back into form. Until I tell him the new part. The part Breaker doesn't know about. The one I decided on when I realized what was at stake.

When I finish, Motor's brow furrows, like he hasn't heard me right.

"You mean"—he shoves at his glasses—"if this whole dumb thing works, then...?"

"Yep." I nod. "You'll be a hero. It all depends on you."

Which was exactly the opposite of what Breaker suggested I do. But if one thread could unravel a sweater, surely it could bind one together as well.

"Now come on," I say. "Breaker and Mouse are probably waiting for us, but are you sure you don't want to shower before we leave?"

"Nah. Showering's for septic tanks."

I consider insisting. A red pimple is forming on Motor's cheek, probably from all the accumulated grime and oil, but I let it go. As I follow Motor back to our room, he keeps smiling at me over his shoulder. Right outside the door, I pull him to a stop.

"Motor, where did you learn that saying? Calling someone a septic tank?"

"I dunno. Everyone says it, duh, you dumb, smelly septic tank. See?"

I snap my fingers and point at him. "Don't push it."

As soon as I'm through the door sparks ring out next to my ear. Horrific pain radiates from my neck down my spine and along every nerve in my body. Out the corner of my eye, the gray male from reception takes out a needle and jabs it into my arm.

He's so close, I could...

"Oh, don't bother plotting, sweetheart. You're paralyzed."

I swing my eyes to Motor. He's crouched on the floor with his hands over his head. Rough hands catch me as I fall.

1:44:12. 1:44:11.

They're early, I think. Then, everything goes black.

55

When I wake, I'm lying in a hospital bed in a windowless room. It feels like I'm hundreds of miles beneath the dormitory floors. Yet there is a sound.

Click. Click. Click. Click.

It can't be.

My entire body feels wrung out, yet I clench my fists and manage to turn my head slightly. My heart beats faster even as my body goes limp.

For there, unbelievably, is my grandmother.

56

For as long as I can remember, my Grand Mati has looked the same. Strong and graceful with flawless glowing skin and perfect posture. If anything, as she's aged, she's become younger. I commented on this once, making her laugh.

"What can I say, Spark Plug?" She winked. "We have good genes."

Now she's sitting next to my hospital bed in a plush chair with her legs tucked up under her, clicking her pen. Her shiny dark brown-and-gray braid twists down her shoulder, curls escaping wherever they can. A reading lamp casts a warm yellow glow on her as she peruses a tablet, the screen filled with data sets. It's almost like I've woken from a strange dream and am back home. Although I couldn't be, because at home our lamps never worked.

Nor was I ever drugged or electrocuted in the neck.

When I shake my head to dispel the grogginess, she is immediately beside me, one hand on my arm, the other stroking my forehead.

"Thank goodness," she says quietly. "How are you feeling?"

How am I feeling?

"I was electrocuted." I try to touch my neck, only to find that my arms and legs are zip-tied to the bed. A cry escapes me. "Grand? What are you doing here? What's going on?"

"Don't be afraid. Everything is all right. There was simply a miscommunication. I told them I wanted you to wait in my quarters. I don't know why they placed you in the general population. They're all a little afraid of you, honestly."

As she was the morning the beasts raided the island, she is purposely calm. But now, like then, I don't need calm. I need outrage and horror and her I-will-murder-you face from that time Su and I used her favorite bathrobe to make ourselves turbans. Also, *her quarters*?

"How is everything all right?" A strangled sob comes up my throat. "You've been lying to me. For my entire life. The mob. The Fortress. The labs. It's all you, isn't it?"

Grand liked to say that the simplest, most logical answer was usually the correct answer. Well, then what was most logical? That the Seventeen Year Truce was coming up and our matriarchs had no recourse against it? That they trained us to be fighters our whole lives and at this crucial moment in time had no plan? That fees were the only ones who knew how to make babies, yet males managed to coerce my fiercely independent and loyal brethren into making more males all these years?

Or was it most logical that males weren't behind any of this?

Fees were.

Unflinchingly, she says, "Yes. They're all various backup plans in case the divide failed. The Fortress is the oldest of them."

"But why? Why are you making more males?"

"After we escaped Buffalo, most fees couldn't yet conceive of a future where we didn't have males. But when those young beasts attacked our fees on the island right after the divide, some of the mothers began to imagine a future where beasts were less beastly. What if we could raise young beasts in our own image?"

Beasts. The word hurts my ears now.

"But you aren't *raising* males. You're messing with them."

Again, a curt nod. "One of our geneticists teamed up with a hormone replacement therapist who worked in the same building as NeuYue labs. The goal was to erase a beast's testosterone and libido."

"Grand," I interrupt sharply.

But she cuts back just as quick. "Fees have dealt with the repercussions of a beast's hormones since the dawn of time. Let them, for once, make do. And if you can't curb your moral indignation, we won't be able to continue this conversation. The choice is yours."

Whenever Grand and I argued about Twofer, Liyan always told me, *First and foremost your grand is a scientist. Her clinical nature requires her to be callous and narrow.*

I take a deep breath. Her eyes do not leave me. I curtly nod for her to continue.

"Our first trials weren't on infants. They were on the beasts who hurt our fees. Unfortunately"—she clicks her pen, her eyes steely—"all those beasts died. Mayor Grim, however, actually supported the research. *He* suggested we do the trials here, and while he was alive, he sent us a few more particularly violent beasts to work with. Some of those cases were quite successful. Rage, for instance. But then Grim was murdered, new subjects were no longer forthcoming, and the team decided it would be more productive to begin the process in utero."

"But this place is horrible. They use this sound torture to keep everyone under control and drug everyone and—"

She cuts me off. "From what I understand, the Fortress offers plenty of exercise, free time, stimulating classes, nutritious meals. I'll grant you that Doctor and his brother are a little . . . eccentric. But we both know there are worse situations out there." She softens. "Besides, no one will be here much longer. Glori, there's something I've been keeping from you. . . ."

"Yeah, no waste, Grand," I say loudly, pulling against my restraints.

She frowns but doesn't scold me. I guess a lifetime of lies earned me that much lenience. Instead she slips off my bed and retrieves a pocket-knife from her bag. I flinch when she flicks it open, but she only uses it to cut my zip ties.

"This is not how I imagined telling you, for the record." As I rub my wrists, she resumes her seat on my bed and worriedly chews on her lower lip. "I only kept it from you because I wanted you to have as normal a life as possible. Whatever normal means nowadays. The thing is . . ." She takes a deep breath. "Two Five wasn't the first child conceived after Nuclear Night."

"Obviously."

Her left eyebrow shoots up at my tone, but she continues. "I'm not talking about the lab babies or the beasts here. I'm talking about you. You were the first child truly conceived after the Night. I know you've always wondered why Majesty had you when she was so young. Well, it wasn't technically her idea." She hurriedly says, "Though it was with her blessing."

"Blessing to do what?"

"To combine one of her harvested eggs with a sample of synthetic sperm that Auntie Shereen and Auntie Jean created. Glori, *you* were the last child NeuYue conceived before we moved to the island."

I can hear Majesty screaming at my grand, *In what sense is she mine, Mother?* No wonder she never felt or exhibited any attachment to me. Willing or not, what was I to her but a science experiment?

"Why would you ever, *ever* choose Majesty as the sample?"

Majesty, who was temperamental even before she was snatched. Majesty, who I remember being innately angry, the way other fees were kind or funny. A wildly emotional being, laughing and verbose one minute, brooding and stormy the next. My grand stops clicking her pen.

"Because Majesty was conceived the same way."

Like Su with her Rubik's Cube, my brain twists as I rapidly put all the pieces together.

"So I'm the first fee made from synthetic sperm born of a fee made from synthetic sperm, born of a CRISPRed fee?"

She smiles. "Tongue twister, isn't it? We needed to wait until you were out of puberty to make sure you could have children of your own and that there were no latent mutations. Ideally, we'd wait until you were in your twenties or thirties and make dozens of other fetuses similar to you in the meantime. We are doing that now, of course. But back then, we only had you and we only had seventeen years. Glori, I've always told you that you're my special girl."

But that's only dressing it up, because what I *actually* am?

Is my Grand Mati's solution to the divide.

"You're saying that we don't need males anymore?"

In spite of everything, Grand laughs. "Some would argue we barely needed them in the first place. But yes. That's correct. At least in the macro scheme of evolution, males have officially outlived their usefulness."

57

"**M**ajesty was never snatched, was she?"

"No," Grand says quietly. "She came to the beasts' side willingly, albeit against my wishes. This was six years ago. Six years before the truce expired. The males were going into yet another election. Over the previous decade they'd had a new mayor nearly every two years. The other elders and I felt it was only a matter of time before one of them got it in their head that they wanted us back. Altering them wasn't working. Removing a male's testosterone and libido didn't make less beastly beasts. It made sickly, depressed ones. We needed a new plan.

"As you remember, when you were growing up, Majesty was our fiercest fighter. When I suggested we infiltrate the males, she volunteered to do the reconnaissance. I protested, but she went regardless. Thanks to her PTTs, we found out about the cameras, that the beasts still used a cash-based economy, and that they hadn't moved on from the Night the same way we had. She's the one who told us the mob was the alliance we needed."

"The mob? Rage has been trying to kill me the whole time I've been here."

"From what I understand, he tried to capture you—a few times—to send you home. How do you think I even knew you were missing?" Her eyes tear up. "First Twofer, then I came back to an empty house . . . I thought they took you, too."

"No," I say, surprised. "I left a note."

"Where?" I tell her, but she shakes her head. "No. It wasn't there. Thankfully, Rage messaged the second he realized it was you in the tunnel. But you escaped. He tried to bring you in at the steam station. But you escaped. He almost grabbed you at the mayor's office when he went to find out if Chia hired mobsters to murder our fees . . ."

"And we escaped," I finish for her.

She nods. "Rage is the only reason the Fortress has been possible all these years. He's found us trustworthy guards. He offered to take our graduating males, protect them after they left here. He also found Majesty after she went missing."

I suddenly feel sick. "Please tell me Rage isn't Twofer's father."

"Two Five should be so lucky, but no." She plays with her braid. "Rage is gay. Maj was supposed to be gone for only a week. Two, tops. But then all her PTTs stopped. We lost her for three months. I thought she was dead. Rage found her beaten up and knocked out in a back alley downtown. He nursed her back to health, or some semblance of it, and delivered her to us at the bridge."

"What happened to her?" I ask, enthralled.

I've never heard any of this.

"She's never said."

"And the labs. All those baby fees . . ."

It was one of the things that hadn't made sense to me. If fees thought the labs were destroyed, how come all the Miracles and every year above us were still learning the science behind ex-utero births and CRISPRing? Now I knew. We learned the science because Grand was confident that one day we'd put it to use.

She nods. "We'd never have the level of weaponry the males have. Even if the mercenaries scavenged towns miles away, I refused to be a gun-based society again. So we used our intellect instead. Fortitude's crew didn't torch the labs. We did. In ways that wouldn't matter. On buildings that had no use. We wanted everyone to think the labs were gone. To give us time and space to breathe, to assess. We took the girls in gestation and gave the boys to the men we trusted. Ansel. Sarge. Zeno. Chia…"

"Chia?" I sit up straighter. *Reason.* "If you trusted Chia enough to give him a child, why not ask him for your labs back? Why all this secrecy?"

"*Ask* Chia to return *our* labs?" She snorts. "Just as he is 'asking' us to move into internment camps? Nope. I am done asking beasts for permission. For the first time in the entire history of the world, our power is our own. We decide where we live. We decide whether or not to procreate and in what manner. We are done giving up everything for nothing in return. Glori, this is bigger than the labs or the divide. It's not about gender for me. At least not anymore. It's about freedom. Power. Our entire future."

As she talks, she grips my hands imploringly. I've forgotten how intense her gaze is. How vivid and bright that gaze sees our world. Everything is possible to her. It's infuriating. Sensing my displeasure, she releases my hands and takes a thermos from her bag.

"Hē cha," she says in Mandarin.

It's our family's joke. What Liyan always says, regardless of the malady. *Drink tea.* Tea makes everything better. Maybe it does. What she pours smells like herbs and strength and home.

"What now?" I ask tightly, even as I gratefully take the cup she offers and drink the whole thing down despite the scorching temperature.

"Simple. I'm going to take over the city and insist Chia and the other beasts leave."

I laugh, but she's serious. "Do fees know about this?"

"Of course. With the exception of you and the Miracles and a few others of our youngest generations. We didn't think it was a healthy way for you to live with a potential war looming on the horizon. Although we prepared you all as best we could."

"And what does all of this mean for Mouse?"

"Mouse?" Her brow furrows.

"Twofer."

"Glori." Her lower lip trembles. "I didn't tell you on the island, because I didn't know how. Of course, if I knew you'd chase after him, I would have immediately, but Spark Plug . . . Twofer is dead. The mercenaries found his body on the beasts' shore. The beasts killed him."

I let out a shocked laugh. "No, they didn't. He's *here*."

Her entire body quakes like someone shook her. "What?"

"Yes. Why else would I be here?"

"I haven't had a chance to ask." Her eyes fill with tears. "Glori . . . you've actually *seen* him?"

"Yes, and talked to him and hugged him. He's here and he's fine. He even . . ." My voice breaks. Wiping at my eyes, I take a deep breath and continue, "He even gave himself a name. Mouse Scooter. And he's made friends."

Holding a trembling hand to her lips, she clears her throat and in a raised voice says, "Doctor, I'd like a word."

A moment later, there's a gentle knock. The door pops open.

"Ma'am?"

It's Doctor, but not the neat, blue-suited male from the screens. This doctor is wearing the same sweat suit the wards wear. His hair is long and gray and sits messily on top of his head in a wild knot. He is openly sweating, and red dots pepper his hands and face. No wonder he chose to appear as the blue-suited version of himself. This male is a slob. He blows his nose into a rumpled handkerchief. Grand doesn't try to hide her shudder of disgust.

"What do you know about a child being dropped off here a few days ago?" she asks.

He nods. "Yes. That happened. It must have slipped my mind, getting all the Sixteens ready as we have been. Why?" he asks innocently. "Is he of interest to you?"

"A young child that we did not birth? Of course he is of interest to me. I want him brought here. Immediately."

"Also, my friend Sway," I quickly add.

Grand looks to the doctor expectantly. What passes for mild shock crosses his features but evaporates as a violent, phlegmy cough wracks his body.

He dabs at his forehead with his dirty handkerchief. "Beg your pardon. I haven't been feeling well, except if my recollection serves, Sway was released. Same day Glori came in."

I shake my head. "No, he's lying. Breaker heard him. Downstairs. Screaming."

The doctor calmly gestures to the room around us.

"We are downstairs. Do you hear screaming?" He presses a finger to his ear. "Ma'am, my brother informs me that the mayor and his patrol have passed the tollbooths. It is time. Perhaps for now, the little one should be left where he is? He is sleeping, after all."

"Fine," Grand replies, even as I protest.

She gives a curt nod of dismissal. With a flat smile, Doctor makes a faint bow. When the door closes behind him, I scoot closer to my grand and clutch her arm.

"Grand, something isn't right," I whisper urgently. "I don't think everything is working the way you think it is. He is absolutely lying. Plus, the mercenaries lied to you about Twofer and I saw Misère and Muerte kill Rauha."

Her shock is so great, it brings her to her feet.

"Rauha?" she asks softly. "When?"

I swivel to look at the wall for Motor's timer. I have no idea how long ago it was.

"On my transport ride out here. They were with mob that were dressed as patrol soldiers when they did it."

I move to stand, but the motion makes me woozy. I immediately sit back down. My eyelids suddenly feel heavy but not naturally. Like I've been drugged. I look at the empty cup in my hand. Hē cha. When would I learn that my grand was a master of sedation?

"Oh, Grand," I say quietly.

"I'm sorry, Spark Plug. I didn't know Twofer . . . Forgive me"—she smiles—"*Mouse* was here. But now at least when you both wake up this will all be over. I'll leave word for him to be brought to you as soon as he stirs. And I'll look into your friend as well."

I frantically grip her hand. "Fees think Reason told the males we had Mouse in the first place. No. That's not right. I have to warn you to watch out."

My words aren't working. Grand is in danger. But all I want is to lie down.

"You don't need to warn me about anything," she says, laying me back and tucking me in. "You need to rest. When I return and you've had some sleep, we can go around and around on all of this. As many times as you need to. Now please don't worry. I'm not so foolish as to think I'm the only one with backup plans. I'm well prepared." She smooths back my nonexistent hair, then kisses my forehead. "I hope one day you'll know just how much I love you."

This is my chance. To tell her that I love her, too. Even through all the lies and deceit. Because even though I am furious and disgusted and betrayed, this is my Grand Mati. She has stood by me my whole life. Loved me, tucked me in, made me laugh, made me *me*. Grand because she simply is. Every single thing about her.

What is love, if it is not stronger and deeper than anything else?

She pauses by the door to give me one last look. I want to say that I love her, too. In spite of everything. Regardless.

Always.

But I don't. So she leaves.

58

I wake to silence. When I swing myself out of bed, my head pounds a hundred times worse than it did from drinking with Sway. The floor is cold on my bare feet. On my grand's chair there are now freshly folded clothes. I hurriedly put on the sweatshirt and leggings, then notice a pair of boots beneath the chair. Non-ridiculous, low-heeled, synth-leather boots that actually fit me. I now totally get what Comma meant about happy crying. When I stick my hands in the pocket of the hoodie, I touch plastic.

My grand gave me a keycard.

Even better is what she left hanging on the doorknob.

My pack.

Grand said it would all be over when I woke. Angry as I am, I hate how ominous that sounds. I also hate that I have no idea if a few minutes, hours, or days have passed since she said it. Regardless, Mouse has definitely been waiting longer than we planned. If we even still had a plan. Or needed one. My Grand Mati ran this place. For a moment, I feel tremendous relief. My role here is done. She'll fix everything.

And then I swipe my card and step out into the hall.

It is sterile, white-tiled, and so perfectly silent that I immediately have flashes of my childhood nightmare. The Night has happened again and I'm the only remaining survivor.

"Grand?" I call out.

Nothing. The Butler system must not function down here, because the walls stay wall-like. Regardless of my situation, I can't help but give a silent thanks be that I am alive post-Night and my home will never talk to me. As I move down the long white hall, slipping my knives into place, a faint beeping sound grows louder.

"Hello?"

Nothing.

Up on my right, there are two identical doors, both with frosted glass windows. One bears a picture of a fee in pants. The other a fee in a dress. The beeping comes from behind the door with the pants fee. *The Room with the Pants*, just like Breaker said.

I push on the door. I don't need my keycard. It isn't locked. As if whatever's inside is no longer a threat, or won't be escaping. I both desperately do and do not want to see what's on the other side.

At one time, it was a bathroom. The toilet now has a tray of equipment resting on it. Dirty scalpels and rods, and the same pre-Night pastry torch that our library loaned out even though the butane canister stopped working ages ago. Power tools and a tattoo gun hang along one wall. Branding irons another. The garbage can next to the sink is filled with bloody rags. But these are all quick, fleeting observations because my eyes are instantly drawn to the gurney that's pushed into the corner of the room and the body that lies on it.

"Oh my mother," I whisper.

It's Sway; dressed in hospital scrubs. His head is tilted back on the pillow, his mouth hangs slack. One arm flops off the gurney. I rush over and shake him. He doesn't respond.

I'm too late. A sob burbles up in my chest.

"No, no, no," I murmur.

I cup his cheeks in my hands.

Suddenly, his eyes fly open.

"Staring," he bursts out.

I shriek and leap away from him. His eyes gleam brightly, and then *he grins at me.*

"Were you faking being dead?" I whisper, horrified.

"I figured I'd never get a more perfect chance." His grin has the audacity to widen. "I *had* to."

I leap at him, pounding on his chest. "I am going to murder you."

"Boop!" he cries out defensively, shielding himself from my blows. "Boop. Boop. Boop."

Managing to grab my wrists, he pulls me to him, and next second, I'm curled into his lap. He hugs me tightly, rocking us back and forth as we both do some version of relieved crying.

"Someone told me you were screaming," I whisper into his chest.

I feel him shake his head. "No. They gave me some kind of shot when I first got here, but other than that and a wicked chipped tooth from when they darted me, I've been left alone. No food. No visitors. Nothing. So I tried that thing Su said, about making a terrifying situation less terrifying by doing something ridiculous. I've been singing."

"Singing." I laugh. "Not screaming."

"Show tunes, nineties punk rock, and Korean rap. Now I kind of feel insulted actually."

I push away from him. "You're telling me you've been sitting in an unlocked room with access to scalpels..."

"Gruesome bloody scalpels," he corrects.

"And it never occurred to you to escape?"

"Sure it did. It also occurred to me that I am a terrible fighter. Did you find Twofer?"

I nod. He lets out a whoop of excitement.

"He goes by 'Mouse' now."

"Mouse? That is not a male name."

"I know, isn't it great? Sway, my grand's here. This whole place is hers, but she said she'd send Mouse to me and he isn't here and I think Chia is coming and there's so much I have to tell you. But first we have to go get Mouse. Unless of course you'd like to stay here?"

"Nah, the bloody scalpels and I will always have our fond memories." He grabs my hand as I untangle from him. "Glori, promise me something?"

"Yes. Anything."

He leans his forehead against mine but gently this time. Like we do back home.

"Promise me we'll never leave each other ever again."

I smile and quick-brush my nose against his, and just as I'm about to tell him that I do—I promise—all the lights shut off.

There is no ambient or emergency lighting. We are in utter darkness. In a basement.

"At least we're together now," I say.

Which is when the voice begins to shout: "LOCKDOWN. LOCK-DOWN. LOCKDOWN."

59

"I wonder what mode this is," Sway shouts.

"LOCKDOWN. LOCKDOWN. LOCKDOWN."

He holds on to my shirt as we edge out into the hall. There is a door at the end of this corridor. Hopefully it leads somewhere that goes up. As we inch along, I hold my keycard out in front of me and blindly wave it in the air. A few steps farther, there is a hiss. The door pops open. Beyond it are red emergency lights and a stairwell.

"Thanks be," I holler.

"Yes, thank you, Glori," he shouts back. "Geez, you are such a praise seeker."

I am too grateful to be back around his idiocy to correct him. We take the stairs two at a time back up to the cafeteria floor. Breaker's maps showed that the apartments on each floor fanned out around a central hub on each level. The yard was the hub on the second floor. The cafeteria was on the third. The theater on the fourth. And so on. The halls leading to the cafeteria are all thoroughly deserted. And in almost every hallway, all the apartment doors are open. All the rooms are empty.

"Glori, I don't think anyone is here."

That *had* been the plan. But Grand had also said no one would be here much longer. I start to run.

Please let them be there, I think. Please.

"LOCKDOWN. LOCKDOWN. LOCKDOWN."

When we get to the cafeteria it's as empty as the rest of the building.

"Mouse!" I yell.

No reply.

"Motor!"

Same.

"No. No, no, *no*."

I pick up a chair and lob it across the room. It crashes against the wall. What was I expecting? That Mouse would use his little five-year-old male brain to figure out a way to hide this whole time? That Motor wouldn't quit on him and that *he* would figure something out? Well, yes, that's exactly what I wanted them to do.

"Maybe your Grand has him," Sway says as I lob another chair.

Not if she was going to meet Chia. She would never put him in that kind of harm's way. Although she did leave us here.

"Glori, look."

Sway points. A door has popped open on one of the cupboards that runs along the wall.

Once, before Two Five was born, we had three months of heavy rains cut only by intermittent slushy snowstorms. It was week after week of permanent gray skies and stiff, freezing hands and feet. When it began to feel like it might be better to end our lives than wake up to one more day of such bleakness, there were still a few more weeks of it. Then one morning, the clouds cleared. Patches of blue dotted the sky and suddenly a vibrant double rainbow soared over the entire neighborhood. I never imagined I'd see anything more gorgeous.

Yet the two males who now tumble out of the cupboard are, without question, a million times more beautiful. Motor wields a butter knife. Mouse gives me a happy thumbs-up.

I fly to them and grab them both up, clutching them tightly. And it is right then, as I hug Mouse to me, that I finally, truly understand the layers to what my grand has done. She has made difficult, awful decisions. But she did it for us. Just as I would do anything for this male. I would sacrifice my very life to protect him. And woe to the being who tried to cause him harm.

"We hid when the alarm started going off," Motor shouts into my ear.

"Motor said you wouldn't come," Mouse shouts into my other ear. "But I said you would. I said we had to wait."

"Glori." Motor whaps my shoulder so he has my full attention. "It wasn't me. I didn't turn you in."

"I know, Motorhead. I wouldn't care anymore if you did. You are both mine, do you understand? And I will never ever let you out of my sight or let anyone hurt you ever, ever again. From here on out we stay together always. Got it?" I nod to Sway. "All four of us."

Motor's eyes well with tears, and he wipes them with his arms, forgetting to take his glasses off first. I ruffle his shaved hair, then kiss both their foreheads.

"Gross," Motor mutters with a goofy smile.

Mouse tugs on my arm. "You mean all five of us. Want to see what I brought?"

Before I can answer, he waves across the cafeteria at a cabinet door that's slightly ajar. I'm about to ask what he's playing at when the cupboard pops open and the little male with the big head tumbles out. A dozen pots and pans clatter out with him. When he gets to his feet, he throws his arms wide.

"Ta-da. It's me!"

"Glori, this is Hercules," Mouse shouts over the voice, then in a rush adds, "You said whatever I brought had to travel well. Hercules travels super well. Can she come?"

"Well, *he* certainly isn't staying here."

Mouse shouts, "She said you can come!"

"LOCKDOWN. LOCKDOWN. LOCKDOWN."

"Now can we please get the bump out of here?" Sway yells.

"We can't yet," I holler back. "We're not all here."

"You mean there's more?" Sway asks.

I nod because sometimes you *can* protect everyone. It just takes a little more work. I look to Motor. His brow is furrowed. He pushes up his glasses. Or at least I hoped you could protect everyone.

"Duh. There's everybody."

60

Breaker's plan before the guards electrocuted me and then my grand drugged me into a brief comatose state was simple. Keep quiet. Rescue my brother and Sway. Then leave. My variation went something like this: Keep quiet. Rescue my brother and Sway and *everyone else*. Then leave. Because every time I considered what was at stake, it wasn't a question of Mouse's or Sway's or Motor's life. It was a question of our very humanity. And what it would mean about mine and any future I might make, if I saved only the ones I love and left everyone else to suffer. It was the same choice all of our elders had. Male versus fee.

For me it was easy. I chose both.

So I did dispose of Motor. I disposed of him to spread the word that we were *all* leaving. If we could sneak out four of us, why couldn't we sneak out just under a hundred? By the time the guards and Doctor woke up and realized everyone was gone, we'd be miles away.

"Except," Motor says as we tell Sway all this on the stairs up to the top floor, "Glori got fried in the neck and never came back. So, when I got to the cafeteria, Breaker and I decided to improvise. Well, first Breaker threatened to murder me if I was lying. Then we improvised."

We stop when we can climb no higher. I briefly wonder if they at least started building the swimming pool on this floor. I take a deep breath as Motor pushes through the stairwell door. On the other side is a massive, cavernous space of concrete floors and steel beams. Since the Butler hadn't been installed on this level, I can still hear the lockdown alarm, but it is finally—*finally*—quieter.

"Whoa," Sway says softly, and laughs, awed.

I know the feeling. I take his hand. Males of every age group are sitting on the ground, hugging their knees and holding various trinkets they intend to take with them. Board games. Extra clothes. Books. A few Sixteens rush to their feet when they notice us, wielding knives the cafeteria workers used to cut meal. A murmur that is only my name goes through the crowd. As I look around at all the faces, I feel a tremendous sense of panic. What am I expecting these males to do now? Grand was right. There are far worse places than this out there. What could I offer them?

"Sway, what have I done?" I ask.

"LOCKDOWN. LOCKDOWN. LOCKDOWN."

"You gave them the power to make their own choices."

Breaker comes forward from off to my left. He wears the faintest of grins.

"You ain't been murdered yet, Walk-In. That makes me . . . glad."

"Likewise, Breaker. Were the guards a problem?"

"Turns out," Breaker says with a cough, "there's a lot more of us than there are them."

He gestures to a corner where the guard I saw outside the Littles' room is sitting cross-legged with his arms tied behind him. The males used old sweat suits to do it. Though, telling from the fierceness of his glare, I'm quite certain he's a she. She must be the geneticist who teamed up with Doctor. Honor. Such a very fee name.

"You're too late," Honor calls out. "You think you're saving them, but you aren't. She has a different plan and she won't be happy when she finds out about this."

"Yeah, well, plans change," I call back, then ask Breaker, "And the rest of the guards?"

"Oh," Breaker says. "They're all kinda, like, dead."

61

The Sixteens and Fifteens each take one of the Littles. Sway takes Hercules. I pick up Mouse and hold Motor's hand. No one objects that they are too big for this kind of treatment. Mouse sucks on his thumb. Moving like Reason's pack of dogs, none of us more than an arm's length apart, we take the stairs down to the first floor. Breaker tells us how Maximum found one of the guards dead in the hallway to the yard, covered in red sores.

"That must have been what they were vaccinating against," I say.

I'm suddenly glad Mouse convinced a Sixteen to give a shot to Hercules and wonder why my grand decided not to vaccinate the other Littles. I think of Liyan's words again, how first and foremost Grand was a scientist. Maybe that made her callous and narrow, but not cruel. She wouldn't simply let little males die if she could prevent it. But while I'm still naive enough to think this, I'm not dumb enough to say it out loud.

What I do say—blurt, really—is: "Doctor is sick, too."

Fast as his name's out of my mouth, the emergency system shuts off.

The halls are now pristinely, anticipatorily silent. I immediately prefer the noise.

"Thank heavens," Sway says, tapping a beat out on Hercules's back. "I'll be humming that sucker for weeks. Lockdown. Lockdown. Lockdown."

As dozens of males make a shushing sound, the wall flickers and Doctor is alongside us.

This is no prerecorded message.

"Children, what do you think you're doing?"

"It's only a screen," I whisper, hoisting Mouse and pulling Motor in tight to my side. "Let's go, everyone."

The males don't move. Doctor walks up and down the hall so they all can see him.

"You don't have to listen to him," I murmur, only to think, Bump that. Then I'm shouting. "He's not even there. You don't have to be quiet anymore. Come on, let me hear it."

"Woo," Breaker says mildly. His voice barely above a whisper.

A short male with dimples tries one next, a little louder. "Woot."

"Woo-hoo," Motor says, and then shouts it. "Wooo-hooo."

And then everyone does. We're jumping and shouting and running and woo-hooing. Doctor follows along next to us, but we don't pay him any mind. Although I imagine he'll be dead soon anyway, whatever power he had over the boys is now gone. We don't quiet down until we get to the Fortress's lobby, where, as one, we skirt the slumped-over, diseased body of the gray reception male that's next to the dais.

"I believe he's dead," Breaker says.

"Excellent analysis, Sherlock," Sway replies.

Before I can think twice about it, I hand Mouse to Motor, then hurry to the gray male and pocket his red glasses. Since old habits die hard, I also pat him down and am instantly rewarded for my scavenging when I find a portable in his inner breast pocket. I toss it to Sway. He immediately sends a series of PTTs. When I rejoin the males by the blast door, Mouse reaches for me. Kissing his hot little head, I take him back, handing off my keycard to Motor in return.

"Motor," I say loudly. "You have saved every male in here. You are a true hero. So will you please do us the honor of letting us escape?"

He rolls his eyes and mutters under his breath, "Oversell it, why don't you?"

But then he grins and slaps the keycard against the blast door's scanner. "Let's get the bump out of here."

With a *whoosh* of air that makes everyone hop back, the blast doors fly up. The reinforced steel exterior door pops ajar as well. I kick it open.

Motor's nostrils flare.

"It smells, Glori." He pushes the door open wider and steps outside. "It smells like smells. And it's so cold."

The night sky is a deep black. There is the monster truck with enormous tires smashed into the front of the building along with fifty other crashed cars. A cold mist hangs in the air as a light freezing drizzle begins to fall. *This.* This is Motor's first view of the world.

"It's nothing like the yard," he says, pushing up his glasses.

Then he holds his hands out and throws his head back and laughs. Ever so slowly he spins in the cold, wet air. Sway and I put the boys down as the other males rush out around us. And then we, too, stand there arms out, letting the rain splash our faces. Hercules and Mouse mimic us, only they flap their arms like wild, clumsy birds. My eyes find Breaker. His head is thrown back as well, but his eyes are closed and he is smiling.

Suddenly, there is the squealing of tires, bright lights, and a very loud car horn. A sleek black SUV drives at us full speed, then drifts and arcs to a perfect stop not a body's length away.

The passenger-side window rolls down and a finely dressed figure with a Majesterial horn hanging around his neck leans out. Half his head is now dyed the palest of pinks, the other half kept naturally black.

"Don't think because I'm happy you're alive," he calls out, "I'll overlook what you have done to your hair. That is not a Comma-sanctioned haircut."

"Is Comma always your backup plan?" I ask Sway.

"I mean, I don't have that many friends." He looks around at all the new males. "Though I guess the number's growing."

We run to the SUV. I hug Comma so hard, I nearly pull him out of the car.

"You actually did it," he says, affectionately patting my cheek when I release him. "You marvelous boy. No, plural. All you marvelous boys *did* it."

I feel a tug on my sleeve. Half the males have come over to ogle the car.

"Is this a Rinspeed SUV Aqua?" Motor asks with awe.

"How do you know what a Rinspeed is but not real food?" I ask.

"'Cause meals can't drive underwater. Duh."

"I have never seen nothing more beautiful," Hercules whispers, stroking the fender.

As Sway and Comma lock in a tight embrace, the driver pulls himself out his window and sits on the car door, looking over the hood at us. He's wearing driving goggles that he now pushes up onto his forehead. They do little to hold back his wild curls.

"When you said you'd wait for us at Rugged's," Sway calls out, "I didn't think you meant in the Rinspeed, Reason."

"It's the end times, bruth." Reason laughs, pausing to high-five some of the younger males. "Of course we brought the Rinspeed."

"Comma, your old man . . ." Sway says.

He nods. "I know. I'm okay. I'm mean, I'm very much one hundred percent *not* okay. But Reason and I laid him to rest, and Rugged did say every day was a gift that might have to be returned at any minute. I just..."

As Comma chokes up, I reach out and take his hand. He squeezes it and bites his lip. There will be tears for his dad, but not here or now. Reason meets my eyes over the hood.

"How's my puppy?" I ask.

"Happy to see you alive," he replies, then blushes.

"It's still *my* puppy," Sway says, exasperated, as Comma looks at the three of us.

"Well, this is very *Unicorn Warrior* season four," he says.

After a hefty throat clearing, Reason tells us that there's room for all the males in the apartments above Euphoria. Except the Rinspeed only seats six. I look at all the cars that line the corpse road. It's not like we're short on transportation. Only drivers. But then Breaker and Maximum tentatively shuffle up to our group, like they hate to interrupt. Comma curses under his breath when he sees Maximum's facial burns.

"Don't worry, dolly," he says. "Paisley goes with everything. We'll make it work."

"Okay," Maximum whispers. "Thanks."

"Walk-In," Breaker says, "we've had numerous lessons on the mechanics of operating and repairing vehicles. You lead and we'll follow. Kinda, like, to the ends of the earth."

"Wait," Sway says. "Who's this guy again?"

"Good," Reason says. "Let's get a move on. If Chia's mood is any indication, I have a feeling World War Four is about to go down. I'd like to be safely inside when it does."

62

In the rearview mirror, a caravan of ten cars snakes behind us. Each filled with males and Littles. It only took us a few short minutes to find enough working cars for Breaker and his crew to drive. Then, after doing a three-point turn that crashed him into an equal number of stranded cars, Breaker pulled alongside us, the slight raise of his lips equivalent to a mile-wide grin. The other Sixteens only too happily followed suit.

Inside the Rinspeed, everyone gets caught up just as quick. Matricula is working with the mob. She has control of the labs. The Fortress, too. Thanks to Rage's suggestion, the Fortress is now a farm for the mob. The mayor is about to be given an ultimatum. And that's pretty much that.

Reason tells us that late last night Chia received a PTT telling him to meet Matricula here. That she wanted to talk. But only now do I realize I never asked my grand *how* she intended to get all the males to leave. Just as Chia didn't know how to get fees to his side, what threat or offer could she possibly make to have him relinquish an entire city?

"Maybe she'll offer him the fees in the lab," Sway says when I bring this up.

Comma snorts. "Did they lobotomize you in there? This is Queen Bee Matricula Bumping Rhodes we're talking about. She does not sacrifice her drones."

"It doesn't matter what the offer is," Reason says. "Chia's bringing full forces. Matricula doesn't stand a chance."

Sharply, I say, "I think it's time you stop underestimating us. Stop underestimating her."

The car falls silent.

Once we're out of the golf-course grasses, Reason detours around the corpse-road cars by slowly driving on the old suburban sidewalks. As Comma and Sway quietly discuss the repairs that need to be made to the steam station thanks to Rage's attack, Motor stares out the window, a hint of a smile gracing his sour features. Hercules is passed out on Comma's shoulder, breathing so heavily it's like he's trying to blow up a balloon. Mouse is curled in my lap, his eyes burdened with sleep. He reaches up and plays with my paperclip necklace.

"I need more clips," he murmurs. "Our family got bigger."

"We can get them." I kiss his forehead. "Mouser, I'm sorry no one was ever very nice to you at home. I should have done more about it. Years ago."

"It's okay." He yawns. "I know they loved me. Grand told me so every night."

"What? When?"

"Every night," he says, like I didn't hear him the first time. "After she finished reading to us, she would tuck us in, then kiss each of our heads, and tell us she loved us."

I shift him so I can see him better. "When did she read to us?"

"Every night," he says again with even more emphasis. "She didn't if she thought we were awake. That's why I always pretended to be sleeping. I thought you were, too. I didn't think anyone snored that loud for real."

I tickle him. The last few years, Grand rarely came home before Two Five went to bed. I knew it was to avoid him, but maybe it wasn't for the reasons I thought.

Suddenly, Reason curses.

Sway says, "Kill the lights, Rea."

Motor leans forward, peers through the front windshield, and says, "Is it too late to decide I wanna stay at the Fortress?"

Soldiers in mismatched uniforms are working to move seven huge transports into position. Except, unlike the transports at the art museum, these aren't gangly or hodgepodged together. In fact, as the soldiers park horizontally across the road, the transports gleam as if they're brand-new. Reason puts the Rinspeed into park.

"Those are safety officer uniforms," I say. "Fees."

"Where the bump did Matricula get tanks and Humvees from?" Reason asks.

"What are we looking at?" Comma asks, squinting.

"Really, Com?" Sway grunts. "You're too vain to wear your glasses even for this?"

"Oh!" I pass over the red eyeglasses I swiped off the gray male.

Comma flips down the mirror on the visor. "Now, *these* are cute. And a bit strong. But oh my Gorges of Great Yonder, look at all those fees. I didn't know y'all liked getting so much ink."

I peer through the windshield. The SO soldiers are wearing the riot gear that our mercenary Niraasha scavenged years back on one of her far-roaming missions. None of the outfits match and some of the officers aren't wearing full suits of the gear at all. Just a chest plate or helmet. It's these fees I focus on, because Comma's right. All their visible skin is covered in tattoos. I look to the others in the riot gear. A few of their faces are badly scarred.

"Actually, maybe those aren't fees," I say.

Of course, Grand wouldn't put fees in harm's way, but she would borrow their uniforms. She brought the mob to fight alongside her instead. Or rather, behind her. Because there, past the Humvees and ahead of the group by about ten feet, is my Grand Mati. She's wearing the same protective riot gear as the rest of them, yet a luxurious black cloak swirls down to her feet. In her right hand is her electric cattle prod. She no longer looks soft and comforting like she did a few hours ago. This Matricula Rhodes is prepared for war.

"Who is that marvelous fee?" Comma whispers.

Craning his neck, Mouse says, "Oh, that's my grand, Matricula."

"Grand Matricula?" Comma swivels in his seat and glares at me. "Tell me that's not the same thing as Grand Mati?"

I nod. "Matricula Rhodes is our grandmother. I didn't tell you before because I thought you two would sell me out if you knew who I was."

"Why?" Motor asks. "How much are you worth?"

"Glori, she didn't bring enough people," Reason says. "Chia has more soldiers at his poker night. Where's all the mob's guns?"

"Grand hates guns."

Though half the mobsters masquerading as fees are holding Tasers, the rest have knives, bats, and bricks. Despite the fancy vehicles, this is a cobbled-together army in borrowed clothes with homemade weapons. The mercenaries aren't even here. It makes me wonder if Grand was genuinely shocked that Rauha was murdered or if she was simply shocked I'd found out, because I can't believe, even despite all the evidence in front of me—*they aren't here*—that the mercenaries would ever go against my grand.

"Then why not at least take on Chia at the Fortress?" Sway asks.

"With what?" Comma asks. "Other than those tanks, Matricula

clearly has no weapons. Chia has my dad's entire arsenal. It *has* to be close combat. Otherwise he'd starve her out."

"But why here?" I ask. "She must have wanted it to be here."

When Sway and I walked from Rugged's, we wondered why no one had moved these cars. Even for the simple sake of receiving deliveries, a car-free road would have been so much easier. My gaze sweeps the road again. All the cars have four or more bodies in them.

"A transport could never get through," Sway says.

"And anything electric would never hold a charge this long," Reason adds. "We swapped out batteries for the Rinspeed at Rugged's."

"Um, you guys..." Comma says.

"She's making them walk," I say, unable to hide my pride. "From the last transport stop, that was almost three miles. They'll be exhausted when they get here."

"Guys!" Comma adjusts his glasses, then taps on the window. "That's Fuego."

We all look out the rain-speckled side windows. There are males sneaking past the Rinspeed through the front lawns and backyards of the houses next to us. They're wearing patrol uniforms. Comma points at a scrawny boy with an acne flare-up on his cheek who's bringing up the rear. Matricula set up a roadblock facing west, but Chia's forces snuck around and are coming in from the east, from behind them. Matricula has twenty-five soldiers and a few tanks. But Chia has hundreds of soldiers. Their uniforms are all freshly pressed. Even more impressive, they all have guns. Every single one.

"It's going to be a slaughter," Reason murmurs.

But I refuse to underestimate my grand again.

"I don't think it's the fees we should be worried about."

63

When the last patrol soldier passes us, the males and I slip out of the Rinspeed and creep forward into the encroaching dawn. Gesturing for Breaker and the other males to stay in their cars, we leave Hercules sleeping on the seat because he's still dead with exhaustion. The rest of us crouch by a van that's crashed into a lamppost. It's about a hundred feet from Matricula. Just as we lie on our bellies, there comes the sound of over a hundred guns being clicked into kill mode.

Through the misty rain, Chia emerges from the backyard of the house right next to where Matricula is standing. He's wearing dented body armor and a mangy fur coat. A fat cigar juts out of his mouth. If Matricula is surprised to see him, she doesn't show it. Instead she holds her arms open, welcoming, as if she's offering his entire army a hug.

"Chia, you got fat," she says.

"You try to manage a city of beasts with a trim physique."

Grand lets out a bark of laughter. "I take it you're here to agree to my terms?"

"That's the funny thing I've been trying to tell you. Turns out, none of my constituents want to move to Hamburg. They don't care so much that it's attached to Buffalo's power grid or still has scavengeable goods, as you so kindly pointed out. See, they never did finish building that skyway connector over to the city. The commute would be a nightmare."

"Except that is the whole point," Grand says. "You won't be coming back."

Chia inhales on his cigar. Holds it.

"I think we'll pass. Are *you* here to agree to *my* terms? 'Cause it seems to me you literally brought knives to a gunfight. I thought fees were tough nowadays, Matricula. Aren't you all trained in some kind of chewed-wings technique?"

"It's pronounced *wing chung*."

He tilts back his head, exhales smoke.

"My mistake. I didn't kill those fees on the island, Mati."

"Do you mean this past week or seventeen years ago, Bear?"

"Bear." Chia laughs. "I haven't heard that name in years. But yes. Both. Either. Look, I don't want a war, but I was told you're using the labs again..."

"That would be me," Reason whispers. "Sorry."

"...making babies behind my back, cutting me out. You're lucky I'm being gracious enough to meet you. But the divide ends here. Tonight. Come on, Mati, aren't you tired of having no one to help you open jars? You have my word. Every fee that comes over will be safe."

My grand smiles tightly. "We learned the turn-over-and-tap-on-the-counter technique years ago, Bear. But I extend the same offer to you. Move to Hamburg. Start over. In time, I will bring you children. You can make good lives out there. I promise I'll keep you safe."

"From what? Your angry fees with bricks?"

"Silly boy. These are not fees." She gestures to the mob males in SO uniforms. "*These* are fees."

The doors of the Humvees open. Out of each one steps a mercenary in red.

"Say hello to Misère, Niraasha, Itami, Muerte, and Annihilation."

"Ohh." Sway pats my shoulder. "*Ann*—now that makes sense."

Misery. Despair. Pain. Death. Ann.

At her words, the mercenaries all go into their battle stances. Brass knuckles fully on display, Misère twirls her baseball bat with the embedded nails in a figure eight. Niraasha hefts her battle-ax, executioner-style. Muerte, arrow nocked, stands perfectly straight and then draws her bow and leans back in a ready-aim-fire crouch. Itami twirls her double blades in the air, then lunges to the side, holding one blade in front of her and the other above her head. And Ann? She simply stands there, tapping her lead pipe in her hand, shifting from foot to foot in anticipation. She begins her fights sprinting.

It is a terrifying, dreadful sight. Instantly, my reservations about their loyalty vanish. I am utterly relieved to see them. Never in my life have I been so proud to be fee.

"Glori," Motor says, "remember that thing I said about Buttercup? I've changed my mind. I want to be one of those when I grow up."

Mouse shakes my arm.

"Hang on, buddy. I'm listening."

I count off the patrol soldiers. Even with the mob behind them, the mercenaries would still need to take on roughly twenty males apiece to make this an equal fight. That could be doable. Just. If the males didn't have so many guns.

Chia raises an eyebrow, then laughs. "Girls in leotards?"

Suddenly, a faint cough comes from inside the van we're hiding under.

"Sway, weren't all these cars empty when we walked in?" I ask.

"Yeah. Not the ones far out, but all these that were close to the Fortress..."

Matricula whistles, and as one, all the doors of every car for a quarter mile swing open. Mob members pour out, at least four per car. A few of the mayor's soldiers lower their guns and curse. A handful moves in tighter around Chia. And, as he continues to puff on his cigar, I have to give the mayor credit. It can't be easy staying calm in front of such a terrifying sight.

But his cool burns off when Rage steps out from a Humvee and hands Matricula a cage with a rat in it.

"Thank you, Kiku," she says.

Sway, Reason, Comma, and I all whisper, *"Kiku?"*

"You son of a bitch," Chia grunts.

"Right now," Matricula says evenly, "the rest of Rage's crew is downtown with cages identical to these. If they open them, you will all be sick in a day. Dead in two. The virus is airborne and ravenous. If you come any closer right now, you will be in trouble. Of course we have plenty of effective antidote. Every fee was inoculated years ago. It's in our labs. But if you so much as look in the direction of Grand Island, we'll blow the bridge. And you will all die. If you do not all vacate the city in the next twenty-four hours, we release the rats and you all die. If you ever come back to the city without our permission... you get the picture. I suggest you start packing."

"Rage, bruth," Chia says. "I can give you whatever she's offering and more."

Rage simply smiles. "I think you had time enough for that, *bruth*."

Shrugging off his fur coat, Chia reaches behind him and yanks two pistols from holsters that are strapped across his back. His patrol soldiers follow suit and bring their guns up. They look lethal but also nervous and tired. Only adrenaline is keeping them fueled right now.

"This is your last chance, Chia." Matricula swings her cattle prod up. "Leave."

Mouse pats my arm again. "Glori, I don't feel so good."

Half paying attention, I put a hand to his forehead. He is teakettle hot.

"Mati, you know I can't do that," Chia says.

He's not laughing now. Half of Matricula's soldiers switch on stun guns. The dark street becomes aglow with their humming blue lights. Sway rolls up Mouse's sleeve. His little arm is covered in red splotches. My eyes meet Sway's and I can't help noticing, on the side of his face, three of the same marks.

"No," I say.

How could this be? Mouse said he, Hercules, and all the big boys at the Fortress got a shot. Yet the gray male and all the other guards were dead. I can hear that guard, Honor, saying we were too late. That *she* has a different plan. Did she mean my grand? What if the adult males were instructed to take the vaccine first? And what if the shot wasn't a vaccine, but the virus? My mind spins. Grand Mati said it would take two days for the virus to kill the males. How long would it take to devour a weaker, younger immune system? My males aren't sick. They're dying.

I clutch Mouse to me and run. Through the mob, around all the patrol soldiers.

Behind me Sway shouts, "Don't shoot. Don't shoot."

Until I am standing between Grand and Chia.

64

"**D**on't shoot," Sway wheezes, running up behind me, hands held aloft.

"Don't shoot," Reason says, running up as well. "Don't shoot."

"Stand down," Chia barks. "Reason? Sway? What's going on?"

"Glori?" Grand gasps. "What are you doing here? What's wrong with Twofer?"

As dispassionately as she's been playing this, I can't help noticing that for the first time in her life, she looks her age.

"He's sick, Grand. Mouse has the virus. You *gave him* the virus."

"I did no such thing. That's not possible. This"—she hefts the rat's cage—"is as close as the virus has even come to the Fortress."

Holding a hand out to Chia—*don't shoot*—she sets down the rat and comes toward me. When she gets a better look at Mouse, her face pales. Her shock doesn't make me feel any better. This wasn't intentional. Which means she has no backup plan for fixing it.

"You lying, cheating bitch," Chia growls. "You're 'going' to release a virus? Three of my best men are already dead from that."

Grand snarls back, "I swear to you, I didn't do this. I gave strict orders that the virus was not to be released without my word."

It's one of those moments where things could go one way. Where my Grand Mati could promise it wasn't her. That she had plans for world domination, but they didn't include murdering little boys. It could be where Chia admits that taking a blow to his ego and accepting defeat is better than losing more lives. Ever so briefly, I wonder if in the old world, when there were still plentiful goods and resources and life, if people back then took the time to listen, learn, and understand. Because they don't now.

For a single moment, it looks like things could go one way.

They quickly go another instead.

65

We are thirty feet apart, my grand and I, when a soldier in a sleek, skin-tight body suit steps forward from the platoon of mob behind her. Her suit looks like one of the mercenaries', only it's a pristine ivory and she's wearing a bulletproof vest over it. As Grand glares at Chia, the ivory soldier reaches behind her and draws a samurai sword from the sheath on her back—a proper katana, exactly like the one that hangs above our fireplace. Exactly like the one Liyan carries with her.

"No!" I shout.

I am fast, faster than any human I know. Handing Mouse off to Sway, I charge forward. I am twenty feet from my grand as an arrow flies from Muerte's bow and sinks into Chia's shoulder. He grunts in surprise. The cigar falls from his mouth. Muerte follows with another that hits his chest near this throat, right above his body armor.

Reason screams. Many are screaming now. One of them is me.

I am ten feet away—my hands outstretched—so close, but not close enough—as the ivory soldier drops to one knee and stabs my grand. Up beneath her protective armor, up through her rib cage. Grand looks down in surprise, not at her wound, but at the fee who made it. Then she crumples.

And everything is chaos.

66

As one voice, the mercenaries shout, "Attack!" and Chia's patrol opens fire. Everyone ducks. Abandoned car doors are thrown open as both sides take cover. The mob all carry pipes, Tasers, and homemade shivs. It's not a fair fight, but as is evident by the erratic spray of gunfire, Chia's soldiers will soon be out of bullets. When they are, it won't be long before the howling, shrieking mob falls on them. Or before the tanks start firing. The air is filled with smoke, hate, and death.

Reason and Comma run directly to Chia. But I only have eyes for the ivory soldier. I can't call her Liyan. Maybe because I can still hardly believe I just watched her murder my grand, but also because I won't be able to kill her if I think of her as the person who's been my surrogate mother all these years. And I do intend to kill her.

She is only a few yards away, and she's waiting for me. Sword drawn, she falls into a defensive crouch I'd admire, if I didn't so badly want her dead. I pull out Mama Bear.

"Glori, no!" Sway shouts. "Your grandma needs you. This is more important."

"Jackal," the ivory soldier shouts. "Take her down."

Jackal grins and nods but then is immediately overtaken by two patrol soldiers. I glance back: Mouse is kneeling by Grand, his hands lightly resting on her chest, shaking. When I look to the ivory soldier again, she is fleeing into the woods like a coward. All five mercenaries are fast on her heels. Itami snuck me packs of chalk and together we'd color over as much gray pavement as we could around the cul-de-sac. Muerte taught me how to use that chalk for hopscotch instead. Niraasha showed me how to walk on my hands. They'll never let the ivory soldier get away with this.

Moments later, all six of them fly from the woods on sleek motorcycles. My heart soars with gratitude, until I realize it isn't a pursuit. The mercenaries ride grouped around the ivory soldier in a protective blockade. Even though I knew they killed Rauha and lied about Twofer, the betrayal still takes my breath away.

I slide to my knees in the mud next to my grand. Sway is trying to stop the blood flow by pressing his sweatshirt to her gut. For half a heartbeat, I wonder if her injury is repairable. Maybe the sword missed all her major organs. But then we take off her body armor and see that my Grand Mati is soaked in red from her neck to her waist.

"Shui?" she asks, staring at Sway's necklace. "They told your mother you were dead. To make her more docile. She killed them and then came to us."

"You know her?" His eyes flick to me, then back to her.

"You look just like her."

"Who . . ." Sway says, but Grand's eyes shift to me.

I take one of her hands. She places the other against my cheek. One of Chia's soldiers stumbles past with a pipe sticking out of his chest.

"Gloria, my Glori, my Gloria. Did you know that I named you after one of the greatest fee crusaders in my lifetime?" Each word is a struggle. "I didn't release the virus."

"I know, Grand, but that's not important now. Where is the vaccine?"

"Our labs . . . on the island. There's plenty. Get Two Five home." Her eyes flick around the battlefield. "All of them."

She coughs. Blood flies from her mouth. She prepared us for everything except this. I've never even seen her sick. I don't know what to do. A tiny red bubble pops next to her mouth.

"I wanted to keep everyone safe." Her eyes shift to Mouse. She smiles. "Grand loves you . . . Mouse."

Tears stream down his face. His little lower lip quivers, then he inconsolably collapses over her. She rubs his back. I stroke the hair away from her face.

"Grand, I'm so sorry I left without talking to you about it first. I'm sorry you came here for me and now all this. It's all my fault. Please don't leave us." My voice rises into a wail. "I don't know what to do without you."

She squeezes my hand. "My special girl. You will be great."

She smiles, but then her expression turns panicked, her eyes distant. Sway's hands shake as he continues to try to stop the bleeding. We all knew death could happen at any moment. But she is not ready. Neither am I.

"Glori, look out for your mother. I never . . . I never . . ."

"I will, Grand," I promise. "I'll look out for everyone."

Then she is gone. Nothing more than another body. And there is no time for mourning her, or there will be others.

67

"**G**lori! A little help?"

I place Grand Mati's hands across her chest. Fifty feet away one of the same wolf-bear-tiger beasts from the train has cornered Comma. He is frantically waving his unicorn horn at it, trying to keep it at bay. Motor is behind him, pressed to a car. With all my might, I fling Mama Bear, then Slim. They both clip the beast's back thigh. It howls with pain and rage, then lunges past Comma and grabs Motor by the arm, shaking him like the easily won piece of meat that he is. Motor shrieks. Comma stabs at the creature with the horn. I'm halfway to them when two shots ring out and strike the beast in the head. It drops on top of Motor, dead.

"Get it off me," Motor screams. "Get it off me. I'm covered in brains!"

"Could be worse, you could be covered in your own dead."

Behind me, Fuego is holding a smoking shotgun. He is scrawnier than Sway with a ratlike countenance and a thin line of hair above his lip that looks drawn on.

"Fuego!" Comma effuses. "You saved my life."

"Yeah, well." Fuego kicks his chin up with a nod. "That's how I do."

I run to Motor and push the beast off him.

"I'm not sure I like outside life so far, Glori," he whimpers.

I push up his sleeve. The bite wounds are superficial. The virus sores are not.

"Call me later?" Comma calls after Fuego.

"I'll probably be busy," Fuego shouts, then he takes off, fleeing into the woods.

"Burned again," Comma says as one of the sleek Humvees explodes with patrol grenades.

It drops us all to our knees. The sky is lit with flames and smoke. The wet dead trees hiss and smolder as they try to catch fire. Still the sky spits rain at us.

"Glori," Sway yells. Mouse's arms wrap his neck like a too-tight scarf. "We have to go."

"Where's Reason?"

We spot him at the same time. Reason has dragged Chia alongside one of the tanks. He is bent over him, sobbing. Which means he doesn't see Jackal coming up behind him.

"Sway, take the boys to the car." I hand Motor off to Comma. "Comma, message everyone you know and tell them to get to the bridge. I've got this. Sway, now!"

I skid to a stop in the mud next to Reason and block Jackal. He just has time to grin at me before he is tackled from the side by Breaker. But Jackal has a knife. He slashes at Breaker. And then a shadow falls on the group. Rage. He grabs Jackal by the back of his neck. Next second, he violently twists his head, then drops his limp body to the ground.

"Rest in peace," Rage says. "Uragirimono."

Traitor.

Breaker and I stare at the body, stunned.

"Whose side are you on, Rage?" I ask as I pull Reason to his feet.

"Matricula was my shugo tenshi," Rage replies. *Guardian angel.* "She saved me from the streets when she accepted me at the Fortress. I have never meant you harm. We have been betrayed, too. Yesterday morning, the mercenaries dispensed a 'vaccine' in the tunnels. Every mob member was given a shot. But I do not think it was vaccine."

He rolls up his sleeve. His arm is peppered with sores. I was right. All the males at the Fortress were injected with the live virus. Mouse, only because he convinced them to. Hercules, as well. Why they didn't "vaccinate" the other Littles, I don't know. Maybe with their young immune systems they wouldn't last long anyway. Maybe the ivory soldier didn't want to waste any doses.

"I can get the actual vaccine," I say. "It's on the island. The fees won't blow the bridge if it's me. Meet us at the base of the bridge with as many males as you can bring."

I grab Rage's arm. My hand looks tiny on it. He flinches at the contact. "Bring mob *and* norm males."

He nods curtly. Then, at the top of his lungs, shouts, "Yameru!"

Every mob arm raised in combat falls. Weapons are dropped. I think about what they taught the males at the Fortress. *We do as we're told. Always. Without question.* I try to rouse Reason to tell him to call off Chia's men, but it's clear there are very few left standing and that Reason is not capable of command right now. Rage moves off to help a mobster who is being punched in the face by a patrol soldier.

The Rinspeed roars to a stop alongside us. Sway looks tiny in the driver's seat.

"Breaker," I say, "get everyone into those Humvees. Then follow Rage back to the city."

He nods once, the way he does, then is gone.

"Your grandma sure had all her bases covered," Reason spits as I help him into the backseat of the Rinspeed. Comma cradles Hercules. It's clear now he isn't sleeping. He's unconscious. His entire torso is covered in spots. I could remind Reason that my grandma was just murdered by her best friend. That this wasn't her. But now isn't the time for debate.

"Sway, drive to the bridge like our lives depend on it."

"Yeah," Motor says, a smattering of red spots on his cheek. "'Cause they do. Duh."

68

Buffalo is burning.

Despite the numerous hours it took us to get to the Fortress in the transport, it takes Sway twenty-five minutes to get back to the city in the Rinspeed. I guess that's what a hundred and twenty miles an hour gets you. Breaker and the Fortress males keep up in the Humvees behind us, only occasionally crashing into abandoned cars. But we still aren't fast enough. Everywhere on the downtown streets, norm males lie dead. As we drove, Comma's portable exploded with reports from his friends in the city. Apparently, fees weren't the only ones with duplicitous traitors in their ranks. Jackal's resentment toward the mayor ran deep, and he convinced some of his brethren that the norms moving to Hamburg, as Rage insisted they would, wasn't nearly enough retribution for driving the mobsters underground all these years. A group of his like-minded contingent was now on a killing spree, attacking every norm they met.

It's what our teachers always warned could happen to us.

Occupation followed by slaughter.

At Reason's insistence, we stop at Euphoria to collect more males.

Glancing at Hercules, I start to protest, but Sway murmurs that it's on the way. The Rinspeed's tires skid to a stop on the slush out front. The entry windows are all shattered. Reason's posters lie scattered and sopping on the sidewalk. Wreckage is sitting on the front steps. Eugene the hologram sits beside him. Wreckage's hand is on his belly. Dark red blood blooms beneath it.

"We don't have much time," I say as Sway throws the car in park.

Mouse is holding Hercules's hand, telling him about what bread tastes like. Motor is humming quietly to himself.

"Ah, hey, Sway. Hey, Reason. Things are crazy." Wreckage takes his hand away from his shirt. It's covered in blood. "I've been shot."

"We can't leave him like this," Sway says.

Behind us, a block away, there is a massive explosion. Ash falls like snow. Reason's portable crackles. "They've breached the power plant." Comma's, too. "City Hall is down." As soon as one message ends, another comes through. "They've taken over the farms."

"They're in my building."

One is just screams.

"Can I be of assistance?" Breaker stands over Wreckage.

"Not unless you have a medic with you," Sway snaps.

Breaker pivots and starts murmuring to the male next to him.

"Breaker!" I holler. "It's okay to use your outside voice now."

A faint light comes to his expression, and then he's shouting, "Fuerza! Over here."

A Sixteen comes running. He pushes Sway aside, takes out a cauterizing gun and bandages from his pack. He kneels next to Wreckage, speaking to him in his calm, flat voice.

"Where'd Reason go?" I ask.

"There." Mouse points.

An extended-cab pickup truck on swamp tires with enormous matte-black rims drives out the front of Euphoria. The inside is packed with dazed-looking males. More fill the flatbed along with an army of dogs. Reason pulls up next to us, Mastodon wedged onto the seat beside him, Carrot in his lap. Reason's moonlit eyes are numb, steely. I see now how fees have held their grudges for the last seventeen years. I can't see Reason ever forgiving us.

Yet he leans across the passenger seat, meets my eyes, and calls out, "Same team?"

"Same team," I confirm.

And then he hands down a familiar black fuzz ball with white paws. I kiss its head and pass it back to Mouse.

"Look, Mouser. A puppy for you to take care of."

"Like from the labs," he says weakly.

I don't know when he was taken to the labs without my awareness, but he's right. I knew I'd been around dogs before. Only they weren't dogs. They were the wolf-bear-tiger creatures. What couldn't CRISPR do?

The puppy licks his face. Mouse smiles. "Let's call him Lucky."

"Fine." Sway sighs. "It's *his* puppy."

As Sway maneuvers the Rinspeed back out into the streets, bodies as numerous as potholes, I notice the red dots are now peppering his neck and arm.

"We're going into this fight empty-handed," Motor says. "You know that, right? We have a few dogs. They have those red assassins."

"Yeah," Sway says. "But we have something even more lethal. We have Glori."

"Oh, great." Motor makes a fart sound. "Then we're definitely gonna lose."

69

In the mist and rain, standing in the slush of the previous day's snow-storm, a lone red figure waits for us in the middle of the bridge. A battle-ax is casually slung over her shoulder.

"Which one is that?" Comma asks.

"Niraasha," I say.

"Despair," Mouse adds, Lucky teething on his finger. "Niraasha's battle card nickname is the Farmer, because she harvests bodies with her battle-ax like farmers harvest wheat. She has high endurance and strength, but her kill score is only fifty percent of the others."

"Scythe," Comma murmurs, Hercules passed out on his shoulder. If Comma didn't have the virus before, he does now. "Farmers use scythes, not battle-axes, you silly goits."

"Battle cards?" Motor looks at Mouse blankly. "You made game cards for them?"

Mouse nods. "Like Pokémon but bloodier."

Two twin lane truss arch bridges used to span the Niagara River between Grand Island and the mainland, but fees blew one of them when they originally fled. Now they are prepared to blow the other. Corded along the rails of the bridge are circuits that attach to wires that disappear underneath the beams, where, I'm assuming, they meet some form of explosive. Behind Niraasha metal parking spikes lie across both lanes of the bridge.

Fees had backup plans that went three backup plans deep. If the males had rallied before the virus could take effect, we'd simply have blown the bridge. The males would be too sick to find boats and battle the river current. Which meant the fees could safely wait it out on Grand Island until all the males were dead, then cross at their leisure to take the city back. I wonder how many other fees knew about this plan. I wondered if they knew the ivory soldier had prematurely put it into effect. Or if they had known this was the actual plan all along. If they had been all right with it.

A sharp pain cuts through my chest when I realize I'll never be able to ask my grand for her version of the story. And suddenly, I am furious.

Reason pulls alongside us. I hear him tell the males in the truck to wait. His pack does not. They immediately jump down from the truck bed and fan out in front of our vehicles in a perfect, growling line. Sway reaches down by my feet and hands me a Taser.

"I took this from the battle," he says.

I roll down my window and chuck it as far as I can. It sails over the bridge railing into the water below.

"Sorry. I've seen enough of those to last me a lifetime. Besides, I won't need the help."

I get out of the car. For better mobility, I take off the bulky sweatshirt Grand left me. Now I'm only wearing my tight tank top and leggings. Motor climbs into the front seat.

"You all cross under the bridge in the Rinspeed," I say. "I'll meet you on the other side."

"No," Motor says.

Sway nods. "We agreed never to separate. You come with us."

"If I do, Niraasha will be waiting for us when we get there. And we're not separating. We're taking different routes to the same location. Sway"—I beg him with my eyes; the males will die if he doesn't leave me— "what's the point of an underwater car if you don't break it in?"

Reason comes up next to me. "The pack and I will stay with Glori. We've got this."

Comma passes forward all of his rings. I start to protest—this is hardly the time for pretty—but he closes my hand around them.

"Slice that nag into ribbons."

"Go," I urge.

"Glori," Mouse whimpers from the backseat as Sway puts the car in reverse.

"It's okay, buddy. Niraasha and I are just going to talk."

I wave to them as they leave.

"We'd better survive this," Reason says, taking the cap off his crutch, revealing the spike beneath. "I really want to ride underwater in that car."

I let out a bark of laughter. Then bounce a little on my toes. Wobble my head side to side to loosen it up. Mastodon is between me and Reason as we walk forward to meet Niraasha. We both put a hand on his head. It calms me.

"Hello, Auntie," I call out as I put on Comma's rings. "I need to get through here. The males are sick, and I need to access our labs to cure them. Whatever happened to make you turn against my grand..." I choke on my words. "You've always protected me. You've always been my friend."

I think of Niraasha sprawled on my bedroom floor building paper castles. Singing me pre-Night pop songs. Teaching me how to dance.

It wasn't only my Grand Mati who was double-crossed.

"Unfortunately, little bee," Niraasha calls, "this is bigger than our friendship. And it has been a long time since I served your grandmother. I can't let you cross."

I nod, expecting as much. "That's too bad, because I wasn't asking for permission."

My hand goes to my hip and comes up empty. Slim is missing. Waste. She *and* Mama Bear are both back in the woods, probably still thigh-deep in that wolf-bear-tiger's leg. I pull out Baby Bear.

Niraasha smiles. "Glori, I trained you," she says. "We both know you won't win."

She did train me, but so did Itami with her knives and Misère and Ann with their incredible hand-to-hand. Muerte with her bow. And even Liyan with all my daily wing chung lessons. Grand made sure of it. Thanks to her, I am a very diversified fighter and I have one great advantage. I know everyone's weaknesses.

"Glori," Reason says quietly. "I can send the pack."

I shake my head. I don't want them getting hurt.

"Don't worry, bruth," I say. "I have no intention of losing."

And then I run at Niraasha full tilt.

70

Niraasha is a beautiful fighter. On my approach, she swings the ax in a slow, almost lazy circle over her head, then brings it down with breathtaking quickness. I barely roll under it before it is grazing the ground near my feet. I'm scarcely back up, and she is swinging again. This time I spin away, but it catches me across the back. I feel my skin open up. Right below my shoulder blades. Reason shouts in concern. I can tell from her eyes that underneath her balaclava, Niraasha is smiling.

"You're too late, little bee," she says as we circle each other. She isn't even breathing heavy. I can't say the same. "The ivory mercenary is just getting started. And she'll never stand down."

"Then I guess she'll be falling down."

"Nice," Reason says.

Blood is soaking the back of my shirt. I feint in with Baby Bear. Choking up on her ax's handle, Niraasha swings. Maybe she's not winded, but there is no getting around how unwieldy her weapon is. The ax is too heavy to quickly parry.

Plus? She drops her guard when she swings.

I dodge her first swing, and this time I don't dance away but instead duck in close and stab Baby Bear into her thigh. As she cries out in pain, two-handed, I snap her right wrist. Her ax immediately falls from her grip. Even an elite mercenary assassin can't fight with a broken wrist.

Except that's not true.

Springing forward, she pulls up her balaclava and sinks her teeth into the flesh above my collarbone. I scream in pain even as I know I'm lucky. She was going for my throat.

"Attack," Reason shouts. "Attack."

The dogs lunge, snarling and yipping at her. Niraasha cries out, a chunk of my skin falling from her mouth. She tries to curl herself into a ball as the dogs rip at her. Red splatters the slushy snow.

"Stop!" I shriek.

"She was going to kill you," Reason shouts as the dogs continue to attack.

"Please stop them."

"Halt!"

Instantly, they stop. Sit. Lick their paws and one another's faces. I run to her. Help her sit up. Niraasha is shaking, her entire body a mess of puncture wounds and torn flesh. Yet I touch her cheek. The dogs have shredded her mask. But they did not do the majority of damage that is underneath. Niraasha's face is a mess of scars. Like someone took a sharp knife tip and carved lazy circles over all her features.

"What happened to you?"

"The beasts, you fool." She spits blood on the ground. "You'll be sorry for this."

I can't tell if she means because I hurt her or because I teamed up with the males. We drag her to the bridge rails, then bind her wrists with zip ties that Reason carries in his pack.

"Did you think this was all over nothing?" she shouts after us.

But I've already put her behind us.

With the dog pack swarming around us, Reason and I hop over the parking spikes. At the top of the bridge, we look back at the city. In the distance there is only smoke, but out of that snakes a line of cars. Rage, Breaker, and Comma did well. The males are on their way. When we get to the foot of the bridge on the fee side, Sway and the other males are waiting for us outside the Rinspeed. Sway is pacing. The other males don't have the energy for it.

They cheer when they see us. Motor and Mouse run forward and throws their arms around me.

"You should have seen her," Reason calls out as I pick up Mouse. "Glori was incredible."

"I know." Sway jogs up. "She's mesmerizing and terrifying in equal measure. Is that a bite mark?"

"We have a problem," Comma says. "The Rinspeed's battery died."

Suddenly, behind him, there are blue flashing lights. I squint. An ambulance is lurching toward us, as if whoever is driving is still learning the difference between the gas and brake. It stops ten feet from the Rinspeed. A fee hops out. She's brandishing her hatchet and a police baton. She is either the best thing I've seen in hours or the most traitorous.

It's Su. The daughter of the woman who killed Grand.

71

"**D**on't come any closer, Su," I shout.

"Glori, it's me," she says, stepping forward.

"How did you know we were here? Did the mercenaries send you?"

"*I* called her," Comma says.

"Grand was murdered. The fee who killed her used a katana. Our katana."

"Holy waste." Su stops walking. Her hatchet drops to the ground. "Glori, I didn't know."

"Where is Liyan?" I ask.

I remember Grand and Liyan cackling together when Su and I were younger. Putting on that old Celia Cruz CD while they cooked, dancing. Playing endless rounds of double solitaire. How Liyan protested when we moved to the cul-de-sac. How she protested when we decided to stay. And then how she kind of just gave up protesting. When was the last time I even heard her and Grand speak? Let alone sit out back gossiping over an evening tea?

"Su?" Wiggling out of my arms, Mouse runs to her. "It's me. I went to a Fortress. And Grand got . . . And now I have a puppy and a virus. And Glori says we're all gonna die."

Su puts a hand against his forehead and notices the dots. "He wasn't vaccinated?" she asks.

I remember Su staring at those rats in the lab. I thought she was horrified over the dead animals. But she wasn't seeing those rats. She was envisioning males. She knew about the virus.

"No," I say. "The opposite. He was injected with the virus, and you've known about this all along."

"I knew about the truce. And the virus. It was supposed to be a worst-case-scenario move. I knew about the labs." She nods. "I knew everything. Ma told me it all. She wanted to tell you, too. Except Grand wouldn't let her. But I didn't know they teamed up with the mob. And my mom never once said that she was plotting against Mati. She loved her."

Tugging Mouse by the hand, I start walking around her. Toward the labs. We've lost too much time already. The males silently follow behind me. Su's mom killed my grand.

There is no coming back from this.

"Wait," Su cries out. "I know where the vaccine is. I've seen where they keep it. Don't leave me here, Glori. Please. I can't lose all my family in one day."

Sway reaches out and takes my hand.

"This could be a trap," Reason says. "She could be trying to get us to lower our guard. Lead us exactly where the ivory soldier wants us to go."

Instinctively, I check my perimeters. All I see are tall grasses and trees and rain.

Sway squeezes my hand and says, "Grudges are what got us here in the first place. You can fight it out later. Right now, we need her."

"And we really need that ambulance," Comma adds.

I have told Su my every thought, every worry, every daydream for the entirety of our lives. Yet she knew about everything. *Everything.* And kept it from me.

"If I find out you're lying..." I say.

"I'm not," she says stonily.

"I can't promise you I'm not going to hurt your mom when I find her."

"You know I won't let that happen. All I ask is you at least hear her out."

We lay Hercules down on the gurney in the back of the ambulance. Saying he can't bear losing any more people he loves, Reason makes his pack stay with the Rinspeed, then scavenges in the ambulance for something to temporarily bind my back wound. My collarbone will have to wait until later. Sway sits up front with Su, Motor on his lap. I hold on to my Mouse. He holds on to Lucky. Because when Mouse asked if the puppy could stay with us, no one could bear telling him no right now.

"Besides," Comma says, stroking Hercules's forehead, "we literally need all the luck we can get."

"Everyone, buckle up," Su says from the driver's seat. "Next stop, the labs."

A whirring sound comes from the dashboard. The CD screen says it will be playing Track 1 of Classic Mix. Staccato drumbeats come out of the speakers. Then my girl Bee starts singing about girls. Girls running the world. Checking her mirrors one more time, Su flips on the ambulance lights and turns up the volume on the stereo.

"I feel like I've come home," Comma says.

And then Su floors it.

72

H ardy, cold-weather wildflowers pepper the road as we speed toward the labs on Grand Island Boulevard. The deep maroon-and-purple flowers were one of Matricula's first planting successes. It is little consolation that they are here and she is not. Benches are set out along the road next to bike-borrowing huts. Faint wonder etches Sway's expression as he looks out the window.

"It's so pretty here. And clean."

I never had anything to compare it to. Without all the vehicles, it's quieter, too. And it smells crisper. Already, I feel saner. Or at least, as much as circumstances allow.

When we come to the outlaying streets of the neighborhood, Su slows down. I see now what Sway meant about the world seeming fresh when seen through new eyes. Fees are talking over the fences of the houses directly across the street from stores that all have fresh coats of paint. Blue Bicycle. Grow Food. Mighty Taco. Despite all the windows being boarded up, you don't have to guess that this is where people live. It is full of life and energy, and it feels safe and, I imagine, exactly what neighborhoods felt like before Nuclear Night.

I've come home. Only maybe it isn't home anymore.

"Solely a suggestion," Comma says, "but perhaps it's better not to drive the route saturated with fees."

"Now, why didn't I think of that?" Su replies, checking her mirrors. "This is the only way, Shaka Blue."

Comma claps his hands. "A *Unicorn Warrior* reference *and* put-down? Color me Horned."

Su drives slowly as if that will call less attention to us. Up ahead, a fee is leaving the co-op, a canvas bag filled with her allotment of weekly groceries. When she sees us, she sets down the tote and takes a crowbar from it.

"Told you we weren't starving," I say to Sway.

The PTT network must have begun. The warning has gone out. Around and ahead of us, the street and sidewalk are filling with fees carrying homemade weapons. A car full of beasts has made it over. Wait until they see all the others waiting on the other side. Su rolls down her window.

"It's okay," she shouts. "It's okay."

Sway waves a white sock out his window. The fees fall in and walk alongside us. I know all these faces and yet I don't. These faces want to kill six of the eight of us.

"Maybe we should drive faster now," Reason says.

But Su keeps it steady—lurching yet steady—and we pass through the neighborhood unharmed. Su puts on her blinker. We make a right. She speeds up just as the sky ahead of us abruptly, drastically brightens.

"The lab's lights," Su says. "We're back on the power grid."

When the fees moved to Grand Island, they co-opted an old car dealership on Alvin Road that had a good number of solar generators. Normally, it was the best-lit spot on the island. But now it positively glows. Our own mini city. Suddenly, Su slams on the brakes.

"Geez, Drivers' Ed, learn your pedals," Sway snaps as he and Motor crash into the dashboard.

Unfazed, Su peers through the haze and curses. Ann stands in the middle of the road where Whitehaven meets the I-190. Behind her, about a half mile away, are the lights of the labs. She twirls her lead pipe in front of her, then behind, then tosses it above her head and catches it.

"Annihilation's battle card says she used to be a cheerleader," Mouse says. "In something called college, she became something called an Olympic Silver Medalist in karate. She has a one-hundred-percent kill rating."

"Come along, little one," Ann calls out. "Let's get this over with."

"And she's always been the chattiest," he finishes.

Ann taught me to do a double layout flip. She gave me fancy hair braids. (That Grand, without fail, took out later that same night.) Of all the mercenaries, she wore the only balaclava that showed her mouth. Tonight, as ever, her lips are decorated in bright red.

Su revs the engine. "I can try to run her over."

"Yes," Comma says. "Do that."

Mercenaries are holy. You didn't spar with them lightly, let alone threaten to kill them. I try not to be touched by the offer. I shake my head.

"No. One of you will only get hurt. Are there jumper cables in here?"

Su nods. "Under that bench seat."

Reason lifts the seat. They're sitting right on top, perfectly wrapped.

"Su, don't wait for us," I say. "Get them that antidote. Sway, you stay with Mouse. There's no one else I trust more with him. We'll be right behind you."

"Jumper cables?" Motor shouts as I hop out of the ambulance. "I mean, why not just attack her with a piece of string and some lint?"

Reason also hops out of the ambulance, spiked crutch in tow.

"Sorry, bruth," he says to me. "As far as I'm concerned, we're on a winning streak." As soon as we walk away from the ambulance he asks, "You sure this is a good idea? You're hurt and you look like hell."

Su drives the ambulance around us in a wide berth.

Ann is dancing in the road ahead of us. This is fun for her.

"Good," I say. "It'll give her even more confidence."

Because you know what Ann's weakness is?

She's used to winning.

73

Ann is even stronger and faster than I remember. Maybe because most of our lessons she spent lying on her back, with her feet kicked up on a porch rail or couch, telling me about her old karate wins and all the foods she most missed.

"I am telling you. Sponge candy? Would blow your mind."

I try to fight her with the cables first, using them as a makeshift lasso. But she literally skips away from them, darts in, and punches me in the chest. Using Misère's famous sidestep move, I whack her as hard as I can on the back of the neck. It momentarily jostles her equilibrium. It also pisses her off.

I don't even see the combination of kicks she uses next. I only know they bring me to my knees and give her enough time to step in and break my left arm. My ulna snapping sounds as loud as when Mouse and I jumped on tree branches to break them down for burning. My vision blurs and fills with sparkly lights, like I'm back in the mob's tunnel.

"That's for Niraasha," she whispers, hovering right over me. They must have had eyes on the bridge after all. But then her gaze softens and she whispers, "Your turn."

I hesitate only a half second before I bring my head up as hard as I can, right into her face. She takes a step back, her nose spewing blood. Her mouth missing teeth. Still she manages a grin before she blinks twice, then falls over like a downed tree. Completely knocked out. With shaking hands, Reason zip-ties her wrists.

"What just happened?" Reason asks.

"I think she let me win," I reply.

His eyes flick uncertainly to my arm. I hold it gingerly to my body. Even the bullet didn't hurt this bad.

"I mean, it had to be believable."

From the labs comes the sound of glass breaking; shouting. We run.

All the cars are still out front of the old dealership and have been for years. But now the lights that have always been strung above them glow merrily. The tractor-trailer truck that Grand used to transport the SymSac fees is still jackknifed out front, just how she left it almost eighteen years ago. We run around it and immediately see what the glass-breaking sound was. Su drove the ambulance straight through the entrance doors.

"What the . . ." I ask.

Reason and I step over the broken glass.

The labs are like walking into the future and the past all at the same time. The car dealership cubicles are still set up, only behind them are all manner of gleaming stainless-steel and chrome equipment. It is all pre-Night old, but since nothing like it has been manufactured in years, it might as well be cutting-edge new. The room is brightly lit with freshly mopped black laminate floors. Fees' daughters' drawings hang along a far back wall. Compared to the university labs across the river, this setup is laughable.

What's happening in its midst is anything but.

Su and the boys are huddled in front of the ambulance with their arms up in the air. A dozen lab techs have the same number of loaded crossbows aimed at their chests. Half of the crossbows swing toward Reason and me when we enter the room.

"Wow, you're good," Comma says, his gaze feverish. "We've barely parked. Remind me never to get on your bad side."

"So," Sway says, "they sent a welcoming committee."

"There isn't time for this," I say to the lab techs, clutching my broken arm to my chest. "Su, take us to the vaccine."

No sooner do I move into the labs than two fees come forward from the rest. Eugenie and Maluhia. They were one of the co-living sets that coupled off years ago. Eugenie has worked alongside Grand from the very beginning. The fact that she wasn't killed with the other elder fees the day Mouse was taken can only mean she does not agree with my grand. Their daughter, Cinnamon Toast, is a few years ahead of me. Su told me she placed into the labs. Now she towers over her moms, bodyguard-style.

"Hold it right there," Eugenie says. "We've had word that you were turned. Working with the mob to liberate the beasts. That you lured Matricula to you. That you're complicit in her death."

I breathe a sigh of relief. They're not all in on it, then.

"I'm not trying to liberate the males," I say. "I simply need the vaccine that will cure all of them. Wait. Yes. Actually, I guess I am trying to liberate the males. Auntie Eugenie, Auntie Maluhia, this is my brother, Mouse. You haven't met him before because we've been living outside the neighborhood for the last five years so we wouldn't disrupt anything over here. Say hi, Mouser."

"Hi, Mouser." He waves and laughs weakly.

Cinnamon Toast backs away and hurries into the labs.

Su warns, "Glori."

"I saw her," I reply. But I keep my focus on my elders. "And these are my friends. They're boys. Not beasts."

"I can attest to that," Su says. "These males are not *that* terrible."

"Thanks for the strong vote of confidence," Sway mutters.

"Say hi, boys."

"Hi," they all say with varying levels of enthusiasm.

Maluhia nods at Hercules, then murmurs to Eugenie. My ears distinctly pick up the words *the Fortress*. But no one else has lowered their crossbow. I don't know what to do. I scream with frustration.

"We don't have time for this."

"I hear that."

Cinnamon Toast is back. Over six feet tall in the sixth grade, she's always been magnificently strong with a personality and will to match. Before I left school, she was the only fee who could best me in wrestling. Seeing her loom over me now, I imagine that's still the case.

"Glori." She nods to the males. "This your family now?"

I lift my chin. "It is. Mouse has always been."

"Okay." Cinnamon glares at the labs techs and barks, "You heard her. Glori said her family's in trouble. Are we not helping our own anymore? We've had safety precautions for the Seventeen Year Truce in place for years, but biological warfare was only ever mentioned as a true last resort. This was *not* part of the plan. This is not us."

As if it was their very consciences shouting at them, all the fees jump into action.

Maluhia drops her crossbow and comes forward first. "Oh, for heaven's sakes, give me that little one. She doesn't have time for the vaccine. She needs CRISPR antiviral fluids."

"This is a boy," Comma says, rocking Hercules side to side. Hercules's eyes flutter briefly open. He registers Maluhia. Smiles. Then closes his eyes again as if to better focus on his labored breathing.

"You take her from the Fortress?" Maluhia asks, taking Hercules from Comma. "Then it's *her* life. All the little ones there are girls. First ones made by the fees that went across six years ago. I can't believe they let her get that virus. Don't worry, beast. I'll give her back. Maybe."

Mouse tugs on my tank top. "Told you. *She.*"

That was why they kept them separate at the Fortress; why they had a better existence. I'm about to ask why they were sent there at all, but I know all the answers. Chia's cameras. Never mind trying to get multiple infants from the heart of Buffalo to the bridge unnoticed.

Around us, all the other fees get to work. One takes the tray that Cinnamon is holding. Another swabs down the boys' arms. As Reason gets his shot he tells Eugenie about all the males that are lining up at the bridge and convinces her to organize a triage. Only once it's decided that Sway, Comma, and I will stay back with the younger boys and get medical attention does Su offer to go with Reason.

"Cinnamon, you'll take good care of Glori?" Su asks.

"I won't let her out of my sight," Cinnamon Toast says.

Su nods, relieved, and begins packing the ambulance as Cinnamon kneels and hands Motor a lollipop.

"What's this?" He looks at me skeptically.

"The best thing you've ever tasted," I reply.

Motor grunts, then sticks the whole thing in his mouth. Wrapper and all. Mouse finds it hysterical, though his laughter is weak. Cinnamon shakes her head, bemused but also worried. She's just saved males. Everything is going to change now. And she helped make that happen.

"Thanks, Cinn. And here I thought you never liked me."

"You kidding? I was intimidated as waste by you. A fee not made by beasts? We were awed. I always knew you'd do big things. Respect, little fee."

"Wait. You mean everyone knew my background? I only found out today."

"They never told you?" Cinnamon's eyes cut accusingly to Su.

I kneel next to Cinnamon as I take the wrapper off Motor's sucker. Mouse is playing with Lucky, throwing a ruler for him to retrieve. Multiple fees stand around watching him with expressions of awe.

"It doesn't matter now," I murmur, then ask, "Where is Liyan?"

Cinnamon quietly replies, "Amusement park."

It only takes a few minutes to load everything. Everyone is told to stay safe. Be on watch. No one in Buffalo has time for long goodbyes, so we keep them short. Su hangs out the passenger-side window. "Glori, maybe I should stay back with you."

"No. Go be of use and help administer the vaccine. The males need someone that is at least partially sympathetic to their side. Besides, what will you do here? Watch me get a cast?"

"And my mom? You aren't . . ."

Before she can continue, I hug her tightly. Then hold her face in my hands.

"I love you. We'll sort this all out when you get back. Nothing is bigger than us, right?"

She nods, smiling like that time Liyan surprised her with a trampoline on her ninth birthday. As I always do whenever Su smiles, I can't help thinking how right Liyan was when she named her. (Regardless of how much Su hated it.) Sunshine. Her smile lights up the world. Yet it does little to deter me from what I'm about to do.

As Su, Reason, Eugenie, and a handful of other fees drive away, Comma slips a sling over my forehead. As he gently settles my broken arm into it, he tells me it's fashioned from his favorite unity scarf. Not so that I'll be careful with it, more so that I know it will take care of me.

"We aren't staying in the labs and recuperating, are we?" he asks.

Out front, Sway pulls up in a bright yellow, freshly hot-wired Mustang. A car dealership price tag still in the window. Cinnamon tosses me a billy club. Motor calls shotgun.

"Bump no, we aren't."

74

FANTASY ISLAND

NIAGARA'S AMUSEMENT & WATER PARK

"Y'all had an amusement park over here and you didn't invite us?" Comma asks.

"It's not like it was open for business. We've never had the electricity to spare."

"Apparently you do now," Sway says.

We park the Mustang right against the front gates. Leave Lucky in the car. The entrance to Fantasy Island is styled after an old red barn. Behind it, the park literally gleams, a happy glow of fat yellow, red, and white lights against the wintry black sky. All the turnstiles are locked, but the gate on the end is open.

"What's a water park?" Motor asks.

"Water parks were like swimming pools but even better," I say.

I'm carrying him piggyback-style and really, really wishing I'd forced him to shower. Sway has Mouse. Maluhia tried insisting we leave the boys at the lab with Hercules. But we felt safer together, even if where we were headed was undeniably more dangerous.

"Water parks had these slides filled with water that you went down in your bathing suit. And a lazy river that you floated on in a circle raft. Or at least that's what the brochures in the ticket office showed. Before we burned them."

"Pre-Night was so weird," Sway says.

"What's a slide?" Motor asks. "And a raft? And what's a bathing suit?"

"Oh, this is going to be fun," Comma says. "He's worse than a fee."

Carnival lights blink haphazardly from every ride and game booth. A few rides still blare music. Bass-heavy tunes that do little to enliven the desolate park, kind of like putting perfume on a corpse. Something called a Tilt-A-Whirl spins and dips its empty cars on a circular platform. I catch a flash of red in one of them, but when I wait and really look at all the carriages, they're empty.

I try to imagine the amusement park when it was a happy place, with fees eating popcorn and whatever kielbasa was, drinking something called slushies. The air filled with squeals of joy and not the tinny sound of the rides' ancient sound systems. But the emptiness is too much. Maybe there are no bodies here, but this is absolutely a graveyard. We pass a giant ship that makes loud gears-crushing-against-other-gears noises and shudders in place.

"Can we agree to never ever come here again?" Sway asks as the wind picks up.

"Yes," I say.

"Oh, I don't know." Comma shivers. "It kind of has that quaint someone's-gonna-stab-you vibe."

Sway's portable chirps.

Reason says, "We're at the bridge. About a hundred males are waiting. The mercenary is gone. Be careful."

We pass the swings ride. I half expect to see my mother on it, like I have so many times in recent years, spinning and spinning, but they all sway empty in the breeze. Then it is around the bend, and we are at the slide. It is nine lanes across, with three large bumps. Each lane is a bright purple, teal, or pink plastic that remains remarkably vibrant. They used to have burlap sacks for fees to sit on, but we repurposed those a long time ago. The times I brought Mouse here, we used old sweaters to slide on.

At the top of the slide is a little wood house that used to maintain rider lines but now is headquarters for the movement to wipe out males. It is the perfect defensive spot. There is no getting up there without being attacked. I know this because that's what Itami said the countless times Mouse and I tagged along with her during her lesson shift, which always fell on the EMS staff meeting day.

"Your mercenaries had staff meetings?" Comma asks when I tell the males this.

"Well, what else should they have called them?" I reply.

After setting Motor and Mouse down in a hot-dog stand, where they curl into each other for warmth, we approach the foot of the slide. This time neither male wastes his breath telling me not to fight.

"Stay put, males," I say, then walk up the first hill of the slide.

"Not on your life," Sway replies, and tries to follow me only to immediately slip back down the incline. "No fair. You've had practice."

He moves instead to the stairs off to the right of the slide.

"Knock, knock," I shout, tapping Cinnamon's billy club against the slide.

Immediately, Misère, Muerte, and Itami step out from the cabin. They simultaneously draw their weapons.

"I am here to speak with the ivory mercenary."

"But she does not wish to speak with you."

Itami takes the center lane and slides down the first hill, then waits for me with her double fighting knives drawn. Muerte with her bow and arrow and Misère with her bat each take an outside lane but remain at the top.

"Please, don't do this," I say, slowly climbing up the slide. "You've killed off almost all the males. You killed Grand. There are no more enemies for you to fight."

And what I think but don't say is that even more than wanting revenge, my males and I will never be safe unless we come to a resolution.

Or I kill all the mercenaries.

"Sorry, Glori," Muerte says. "But we swore. We swore we would bring about this world no matter what. Even if it meant hurting ones we loved. For the future of everyone."

"I know you don't believe that or you wouldn't have let me run away back at the transport. And happy futures don't start with murder, Muerte."

"No more talking," Itami says.

Leaping over the second hill entirely, she comes straight for me, knives flashing. She's only a few feet away when her name rings out.

"Itami!" Then even happier. "Itami! Itami! Itami!"

Mouse scampers up the slide, faster at it even than me. He meets Itami as she skids to a stop in front of me. Throwing himself at her legs, he stands on tiptoes and barely manages to kiss her belly.

"Otokonoku," she says.

All the other mercenaries kept their distance from Mouse but not

Itami. She made him origami cranes and sailboats. She swung him through the air by his arms until they were both dizzy from laughter and velocity. She carried him on her shoulders and let him pluck leaves from trees, then made crowns out of them.

Not feeling well despite his newest shot, Mouse is not his usual chatty self but simply stands there holding on to Itami. Or maybe he is too afraid for words.

"I don't know what to do." Itami looks to the other mercenaries.

"I will take it from here, sisters. You have done enough."

It's Liyan. She no longer wears the ivory mercenary suit. The clothes she changed into are disheveled and bloody. Bruises mar her face and she looks like she's been crying. Yet she stands straight with her arms clasped behind her back, her head held high.

"Leave or we will kill you. Keep your mouth shut and we will let you live."

There is so much I want to say, and yet I can't speak.

"How do we know you'll keep your word?" Sway asks from his position on the stairs.

Her eyes move to him. She frowns. Then does a double take.

"Shui?" she asks, simultaneously stunned and hopeful.

Sway's hand goes to his necklace. "Mama?"

She nods once, definitively. This is probably not the heartfelt reunion Sway had hoped for, but he didn't know Liyan. And yet, he does not look the least bit disappointed. Despite the tremendous height difference, it is almost laughable how similar they look. How did I not notice this before? But also, why would I? Liyan had told me countless times about her flight from Beijing to the States. I knew the wealthy businessman let her bring her family. I knew she flew over with both of her parents, but I never knew that family included a son.

Comma stage-whispers, "Why is she saying his name wrong?"

"In Mandarin *shui* means water," I say. "*We've* been saying it wrong."

"Because in a time of death," Liyan says, "he gave me life."

Pulled forward by her longing, Liyan turns ever so slightly. She's not clasping her hands behind her back, they're bound there. Hearing my surprised breath, Liyan's eyes cut to me.

"Glori," she hisses. "Get them out of here. Now."

The next second, she is sprawled flat on the ground, blood coming from a wound at the back of her head. Sway shouts and runs out onto the slide just as the ivory mercenary steps from the hut. Unsheathing the katana from her back, she holds it to Liyan's neck. Sway immediately stops where he is, a few feet away from me.

"That's better," the mercenary says.

Stepping over Liyan's body, she takes off her ivory-white balaclava and shakes out her wild hair. She laughs at my expression.

"Hello, Glori," she says. "I'd hoped you were dead."

It's my mom.

75

"**Y**ou . . . talk" is all I can think to say.

I glance back at Mouse. Itami has a hand on his chest, holding him to her leg. He notices Majesty but continues playing with Itami's short knife. There will be no scampering up the slide to greet her.

"Yes, well. Thanks to your grand, you and I both have IQs higher than the average norm, so I learned talking pretty early on in this voyage we call life."

Twice Majesty has suffered atrocities at the hands of males that were so vicious we never spoke of them. She was our most ferocious fighter. Our most temperamental fee. I am and am not shocked that she did this. And yet, in this moment, what I truly can't get over is her voice. It's as clear as day. And the longer I stand there, so is the truth.

"You took my brother?"

The morning they came for him, Majesty spoke to me for the first time in months. I see now that she was keeping me inside, preventing me from helping him. And it worked.

"The mercenaries took it, yes. We've had this plan in mind for some years now, without an idea of when to put it in motion. But then I saw you bike away with it that night and I knew the beasts would eventually see footage of you two, and I knew my moment had come. So I placed a PTT to Jackal. I believe you two met. Jackal enlisted two of the mob's more unsavory affiliates to do a necessary job I had been dreading for some time."

"You mean murdering LaVaughn, Josie Baker, Ruth—"

She cuts me off. "Your Grand's biggest supporters. Yes."

"Fees that would never let you get away with this."

"Fees that would have had qualms, yes."

"Like Rauha."

"Believe me, I took no joy in it. Not when there are so few of us left and we'll all be so vital to the rebuilding, but it was your Grand who always said fees never played dirty enough. With her council dead, I knew Matricula would finally feel the necessary rage to enact the measures she'd been vacillating on for years. And the beauty of it was, those fees wouldn't be here to dissuade her from it. They were her conscience all those years, and I took them from her."

"Then why take Two Five?"

"Because I wanted Matricula to think everything she'd worked so hard for was at risk. Her labs. Her family. Every fee's future. I wanted her to see how ridiculous it was to lose everything she'd worked toward because she felt attached to one single beast. I took it because I wanted her to stop making concessions and go forward with what she originally conceived—a beastless existence—without *it* clouding her vision. What I *hadn't* expected was that taking it would drive you out. Thanks be for small miracles, I guess. I found the note you left her, by the way. Got rid of it. Couldn't have her going right after you and the little beast."

"His name is Mouse."

"And it is supposed to be dead." She glares at Itami. "You *volunteered* to do it."

"The Fortress seemed like the more humane option," Itami says, glaring back at Majesty. "I thought we could raise him with the other little fees."

Majesty snorts. "You know that would never have worked."

Itami shrugs and says simply, "I couldn't do it."

"But all these years," I say to Majesty, "you've been acting so . . ."

"Comatose?" She nods. "If you haven't yet tried it, I highly recommend the sedative we use in the Fortress's milk. It's the only thing that makes living on this moldy, isolated speck of the earth bearable. And what better way to convince your Grand to follow the morally taxing path she'd chosen than to have her daily see evidence of how beasts break us. It was a blessing when those beasts jumped me on the other side. Not only because Rage found me, but because it confirmed everything your Grand already knew about what beasts have at their heart."

There's a manic brightness in Majesty's eyes and words. She keeps worrying her lip with her fingers. Only a few hours ago, she killed her own mother. Even if you were completely insane, that had to take some kind of toll. Except I don't think Majesty is insane.

"But then you killed her anyway." It comes out a whisper.

"I didn't want it to come to this," she replies equally faintly. "But it was necessary. If you had only stopped eluding us along the way, your grand wouldn't have had to die. Right now, she'd be waging a furious war against the beasts. *You* could have been the spark that ignited our cause." My eyes go to Muerte, but she won't return my gaze. She *had* been ordered to kill me back at that transport. "I've been saying it ever since the Night. The only way for fees to have the fresh start we all keep bandying about is for all the beasts to die."

And then something weird happens. I start laughing. It's not a healthy laugh, but I can't help it. Sway takes a step toward me.

"The tea party ain't over yet, Mad Hatter," he murmurs. "Keep it together."

But I only have eyes for Majesty.

"Glori," Majesty presses, then gestures at Sway. "You think you want this because you don't know what you are taking us back to. We have been bred to be subservient. Did you know that when beasts and fees were in a car together, the beasts always drove? That we were called the weaker sex? That when an older fee dated a younger beast she was demeaned for it? They called us hysterical in our anger. Aggressive in our firmness. And no matter how 'honorable' a beast was, when it got together with its friends, they spoke about and looked at us like we were meat. All the while in our homes we were expected to take on the bulk of the housework and the child-rearing *and* offer our bodies up at their will without complaint or question and be derided as low performing when we chose not to.

"All that vague waste Matricula spewed about our power being our own? What power? We never had any. We have been in servitude since the dawn of time. And as long as we exist alongside beasts, no matter how much you delete them from our culture or teach young fees effective takedown moves, we always will be. On that, at least, your grand and I agreed."

Sway holds up his hand. "For the record, I would never compare a fee to meat. I mean, a complicated board game, maybe."

"A pair of high-heeled shoes," Comma calls out from the foot of the slide.

"Shut it, beasts," Majesty says.

"Grand never wanted *this*," I say.

"Your grand was the most consistent human I've ever met. Even now, you love these beasts, but I'm sure you feel guilt for it. I felt guilt for it when I was on the other side and in a moment of weakness ravaged that beast with the gorgeous red beard."

"Quarry?" Sway spits. "That's your type?"

She ignores him. "But not Matricula. She knew what she wanted to do, she knew why, and she went about it without guilt, never losing sight of the goal. Until Two Five came along."

Majesty glares at him now. I have never seen such hate.

"I told her to send it across. But she insisted on keeping it. Not for me. For you. And the longer Two Five stayed with us, the vaguer Matricula's waste became. Reading to you both every night..."

"Told you, Glori," Mouse sniffs. "Every night."

"Instead of backup plans that involved erasing the beasts, she began talking about relocating them. I decided that to truly start over, we needed a plan that rebooted the entire system." She rolls her eyes at my confused expression and quickly says, "'Reboot' is terminology that related to computers, the internet, and streaming services when the Wi-Fi went down. Just think, Glori, of how lovely it will be to walk alone, at night, in the pitch-black without an ounce of fear. Maybe I will be seen as a villain in all this..."

"Oh, that is certain," Sway says.

"But I was never meant to be a mother. I was an experiment right from the beginning. *I* was meant to be the reboot. I am our future. The first child of the god that was Matricula Rhodes. I am the new Adam, and I'm not sharing my rib with anyone."

"The only problem is," I press on, "the males you're killing are not all the same as the males you escaped from all those years ago. You must know that." I look to all the mercenaries and then to Mouse. "I know you all do."

"Oh, Glori," she says softly. "You're only proving my point as to why your Grand and her court had to go. The beasts are all *exactly* the same. Ladies, do you mind showing Glori what these males we deemed *good* did?"

As one, the mercenaries peel off their balaclavas.

"Oh my." Comma gasps.

Misère's curls are cropped close to her head in a tight Afro, which does little to hide that she's missing an eye. The skin around Muerte's cheek has been badly scarred, not from radiation, but like someone held a flame to her face. But Itami is the worst. Lovely, smooth black hair hangs over the right half of her face, only partially hiding what looks like badly healed, smashed bones. The damage starts from her right cheek, goes over her nose, up to her forehead.

No wonder they so readily embraced becoming killing machines. They were the fees that I've heard about my whole life. The ones attacked by the males Matricula allowed onto our island on the night that no fee speaks about because it was too horrific.

"The night we got to the island," Itami says, "Rabbit said, 'Let's play Truth or Dare.'"

"Gorilla brought beers," Muerte adds. "Made out with Ann, while Pig locked the doors."

Majesty nods and continues, "Bear's first question—Bear, whom you know as the illustrious Mayor Chia—Bear's first question was who shot Fortitude. I told him the truth. It was me. I killed that son of a bitch."

"Oh my honey-hued horn," Comma whispers.

"And then they beat you," I finish.

"Beat us?" Majesty laughs and twirls the katana in her hand. "No. Then they began executing us. Wolf decapitated Hope and Merry with a tomahawk. And no, tomahawks do not make clean cuts. Rabbit carved up Niraasha and Misère. Pig burned Muerte and Ann. Gorilla beat Itami. We fought them off, but we weren't strong then like we are now. Bear ran. He claimed he was going for help. Maybe he was, maybe he wasn't. Regardless, as of this evening, with Chia gone, they are finally all dead.

"I know we have lost a lot. Maybe our own humanity in the mix. But I am doing this for Chardonnay and AC and Cookie. For all the fees who will come after and who will never, ever have to be held back or held down by beasts."

"Maj," Misère murmurs, "you're getting upset."

"What happens now?" I ask.

Majesty's eyes flash with emotion.

"I can't let you go, little fee. I'm sorry. This is war, and anyone who sides with the beasts must lose. I know I have not been a good mother, but I can make the end quick for you. I can at least do that."

"Majesty, that is enough," Itami says, then sends Mouse down the slide to Comma. "Our mission has always been to protect our own at all costs. Glori is our own. That little one"—she points at Mouse—"*is* our own. I've watched him grow. We've *all* raised him. He is no different than a fee."

"Itami is right. What is the point of all this sacrifice," Muerte adds, "if we end up here? Murdering our loved ones? There has been enough death today."

Now they approach her. Not to hurt her but to stop her nonetheless. Faster than a termite infestation, Majesty swings her katana and cuts Muerte across her chest. As Mouse shouts for her not to, Itami advances.

Majesty throws the katana away, reaches behind her, and pulls a gun from a holster behind her lower back.

"If you're not with us, you're against us."

But she doesn't aim for the mercenaries.

Instead she points the gun at my heart and fires.

76

Like Mouse rolling into a ball whenever we ran defensive drills, instead of being useful and trying to dodge the bullet, I close my eyes and brace for death. The billy club clatters to my feet. But I do not feel any pain. I *do* hear a wet rasping sound. When I open my eyes, Sway is at my feet frantically clutching at his abdomen, blood oozing between his fingers. He leapt in front of the bullet.

"No!" Comma screams.

He races up the stairs. Majesty looks at the gun in her hands. Then at Sway. I roar. She trains the gun back on me. Before she can fire, she is falling backward off the slide. Her arms pinwheeling frantically in the air. Liyan has crawled up behind her and swiped her ankles out from beneath her.

"Waaaaste . . . !" Majesty shouts, then drops from sight.

A moment later, there is the horrible thump of a body hitting the ground.

Then there is nothing.

As Liyan collapses, I sink down to Sway. Comma already has his head in his lap. Itami is rocking Mouse at the foot of the slide.

"Someone go for help!" I scream.

"Glori." Sway looks down at his belly, then up at me, and gives me a wobbly smile. "I met my mom."

I get it then. Exactly what life is. It is nothing. We are here and then we are gone. And all the drama we get into, the passions we fall in and out of, the friendships we make and break, they are supposed to impart significance. But there is no significance. Life is lovely, awful, and fleeting. The only power we truly have is how we choose to face it.

"At least now I won't steal your snapbacks anymore, Com," he says.

"You can have them all, you silly goit," Comma murmurs, stroking his hair. "Don't you dare leave me, or I swear I will bury you in a polo shirt and khaki pants."

Sway clutches my hand. I kiss it. Then I kiss his thin lips. His smooth forehead. Then I finally, finally, kiss the freckle that is right below his eye. When I do, he whispers something so quiet, I wouldn't have heard him if my ear hadn't been right next to his mouth.

"Glori, I don't regret a second of knowing you..." He gulps air; it is meant to be laughter. "Okay...maybe this part. *You* are very everything."

And then his eyes flutter closed.

SOME WEEKS LATER

When you don't know what to do or where to go, you go home.

Only I didn't know where that was anymore.

While Eugenie, Breaker, and Su dispensed the vaccine at the bridge, Reason rode through the city in the ambulance, distributing it to anyone left alive. But Buffalo is a large city and males didn't believe in habitation zones and Rage wasn't able to prevent all the mob from attacking norms. Or vice versa.

When he was out of vaccine, Reason went to Quarry and tried to convince him not to retaliate. But in this critical moment, the Influencer had no influence. Two days after we escaped from the Fortress, Quarry and a small group of surviving norms arrived in armored Humvees at the remaining Grand Island Bridge with rocket launchers, grenades, and assault rifles looking to avenge the deaths of their families and friends.

"You will pay for this," Mouse's father shouted through a bullhorn.

And then they all drove forward.

Fees blew the bridge when the males were halfway across.

Thanks to the Rinspeed and multiple trips, our small group had fled the island the day before. We watched the bridge explode from the rooftop of the steam station. Shortly after, in the faint morning sun, there were bright bursts of colorful lights. *Fireworks*, Liyan said. I couldn't help wondering which fee had stashed them away all these years just waiting for the downfall of men.

That was many days ago now. I haven't been down on the ground since. Part of me wants to go home. We've heard Grand Island is primarily empty. It turns out we weren't the only family that had an emergency boat stashed at the shore. Eugenie is governing now, and she's relocated most of the fee families to the exact same mansions that Chia had cleared for us. They are ideally located, spacious, and well preserved. Just as with the divide, not all fees went with her. A few defected, choosing to take their chances out in the wild world rather than stay in a city that reeked of fresh death, and live with fees who might or might not be complicit murderers.

I am vaguely curious to see what the fees plan to do with Buffalo, how well this new society works. How much power they allow the few surviving males. But for now, pulling up the ladders is all I can stand. I want nothing more than to sit on this roof as I am now, with my glass of sun tea, remembering the dead and being thankful for the living.

Mending, Liyan calls it.

Honestly, there isn't a lot of time for even that.

Living with three children makes thinking about anything other than feeding, clothing, and reprimanding them a luxury. I see now why fees set up cohabitation families. It takes at least four adults to maintain any semblance of sanity around little ones. From what I hear, the fees don't have their hands any less full having absorbed the Littles, the Fortress males, and soon the newborns from the labs. I like to pretend I can hear all those young voices on the wind, that they mean we have a new happy future ahead of us. I can't say it always works.

Even as I have the thought, the roof door crashes open.

I reach for Baby Bear, the only knife I have left, but then a wiggly black blur with four white paws shoots out and runs straight to me. A male comes out behind him, sitting on his hover board. I wonder if there will ever be a day when I do not reach for Baby Bear at the sound of a loud noise or when I step into a dark room.

Probably not. And I'm okay with that.

There's so much to protect now.

"Don't go getting all stabby," the male says. "It's only us."

As Lucky sprawls at my feet, imploring me to rub his belly, the male scoots from the hover board to my bench. A long time ago, someone carved *JB Loves LB* into the wood seat. He runs his fingers over the lettering. The first night we were back, Reason and I moved the bench away from the edge of the building and placed it at the heart of the orchard instead. The fruit trees had begun to shoot out bright green leaf clusters. It was going to be a magnificent show. Plus, I think we all needed to be a little more inward facing. Literally. No one wanted to look out on the city now. So much of it had been destroyed.

"Breaker's here."

"Visiting the puppies?" I ask.

"Yeah. Rage dropped him off. He said the fees got the solar fields at the farms back up and running."

I shrug. "Good for them."

"You can't be mad forever. What happened wasn't any of their faults. And they took in all those Littles and Fortress males like it was nothing. Besides, we still have so much."

Except I was so close to having nothing.

He holds his arm out to me, and I curl into the warmth and safety of it.

Grand always told me that there was passion and there was love. And the two things should not be confused, though they often were, to disastrous consequences. Passion, Grand said, was sensational, like a burst of lightning. Gorgeous, vibrant, but fleeting. She said it could strike interchangeably among any number of people. Whether they liked it or not. Beasts craved the heat of passion and often were blinded by the brightness of it. It was what made them so unreliable, so fickle.

Love, on the other hand, was like a stream. It was tricky and complicated, winding this way and that. It ebbed and flowed depending on the season. It was entirely possible to hate a person you loved—Grand especially told me this whenever Su and I fought—because love changed with time, but regardless, it would always be there, a current that never ran dry.

I hardly know anything anymore about how the world works, but I know I love this boy.

"I love you, *Shui*."

It's been about a month, and not one single day has passed that I'm not still surprised he's alive. He kisses the top of my head. "And I love you, *Gloria*. Still. Now. Always. Even though it's only been a whole five minutes since the last time you told me."

He can tease me all he wants.

I will never waste the chance to tell someone I love them ever again.

We have Motor to thank for the fact that Sway is alive. When I walked up the slide to square off against the mercenaries, Motor told Mouse to stay put, then, like the hero he was born to be, he raced back to the Mustang and drove it through the remaining front windows of the labs, where he told the first techs he saw to grab emergency medical supplies. That I was fighting the ones in the red and was definitely going to die.

Luckily, his utter lack of confidence in me meant that when Majesty shot Sway, Amelia and Frida were already running toward us with bandages and a blood transfusion kit.

"Sooo," Sway says, "what would you say if I asked you to close your eyes and come with me and not ask why, because we might have a surprise for you?"

"I'd say I knew it was too quiet."

Sway's kid sister, Su, still PTTs her friends daily. She says now that fees have access to the males' broadcasting tower, Eugenie has already picked up signals from other cities. Faraway places, with strange-sounding names like Omaha and Minneapolis. Su says that Eugenie is worried people will come looking for us, that she and her common council are discussing continuing Rugged's weapons program. Su says this to Comma mostly. She and I are still a little wary around each other. Though I understand why she kept so many things from me, I can't quite accept it. But we'll get back to where we were. Life's too short not to.

Comma says there's enough supplies on the rooftop to last us at least a year. Reason says we should try somewhere new. "*The Magic Kingdom,*" Motor always interjects. "*It's the most magical place on earth* and *Mickey lives there.*"

"*Lived,*" we all correct.

Regardless, Reason says, we should find a place that doesn't have our history. But then Liyan reminds us that wherever we go, whomever we meet, they'll simply have a different history and that it will most likely be equally unpleasant.

After the Night, even okay people did bad things.

Now Sway gently knocks on my temple with his fist.

"You're stuck in there again," he says.

Before I can reply, he struggles to his feet. Behind him, a partially blue sky is visible through the haze. This morning the thermometer outside the kitchen window said it was already eighty-seven degrees outside.

"Come on, this is a good surprise. I promise."

With Lucky in the lead, we cut through the wheat field on the hidden path but then veer in the opposite direction of the garage with all the cars and motorbikes.

"Coming in hot," Sway calls out.

In reply, there is giggling and Comma shushing everyone. Sway tells me to close my eyes and then pulls me from the wheat.

"Surprise!" my family shouts.

"You can open your eyes now," Motor says, sounding like he's eating. "Duh."

Motor is *always* eating. Since we crossed the river, he's already gained ten pounds. I open my eyes and immediately look at Sway.

"Is this real?"

He nods, then lightly tugs on my chin. "There it is."

He means my smile. I never thought I'd find it again. But there is no not smiling at the spectacle in front of me. We're standing on a part of the roof I have never seen. All my mees—Mouse, Motor, Hercules, Reason, even Breaker—are standing in a line in their underwear, giggling. Comma has on a robe, which he now drops, to reveal bright blue chest hair and tight matching blue swim trunks with sparkly silver stars on them.

"Ta-da!" he says. "What do you think?"

Behind them is an enormous aboveground swimming pool that is filled to the brim with only slightly murky water. Liyan and Su are watching from lawn chairs set up next to it.

"You got me a pool," I say, blinking back tears.

Sway nods. "Less bodies. More pools."

"It's filled with filtered rainwater," Mouse says, "so it's okay if we swallow it."

"And we won't drown because everyone is here," Hercules says.

Mouse and Hercules are both in water wings. Simultaneously, they look to Liyan. She nods at them as if they've been over this many, many times already. Fear. It's what my little mees have been left with. And who can blame them? But we're all working on it. More than Sway or Reason or Su or me, Liyan runs our pack.

The night we returned to the steam station, when we were finally alone, I apologized for doubting her. She apologized for not realizing what Majesty was up to. And we promised each other that to the best of our ability we would try to make the decent and good parts of Grand's mission stick. With all our pronoun confusions, she's the one who decided we all might as well be mees. (*"Yeah, otherwise, we're a bunch of fales,"* Motor snorted.)

Sway now describes us all solely with the neutral Mandarin pronoun. Ta. It'll take me some time to get used to saying, but I think it's perfect. No more him. Her. His. Its. He. She. Just ta. We are all male and fee and something altogether different and new.

We are our own fresh start.

"Don't you like it?" Reason asks as my smile leaves me again.

My first thought on seeing the pool was that Grand would love this. I try to shake off my gloom. Looking at Motor's pudgy belly makes it easier.

"I do. I only feel bad for how soaked you're about to get. Suze? Ready, aim, fire?"

Su looks up from her book—she is never without a book now—and smiles brightly. "Oh bump yes," she says, tossing her book aside.

And then she and I run at the pool, spring up, and cannonball into it.

The water is practically hot. I come up, gasping. My broken arm didn't like that, but it's worth it to hear the males squeal and see them dripping wet.

Mouse and Hercules need no further convincing. Within seconds, they are up the ladder and flinging themselves into the water. They come up coughing. Hercules immediately paddles over to Su. They rub noses. Motor tentatively clings to the ladder, looking at the water with displeasure, but then carefully lowers himself in and stands clinging to the wall.

"This is fun," he says. "It's like bathing in sweat."

Suddenly, he's five feet in the air. Reason has slipped into the pool and now has Motor lifted above his head. Mastodon, Carrot, and Eggnog, along with Lucky and the rest of the pack, run around the outside barking.

"Don't do—" Motor shouts just as Reason dunks him beneath the water.

Motor comes up sputtering, then lurches toward Reason. "Do it again!"

Mouse swims over and clings to Reason's back, not wanting to go underwater but not wanting to miss out on the action. Breaker, meanwhile, sits on the edge of the pool holding as many puppies as he can fit in his arms, one corner of his mouth upturned. Despite the fact I constantly tell him he can live out loud now, he remains the most reserved of my mees.

"*Feeling things here,*" he's said, putting a hand over his heart, "*still just feels right.*"

But now he's giggling with the rest of them, like children. Because they are.

Declaring that he can't get his stitches wet, Sway lies on the blanket with Liyan. In the last month, his hair has grown out. She puts it into a mini-topknot. Then kisses the side of his head. His smile is pure joy.

"Oh bump no," Comma says. "I am not about getting dunked. Auntie Liyan, scoot over."

"Don't be such a goit," I call out, splashing him with water.

Then we're all splashing Comma, until he gets angry and grabs his clothes and stomps away. His tiny tush makes me laugh. I shout after him, "Queue up season five."

He holds a thumbs-up above his head.

"I love you, my mees," I shout, only to immediately receive a faceful of water from multiple directions.

Laughing, I look at all the paperclip necklaces on this noisy, boisterous, chaotic family of mine. And I can't help thinking how right my grand was. Our power *is* our own. But when I repeat this to my pack every night after I read to them, kiss them, and wish them sweet dreams, I change it a little bit.

Together our power is our own. Now go do something great with it.

The End-ish

ACKNOWLEDGMENTS

My first draft of *City of Beasts* was completed back in 2009. After reading a handful of articles about how we raise boys and girls differently and how that adversely affects us all later in life, I wondered what girls could and would be like if we were raised entirely separately. Daydreaming about how this might realistically happen—nuclear war, obviously—and I was off and running. Ten years later, with hundreds of revisions under my belt, plus my debut novel out in the world, *City of Beasts* came to fruition. They say writing a book is torture. They do not lie. And yet I am still reading articles about how girls are raised to be perfect instead of brave.

First and foremost, thank you, Mom. You've read almost as many versions of this book as I've written, each time with great enthusiasm. I couldn't have done this without your cheerleading. Eternal gratitude to my editor, Kieran Viola, who had the courage to say "How about one more round?" when she knew I was fried. I am incredibly proud of this book because you made me do the work. To my agent, Sarah Burnes, for saying "This is the one!" And to my Hollywood agent, Mary Pender, who, as Glori would say, is very everything and tough as nails besides. Thank you to my foreign publishers and my entire Disney team, especially Mary Mudd for the extra eyes, Vanessa Moody for the killer tagline and all the copy editors who made this book make sense.

Thank you to Naoko Howard, Debbie Michiko Florence, and Debbie's mama for checking my Japanese. Kelly Cycon for setting up my labs. To the *MIT Review* for all the inspiration. And again to my mom for all the research field trips and her last-minute eyes that caught so much.

City of Beasts is my love letter to my hometown of Buffalo, New York. While it is now being picked as an optimal place to survive climate change, I've *always* thought Buffalo was the best place in the world to grow up. We are a hardy, proud, and friendly lot. I'm sorry I decimated 99 percent percent of your population. To my Charlestonian mob. All you Short Grain and Jackrabbit Filly supporters, plus our community of chefs, servers, managers, bartenders, dishwashers, farmers, vendors... *my people.* I am unbelievably lucky that there are too many of you to name. But your encouragement and your faces and the fact that so many of you bought my book, means the world to me. Let's celebrate!

Massive thanks to Jonathan Sanchez and everyone at Blue Bicycle Books for the prodigious support. Also, to the women of both the Itinerate Literate bookstore in Park Circle and Rust Belt Books in Buffalo, samesies.

Broadly, thank you to the NYPL, the BPL, and the CCPL for keeping me so well read and to all the librarians, teachers, booksellers, and festival coordinators who have read my work and passed it along. Y'all are THE BEST. Much love to Notre Dame Preparatory School in Baltimore. Sometimes you form immediate connections with people—in this instance I bonded with an entire school. Many thanks to Emily McCaffery for making that happen.

To Dhonielle Clayton, Britta Lundin, Danielle Paige, Sara Shepard, Kinsey Gidick, Jen Choi, and all the other writers who have made me feel human in such an extraterrestrial world. Special thanks to Ryan Graudin for her friendship and especially for that last-minute read.

To everyone in my family, especially my sister Annie, who loved this book from draft one and made me keep that ending. To my dad Bill for making life punny. My sister Amanda for all the beauty she puts into the world. To my in-laws for having our backs, always. To my sister in life and in law, Natalie, a true king amongst us, thanks for keeping me in the know, bruh. For my stepdad, Jim, who passed away suddenly during the rewrites of this book. Thank you for a lifetime of support. You are missed. And because I truly can't thank you enough, thanks Mama. *You can do this.*

To my husband, Shuai. Thank you for enduring the sweeping highs of *I finally did it* to the frustrated tears of *I'll never get it right*, especially when they were only hours apart. I will never know what I did to deserve you, but I am so very grateful you're mine. Then. Now. Forever.

And thanks to y'all, the readers. It's such a privilege that I get to do this. I am eternally grateful.

The future is fee, baby. Hear her roar.